THE PERFECT CRIME

AROUND THE WORLD IN 22 MURDERS

Edited by
Vaseem Khan & Maxim Jakubowski

HarperCollins*Publishers*

HarperCollins*Publishers*
1 London Bridge Street,
London SE1 9GF

HarperCollins*Publishers*
1st Floor, Watermarque Building, Ringsend Road
Dublin 4, Ireland

www.harpercollins.co.uk

First published by HarperCollins*Publishers* 2022
2

A catalogue record for this book is available from the British Library

ISBN: 978-0-00-846232-1 (HB)
ISBN: 978-0-00-846233-8 (TPB)

Typeset in Bembo MT Pro by
Palimpsest Book Production Ltd, Falkirk, Stirlingshire

Printed and Bound in the UK using 100% Renewable Electricity
at CPI Group (UK) Ltd

MIX
Paper from
responsible sources
FSC
www.fsc.org
FSC C007454

CONTENTS

INTRODUCTION

NEW VOICES, NEW LANDS, NEW COLOURS

Few would dispute the fact that, until a couple of decades ago, crime and mystery writing was essentially 'white', both in terms of the craftsmen and women practising its art and, slightly less so, in readership. Historical and social reasons for this abound; nonetheless it was a matter of regret.

This deplorable state of affairs was compounded by the fact that Black, Asian, Latinx and other cultures and ethnic minorities tended to be represented by white writers, albeit with a great respect and affection for their protagonists and social canvas they wished to introduce to a previously ignorant readership. Expatriate Englishman Arthur Upfield featured a police detective of aboriginal descent, Napoleon 'Bony' Bonaparte, in his Australian novels; American John Ball created Virgil Tibbs, the Black cop who was later played by Sydney Poitier in the screen adaptations; H.R.F. 'Harry' Keating wrote a series of novels featuring Inspector Ganesh Ghote of the Bombay Police long before he had even set foot on the Indian continent; that epitome of early Black power, Shaft, was invented by another white American, Ernest Tidyman; the wonderful Tony Hillerman gave

1

us unforgettable characters toiling between good and evil on Indian reservations . . . There are many such examples, which today might be construed as dubious, but to some extent these books introduced a general mystery readership to new cultures and in doing so helped pave the way for a future generation of writers who would reclaim their appropriated heritage.

Naturally, there were several pioneers who defied tradition. Rudolph Fisher's *The Conjure-Man Dies* (1932) is believed to be the first crime novel by an African-American author. Recently republished, it is a fascinating tale of two misfit Black cops in Harlem; sadly, their exploits never progressed as the author died young. The Harlem novels of Chester Himes, featuring another dynamic duo, Grave Digger Jones and Coffin Ed Johnson, were written when the author was an expatriate in Paris. Himes' novels are now considered classics of the hard-boiled genre. Less well remembered are the crime novels of George S. Schuyler (an early exponent of Afrofuturism), written under the nom de plume William Stockton.

And then came Walter Mosley, whose debut *The Devil in a Blue Dress* introduced the reader to Easy Rawlins and alerted the publishing establishment to the untapped potential of writers of colour. Following in his wake came Barbara Neely, Gary Phillips, Eleanor Taylor Bland, Hugh Holton, Gar Anthony Haywood, Carolina Garcia-Aguilera, Rudolfo Anaya and Steven Torres, amongst others.

Meanwhile in the UK, Mike Phillips broke through with his Sam Dean series, which won a Crime Writers' Association Dagger in 1991. The dam having been breached, others followed, including Teddy Hayes, Leye Adenle, Tade Thompson and Oyinkan Braithwaite.

Both Vaseem and I are on the board of the Crime Writers' Association, and we have been privileged to witness an explosion of crime and mystery writing by writers of all colours and ethnic backgrounds, winning awards and enjoying critical acclaim, as well as opening up a whole new readership in the process.

Back in 1995, American writer and critic Paula L. Woods welcomed the emergence of African-American crime writing in an excellent anthology *Spooks, Spies and Private Eyes*, which was half historical and half contemporary, and included two of our contributors, respectively Walter Mosley and Brit Mike Phillips. We felt the time was right for another great festschrift of how our genre has evolved, and so this volume is a celebration of new voices in the genre.

In an effort to highlight how diverse crime fiction has become, we cast our net as far as we could. Gathered together in one volume for the very first time are authors from a variety of cultural and ethnic backgrounds, including African-American, Asian, First Nation, Aboriginal, Latinx, Chinese-American, Singaporean and Nigerian.

There was no way all the writers on our personal hit list could be featured. Some had too many commitments to deliver a brand-new story within our deadline, while others felt more at ease with novel-length fiction. But all were supremely encouraging and offered suggestions of other writers who could take their place, so a bow of the fedora to Dorothy Komsoon, Dreda Say Mitchell, Sujata Massey, Kellye Garrett, Courttia Newland, Attica Locke, Nalini Singh, Khurrum Rahman, Steph Cha, Joe Ide and the late Eric Jerome Dickey, who sadly passed away before he could write his story and will be sadly missed.

We would also like to extend our thanks to Ayo Onatade and Craig Sisterson, two respected genre critics who proved most helpful in making suggestions for authors to be considered and helped us get in touch with some of them. And of course to our editor Julia Wisdom at HarperCollins, who immediately connected with our book proposal and showed great enthusiasm while garnering invaluable in-house and international support for the book.

Maxim Jakubowski

. . .

Watershed moments. Bright new dawns. Over the past two decades there have been various initiatives to bring more diversity into the publishing industry. Most have proven to be stillborn, poorly executed, or swiftly run aground on the shoals of antipathy. This time feels different. This time the stars have aligned, the desire to create a more equitable publishing environment matched by a wider desire to engineer a fairer society. If the Black Lives summer of 2020 taught us anything it is that it is no longer enough simply to *talk* about the need for change.

Diversity in the publishing industry holds a very personal meaning for me. I wrote my first novel aged seventeen. Over the next twenty-odd years I wrote six more novels, collecting enough rejection letters to wallpaper a house, until finally receiving a four-book deal for my first crime series set in India.

The interesting thing about that long journey is that only one of those novels featured *any* non-white protagonists. As an avid reader, I had taken on board the idea that books of the type I was trying to write – genre fiction/commercial fiction – simply didn't feature non-white characters. In my mind, I could only hope to be published by writing white characters because those were the sorts of characters readers wanted to read about.

Of course, my thoughts on this have changed dramatically in recent years.

INTRODUCTION

In the summer of 2021 my seventh novel, *Midnight at Malabar House*, won the Crime Writers' Association Sapere Historical Dagger, another marker of the unwavering support I have received from the crime fiction industry. The genre is leading the effort to bring more new voices to the fore and should be commended.

The case for diversity is overwhelming. If we believe in a fair society, then we must recognize that barriers disadvantaging certain groups *do* exist, whether conscious or unconscious. More importantly, fiction – especially crime fiction – provides a lens onto society. Literature is a powerful means by which we can change that society for the better. As individuals, we often formulate our views about the world through artistic media. Thus, when we underrepresent minority backgrounds in our artistic output, we run the risk of aiding divisiveness rather than helping to correct it.

The industry makes assumptions about audiences. One prominent assumption is that white readers won't relate to stories about non-white characters. Because of this we end up with the phenomenon known as *comping* – the comparing of books that might be published to those already published as a way of judging how successful the new acquisition might be. Clearly, this leads to a vicious cycle – white books succeed because they're the only ones published and the only ones used as barometers by which to judge other submissions.

This attitude works its way up and down the chain. Agents become afraid of taking on books that don't fit this model – what's the point if you can't sell such books to a publisher? At the other end of the chain booksellers fear that their regular customers won't buy such books.

Yes, some stories *need* to be told from certain cultural perspectives and wouldn't make sense if you shoehorned in a diverse cast of characters for the sake of political correctness. But the fact is that an industry based purely on human imagination does itself no favours by setting limits on that imagination.

The world is changing. A new generation of readers are emerging who *are* attuned to diversity, who live in a globalized, interconnected world. Similarly, many traditional readers, for want of a better phrase, are increasingly willing to take risks.

My personal opinion is that the publishing industry is making a genuine effort. Talking to people across the industry, I'm convinced that change is an important part of their agenda. This anthology is a case in point. HarperCollins have helped us put together a collection of established writers and emerging stars. For me, personally, it has been exciting reading their contributions and their commitment to the task at hand – which is to achieve agency for their writing.

Readers have an incredibly important part to play in this. The industry responds to readers' buying choices. If readers are willing to take a chance on books featuring diverse characters, the industry will take heed. In other words, readers can directly contribute to a more level playing field, and thus, hopefully, help create a broader canvas for us all to enjoy great books.

What I would really like to see is the industry continue to champion writers from different backgrounds – but to forgo restricting them with the proviso, we will back you, but only so long as you write in your own cultural playpen.

I believe those solutions can only come via a coordinated effort involving all those with an interest in creating a sustainable, vibrant, and equitable publishing industry.

I am, first and foremost, a reader. As a reader, I want to be challenged, excited, intrigued, mystified and titillated. I can honestly say that I have never felt more hopeful about the future of the industry.

Vaseem Khan

THE MAYOR OF DUKES CITY

S.A. COSBY

Marcus pulled out his ink stamp with one hand and a wad of ones with the other. He'd glanced at the girl's ID with his good eye while she and her two friends took selfies and debated whether the pics should be tagged 'Girls Night Out' or 'Birthday Celebration' on Instagram.

'Eight dollars is your change. Have a good night, ladies,' Marcus said.

'You gonna buy me a shot? I'm doing twenty-one for my twenty-first,' the birthday girl said. She smiled at him and for the briefest of moments he felt the leather skin around his heart pulsate. She was small-town pretty in that way that made the local boys forget about condoms and nineteen years of child support. She was seven years younger than Marcus. Their ages were close enough to avoid any concerns about impropriety. Except it was bad news if a bouncer got too friendly with the patrons. Especially in a small town. Especially if bouncing was the only job you could get because you were blind in one eye. And especially if the last time you got involved with someone you got heartbroken.

7

'Maybe later. Have a good night,' Marcus said. The girls slipped by him, all giggles and swagger. Birthday Girl made sure to touch his bicep as she made her way into the bar. She got close and Marcus could smell her perfume. A bellicose, fruity scent that lingered long after she had clicked away on her stiletto heels.

'Shit, she did everything but drop her drawers, Mayor,' Trent said. Trent was the other bouncer working tonight. He was shorter than Marcus but built like a fire hydrant. Two hundred pounds of muscle packed on a 5'6" frame. Trent walked around strung up as tight as an over-tuned guitar begging for someone to strum him the wrong way. Marcus didn't like working with Trent. He was fairly sure the kid was juicing. Add that to the 2x4 chip he had on his shoulder and that all but guaranteed they'd end the night with blood on the floor. But Lonny was the owner and Trent's uncle, so that pretty much meant Trent had carte blanche to take out his little man frustrations on drunk rednecks every other weekend.

'Not good to piss where you eat,' Marcus said, conveniently ignoring the fact he had fallen in love with a girl who was in the bar five days out of seven, until the day he found her . . .

No. Marcus wouldn't think of that yet. Those memories would be waiting for him later tonight when he fell across his bed and closed his eyes. They waited in that Stygian darkness to be rendered in Day-Glo garishness. Neon reds and blues that spilled across the back of his eyes.

'Well let me get your leftovers. I ain't got none since before the fourth of July. Shit, I'd bang the crack of dawn right now if it stood still long enough,' Trent said with such bitterness Marcus winced.

'Get the door. I'm gonna take a lap inside,' Marcus said.

'Ha! Go get her, big boy,' Trent said. He winked at him. Marcus shook his head and went inside. Marcus wasn't shocked that Trent thought he was going in to stalk Birthday Girl. It never occurred to Trent to do his job, so he thought everyone else felt the same.

The interior of The Lookout Bar and Grill was laid out in an exaggerated upper-case L. The bar was in the center of the L with a bandstand near the bottom. Weathered leather booths lined the walls and twelve rickety tables with uneven legs filled the main causeway. It was still early but most of the tables were occupied, as were a lot of the booths. Pittsville County only had two bars, The Lookout and Coppers. But Coppers could never seem to keep their liquor license current, so most people ended up at The Lookout if they didn't take the two-hour drive to Richmond.

The lights were low and someone had played the latest country pop confection on the jukebox as the band set up, but Marcus could still read the crowd. It was all about body language and posture. Imminent violence charged the air like a thunderstorm. Marcus had learned how to read currents and prevailing winds. Often he would defuse a confrontation before a blow was thrown. It didn't hurt he had a legitimate rep as a bone breaker. When he'd first come home and started working for Lonny, he was sure his rep would mean endless duels with guys he'd gone to high school with, trying to show off for their girlfriends or wives. If anything, it was the opposite. Since he'd come back with his tail between his legs, he was welcomed into the fold with open arms and knowing nods. He was just another big fish who had left his small pond. Life had judged him wanting and thrown him back.

Desiree didn't feel that way.

'Why don't you get surgery for your eye? Get back in the ring.'

'The cage,' he'd corrected her as she lay across his chest like a lounging cat.

9

'Whatever. You should do it. I know you don't want to spend the rest of your life tossing Tylers and Chads out into the parking lot.'

'It pays the bills.'

'More to life than bills, Marcus.'

She'd been right. There was love. There was death. He'd found both with her.

'Mayor! Da Mayor of Dukes City! When we gonna spar, big man?' Jody Mickens said. He stumbled, caught himself, then held his hand up palm out, waiting for a high five. Marcus slapped his palm with a touch more vigor than was necessary. The more Jody drank, the more invincible he thought he became. Marcus wanted to remind him, even if it was subconsciously, that he wasn't invincible. He was frail and soft, and if Marcus felt like it, he could break him as easily as he broke an egg for his morning omelet.

'Damn, man. You trying to break my damn hand?' Jody said. He laughed but it was hollow around the edges.

'My bad, Jody. Don't know my own strength sometimes,' Marcus said.

'Yeah, I see that. Let me buy you a drink, man,' Jody said.

'Maybe later. Darlene waving for you,' Marcus said.

'She just want another margarita. She trying to outdrink me,' Jody said, before lurching over to his wife and her sister. Marcus had seen Jody and his sister-in-law in The Lookout without Darlene more than once. It amazed him how people thought they could keep a secret in a town with less than ten thousand people. But then again, people kept the secrets that really mattered. The kind of secrets that got you the needle in your arm or a ride in Ol' Sparky.

'Why does everyone call you Mayor?' a voice said behind him. He turned and saw Birthday Girl leaning against the bar. Her pupils were as big as dinner plates. The brown ringlets of her hair framed her face and gave her a doll-like countenance. By the look of it, she was at the crest of a high from a ferocious bump of coke.

'It's just a nickname,' Marcus said.

'I can see that. But why do they call you that?'

'I used to fight. MMA fighting. During my first fight a commentator said I was taking the guy to Dukes City and the other commentator said I was the Mayor. Name just stuck,' Marcus said.

'You used to fight?' Birthday Girl said. Marcus shrugged.

'Yeah, for real. Mostly regional stuff.'

'Nah, I believe you. You look like you could snap me in half like a breadstick,' Birthday Girl said.

'I don't hit women. I've never hit a woman in my life,' Marcus said.

But somebody around here does, Marcus thought. Desiree's face floated up from the depths and danced in front of him. He could almost see the maroon string lights illuminating her honey brown eyes.

'I mean, if you used to fight what you doing here? No offense,' Birthday Girl asked. Marcus stared past her to a couple in the corner of the bar. The woman took her index and middle finger and pushed them against the man's temple. The man rolled his eyes and stared up into the ceiling. Marcus hoped he was looking for the angels of his better nature. If the guy raised his hand, Marcus could close the distance in two long strides. A few of the more unruly patrons of The Lookout had found out he was deceptively quick.

'Huh?' Marcus asked.

'I said what are you doing here if you're some big bad MMA fighter? I mean, unless you don't want to talk about it,' Birthday Girl said.

'You could always google it, but the short version is I got

poked in the eye during a fight. Everybody pretty much knew the winner was going to the big leagues. I had the guy. Like, I had him. One more body shot, he would've folded, but I tried to show off. I went in for a slam and he jammed his thumb in my eye damn near to the knuckle.'

'Oh God.'

'Yeah. Detached my retina and damaged the nerve. So, no big leagues for me. I came back home,' Marcus said.

'Aw, I'm sure that's not true.'

'You sound like my ex,' Marcus said, instantly regretting it.

'Your ex? If she your ex that means you're single. Unless y'all still friends with benefits,' Birthday Girl said.

Marcus sucked his teeth.

'No. She's dead. Been dead for almost a year.'

'Jesus Christ. I'm so sorry. I'm such an idiot.'

'You didn't know. You probably heard about it though. She was Desiree Bowles.'

'Oh shit. That's the girl they found in the creek behind the building here. Damn. I mean damn, that's so messed up.'

'They didn't find her. I found her. We'd been broke up for a month. No one had heard from her for a couple days. I was taking the trash out before we opened for the night and I saw a whole flock of buzzards in the trees back there. I don't know why I went to check it out. Maybe I kinda knew? Subconsciously, you know? This was the last place she'd been seen. On my night off. My one night off,' Marcus said. He wondered if Birthday Girl could feel the guilt emanating from him, the insatiable regret that filled him like sand in an hourglass. Tick tick ticking away every day. Each grain inscribed with the idea that if he'd been there, he could have saved her.

'You wanna drink?'

'It's your birthday.'

'Yeah, but I think you need it more than I do. I can't imagine finding my ex de . . . finding them like that. Come on, do a shot with me.'

'Maybe later,' Marcus said. The Temple Pusher was now in the personal space of a woman standing near the hall that led to the bathrooms. The guy was nowhere to be seen.

'All right, Mayor. Don't leave me hanging.'

'OK, Birthday Girl. I gotta go handle something,' Marcus said.

'Kristen!' she yelled as he went to disentangle the two women near the bathroom.

The band started up a few minutes after he and Trent tossed the two women and the guy. The three of them continued to argue in the parking lot The Lookout shared with Pets A Million and Beads Beads Beads, Linda Danvers' craft shop.

'Should we call the cops? Or do you want me to go over there?' Trent asked. Marcus looked up at the night sky. The stars looked like pinpricks in a bolt of black suede.

'No. They just yelling. It'll be OK,' Marcus said. Would it be OK though? Or would it escalate? Transform from a simple romantic squabble to a deadly encounter in the blink of an eye?

'Kiss my ass, Lavon. You told me y'all was just friends!' a voice said from the far end of the parking lot. A few seconds later a two-door sports coupé with BRWN SGAR on the license plate went roaring past Marcus and Trent. The car paused for the briefest of moments before it merged into traffic.

'That took care of itself, I guess. I wouldn't want to be Lavon tonight though,' Trent said. Marcus caught a note of disappointment in his voice. They were halfway through the night and he hadn't had a chance to really flex his muscles. Tossing the love triangle had been light work.

'Yeah, he gonna be on the couch tonight. I'm gonna take another lap,' Marcus said.

'Just ask her for her number, man,' Trent said. Marcus shook his head. The atmosphere in the bar had shifted significantly in the last hour. Bodies gyrated on the dance floor in desperate rhythm. Strangers had become friends and friends were trying to find the path to lovers. The band was tearing through a bluesy number that only threw more logs on the fire of sexual tension that was slowly consuming The Lookout. Marcus posted up near the bar and scanned the dance floor. He wasn't looking for Kristen to get her number. There was a wildness and a willing-ness about her that reminded him of Desiree. Not a naivete but a hedonistic sensibility that attracted lovers and predators in equal measure.

He heard a throaty laugh that rose over the music like an opera singer hitting a high note. He flicked his eyes over to the corner where the laugh had come from. Kristen and her two girlfriends were in a booth with the Larson brothers. Jaime and Justin were a couple of good ol' boys whose family owned the paper pulp mill that employed 50 percent of Pittsville's citizens. They were all laughing but Kristen was the star of that show. Jaime Larson appeared particularly smitten with her.

Marcus let out a sigh. She wasn't Desiree. She was just a girl having a good time on her birthday. She would go home with Jaime or Justin, or with the beginnings of a hangover. Regardless, she was going to be all right. At least for tonight.

Marcus cut through the crowd and headed for the bathroom. He needed to take a leak. As he turned the corner at the bottom of the L he saw Jody standing in the hallway that led to the bathrooms. He was in front of the bulletin board that Lonny used to advertise upcoming events. Lonny was convinced placing it near the bathroom was a brilliant marketing move. Marcus didn't have the heart to tell him drunk people trying not to piss themselves didn't pause to peruse the coming attractions.

Except here was Jody doing just that. Marcus stopped. Jody wasn't just reading the announcements. He was drawing a little bit of graffiti. He had a pen in his hand and was adding his own artistic contribution to the board. Marcus watched him as he chuckled to himself and put the pen back in his pocket.

He slipped past Marcus without raising his head. The liquor was pulling his chin down into his chest. Marcus walked along the short hall and stopped in front of the bulletin board. If Jody had drawn a vulgar work of art, he'd have to take it down and toss it in the trash. He couldn't do anything about what people drew on the stalls, but he could keep the hallway clean.

Marcus peered at Jody's handiwork. He felt his guts twist into a cold knot of despair. The entire length of his intestinal tract felt like it was being crocheted by a demon. Marcus fell back against the wall and put his hand to his mouth.

•

Later, as Trent was helping Charlene and Mandy, the two bartenders, clean up, Marcus pushed the crowd toward the door.

'Drink 'em up! You ain't gotta go home but you gotta get the hell out of here!' Marcus said. For the most part the crowd followed his directions. A few stragglers chugged their beers. A few late-night lotharios tried in vain to seal the deal before the light came up and their true faces were laid bare.

'Hey, man, I gotta dip. Can you finish shutting things down?' Marcus asked Trent.

'Yeah, man, I gotcha. Going to catch up with that little hottie, huh?' Trent said.

But Marcus was already out the door.

•

Jody lived out near Iron Bucket Road in a double-wide trailer down a long dirt lane about sixty yards from the main road. Marcus had driven him home a couple of times over the last few years. His own trailer was five miles away. Since Jody's house was on his way, he didn't mind dropping him off if he was too pie-eyed to drive.

Marcus couldn't ignore the irony. He'd taken better care of Jody than he'd taken care of Desiree.

Jody's truck was parked haphazardly in front of his steps. Marcus went up to the door and gave it three sharp knocks with one hand while waving away the moths and June bugs gathered around Jody's porchlight with the other.

'Who the fuck is it?' Jody yelled.

'Jody, it's Marcus. You forgot your ID. I'm just dropping it off,' Marcus said. He could hear Jody clomping and stomping toward the door.

When he finally appeared in the doorway his pale moon face was dripping with confusion.

'You sure, man? I swear I got it,' Jody slurred.

'Yeah. Come on out to the car,' Marcus said. Clarity made a brief appearance in Jody's eyes. Marcus wondered, was it a latent form of reptilian survival instinct? An animalistic sense of self-preservation left over from the days of caves and mastodons? If it was, it found no purchase in Jody's mind. It flickered out like a candle in a rainstorm.

'OK sure. Nice of you to bring it,' Jody mumbled.

When they got to the car Marcus leaned in the passenger window. He came back up with his fingerless fighting gloves on his hands.

'What you doing, Mayor?'

'I thought we'd get that sparring session in,' Marcus said. Jody laughed.

'Tonight? You must be drunker than me.'

'Darlene at her mom's?' Marcus asked.

'Yeah, she got pissed at me for flirting with Jennifer Lowe. Why are you here again? Where is my ID?' Jody said. Marcus rolled his neck.

'When I found her, she was on her back. One of her pants legs had caught on a root on the bank of the creek. Cops told me people who drowned almost always float face down. Then they found out she hadn't drowned. Her head had been cracked open. Her mama told me the mortician said she had bruises all over her body. Bruised everywhere. The person who did it had even knocked out her front teeth. The cops kept that back.'

'Mayor, I'm sorry about Desiree, but if you ain't got my ID I'm going back inside. I got the bubble guts, man,' Jody said. He started for the trailer. Marcus spun on the balls of his feet and gave him a stiff rabbit punch to the back of the neck. Jody dropped to his knees. He keened like a baby goat.

'Nobody knew about her teeth except the cops and the mortician and me and the person who killed her.'

'You damn near broke my neck, man,' Jody gasped.

'Lonny lets me keep the poster up on the bulletin board even though nobody has come forward. Nobody talks about her anymore. It's like she was never here. But that poster's still up there. She's still with me. She's still in my heart,' Marcus said. He grabbed Jody by his shirt and pulled him to his feet.

'So, you wanna tell me why I watched you black out her teeth on that poster? You blacked 'em out and laughed about it. Explain that to me, Jody. EXPLAIN IT TO ME!' Marcus roared.

'You're crazy. It was just a joke. I didn't cave the back of that girl's head in. Crazy fucker,' Jody said. His breath was coming in ragged bursts. Each exhalation smelled like the exhaust from a car that ran on whiskey.

'Jody.'

'What, Marcus? Let me go, man,' Jody said.

'I never said the back of her head was caved in. But somehow you know that too,' Marcus said quietly.

Jody's face went from alabaster to chartreuse.

'It was an accident, Marcus. I swear it was.'

Marcus hit him with a one-two combination to the ribs. Jody fell to the ground. He coughed once, then twice. Blood, as red as a melted crayon, spilled over his thin lips.

'Time to go to Dukes City, Jody.'

Marcus hit him again.

And again.

And again . . .

THE LAND OF MILK AND HONEY

SILVIA MORENO-GARCIA

In the house with the red double doors there lived an old man and six women, just them and no one else. It was a tattered casona, the zaguán leading to an interior patio with a lemon tree and potted plants. The abode had once been quite grand, but nowadays the wallpaper was peeling and the tiles around the fountain were cracked. A Studebaker Roadster had been left to decay under the onslaught of the elements in the courtyard.

The man of the house was Don Aurelio Heliodoro Vallejo Pacheco and he did not believe in modern notions of women venturing out into the world. Ladies were supposed to be courted in the presence of their family and girls had no business attending a school. A woman's place is in the home, he said. There they could rest safe and sound and far from the dangerous glare of the city's lights. To ensure the women did not stray from the path of virtue and wouldn't be distracted by idle thoughts, he had them knit every day. They knitted booties and blankets and clothes to dress the plaster Baby Jesuses that made their appearance during Candlemas and Christmas. Aurelio sold those clothes through an intermediary, even though he hardly needed the money. The profits were placed in the safe inside the office.

The six women would sit in the living room on faded couches and chairs lined in velvet. The eldest of them was Don Aurelio's sister. Then came his wife, followed by four daughters. The girls had been born two years apart from each other. The youngest one, Ofelia, turned nineteen that spring of 1949.

Something else happened that spring: Don Aurelio broke his leg. Early that afternoon he had gone to collect the rents. Don Aurelio owned two vecindades and he knew that if he waited until Monday the factory workers and assorted riffraff that dwelled in the cramped buildings would have spent their salary on drinks. So he stopped by before they had the chance to hit the cantinas and then, after depositing the cash back in the safe at home, he went out to drink and play dominoes.

It was nighttime when Don Aurelio stumbled outside La Valentina, landed at an odd angle, and somehow broke his leg. Two of his drinking buddies drove him home and called for the doctor from the pharmacist's store, because Don Aurelio did not keep a telephone in his house. He said it was too pricey. Meat was also pricey and he selected the worst and cheapest cuts for his family, but bought juicy steaks for himself. Sometimes he made the women go without meat for a week to economize while he ate out.

The doctor put a cast on his leg and told him to stay in bed. Don Aurelio wailed for a whole day, railing against his bad luck while the women tended to him. Then he calmed down and, remembering that he had to collect the rents, he began to worry about how he would manage that and who would run the errands, because he was the one who bought the food and other supplies.

'Perhaps we could do it,' Ofelia's mother said.

'What, go out there on your own?' Don Aurelio replied. He

took the women to Mass once a month and on their birthdays he allowed them to watch a movie, but they were always at his side.

'We could hire a maid.'

'Do you think I'm made of money, woman?' Don Aurelio asked, aghast.

Although every family of their class had a maid and even the poorer ones could afford a cleaning lady once a week, Don Aurelio had never considered such an expense. Besides, he knew most maids had bad habits. If they didn't steal from you, then they might bring their boyfriend to the house. When there was a maid, the louts of the neighborhood came around like dogs in heat. Don Aurelio was a righteous man and he would not allow such a thing.

Instead, Don Aurelio sent a telegram to his cousin Trinidad. Trinidad had been widowed for several years. She was one of those poorer relations that bloom in every family. She had a son who was hoping to live in the city. A few months before she had written to Don Aurelio, hoping he could find the boy a position, but Aurelio had not bothered replying. Now he invited Arturo to live with him. He would be provided with room and board in exchange for running errands, collecting the rents, and fixing whatever needed to be fixed around the house. He promised the boy a paltry salary which would have been half of what a decent assistant would have cost him.

This is how Ofelia found herself opening the door to Cousin Arturo one warm day in March. He walked in shyly, with a suitcase in one hand and a felt hat in another. He had straight teeth, bright eyes and parted his hair on the left side.

'Cousin O–Ofelia?' he asked. 'I don't know if you remember me, I . . . ah . . . I was at Cousin Magda's wedding.'

Cousin Magda's wedding had taken place six years prior. Their father had taken them to the countryside. She remembered the digging of the pit for the barbacoa, the hot coals and the scent of the smoke drifting up in the air. Her gloves had stuck to her skin under the blazing sun but her father would not allow her to take them off.

'I think I do,' she said, though she really couldn't have told him apart from her other cousins.

He smiled, shy yet cheerful, and she guided him to her father's bedroom. Once he went inside, Ofelia grabbed a broom and began sweeping the hallway, trying to listen to what they were saying. She couldn't understand a single word, but still she walked up and down the hallway, sweeping the same stretch of crimson clay tiles. In the living room the women knit, preparing trousers and shirts for babies and plaster statues alike, but as long as Ofelia pretended to sweep, she could escape the confines of that space and the clicking of the needles.

At length, the door opened and Arturo stepped out. He smiled at her again.

'If you'll pardon me . . . Your father says there's a cot in the little blue room, but I'll need blankets,' he said, and she smiled back.

•

Arturo proved himself to be an industrious, well-behaved young man. He went to fetch tortillas and vegetables and chicken for the consomés that Don Aurelio liked. The milk was delivered, so he didn't need to bother with that. He collected the rent and Ofelia counted the bills in her father's office. She had kept the books for him for a long time now because her father said her mother had grown scatterbrained.

Arturo set up bait and poison for the rats that had been nibbling at their food, decided to clear the damp rooms full of junk and broken furniture in the back, and began repairing the old car.

Don Aurelio's house was a place without tenderness. But Aurelio's father had fancied himself a poet and in the dusty books that nobody else ever bothered to clap open, Ofelia had found words of passion. When her father discarded the newspaper on the table after his breakfast, leaving coffee stains at the edges, she carefully read the pages instead of merely paying attention to the headlines as he did. And when her father took them to see a women's picture, which he thought to be suitable entertainment, rather than focusing on the moral of the story – for wickedness was punished in the last reel – Ofelia reveled in the sin.

And that is how, despite Don Aurelio's talk of temperance and morality, Ofelia found herself admiring the strong arms of her cousin, fixating on the fullness of his lips and wanting to trace the beads of sweat that slid down his throat as he worked around the house, going into rooms that Don Aurelio could never be bothered to care for despite the fact the house was damp and old and needed constant attention. For the first time in years fresh paint concealed the mold that had once bloomed by a leaky windowpane and rolls of wallpaper which had been stuffed in a corner and forgotten were carefully pasted onto naked walls.

By the end of April, Don Aurelio's leg had healed, but he didn't take up his chores again. Instead, he headed to the cantina earlier, ate out more often, and decided that Arturo would become a permanent addition to the family. For a few years now he had feared he would have to marry off at least one of the girls, to ensure someone could take care of his properties. He could not conceive that the women might manage on their own, but he also feared what a strange man would want. Although dowries were relics of yesteryears, none of his daughters was particularly pretty. Ofelia was the most attractive of the lot, but even though the gap in her teeth was more charming than off-putting, the girl was so quiet. She hardly said a word. Besides, she was as flat as a board and Aurelio, who fancied hour-glass shapes and prostitutes with large breasts, couldn't imagine that any man in his right mind would settle for a flat little thing when he could avail himself of something better.

What Aurelio feared, in short, was that any suitor would want money to accompany his bride. Now, with Arturo there, Don Aurelio could rely on a man to watch over his affairs without having to spend a fortune on securing his loyalty.

That is how, the first week of May, Don Aurelio had Arturo moved to a nicer room with a real bed instead of a cot and a wardrobe to replace the old crates where the boy had placed his clothes.

•

Spring turned to summer and Ofelia spied on Arturo from the shadow of the lemon tree as he stood in his undershirt, fingers dark with grease. While she scrubbed the flagstones, she watched him, looking down whenever he glanced in her direction. In the evening, when he had his coffee with milk and a few almond cookies, her eyes rested on his hands.

She hovered around Arturo when he was working, finding excuses to be in the same room as the boy. When they talked, it was a succession of quick, polite sentences. But soon they were conversing rather than just exchanging pleasantries.

Ofelia asked him what he did when he went outside, she asked him to tell her the names of the actresses that appeared on the covers of magazines.

'Well, there are many of them. I should just buy a magazine at the newsstand the next time,' he said.

'My father doesn't like us reading magazines. He says they have too many ads for perfumes and make-up.'

'It can be our secret.'

She smiled and when he brought her a magazine, they pored over it together, looking at the glamorous ladies in their mink coats. Ofelia wondered what it would be like to get her hair done or paint her nails. She'd never owned a pair of high-heel shoes, nor a string of pearls.

'You'd look prettier than the lot of them in that dress,' Arturo said when she stared at a photo. She blushed.

They began meeting at night. They didn't discuss it, but somehow Ofelia would end up walking into the interior patio and Arturo was already there, cigarette in hand. Or else she'd lean against the car and he'd come strolling outside.

If it rained, they sat in the car. Just sat and talked. He was as shy as Ofelia and well-behaved. When he spoke at the dinner table it was all *usted* and please and multiple thank yous. In private, he was still coiled tight. Until the night when Arturo's hand crept under Ofelia's thin dress, brushing against her underwear, and he leaned forward, kissing her until they were both breathless.

'It's uncomfortable, sitting here,' she complained, because the car had a bad smell. A rodent or some other small animal had died somewhere inside and the scent lingered.

'I could come to your room.'

'My bed squeaks,' she told him, her voice a whisper.

'Mine doesn't.'

She thought to grab his hand and pull him back into the house, shove him into his room and onto that bed, but there was a loud whistle outside: the noise of the man selling camotes, making his nightly rounds. It startled Ofelia and she ran from the car.

•

That night marked a turning point for them. If she had once sought Arturo, now she avoided him. Ofelia threw herself into her duties, her needles furiously clicking as she worked next to the other women. It was regular baby clothes that they knitted, for now. The orders for clothing for the Baby Jesuses wouldn't begin to trickle in until September, perhaps October. It was still months until the women in households across the city would lovingly dress their plaster figurines and rock them in their arms. They'd dress the child again for Candelaria in fresh shoes and clothes, and again the needles in Ofelia's house would click for that occasion, telegraphing a mute tale, following the patterns they'd knit their whole lives.

But now it was summer. She hardly spoke to her cousin and she went to bed early. If it had been winter, she might have slept soundly, but the rain kept her up at nights. When it rained, the rats came rushing out of the pipes, seeking safety and warmth, and the women set up pots and pans around the house to catch the water from the leaks. In her room, the water dripped; it wouldn't let her close her eyes.

She recalled Arturo's hand on her thigh or his voice, low against her ear. She felt warm and cold, tossing the covers aside, then huddling under three blankets for warmth. The sight of a rat in the kitchen made her cry and when she burnt her dress with the iron she giggled. She was at turns furious, woeful, distracted, serious, listless and frenetic.

Ofelia's mother thought the girl had caught a chill, and told her to rest. A chill was the only ailment Ofelia's mother under-stood, and they did not ask the doctor to come for a visit. Women's illnesses did not deserve scrutiny.

Thus, the girl lay swaddled under one of the many blankets stuffed around the house, staring at the ceiling while the rain leaked into her room and landed in a pot set by the bed, sere-nading her. Finally, Ofelia rose from her bed and walked in the dark until she found a thin strip of light emanating from under a door. She pushed the door open and walked into Arturo's room. He put aside the book he had been reading and she took off her nightgown.

The first time Arturo and Ofelia made love in that room that was blessedly distant from the other rooms in the house; they did so in silence, as though they were enacting a pantomime. They were both too terrified of being discovered to utter a single sound. She didn't even bid him goodnight when she stepped out.

They were cautious, at first. But caution was quickly discarded. If they found themselves alone, they flew into each other's arms, and not only in Arturo's room but anywhere around the house. Some nights she sat on his lap on an old couch that had been stained by the humidity and forgotten in a dusty room, arms around his neck, while on other occasions he shoved her against a wall and she bit her lip in delight. The rain drew patterns on the windows and dripped into the rooms, caressing their skin.

He began to bring her things. First, another magazine. Then a pair of stockings. A little bottle of perfume. She hid them away.

One afternoon, he sat her atop the desk in the office and merrily made love to her while a rat stared at them from a corner of the room. When they were done and he was tucking his shirt back into his trousers he let out a loud sigh.

'I guess I'll have to put out more poison for the rats,' he said. 'But they never die completely. The problem is this house. It's too old and damp and dark. It's dreadful. And to think your father could simply buy a new, nicer place.'

'My father would never buy a new house. He'd say it's a waste of money.'

'I know. Ofelia, I'm going to tell you a secret, but you must promise not to tell your father.'

'What is it?'

She was still sitting atop the desk and Arturo, who had taken a few paces from her, moved back to stand between her legs, his right hand rubbing her thigh. She shivered at his touch.

'I've been putting aside a little money and I want you to go away with me.'

'My father doesn't pay you enough to squirrel away much,' she said.

He chuckled. 'No, he doesn't. But I still find a way to put away some cash. I increased the rents a bit and I'm pocketing the difference. I swear, it's not much per household, but it adds up.'

'But that's stealing!'

'It's like you said, he doesn't pay me enough. He has so much money. That safe is crammed with bills. I bet if we took a bag full of bills he wouldn't be able to tell the difference. And some of that money is yours. He sells all those things you knit and you never see a cent of the profits.'

Ofelia never thought much about what happened to the garments she knitted. She knew, of course, that her father affixed a sign outside their door that said 'Baby Jesuses Dressed/We Knit Clothes for Newborns' and women came by and placed their order. Or else, he sold the clothes to his intermediary downtown. But the money never concerned her. This was simply something she must do, and whether the garments were pure white or brown or red, she must knit them.

'With the car fixed and a little money, we could go anywhere,' Arturo said, although he hadn't bothered fiddling with the car in weeks, too busy studying the contours of her body in his spare time.

'Where?'

'I don't know. But aren't you tired of being locked inside

28

here? I come from such a small town and I hated it there, but it almost feels worse to be in the city when I feel so trapped. And you want pretty things and to have fun, you've told me so.'

She'd told him she wanted to wear make-up and satin and curl her hair. So she nodded and his hands found her face and he kissed her until her hands were at his buckle again and he was pushing into her once more.

•

It was in October that they began taking money from the safe. They justified it using the same principle as before: it was only a little money and her father wouldn't notice it.

By then, Arturo had become surer of himself. Gone was the shy, almost stammering boy of nineteen who had stumbled through the doorway of the house. Instead, Ofelia was greeted by a man who invariably brought her a present every time he went out, then pressed her against a wardrobe or some other piece of furniture and unbuttoned her blouse, his hands on her breasts.

How she loved the look in his eyes when he was aflame, his hair tousled. Of his gifts, she felt less certain. At first, she liked them all very much. Magazines, rice powder, books. Then underwear, a dress, a compact mirror, a necklace, lipstick so crimson it was like smearing blood across her lips.

The gifts began to fill her with a strange sense of dread.

They didn't belong in the dark casona with cracks in the walls any more than the cheerful wallpaper Arturo had put in one of the rooms or the fresh coat of white paint he'd given another. She looked at the plants growing wild in pots and the dry fountain, at the women sitting in the living room with its velvet curtains and the Victrola in the corner, and she knew Arturo's eager face and enthusiasm clashed with everything inside the house, as did his presents.

The gifts he procured for her were like artifacts from another universe, as baffling as a radio would have been to a Babylonian priestess. She hid them, fearful that her father might find them, but also terrified that the house itself might reject them, that it might expel Arturo. He was like an eyelash rubbing against an eye, almost an irritant.

She suffered from piercing headaches that would arrive early in the morning and follow her late into the night. Certain noises aggravated her: the clicking of needles, the ticking of the clock in the living room.

She checked that the gifts were safely hidden inside a chest. She checked in the morning and at night, but sometimes she felt compelled to run into the room in the middle of the day and fling the lid open, to ensure the objects hadn't somehow spilled onto her bed.

The others noticed the dark circles under her eyes.

'What is wrong with this girl?' her father asked.

'She has a chill,' her mother said.

'Again? You're too idle, Ofelia. That's the problem. Knit a few more booties, that'll get your mind back on track,' he said.

During supper she ate two morsels and drank but a sip of water. She felt dread crawling inside her entrails. She couldn't explain it to Arturo. When they lay tangled in his bed together, she'd press her face against his chest and she'd sob and he'd ask what was wrong.

'I don't know . . . it's the house,' she said. 'It frightens me.'

'What frightens you?'

'The noise of the headboard scraping against the wall . . . the noise of the springs . . . our voices. What if they suspect?'

The rains, which concealed all sounds, had departed and the naked night remained.

'They don't suspect a thing. Won't you wear that nice negligee

I bought you? For a few minutes,' he said, pressing the piece of clothing against her hands. 'It's fine. Ofelia, kiss me.'

How she wanted him! And how obscene was the sight of him nude on the bed. His youth was an affront, their kisses sacrilege, but she kissed him nevertheless, searching for the warmth of his body. She thought about knitting a huge, thick blanket, large enough that they both might hide underneath it and be swallowed by darkness.

•

By December the room Arturo repainted had grown cheerless and mold was beginning to bloom again upon its surface. It looked almost like tiny fingerprints, gray and soft.

Don Aurelio sent Arturo and Ofelia shopping for Christmas foods, for bacalao and romeritos and guayabas for the ponche. Two people were needed to carry multiple bags filled with goods, and normally Ofelia found such shopping to be a treat. That year, Don Aurelio couldn't be bothered to go, preferring to spend his time at the cantina where he now played endless rounds of dominoes. But that suited the lovers well enough and she relished the thought of having a coffee with her sweetheart.

The streets downtown were a collage of multicolored piñatas, mountains of fruit, colación, and firecrackers. There were hundreds of people shopping. It didn't matter where you went, waves of humans crashed against Ofelia's body. She clutched her purse against her chest, stood on her tiptoes, tried to speak to Arturo but the crowd was like a roar.

The noises of cars honking mixed with the buzzing of all those voices and the shrieking of radios, the music of the organilleros on the corners, the paper boys yelling headlines about robbers and murderers. Ofelia wished to press her hands against her ears to muffle the sound.

Near the Alameda she saw a grotesque, poorly made Baby Jesus in a shop window, resting in its cradle filled with hay, surrounded by the Three Wise Men. The unseeing eyes and plaster limbs of the figurine made her sick and she turned away in fright, shoving her way down busy sidewalks, blind to nativity scenes and tinsel ornaments, until Arturo caught up with her.

'Ofelia! What's wrong?' he asked.

'Arturo! Don't make me go back to the house!' she exclaimed, clutching at his arms. She thought someone was squeezing her lungs.

'But, Ofelia, we said in the summer—'

'No! Not in the summer. I want to go away this instant. Please, Arturo, please!'

'Ofelia, you're being silly. Don't cry, darling. Very well . . . don't worry, just don't,' he said, hugging her and pressing a kiss upon her brow. All thoughts of having coffee were forgotten. They proceeded with their shopping in haste and it was only when they reached the doors of the house that Ofelia felt that terrible constriction in her chest lifting.

She'd been sick every morning in December, with a sour taste in her mouth lingering until noon, but now she could hardly sleep. She heard the whizzing of fireworks outside their house, as the neighbors organized their posadas, and she recalled the crowd downtown and shuddered.

Arturo purchased a rosca de reyes from the bakery and they sat around the table, drinking chocolate.

She regarded the cutting of the bread with weary eyes. She did not wish to eat a slice, she wanted to refuse to eat, but her mother was systematically handing out plates. Ofelia looked at the bread on her plate and she saw the tiny, pale leg of the Baby Jesus sticking out from the dough.

She had eaten dozens of roscas de reyes in previous years and

32

twice before she'd found the little porcelain Baby Jesus figurine in her slice of bread. It was such an ordinary occurrence that it should not have evoked anything but a smile. Instead, Ofelia pulled her chair back in horror and stood there, mutely, a hand clasped against her mouth.

'Child! What has gotten into you!' Don Aurelio yelled.

She could not say. All Ofelia knew was that the tiny figurine reminded her of the Baby Jesus they'd seen near the Alameda and that brought back the nauseating memory of the people shoving against each other, of the scent of gasoline and perfumes and foods, and the noises of motors.

'I saw a rat,' she lied, though in her eyes she saw only the blinking lights downtown and her tongue was coated with bile.

'Damn rats. Arturo, didn't you say you had bought more poison and baited them?' her father asked.

'Yes, sir, the raticide is under the sink.'

'It's the cold that makes the rats so eager. It's chilly. Someone bring me my cozy blanket,' Don Aurelio grumbled, and Ofelia sat down. She clutched her hands under the table to keep them from trembling. Christmas Eve was fast approaching.

She wouldn't survive it.

She held Arturo in the dark, begged him to take her away. But the hours marched on, inexorably, until she found herself sitting in the living room, with her father half-asleep, drunk already on rum, and the women smiling. Arturo sat in a corner and she tried to look at him, only at him, erasing everyone else.

'It's time to lull the Baby Jesus to sleep,' Ofelia's mother said.

Her sisters were fetching the plaster statue, which had been dressed early in the morning. Ofelia had avoided looking at it, but now they were bringing it into the room. She wished to close her eyes, fearing the horrid, leprous Baby Jesus from the store downtown had sneaked into their home. She'd heard tales of Baby Jesuses that moved at night or whose expressions changed.

Miracles, they said.

Horrors, she thought.

The women were rocking the baby in their arms and they were singing. Ofelia sat still, staring at Arturo, who she could hardly see because he was sitting in shadows. Her mother stepped forward, holding the baby up in her arms, exposing its pale face to Ofelia, and Ofelia felt a spasm of terror cleave through her body.

Her hands were closed into tight fists, which she pressed against her stomach. But it was only the old figurine they'd owned for years and years and she was able to finally breathe in relief. Ofelia's mother turned away, carrying the baby back to its crib.

Then Arturo was there, extending his arms in her direction.

'Merry Christmas,' he said, and she let him embrace her, eyes bright and watery.

•

Ofelia lay under a thick blanket that her sisters had knitted and stared at a crack running down the wall. Children were playing with firecrackers in the street. She could hear them yelping and laughing. Outside, the scent of gunpowder perfumed the air. But the house smelled of old rains that had trickled into ancient rooms for over a century, it smelled of wax and also of forgotten things.

Arturo let himself into her room. Ofelia sat up, startled; she thought him a ghost at first.

'Why aren't you ready?' he asked.

'What do you mean?'

'We said we'd leave tonight.'

She didn't recall that conversation. Ofelia was in her nightgown and he was fully dressed, with a suitcase in one hand. He sighed and set the suitcase down. 'I thought you wanted to leave the house.'

No, she had not wanted to return to the house. But that had been a few days before. Now she was suddenly frightened by the thought of stepping out into the street, of the noise and those firecrackers exploding.

'Ofelia, you need to change and then we have to open the safe and get a little bit more cash.'

'But tonight . . . I'm so tired,' she said. 'And if we were to take any more money I'd feel so bad.'

'Just a few more bills. Ofelia—'

'Arturo, not tonight. I know something dreadful will happen tonight.'

'You're saying that because you hardly ate a thing today.'

'No. I just know it. Because outside . . . and the house . . . It'll never work.'

'You're giving me a headache,' he muttered and pinched the bridge of his nose. 'Let's go to the dining room and you can have a bite and we can go over the plan again.'

She nodded. They ventured into the kitchen and she began boiling water for a couple of coffees. He stood by the door, speaking in a low soothing tone. She didn't recognize half the words he said. The naked bulb above their heads cast stark shadows on the walls.

'. . . and you'll never have to come back here.'

She heard that. Loud and clear. Ofelia raised her head and blinked, realizing what he was saying at last. 'Leave the house forever?'

'Of course. Go someplace new. Someplace better, without nosy relatives to tell us what to do.'

New, better, outside. Far from the house with its cracks on the walls, the scent of mothballs lingering in the armoire, the dry fountain and the broken tiles. Far from Don Aurelio, her mother, her sisters and the incessant clicking of the needles.

But outside there was the terrible, hungry night and the eyes of the porcelain Baby Jesus.

Outside they'd eat her bones and chew on her marrow. She knew it, she just knew it, and she felt that hand crushing her lungs again.

She realized that it was Arturo who had invited this monstrous doom into her home. Arturo and his gifts, which collided with the house, too full of life and vibrant with promise. The house spit them out, rejected them. And Ofelia, born of the house, grown in the house, couldn't exist in the presence of such animated desire and motion.

Now Arturo wanted not only to bring all this wildness into her home but to pluck her free, to toss her into the world.

She'd be smothered.

'Love, the water's boiling,' he said, tugging at her hand.

Ofelia turned her head and moved the kettle from the burner. 'Sit, and we can talk while we have coffee,' she said.

He stepped out of the kitchen. She arranged almond cookies on a plate. She poured the water into the cups, added a splash of milk and the sugar, making the coffee the way he liked it.

Ofelia walked into the dining room and placed the cup and the cookies before him.

'Now, what's wrong? You're all jittery. I don't understand it.'

She sat in front of him. 'It's not safe outside.'

He nibbled at a cookie. 'Not safe how?'

'My father says a woman's place is the home. I can't leave, Arturo. Just stay with me here, let's just stay and forget about going anywhere. Let's forget about the money or driving to distant places. Let's stay.'

Ofelia prayed to God in that instant, begging him to change Arturo's mind. That he might abandon all thoughts of escape and that they would remain together in the dim hallways and damp rooms of the house. Because otherwise . . .

She stretched out a hand to clutch his own. The house didn't like Arturo, but if they were careful, if they tried, maybe the house would grow to tolerate him. He needed to stop bringing those gifts and those maps and stop talking about escape. They must toss away all the things he'd bought her, dig a hole and bury them, there, under the lemon tree.

'Arturo,' she whispered.

She wanted to tell him that she'd seen an abomination behind the glass – that horrible porcelain figurine in the crib. The house could protect them, it could keep their secrets. They must never try to leave it.

But Arturo shook his head and brushed her fingers away. 'Ofelia, no. We're leaving. That's it. We said we would, and we will,' he assured her.

He shook his head again. She watched him, unblinking, as he lifted the mug and drank the coffee laced with raticide.

FOR MARG

J. P. POMARE

I used to sit and watch him, after she was gone. Out there in the bush, there's a spot where the sun passes down through the trees and you can see all the way across his farm toward the house. I'd sit there until I heard the motorbike, or a fence swing open, then I'd make my way toward the fence line and watch on as that funny old farmer would tend his sheep, his property. He'd sit there up on the hill when the air was still on these crisp spring mornings, talking away, sometimes to the dog and sometimes to her. When it was still, his voice would carry down into the gully, cutting through the bush to me. That's how it began. I just wanted to observe him at first. Then something changed.

•

The felt, the wood; *thwack*. The sound echoes through the fog, down over the hills, into the gully. He swings again, this time it's louder, the crack of iron driving through the rabbit's crossed feet and into the fence post. He lets the carcass hang, already hardening in the fist of mid-winter. He sniffs, squints down into the fog toward the back paddock. He thinks of her now. Her star sign in the paper circled in red pen each week, words underlined once, sometimes twice. 'Going to be a good week,' she'd say. Or, 'Might be someone from my past turns up soon.' Everything returns to ritual, habit, belief, but this hanging of a rabbit makes sense to him; scare the pests off with the body of one of their own. He'd shit himself seeing another human on display like this.

As he hacks into the back of his hand, a new thought comes to him unbidden, as if dislodged by the force of his cough: *The devil is everywhere God is not.* His grandmother's words and he hears them in her voice.

'Doesn't make much sense, does it,' he says to Shep, who is sniffing at something along the fence line. He turns, starts back toward the bike. His whistle splits the morning air. The dog bows for one last sniff before trotting back toward the bike. 'Better move these lambs.'

With Shep on the back, he rides the four-wheeler out toward the back paddock, leaving the gate open at the top of the race.

Shep moves the sheep with the aplomb of a conductor. They each emerge one after the other from the fog, then the body of the herd comes through. Ted follows them up the race to their new paddock. He pauses, with the gate closed behind him. His lips move as he counts. Forty-four head between the ewes and the lambs. He counts off just the lambs, squinting as if it might help with the fog. Sixteen, almost ready to fill his freezer. *Sixteen.* One less than seventeen.

'You've left one behind, mate.'

Shep cocks an ear.

'Come on.'

He closes the gate and takes the bike back down to the first paddock. It's an easy decline toward the gully where the fence separates the farm and the road. He parks up and stands on the bike, his knees aching with the balance.

'Where is it, Shep?'

The dog turns its head back to him. He images the lamb with a leg snapped from one of the rabbit holes, or on its side succumbing to the cold. It's nowhere to be seen. He steers the bike slowly over the hard grass along the fence line, watching the wires for a skein of wool. He stops at times, testing the slack, finding it too taut for a fat lamb to slip through. Barring the return of Haasts eagle, he just can't see how a lamb would vanish leaving no blood, no body. Nothing. It's the second time in two weeks. Two lambs, gone.

'Bugger if I know,' he says. 'Come on.'

•

He cooks oats on the burner, warming up his hands near the flames. At the dining table he gets the porridge down quickly. Marg never liked Shep coming into the house, and after she was gone it took a while to coax the border collie through the door but now he lies at Ted's feet beneath the table. The mail has built up, mostly bills. He hasn't put anything away, boxes are out, open still from when he'd searched for photos for the funeral two years ago. He wouldn't know where to start with vacuuming, tidying up.

'What'll we have for dinner, eh?' he says, already thinking ahead to the evening. Night can't come soon enough these days, but the food, *his* food doesn't taste as good as *hers*. He can't even imagine how she'd made those stewed sausages so rich. Even her mash was creamier. He didn't realize what he would miss when she left. Now his hand goes to the cross at his neck, his thumb rolls over it like a tongue over a capped tooth.

'Ted?'

A stitch of panic in his chest. *Did someone speak?* He looks over as if coming out of a dream but there's nobody in her seat. He just sees the farm outside the window. He thinks about her horoscopes again, and goes to the drawer where she kept her things. They're mostly untouched since the funeral, but now he finds the cutting from the day she disappeared. It's circled and marked up like usual.

> There are few things more important to a Libra than a loving, functional, mutually respectful relationship. This time of year sees you reviewing the present narrative around your partnership energy, as you let go of projections and expectations that cloud your view of authentic connection. Today's third quarter moon in Capricorn encourages you to revisit and release elements of your family past that skew your relationship present.

He pauses for a moment before reading on.

> A stranger or new friend may present an opportunity, it's worth considering deeply.

He exhales as he gets up to make a cup of tea. He holds himself up over the bench while the kettle boils. Maybe he'd miscounted. Maybe his eyes were playing a trick. *Sixteen lambs.* Maybe he just forgot. Maybe . . . he's becoming less certain, maybe his mind is changing. He squeezes his molars. Sheep going missing. It happens, maybe it has happened to Rodge.

He goes to the phone, spins the dial and listens to it ring.

'Morning,' Susan's voice comes down the line.

'Susan, Ted here.'

Her voice brightens. 'Hi, Ted, are we seeing you for dinner tonight?'

It's Sunday. Every other Sunday since Marg died he's gone over there. 'Yeah, I'll come by,' he says. 'Can I grab Rodge for a quick chat?'

'Of course.'

A moment passes. '*Who is it? Ted? Right, take over here for me. Eggs are done.*'

'Too bloody early for a chinwag, Ted,' Rodge says down the line. 'Got bacon in the pan. So what can I do you for?'

'Just something happened last night.'

'Go on.'

He doesn't know how to say this, it almost seems silly now. 'I lost one of my lambs.'

He hears Rodge exhale. 'Not the news I was expecting.' Ted feels heat on his neck at the note of laughter in his voice. 'Was cold out last night. Wouldn't be surprised to find ice in the river. Don't worry about the lamb, might be frozen stiff and hard to butcher, just get it up hanging in the shed.'

'No,' he says. 'You don't understand. It's vanished. Gone. There last night and gone this morning.'

'Gone? You sure?'

'Certain. And it's not the first time. I'm down two lambs in two weeks. Woke up last Sunday and noticed the same thing.'

Ted watches the kitchen clock tick, listening to the phone static. 'Both gone on Saturday nights?'

'Yep.'

'You sure now?'

'I counted them yesterday. I count them every day.' Ted's mind whirs. 'What do you reckon happened?'

'I have my suspicions. Which paddock were they in?'

'The bottom one.'

'Down near the road there?' Rodge asks.

'That's the one.'

He clicks his tongue. 'There's a pack of Māoris out near Ngapuna, you know? Wouldn't surprise me one bit if they've got roast on the table tonight.'

Ted snorts. Ngapuna, his mind goes back to a time he drove all the way out there in a rage. 'You reckon it's them, drive over here to wrangle half-fat lambs?'

'Wouldn't put it past them, reckon they're entitled probably. Always going on about the land.'

'Well I was up for the late kick-off and I didn't hear a thing,' he says.

'You watched the All Blacks. Bloody good game, wasn't it?'

'Yeah, be a tougher ask when we head to South Africa next week. Lomu's an animal, isn't he?'

'Genetic freak, mate. Don't build white fellas like that.' A pause. 'Call me cynical, but I reckon the All Blacks had a late kick-off the night when it happened to us. This time of year when the lambs are fattening the rugby's on.' He laughs now. 'Anyway, my breaky is on the table. See you tonight.'

'Yep.'

•

Years ago Marg would hand-feed the old magpie in the garden cubes of frozen mince. She was always sitting out there, waiting for it to swoop down from its nest in the pines. *Careful, it'll take one of your eyes*, he'd always warned her. *I want a tui*, she told him. *I want a native bird to feed. I wish I could fly.* His mind goes to what Rodge said about the Māoris of Ngapuna. Could they be stealing his sheep? He shakes his head, not to rid himself of the thought but out of disbelief. *Who would take a man's meat?* Once again, his mind goes back to that day, flooring the old ute until he arrived at the address he'd found on the back of the envelope.

'Is Charlie here?'

'Who is asking?' the woman had said.

Her aggression took some of the heat out of his anger. 'Is he or not?' he said.

'*He* is not here.'

'Well, if you're his wife you need to know something. He's out there trying to fuck anything that moves, including my wife. You should keep an eye on him, tell him to keep it in his fucking pants, all right?'

The woman's face had changed at that, not in the way he had expected. No sadness, or none he could see. It was a complex expression, but the way her eyes bore into him, he knew she was angry. With satisfaction swelling in his chest, he drove his old ute back out toward home.

•

He goes to the bedroom, opens Marg's old drawers where her clothes are still neatly folded, collecting mothballs. When she disappeared, he didn't go through her things; some warm clothes were gone and a few personal items with her old suitcase. That's why Jack Treloar, the constable from town, probably had his own theories. 'I know you think she might have left, Ted. But you need to be prepared for the possibility that there is another explanation. I'm sure she will turn up and this will all be a misunderstanding, but she's not taken many clothes, money or a vehicle. You think a woman would just set off without her make-up and perfume? You think you could bugger off into the world without a bit of money to make sure you land on your feet?'

He didn't tell Constable Jack Treloar about the letters he

found, the ones he tossed in the offal hole in a fit of rage. He didn't want them to know *why* she was gone. It says a lot about a bloke when his wife leaves for another man. The thought still brings on a crackle of rage at the back of his neck.

•

He drives all the way out to Ngapuna today, before a plan really crystalizes. This time, he's not planning on knocking down the door of 'Charlie,' but looking for who might be taking his lambs. Having arrived, he now feels almost silly. It's Sunday afternoon and nothing is open but the service station. The entire ute trembles when he kills the engine. He doesn't need gas, he's still got two-thirds of a tank, but he fills it up anyway with one hand on the cab and his eyes squeezed against the wind, aimed down the road at the shadowed main street.

When he pays, the cashier pushes a receipt across the counter. He takes it, drops it into the pocket of his shirt.

He goes to leave, but pauses, turns back. 'You ever know a bloke – Charlie?'

'Me?' he asks. 'No blokes called Charlie around here.'

'He left? Maybe a couple of years back?'

'No blokes called Charlie that I know,' he says without glancing up.

He's driven thirty minutes out here, and despite it all he doesn't want to leave without *something*. 'Right,' he says, before drawing a breath. 'You guys get trouble out here with the Māoris?'

The clerk glances up again, a young face but weathered by the country, cheeks pocked. The boy could be a front rower. 'Trouble?'

'Pinching livestock?'

He pokes out his bottom lip and shakes his head just once.

46

Only now does Ted notice the greenstone fishhook nested in the open collar of the man's shirt. *Shit,* he thinks. He's dark-featured, Ted should have guessed. *Probably a mix*, he thinks.

'Nothing like that round here, you might have the wrong end of the stick.'

'Yeah, probably,' he says, flicking his eyes toward the exit. The room suddenly feels hot.

'Where you come from?' the man says.

'Not far.' Ted glances past him to the calendar pinned to the wall below the clock. The corners peel away, the image is a landscape painting. Earth tones, a fine brush, mountains in the distance.

'Sorry,' Ted says, glancing down.

'What for?' The man frowns.

Ted clicks his tongue.

•

He heads back toward the main road and soon he's taking the turn-off, down that old familiar gravel track toward Rodge and Sue's. He passes a bus shelter. There's almost no paint left, and the wood beneath is wind-chewed.

'Lambs can't just vanish,' he says to no one. 'They just can't.'

Rodge was a butcher and for years he was the one to come out and butcher Ted's lambs, but for the last couple of years, since Marg left, it's been Ted who does it. He feels the rope of thick blood leap from the lamb's throats. He carts the guts and organs himself by hand down to the offal hole. Pulling the concrete cover off, he tips it all down deep into the earth. He thinks now about Marg, those letters. They were planning on leaving together. They'd not told anyone. *That's* what the letter said anyway. He's been spending more time sitting out there on the hill at the top of the paddock still talking to her, like she's there with him, her tea-warmed breath misting the morning air. He tells her everything.

•

The following Saturday he hangs an old copper bell from a hook in the tack shed. He attaches baling twine and gives it a gentle tug. The sound of the bell is a muted ting, but loud enough. *Only a man could get in, take a lamb and get out without leaving blood or anything else*, Rodge had told him. Ted hadn't noticed boot prints in the frosty grass that morning, but had he looked?

He runs the twine through the slat windows. He finds the old fencing wire in the back of the shed under a dusty tractor tyre. He ties off a length of it with the twine and runs it along the eastern side of the property between the farm and the road with Shep at his heels. He punches a stake into the soil at the end and ties the wire off. Then at intervals of roughly fifteen metres he uses wedges of firewood to keep the wire half a foot off the ground. *It's tight enough*, he thinks, looking over the paddock down toward the gully and the fence beyond. Wind tousles the pines. This is how he fixes things: he rolls up his sleeves and does it himself.

'All right, Shep. Let's test it out.'

Back in the shed, he dials Rodge's number.

'What can I do you for, Ted?'

'Could you stay on the line and listen for a moment.'

'Listen for what?'

'Just for a bell sound,' he says.

'A bell?'

'I've run a wire along the fence, connected it to a bell in the shed.'

He laughs. 'You've rigged up your own alarm system?'

'Something like that.'

'Better off sending 10,000 volts through fence.'

'And electrocute half my flock.'

'They'd know they'd been shocked, that's for sure.'

'I'll stick with the bell.'

He hears him sniff. 'All right, hurry up, I'll listen out.'

'Two minutes.'

He lays the handset face up on the work bench, and strides out to the roadside, his gumboots thumping. As the wind strengthens, a mist flows from it silently over the grass. He takes a moment to step on the wire, then he hooks the boot under it and lifts it emulating a man tripping. Then gives it a couple of good tugs with his fist before rushing back to the phone.

'Well?'

'Yeah, I heard it.'

'How many times?'

'Maybe five, six.'

'Beauty,' he says. 'Thanks for your help.'

'And you're going to sit out there all night? You'll freeze your balls off *and* miss the game?'

'I'll have it on the radio,' he says. He cares less for the game these days, although he'd never admit it. Since he lost Marg, most things have lost their colour.

'Be good to beat the bastards over there.'

'Especially after last year. Never know, they might poison our food again like the World Cup.'

'We'll see.'

'Right-o, I'll be seeing you,' Ted says, hanging the phone up.

If it came to it, if he was ever backed into a corner, he thinks about how long it would take to get to his rifle. It's possible, he knows, to hold the rifle out and rest the barrel against your temple. To reach the trigger with your thumb. But he's not rehearsed it for weeks. He'd have to do Shep first. That'd be the hard part. But he'd never leave the farm.

•

At twilight, he shoots another rabbit. The same spot down near the fence line at the back paddock. The shot carted the body over itself halfway down the hill while the two other rabbits scattered. As he goes to hang it on the fence post he sees where the last rabbit was, there's only a nail. *Birds have gotten at it*, he thinks. *But where are the bones?* For just a moment he has the feeling that someone is watching him. He looks down at the long greying hairs of his forearms, then up toward the pines at the edge of the property.

•

His alarm sounds. An early riser he always has been, but never this early. He kills it and scratches at his eyes. Shep still doesn't sleep on the bed but he's close, Ted can hear him breathing as his feet find the floor. He pulls on his jeans, a singlet, his flannel shirt and a Swanndri over it all and tucks the last wisps of his white hair into an old hide hat. The rain came late and heavy through the night, the pot on the floor of the kitchen is half full. Turning the kitchen light on, he watches the cockroaches scatter, one under the fridge, one under the stove.

He makes himself a hot cup of tea, and a piece of Marmite toast which he eats in three bites. He takes the torch now, killing the lights inside the house. He pauses at the door for a moment, then heads back into the house for the rifle.

•

The commentary leaps into the shed when he switches the radio on, kick-off is just a few minutes away.

'. . . *at capacity of fifty thousand people, and I can tell you there are a lot of nervous Kiwis in the ground who have made the trip over. Great anticipation amongst all . . .*'

It's possible, Ted realizes now, that even the police are probably focused on the rugby. Those on duty listening to the game in their cars or at the station. The first professional sports team to tour 'post-apartheid' South Africa. *Police are hopeless anyway,* he thinks. Were no use when it came to searching for his wife. They probably laughed about him, some poor old codger, a cuckold abandoned by the wife that was always too good for him. They would have called her flighty, seeking a better life, a *crazy one.*

•

Focusing on the radio, as much out of curiosity as anything resembling passion, he keeps his eyes on the bell hanging above him. He hears his wife's voice and feels a prickle on his neck. *Go back to the house, you old fool.* Another sound outside now, the scraping call of an opossum. He could spotlight it, knock the pest from its perch with the rifle.

•

By half-time the opossum has fallen silent again. With Japie Mulder's try, South Africa are up 15-6. He doesn't hear the bell tinkle, but when he looks up again in the dark, he notices it move. Just a hint. He freezes, suddenly conscious of his heart beating. The bell is turned, the wire is tight as though a foot is still standing on the wire, then it moves again with a single soft ding as it settles vertical again. This is as far as he had planned. He wasn't sure if it would work at all, or if anyone would come, but now he knows he must act. He can't just sit here. Then he hears something. Movement out there in the paddock. The lambs, the herd, fleeing.

It could be a shadow in the wind spooking them. It could be anything. He rises and walks slowly toward the window. He sees nothing but fog. He looks back to the bell now, finding it still leaning. He hears that voice again, not quite external but not entirely in his head. He wishes Shep was here, he wishes someone was here. Marg, with that hair she was always dyeing to keep the grey out of and those eyes that were once so sharp. He still has all the magazines from the travel agents, the cruises and resorts still circled in her black marker. *The places we could have gone.* But it was here on this farm, in the family house arched like a cathedral they stayed. They were never the ones to come home with fresh tans and books of photos. Of all the postcards they have, banded in the drawer with their wedding album, they'd never sent a single one, and it was all she wanted. 'Someone needs to tend the bloody farm,' he says to no one. That's how the arguments always ended.

•

He tightens his belt and takes the rifle with him out into the night. The grass cracks beneath his boots as he makes his way. He opens the gate gently, lifting the latch silently. He's electric with anticipation; someone is out there.

Moving through the paddock, closer, and closer. The flock emerges like fists of white rock through a receding tide of fog. They rise, begin to move. It's too dark, too foggy to count, even if they would stay still long enough for him to get close. He senses something, a presence nearby. There are no headlights on the road. He continues toward the lambs and they part now, flowing away, sending their tentative *bahs* out into the atmosphere. There is one orphaned sound. Not a lamb calling in fear, but one distinct agonizing cry.

It's coming from back toward the shed. He rushes, his boots

thumping and arms swinging. By the time he gets up the hill each breath is pained. But the sound is louder now, with an echo. The heavy concrete cover is missing from the offal hole, the lamb has fallen in there. It must be a five-metre drop at least. It would have snapped legs, unless the rotting offal was soft enough to cushion its fall. But why is the concrete cover off? Another thought comes unbidden: what if it didn't stumble into the hole, what if someone dropped it in there?

He turns. And seems to hear the blow, the crunch, before he feels it. Red, black, and he's dazed. Something strikes the side of his leg and he trips. Then hard hands are pushing him, turning him so his feet lose the earth. He slides in. 'Please,' he calls as he reaches for the edge of the hole, but his fingers don't grip. He tumbles, a steep sudden descent, then a crunch. Pain all over. The smell fills his head, and he feels the wetness of the lamb beneath him. He looks up and sees a face looking down. It's silhouetted by the tinsel of stars. Then the aperture of night closes like an eye as the concrete cover grinds into place once more. He screams but he knows that no one will hear him, no one will come for him. No one ever came for her.

•

We were not lovers. We never planned on being lovers. We met at the library in town, of all places. We were two girls from different towns, with husbands they could do without. It was similar taste in books that brought us together; she would go in when Ted went to the bank and I'd be there most days reading in a quiet corner. We both dreamed of worlds outside of our farms, outside of our husbands. We wrote each other, planned our meet-ups at the library, talked about the books we loved, and soon we were imagining a different kind of life. One full of travel, one where we had each other for company and support, but it was never romantic. So when he arrived at my door, searching for

Charlie, I knew exactly who he was. I wanted to scream at him, 'I am Charlie.'

When I saw the article in the newspaper part of me died like a frost-bitten limb full of phantom pain of a life I would never have and a friend I truly loved. Her letters had stopped. Right when we were making our plans to escape. It had to be him. She wouldn't just wander off without me. I started coming to the farm, observing him, watching the way the guilt bent him towards that hole, where he'd sit and talk. He'd apologize. No one else could have her, that's what he would say. She made him do it, she had to push him. Sometimes he was speaking right at it and I just knew. No farmer can resist a mystery. Ted was always going to find what was happening to his lambs, he was always going to end up down there with them, with her. I did it for Marg.

SUNDOWN

SHEENA KAMAL

I've left Vancouver and come to America, not for the first time. I don't particularly care for it, but it is what it is. There's a vague idea taking root in my mind, of driving all the way down to Mexico, assuming a new identity and living on a beach for the rest of my days, surviving on tacos, virgin margaritas and that surf life.

I'm not a person that such glorious fortunes generally happen to, but there's always hope. I can learn to surf, I tell myself, as I stop at a small-town gas station in Washington state. There's a first time for everything. My dog Whisper is in the front seat of the Corolla even though I've told her time and again it's safer in the back. But she has attitude, and a will stronger than mine.

So she's up front when a stranger appears at my window. She's barking, and all but leaps into my lap to protect me. My heart fills with joy at this evidence that she cares about me and the meals I provide. This is what my life has come to, but it's not nothing to have the love of a finicky bitch like her, and I know how lucky I am.

The stranger has doubts about us both. He backs away from

the car with his hands up. It's an unconscious reaction, I suppose, but it doesn't sit right to see a Black man who's done nothing wrong acting like I'm the police. Which is why I roll down the window an inch to ask what he wants instead of just ignoring him like I usually would. If it's a blowjob in the cab of his semi parked to the side over there, I'll have to politely decline.

At my age, nothing in the world could tempt me in that direction.

But no, it's not a blowjob in a truck. Turns out it's something quite different. 'You just driving through?' he asks. He looks a bit older than me. Maybe in his late forties, with a little patchy beard and kind eyes.

'Maybe,' I say. 'Maybe not.' Doesn't matter how nice his eyes are. I'm not in the habit of explaining anything to men, so why start now?

'What you do is your business, lady, I'm not interested in the particulars. Was just about to get back on the road myself and I saw you pull up. Saw you got that brown sugar, and thought I'd give you the same warning someone gave me first time I drove this route. Don't stay here tonight. This here's a sundown town.'

He tips his cap like a cowboy and gets into the truck. I watch him drive away, headed for the highway. Then I pump my gas and go inside to pay. There's a cop lingering by the energy drinks. A soccer mom in a candy pink sweatsuit emerges from the restroom in the back. When I ask the cashier for the code to get in, he tells me it's out of service.

Now, I could argue and say soccer mom just used it, but of course I know what he means. It's out of service for me. The same brown sugar that compelled the trucker to offer a warning is what's closed the washroom for me. I'm part native, part middle eastern. Just like with the trucker, in white America I'm something other. Something unwelcome.

The cashier is young, maybe in his twenties, but he already knows that racism will get him far in this world. I see him slide a drawer open. From inside, the glint of a gun. The cop moves from the energy drinks to the chips, just a few feet away from me. He's got his hand on his gun, too.

All the air is sucked out of the room. Is this the hill I die on today?

No. Not over a restroom, and not with my dog in the car, wondering where I am.

I pay for the gas and leave. Driving past the sad motel where I'd been thinking of stopping for the night, glancing in my rear-view to see if the cop had a mind to follow me out of town. I'll have to pee in the woods like an animal, but it's a small price to pay for getting the hell away from a sundown town. I'm Canadian, but even I've heard about the Green Book, where in the fifties African American travelers were warned about the safe and not-so-safe places to eat, sleep, and access services while traveling. And I know that sundown towns are all-white communities that still exist de facto today. Where, as you might have guessed, after the sun goes down all bets are off if you've got any brown sugar at all.

Someone just might get the idea to take it from you.

•

I don't want anyone to take it from her, the girl walking along the shoulder, and that's why I stop. We've just gotten back on the road, and immediately there's another problem. I must be cursed or something, because no matter how far I run, trouble always seems to find me.

The girl is headed toward town, and it's almost dusk. So she'll be stuck there after dark, and I can't find it in my heart to keep driving like her life doesn't matter. She's Latina, wearing a men's sweater that goes to her knees and a pair of jeans rolled up at the cuffs. They don't look like her clothes. Her gait is unsteady, as though she's tired or dazed. As my car slows, she tries to duck into the woods, into the protection of the forest, but she loses her balance and falls.

I pull over to help her up, but she scrambles to her feet and starts to run. She falls again. It takes her a lot longer to get to her feet this time.

'Wait,' I call, getting out of the car.

It's only when she sees I'm a woman that she relaxes. Me being a woman doesn't mean she's safe with me, but the fact that she thinks it does is a bad sign. 'I need help,' she says. Her English is accented, but clear.

'Where are you going?'

'I need to go to the police. My friend is trapped.'

I think about the cop at the gas station with his hand on his gun. 'You can't trust the police here,' I say. Even though you can't trust the police anywhere, it seems an important point to be making to this girl, near this sundown town.

'Please, we have to do something! When they find out I'm gone, it'll be bad for him. He was too high to come with me. It's not like I could carry him on my back.' She's speaking quickly, tripping over her words. I wonder if this is a lure of some kind, to rob motorists with good intentions . . . but she's telling the truth. I have an instinct for this kind of thing, for seeing when people are hiding something, and when they're being honest.

I can tell her panic, and her fear, are genuine. 'You think there's a chance they don't know you're gone yet?'

'They were passed out when I left.' Her eyes dart away from mine. She feels guilty for leaving her friend behind. That much is clear.

'How did you end up with them?'

'I went to a party with my cousins yesterday, and I lost them. I was feeling sick so I went outside for some air, and there was this guy. That's all I remember. I woke up in this house. There was a boy with me in a room. He's younger than me, thirteen. They gave us something, some kind of pills. I didn't swallow all of mine.'

She glances at the car, where Whisper has put her head out to see what's going on. 'She won't bite you,' I say. 'How far away is the house?'

'I don't know. Not far.'

'How long have you been walking?'

'Since an hour, maybe less?'

A hundred thoughts race through my head, but the main one is this: people are trafficked everywhere in the world. In Canada, and here, too. This shouldn't happen to anyone, but it hits a nerve when it's about children.

If she's right and they don't know she's gone yet, this boy might still have a chance. 'Can you tell me how to get to the house?'

She nods. 'I'm going with you to get Elias. That's my friend. I'm Raquel.'

'Nora,' I say. 'I'll try to get your friend back.'

'I'm coming with you,' she tells me.

My immediate reaction is no. She's likely to be a liability, and I don't want her anywhere near her kidnappers. But then what? Do I just leave her here on the side of the road?

We've got about an hour until sundown, then it won't be safe here for either of us. I let Whisper out of the car to meet Raquel. She throws her arms around my dog and holds on a little too tightly.

'We don't have much time,' I say.

She wipes her tears away and climbs in the car. In the back-seat because Whisper won't give up the front.

•

Raquel chats nonstop to cover her fear. She tells me her whole life story. Sixteen, moved from El Salvador when she was eight to live with her uncle, his new wife, and her cousins. She's great at school but scared to go there sometimes. It's not always safe. Her mother calls her every Sunday and, since today is Sunday, her mom must be worried about her.

Everything is true except for the part about her mother calling her on Sundays. I can tell by the slight rise in her voice, the tears she's clearly fighting again, that it's not true. Her mom doesn't call her on Sundays. At least not anymore.

She talks about school and her cousins, whom she loves. What she doesn't say is what happened to her in the house we're driving to, and I don't ask. Because I'm hoping that nothing did, that she escaped before anything could. And whatever she's experienced . . . sharing your various traumas can't be forced. Certain ones should never be experienced, especially by a child.

Whatever happened in the house bonded her to Elias, that much is clear. She desperately wants to save him. 'Do you have kids?' she asks.

'A daughter.'

This opens up a whole line of questions about how old my daughter is, where she is, why am I not with her now, et cetera. 'She doesn't speak to me anymore,' I say, and that shuts Raquel up momentarily. She's starting to doubt me again, because any woman who isn't a good mother, who has been banished by her own child, must not be a very reliable sort. I can't say she's wrong, and I can't say it doesn't still ache to the bone. It's one of my various traumas I don't like to discuss.

You could say the reason I picked her up, and I'm on my way to save her friend, is because this trauma still lives with me. You could say that, but I'd deny it.

Raquel directs me to a road branching off the main one. It's rural here, so there are no houses nearby. The closer we get, the more she wrings her hands to keep them from trembling. Then she tucks them under her legs to hide them. I pretend I don't notice.

We come up to a bend in the road, and Raquel tells me this is it. I park the car behind a copse of trees. On the other side of these trees, she says, is a house attached to a junkyard. There are lots of places to hide children, in the junkyard and in the trees. If I were a piece of shit pedophile human trafficker, I'd live somewhere like this, too.

Raquel wants to come with me, but that's a hard no. Whisper wants to, as well, which is more of a battle. I have a stern talking-to with her about watching over the car, and the girl in it.

'You can drive, right?' I ask Raquel.

'Well, my cousin gave me a couple lessons, but I don't think—'

'Get in the driver's seat,' I say, cutting her off only because we don't have a lot of time left. 'If you see anyone other than me come up to the car, drive away.'

'And leave you here?'

'I can take care of myself.'

Something about my expression tells her I'm serious. I'm allergic to violence, given my past, but I'm capable of giving as good as I get. In the army, and when I worked for a PI outfit in Vancouver, I developed certain survival skills. I'm not proud of them but they've saved my life numerous times.

Survival skill number one, never trust the cops.

I've met one or two of them whose hearts might have been in the right place, even though their guns were in their hands.

But in the heat of the moment how can you know what's in someone's heart?

Even without that momentary heat, people are complicated creatures. It's impossible to know and better to keep out of shooting range. This is general good life advice I'd like to impart on Raquel before I go, but there's not a lot of time left for her friend.

I leave the engine running and give her my phone and my password. It's nothing fancy but can make calls and access the Internet. When I leave, she's to look up the right number and call the FBI. Not the police, not in a sundown town. The cop at the gas station didn't give me much faith that he'd care about the trafficking of immigrant minors. The FBI have to make a full report on all cases of heinous acts that come their way, such as hate crimes and human smuggling.

I take a hammer from my toolbox in the trunk. Raquel looks at the hammer, at my worn leather driving gloves. She's even more scared now . . .

Of me or for Elias? Impossible to know.

'I'll be right back,' I say to them. Whisper whines at me, but I throw her a stern glance over my shoulder as I walk toward the junkyard. Behind that is the yellow clapboard house, sitting innocently in the fading light of dusk.

•

Lots of little hidey holes in a junkyard, and when they notice Raquel is gone, it's the first place they'll look. If they're smart, which maybe they are. I've never underestimated the intelligence of evil people. That can be a fatal mistake.

Skirting around the piles of scrap, old appliances and rusted-through car frames, I approach the house from the rear, where it backs onto the woods. Also a good place to hide. I make a note of that, just in case I need it. The forest here is so much like the forests of Vancouver, and the feeling of homesickness is so sharp that I take a few deep breaths to calm down.

Four count inhale, four count hold, four count exhale.

It works like a charm, and I'm back to normal. It's how I know the house is too quiet. There's quiet, and then there's this feeling of expectation. Like something's about to happen. You don't know what or who, but best be on guard.

A quick peek through the windows tells me no one is in the kitchen, but there's a man sleeping in the bedroom just one window away. The back door is slightly ajar, which is how Raquel must have left it when she took off. I slip in the door, thankful for my soft-soled shoes. That moment of gratitude doesn't last.

It all happens so quickly. I only make it a few feet when I hear the click, and I know the safety's now off a gun. There's a flash of movement from the woman holding the gun, and then another from the man who was prostrate in bed just a few moments before I started my deep breathing. Maybe I wasn't as quiet as I thought.

She's coming from a room to my right, trying to aim, while he makes a grab for me from the bedroom to my left. I dip and pivot quickly, throwing my shoulder into his soft gut and, when he doubles over, straighten and drive my knee into his groin.

The gunshot is loud, temporarily deafening. And it's only because I don't feel any pain that I know it missed me . . . but it hit him.

He's on the ground now, and she's standing pale-faced in a faded green robe. She raises the gun again, but the hammer is already in my hand. Before she knows it, it's whipping toward her and hits her in the belly, knocking the breath right out of her. Her cry is an awful thing as she drops to the ground, to join her . . . husband? Man? It doesn't matter. I pick up the gun and back away, keeping an eye on them both as I continue moving, throwing open doors.

There's a boy standing behind the door to the basement, looking scared. Dazed. He seems to be a little younger than thirteen, which makes me that much angrier.

'Elias? Your friend Raquel sent me for you,' I say to him calmly. 'Let's go.'

He hesitates. He's at the top of the stairs, where he must have climbed when he heard the gunshot. 'Or you can stay here.'

The woman looks at me from her position on the ground. There are tears in her eyes. She's in pain and crying over her man, but she might find her anger soon. I want to get the hell out of here before then.

'Come on,' I say to Elias.

I reach for his thin hand with my free one. He takes it. He's all bones and sharp angles. Someone needs to fatten him up, but that's a problem for another time and another person. I pull him along with me to the front door, which leads out to the junkyard.

Now we're outside.

It's only because the closest pile of scrap is just by the door that we're able to hide so fast when the pickup truck pulls in. My eye catches the covered bed, then the Idaho license plate. It's too soon for some curious motorist to come inquiring about the commotion, so it's likely that they were already on their way. Maybe they're involved in this scheme.

I shove Elias behind me as the woman comes to the door screaming that there was a break-in, and her man Dougie is shot. Out of this whole shitshow of a situation, the thing I'm least surprised about is that there's a child trafficker living in a sundown town, and his name is Dougie. From the corner of my eye, I see a man jump out of the truck and go inside. Possibly a 'Billy' or a 'Petey'.

Not that I'll stick around long enough to find out, because Petey has a gun in his hand. I don't want to take a chance that he's better with it than the woman in the house, or that he's better with it than me. Firearms are death. I'm no stranger to them but they make me sick.

I put that out of my mind as I grip the gun I took off the floor in the house in one hand, and Elias's thin bicep in the other, and pull him along. We're ducking and moving from pile to pile. But he's dead weight. Groggy, just coming down from some high. It's a good thing he's so skinny, or else we'd never manage. We haven't made it far when I hear noise coming from the house and Petey call out, 'Come on out, bitch! I know you're still here!'

I think Elias is going to wet himself. He's shaking that hard. He finds his feet in the next few seconds, and it's a good thing, too, because we've only got a few more seconds before this all turns sideways. The way the road bends and curves, and splits off to the highway, we just need to get to the car, and maybe we've got a chance. We reach the spot I think is directly in front of the car, barring the trees.

To get to safety, there's a dash across about twenty feet of open space.

'We're going to die,' Elias whispers.

I'm of a mind to give him that old lecture, that everyone dies. At least if he goes it'll be trying to gain his freedom from . . . whatever went on in that house. But there's no time to get into it.

'When I say run, you run,' I tell him. 'You see those trees right there? Your friend Raquel is on the other side.'

'She's not my friend. Friends don't leave each other.'

'She sent me to get you. And she's waiting. Don't run in a straight line. Get in the car. Don't wait more than one minute for me, OK?'

Our voices are barely a murmur in the eerie quiet of the junkyard. I can hear rustling. A man who's not used to being stealthy, searching. There's still a fraction of daylight left, painting the sky a pale orange.

I give Elias a push. 'Go!'

Turning in the direction of the junkyard noises, holding the gun with both hands. The safety is already off. It's stunning how familiar it feels to me.

You can't just run off to Mexico, it's saying. You live for the action.

I might die for it, too, I tell myself, as I shoot at an old washing machine lying on its side. To the far right of me, to draw attention away from Elias. But I've miscalculated. The sounds I heard were a diversion. The man from the pickup is suddenly behind me, where I thought was safe. I hear his movement and manage to duck as a bullet hits the rusted car frame beside me. I'm ducking and running now, zigzagging through the junkyard, toward the rear of the house. My palms are sweating inside my gloves. If I can get to the trees, I'll be able to double back to the car.

And if they're not stupid, Raquel and Elias will be gone by then, taking Whisper to a brand-new life. If they are stupid, then I just might catch up to them. I'm not sure which I want more. There's not enough time to step carefully, to pay attention to where I'm going, so I shouldn't have been surprised that I'm suddenly on the ground, tripped up by a rusted car engine.

Then Petey's on top of me.

There's beer and stale cigarettes on his breath. He outweighs me by at least fifty pounds, and he thinks that must give him an advantage because he doesn't use his gun immediately. Which makes him stupid, but I understand his thinking. He wants me alive, at least to answer some questions. His big mistake. He doesn't know I'm armed, too.

The woman's gun is still in my hand. I manage to slam the butt of it into his temple and use his momentary loss of control to jerk my shoulders and hips up to flip us. I get to my feet. He's remembered his gun now and is raising it, but I stomp on his wrist and kick it away. He grabs my ankle with the other hand and pulls me to the ground.

I can hear my heartbeat. Feel my breath ragged in my throat.

What follows is a desperate, brutal scuffle for my gun. Rather, the one that belongs to the woman in the house. He's almost got it when I brace myself on my elbows and use the extra support to give me some power as I kick him in the face. He screams and falls back.

There's a roaring in my ears. I think it's my heart again, but no. It's the Corolla, bursting through a gap in the trees.

'Let's go!' Raquel shouts from the open window.

I'm on my feet now, running toward them. There's a gunshot behind me but the car is still moving and I'm still running. Dougie may be bigger than me, but he's not faster. We must be out of shooting range now. When the car slows, the back door on the passenger side flies open. Elias offers me a hand. He pulls me in, and we take off again.

Whisper is barking up a storm but everyone else is deathly quiet. Raquel gets on the highway and we start to pick up speed. 'What the hell were you doing back there?' I say. 'You could have gotten killed!'

'I couldn't leave you. Me and Elias decided.'

'I think I'm going to be sick,' says Elias.

I grab a plastic bag near my feet and hand it to him. Then I turn to Raquel. 'Did you call the FBI?'

'No,' she says.

'Why not?'

'I don't have my papers.'

An uncomfortable, knowing silence fills the car. She doesn't like talking to the cops, either. Any kind of cop. She's undocumented.

'We want you to get back to your daughter one day,' she says. We being her, because she's the one who knows about my daughter.

My breath is still coming fast. I understand what she's not saying. She's hoping that one day she'll get back to her own mother. Or her mother will come to her. 'Watch your speed,' I say. 'You don't want the cops to pull us over around here.'

The daylight finally gives up, and night comes. Raquel eases up on the gas and puts on the lights so there'll be no reason to stop us.

I think my heart is going to jump out of my skin when a police cruiser passes, lights flashing. They're headed away from us, in the direction of the junkyard house. 'Slow down,' I say to her.

'If I go too slow someone will know,' she tells me. She's right, but the tension still won't leave my body. When we get far enough away, I'll take over the driving. For now, she's doing a good job. Whisper puts her head in the space between the driver and passenger seat and whines at me. I scratch behind her ears and do the breathing exercise, while Elias pukes quietly into the plastic bag.

•

The car smells of sick and sweat. Whisper and I are driving through the night because I'm too awake to stop. I want to get as far away from Raquel and Elias as I can.

When I asked them if they wanted to go to the hospital, both refused. I couldn't take the chance of taking them there and having them run away. Into more trouble. Elias wouldn't tell me where he lives so Raquel directed me to her uncle's house instead, just before Portland. I pulled up a few houses away to let them out.

She hugged Whisper first, then me, and asked me to give her my number. Elias watched with his big green eyes directly on my face but said nothing. Both their expressions were haunted, but she was better at hiding it.

'Thank you for saving me,' I said.

'Thank you for saving *me*,' she replied.

Still, Elias said nothing. He put his arms around Whisper and buried his face in her neck. Then gave me a small, almost imperceptible nod that erased any belief that I have ice in my heart. He was still scared, and he didn't trust his great brown savior. That's good. That's the way it should be. Saviors are just people, and are they doing the saving because of you, or because they have some other hidden motivation?

I wanted to say something comforting, something helpful, but that has never been my forte. Instead, I told them to be careful at parties. Later I cursed myself because what I should have said is 'don't go to parties, stay at home, lock your doors and shut your windows, don't trust anyone'.

Which is the soundest advice I can think of.

'Are you going to call your daughter now?' Raquel asked.

'Yes,' I lied.

It was a kindness, that. Because that's what she wanted to hear in that moment. She looked up at her uncle's house and a change came over her. A kind of toughness emerged, in the set of her jaw, her grim expression. She said goodbye to me and Whisper, then reached for Elias's hand. To my surprise, he let her take it. Together they walked to the house.

Only Elias looked back, past me and to my dog. Whisper gave him a little bark of encouragement. She's not terribly affectionate, but she can sometimes be generous with her love.

•

I think of them both as we drive through Oregon. Eventually we stop at a McDonald's for a break. I clean out the car as best as I can with the cleaning wipes in the trunk. Then use the free Wi-Fi to access the Internet on my laptop and submit an anonymous tip to the FBI website. Giving the details of the house and the license plate for the pickup. After that, I send a message to the PI outfit in Vancouver to let them know I gave their number to a girl named Raquel. Should she ever call for help, I'd consider it a personal favor if they assisted her. We're not on great terms, my old employers and I, but they wouldn't turn her away.

'You OK?' I ask Whisper. She yawns and climbs into the backseat to sleep. It's been an eventful day. I wish I could do the same but I'm still too jazzed.

As we drive away, I try to put the events of the past day out of my mind. I hope Elias finds his tongue again, and his light. I hope Raquel's mother calls her this Sunday. I hope they never think of that house, or me, ever again.

These old-growth forests still feel like Vancouver, like home, but I'm not ready to go back yet. I drive straight through them and deeper into the night. Tomorrow there'll be a new sunrise, a new sunset. Best keep moving forward. Destination possibly Mexico, but the truth is I'm not quite sure where I'll wind up. In the end isn't it all unknown?

DEATH IN DARJEELING

VASEEM KHAN

1

The toy train wound its way up from the foothills of the Himalayas, penetrating the curtain of mist that clung to the flanks of the incline. The journey from Bombay to Calcutta had taken almost forty hours on the Imperial Indian Mail, then overnight on the Darjeeling Mail to Siliguri. The narrow-gauge Darjeeling Himalayan Railways train would take a further seven hours to climb up to the network of hill stations, navigating impossible curves and sheer gradients, slowing to such an extent that passengers could jump on and off without the train halting.

Persis had never ventured this far east. Born and raised in Bombay, she had rarely travelled beyond the city limits. That she was here now, in the company of an Englishman, filled her with an odd sense of wonder.

The train jolted around another steep curve. The Englishman in question beamed at her from the seat opposite. 'I've always wanted to visit the tea plantations. One for the scrapbook, I dare say.'

She'd known Blackfinch for less than six months, but, in that time, they'd struck up a working relationship that had already seen them successfully tackle several major investigations. As India's first – and, to date, only – female police detective, she was thankful of an ally, *any* ally. Her own nature tended to the solitary, verging on misanthropic. And yet . . . Matters had recently become complicated. An attraction had reared its head that couldn't be denied nor pursued, not without undermining everything she'd achieved. Independence might have been three years in the past, but in the new India, historical prejudices – on both sides – still counted for more than anyone cared to admit.

'We're not here on holiday,' she muttered. 'A man is dead.'

'Being miserable won't bring him back to life,' countered Blackfinch, and looked back out over the valley. A hoopoe sang in the branches of a tree growing out of the hillside, so close he could have reached out and touched it.

Persis fingered the telegram in her pocket, the urgent summons that had brought her here at such short notice.

Why *had* Byrne been so insistent?

2

She discovered the answer to that question that evening, sitting in the office of Rector Stafford Byrne at the St Peter's School, otherwise known as the Eton of the East. Over a century old, St Peter's had been founded, like others of its ilk, to provide an English public school education in India for the sons of her colonial masters. Its original site had been Calcutta but, back in 1864, the school had been moved to a hilltop overlooking the city of Darjeeling and facing the Kangchenjunga massif.

Byrne had changed little since Persis had known him. An austere Irishman, he had taught at Bombay's Cathedral Girls

School where Persis had navigated a difficult childhood, the daughter of a widower, prickly, aloof, and not given to the social graces that other girls seemed born to.

'Persis, I'm so glad you came.'

'How could I not?' Persis waved at her companion. 'This is Archie Blackfinch. He's a criminalist from the Metropolitan Police Service, currently stationed with the Bombay Force. I thought his expertise might be useful. He agreed to accompany me.'

'That's terribly good of you, Mr Blackfinch—'

'Archie, please.'

'Archie,' nodded Byrne. 'Will either of you take some tea?'

While the tea was being prepared, Byrne explained the situation. 'Jack Murphy was one of our senior tutors. Five days ago, he was killed when he fell from Tiger Hill, a peak not far from here. Jack had been in Darjeeling for six years; he was an enthusiastic and seasoned climber. It is inconceivable to me that he could have been so careless as to slip to his death. Others have suggested that his death might have been deliberate, that he took his own life. I pray fervently that that is not the case. Jack was a Catholic. Suicide would mean damnation for his soul, and I would not wish that upon my worst enemy.'

'There *is* another possibility,' said Persis softly.

'Yes,' agreed Byrne. 'And that is why you're here.'

'What do the local authorities say?'

Byrne snorted, his thick grey eyebrows coming together in disgust. 'We have a small constabulary here. They have neither the wit nor the wherewithal to deal with something like this. They took one look at the circumstances and ruled it an accident. Why go to the bother of an actual investigation when the facts can be made to fit an open–and–shut verdict?'

'How will they feel about my involvement?'

Byrne reached inside his desk, removed a steel flask, and poured a measure of whisky into his tea. 'Persis Wadia, have I ever struck you as the sort of man who gives a fig what anyone thinks?' He held up the flask. 'Would either of you care for a drop?'

3

They shared a light supper with Byrne, and then Blackfinch had scraped back his chair and asked Persis if she'd like to take a stroll around the town.

Catching her former tutor's eye, she'd declined.

'Suit yourself,' he said, and set off jauntily.

'A handsome man,' remarked Byrne as he tamped tobacco into a pipe.

Persis said nothing, acutely aware of the older man's penetrating gaze. Byrne merely stuck the pipe in his mouth and smiled at her. 'People are a mystery, Persis. Take Jack Murphy. As charismatic a man as I've known. He could have worked anywhere. And yet he ended up *here*, teaching the Classics to the sons of men who wouldn't give him the time of day.'

'Why didn't he leave in '47?'

'Loved the mountains too much. They got into his blood. Like they do for many of us.'

'Was he a good tutor?'

They were interrupted by the arrival of a young nun in a black habit. Her face held a quality of ethereal beauty that Persis found disturbing.

'Ah, perhaps Sister Agnes can answer that. Agnes is – was – Jack's teaching assistant. I thought you might like to speak with her.'

4

Agnes Sheehan was twenty and had been working at the school for less than a year, having moved north from a convent in Calcutta.

'The day he died, did Jack seem perturbed?' asked Persis, once Byrne had left to retire for the night.

'No. He was his usual self.'

'Had he been bothered by anything recently?'

'No.'

'You can think of no reason why he might have wished to end his own life?'

'No,' she said. 'He wouldn't do that.'

'What makes you so sure?'

She didn't reply, lowering her eyes to her hands, clasped on her lap.

'What did he do that day?'

'It was a Friday, so we had classes until Vespers. After that, he went back to his quarters. Here at the school.'

'He spent the rest of the evening there?'

She hesitated. 'I don't know. But he did mention that he was going to the club later.'

'The club?'

'Some of the local gentlemen gather at the Hotel King George on Friday evenings. To play cards. To drink.' She blushed at the words as if merely saying them out loud might infect her with sin.

'Was he a popular tutor?'

'Yes. Very much. He was passionate about his subject and he also ran the Scouts during the vacation periods. The boys loved him.'

'Just the boys?'

Her blush deepened. 'I don't understand.'

'I think you do.' Sheehan squirmed in her seat, but said nothing. 'Did Jack have a lady friend? A lover?'

A quick shake of the head. 'Not that I know of. I mean, not that that was the sort of thing Jack would have discussed with me. But Darjeeling is a small place. You hear things.'

'Was there anyone who might have intended him harm? Anyone holding a grudge?'

'No. Jack got on with everyone.'

Persis held her with a steady gaze. 'What do *you* think happened?'

She seemed bewildered. 'I think— I think he fell. I think he simply fell.'

<h2 style="text-align:center">5</h2>

They began in earnest the following morning, having spent the night at the school, twin rooms facing onto the school grounds, single beds smothered beneath clouds of mosquito netting, geckos scuttling across the walls.

After a hurried breakfast, their first port of call was the site of Murphy's death.

The climb up to Tiger Hill took over an hour – the road was too steep, too narrow, and too pitted for motorized transport. They might have gone faster but Byrne had insisted on accompanying them. It was strange for Persis to see a man she had once considered the epitome of male vigour so diminished by the ravages of time. She wondered why he didn't take a rickshaw, but it seemed a matter of pride for him.

They passed the old British military cantonment, deserted since the end of the war, and a cemetery where soldiers lay buried beneath snow for a good part of the year. At Ghoom they turned left, skirted past the Senchal golf course, and onto a rocky road leading upwards to Tiger Hill, a small plateau with commanding views over the surrounding slopes, all the way down to the Teesta and Rangeet rivers several thousand feet below.

Most of the hillsides were blanketed by tea gardens, scores of tea bushes laid out in regimented rows. Beyond the twin rivers, foothills served as sentries to the great mountains of the Himalayan range, with the snow-capped peak of Kangchenjunga spectacularly drawing the eye. Everest was a hundred miles away, just visible, perspective making the great mountain appear smaller than her sister peak.

The air was thin but cleaner and headier than anything Persis had experienced.

'They call it the roof of the world,' said Byrne, catching his breath beside her. 'If you come here at dawn you can watch the sun rise over the mountains and feel God's presence.'

He ushered them towards the edge of the deserted plateau.

'Look down there.'

They peered over the edge and saw what looked like the opening to a large concrete tunnel. Their eyes followed it as it arrowed down the slope some four hundred feet back the way they'd come.

'They're dotted all over the hills,' remarked Blackfinch, sunlight glinting from his spectacles. 'I noticed them on the way up.'

'Yes,' said Byrne. 'Storm drains. They're for the run-off. For when the snow melts in spring and during the monsoon. They keep the water from ruining the tea plantations. Jack Murphy fell into that pipe. They found his body at the bottom. His neck was broken.'

'Isn't the pipe too small?'

'Jack wasn't a big man. Slender as a whippet, as they say. We lose half a dozen children every year in these damned drains.'

Persis watched as Blackfinch dropped into a squat and rubbed his knuckles over the short grass. 'Did the investigators come up here and look around?'

'Investigators?' said Byrne. 'There was one man assigned to the case and if he hung around here longer than it took for him to peer into that drain, then I'm the next pope.'

They waited as Blackfinch shuffled around, examining the terrain.

'Anything?' said Persis.

'I'm not sure.' He turned to Byrne. 'Where's the body now?'

6

The Darjeeling District Hospital was a run-down, whitewashed building that looked like a hotel, complete with a series of pitched roofs and a guard by the gate.

They found the corpse of Jack Murphy cooling in the morgue.

'Have the next of kin been notified?' asked Persis, staring at the once handsome blond man lying on the slab.

'Jack had no next of kin,' replied Byrne. 'At least none that he ever mentioned.'

Persis went through the bag of personal effects that the orderly had handed to her at the door. When he had died, Jack Murphy had been wearing a cotton shirt, a sweater, a winter jacket, trousers, walking shoes, and a watch. Only one item had been discovered in his pockets, a slim leather wallet, containing just over fifty rupees in cash, and a small note.

Persis opened the note. On it, written in a neat hand:

MEDTR EANTH ETIII TMGGL MIHEL

'What does it mean?' asked Byrne.

'I don't know.' But something about the blocks of letters seemed familiar. The strange symbols beneath the text, however, were a complete mystery.

'We'll need an autopsy,' said Blackfinch.

Byrne looked troubled. 'Why? I mean, the cause of death is not in question. He broke his neck in the fall. His head was practically at right-angles to his shoulders when they found him.'

'Nevertheless,' said Blackfinch, firmly.

•

The pathologist was an elderly man by the name of Robert Simms, the smell of whisky on his breath, phlegm rattling in his throat. His protests went on for some time, but in the end, he was bullied into carrying out the post-mortem by the hospital's medical director, a close friend of Byrne's.

Persis and Blackfinch looked on as the body was cut open and examined. Byrne had excused himself from the grisly procedure.

As Simms peeled back the flesh from the cranium, Blackfinch leaned in. 'I want to take a closer look at the damage to the back of the skull.'

'He fell four hundred feet down a concrete pipe,' said Simms drily. 'Does it surprise you his skull isn't in the best condition?'

Blackfinch ignored him and waited while the cranium was revealed and the blood wiped away. Finally, Simms stepped back and Blackfinch bent over the skull, examining it with a keen eye. He gestured Persis over. 'Take a look.' She stepped closer. 'Two depressed skull fractures. The first' – he pointed with his little finger – 'is small and circular, and passed through both tables of the skull, indicating force applied violently by an object with a sharp, pointed end. One side of the fractured segment is elevated over the surface of the skull – you usually see that following a blow from a sharp, heavy weapon that embeds itself into the cranium. A lateral pulling motion when retrieving the weapon causes the elevation. But the second wound' – his finger moved four inches upwards – 'is linear, almost a flat line, about two inches long. It's quite unusual. Now, unless our killer turned up with two weapons in hand, I'd say these blows were made by the same instrument. Something like a claw hammer, maybe.'

'A claw hammer,' echoed Persis.

'*Not* a claw hammer. Something like it.' He straightened. 'While I was up there I saw what might have been drag marks in the grass around the edge of the drop to that storm drain. I can't be sure, of course. The terrain doesn't allow for definitive forensic conclusions, and weather may have had an impact. But, combined with the injuries to the skull, I can say with some certainty that Jack Murphy was murdered. By the time he went into the drain and broke his neck, he was already dead.'

'You're right,' said Simms, suddenly.

They stared at him.

'It's not a claw hammer.' He had moved closer and was staring at the cranial wounds. 'I've seen injuries like this before. Jack Murphy was killed with an ice pick.'

7

They stopped for something to eat before heading onwards.

As they sat in the small teahouse, Persis fiddled with the note found on the victim at the time of his death. She'd always loved codes and ciphers, spending hours chipping away at crosswords and other puzzles with her father, Sam, down in the bookshop that he ran and above which they lived back in Bombay. According to Byrne, so had Jack Murphy.

Blackfinch watched her, kneading his thighs with the flat of his hand. The climb had taken more out of him than he'd realized. He wondered how the locals managed it, up and down all day like mountain goats.

'I think I have it,' said Persis, suddenly. 'It's a block cipher. Look.' She pointed at the letters:

MEDTR EANTH ETIII TMGGL MIHEL

Plucking a pen from her pocket she rewrote the line, taking the first letter from each segment and placing them all on a single line; then repeating the process with all the second letters, and so on, building up a solid 'block' of letters.

MEETM
EATMI
DNIGH
TTIGE
RHILL

Blackfinch squinted at the paper. 'I don't see how that helps.'

'Read carefully,' she said, then, in exasperation, rewrote the block, this time adding spaces.

MEET M
_E AT MI
_DNIGH
_T TIGE
_R HILL

This time Blackfinch took only seconds. 'Meet me at midnight. Tiger Hill!'

'This proves someone lured Murphy up to the peak.'

'Yes. But who?'

'Perhaps these symbols can tell us.' They peered at the odd characters written below the line of letters.

'They *do* look familiar,' mused Blackfinch. 'I've seen something like them before. But for the life of me I can't remember where. It'll come to me in due course, no doubt.'

'There's no rush,' said Persis drily.

8

By the time they reached the Hotel King George, it was almost four. Byrne had sent a messenger ahead of them – and Agnes Sheehan to act as guide – and they were swiftly led to the office of the hotel's proprietor, a tall, big-bellied Scotsman named Grant Mackenzie.

Framed photographs lined the walls of Mackenzie's well-appointed office, images of Mackenzie in the company of celebrities who had graced the hotel over the years. Persis recognized movie stars, business tycoons, and even Mohammed Ali Jinnah, formerly Gandhi's compatriot in the Quit India movement, later to become the 'father' of Pakistan.

She was surprised Mackenzie kept the photo around. Jinnah's was no longer a name many Indians held in high esteem.

'Damned shame,' boomed Mackenzie from behind his desk. 'Jack was a good man.'

'Did you know him well?' said Persis.

'Been here thirty years. I know everyone worth knowing in Darjeeling.'

'Stafford Byrne doesn't believe Jack could have been careless enough to slip into that pipe.'

'Byrne's been hit hard by Jack's death. He took Jack under

his wing when he turned up here. Fellow Irishman, you see. I feel for him. But it doesn't make him right.'

'We now know for a fact that Jack was murdered,' said Persis. 'Someone lured him up to Tiger Hill, then attacked him with an ice pick, before dragging his body to the pipe and bundling him in.'

Mackenzie's face opened in surprise. 'Murder?'

'Yes.' Persis locked eyes with him. 'Did he have any enemies?'

'Jack? Enemies? No. None that I could name, at any rate.'

'He was here on the evening before his death. Why?'

Mackenzie frowned. 'Yes, he was here. But there was nothing unusual in that. It was our weekly card game.'

Persis leaned forward. 'Who else was at this game?'

'Well, *I* was there, of course, but you can cross me off your list. I was in bed all night, sleeping the sleep of the damned – my wife can vouch for that. A little too much whisky, I'm afraid. And then there was Henry Arbuthnot, but he's no good to you. He's seventy-seven and uses a crutch. Can't get around anywhere without the rickshaw-wallahs. He's got as much chance of making it up to Tiger Hill on his own as I have of flying to the moon. That leaves Tom. Tom Maddox.'

'And who is he?'

'An American. He runs a tea plantation a little ways below the town.'

'What happened at the game?'

'The same as usually happens. We drank. We played cards. We drank a little more.' His brow furrowed. 'Actually, now that you mention it . . . There *was* an odd moment. Halfway through the evening, Jack and Tom had a bit of a set-to.'

'A set-to?'

'An argument. I didn't think much of it at the time. I mean, men in their cups, gambling, bound to get a little tetchy.'

'What was the argument about?'

'I'm not sure. We'd taken a short break and I was staggering back from the bathroom when I saw Tom and Jack having at it in the corridor. I think it might have been about money. They clammed up as soon as I lurched into view.'

'A gambling debt?'

'Possibly. Though we never play for high stakes.'

'Did Tom lose money to Jack that evening?'

'In all honesty, I can't recall.'

Blackfinch spoke up. 'Tell me, Mr Mackenzie, did Jack and Tom dislike each other?'

'No more so than anyone else on this blasted mountain.'

9

They made their way down to Tom Maddox's plantation in the company of Agnes Sheehan, zigzagging down a dirt track as the light began to drain from the sky. The slope was steep and cultivated in small terraces.

Maddox's bungalow was called Windermere Villa, a large place set just above the road, with a small garden in front bounded by a white picket fence. A rockery was set in the drive leading up to the house, with a screen of rhododendron trees, and clumps of dwarf bamboo stretching to a shed with a corrugated iron roof.

Behind them, hill women wandered back up from the tea fields, chattering in their local dialect, some of them with enormous baskets of tea leaves on their backs.

Lanterns swung from the house porch, attracting clouds of mosquitoes in the gathering dusk.

The door was opened by a youth, dark-haired, clearly an Anglo, no more than fifteen. 'Hello,' he said with surprise, and then caught sight of their guide. 'Sister Agnes!'

'Hello, James. This is Inspector Persis Wadia and Mr Archie Blackfinch. They're from Bombay, here to investigate Jack Murphy's death.'

Instantly, the boy's face became dark. 'It's horrible, what happened to him.'

'You knew Jack well?' asked Persis.

'He used to take us into the mountains, as part of our Scout training. There's no way he slipped. Someone killed him. But no one will believe me.'

Persis exchanged glances with Blackfinch. 'James, is your father here?'

•

Tom Maddox was in a small office at the back of the house, shirt unbuttoned, a glass of gin on his desk as he pored over a ledger, pen in hand.

Quickly, Persis explained their mission. 'What did you and Jack argue about on the night of his death?'

Maddox leaned back in surprise. He was a tall man, in his late forties, with a lean face, and a hungry look in his ash-grey eyes. His American accent was broad, indicative of an upbringing in the Deep South. 'Who said we did?'

'Grant Mackenzie.'

Maddox scowled. 'It's true, Jack and I had a minor . . . confrontation.'

'What about?'

Maddox hesitated. 'He wanted money.'

'Gambling debt?'

'I didn't owe him a damned thing,' Maddox snapped. 'No. It was a loan he was after. The kind that never gets paid back.'

'Why did he need a loan?'

'He wanted to leave. Darjeeling, I mean. Wanted to move to

the States. Try his luck in New York. Had the bright idea of setting himself up in business, exporting tea out there.'

'Do *you* export tea to the States?' asked Blackfinch.

'I do.'

'So he would have become a direct rival?'

'You could say that.'

'That must have angered you. I mean, the gall of a man asking you for money so that he could undermine *your* livelihood.'

Maddox said nothing, but his silence spoke volumes.

'What made him think you would agree to such a request?'

'The man was drunk. Or insane. I don't know.'

•

As they were leaving, Persis asked their host if she might use the washroom. As soon as she was out of sight of the others, she went in search of James Maddox. She found him at the rear of the house, feeding a small goat tethered to the rear porch.

'She's called Maisy.'

'James, I know this is a difficult question, but on the night that Jack died, did your father leave the house late in the evening, around midnight?'

The boy's eyes blazed. 'No. My father had nothing to do with Jack's death.'

Persis paused. 'Where's your mother?'

'She lives in Calcutta. She and my father are . . .' He stopped, then sighed. 'What's the use? You'll find out anyway. They're separated. But it's only temporary.'

'Why did they separate?'

'She was tired of living in Darjeeling. She wants us to sell up and move to England. That's where she's from. This all belongs to her. It used to belong to my grandfather, but he died out here. My father was his general manager; he ran the plantation for him. Mother and he, well, I guess they fell in love.'

Persis was silent a moment. 'Were you born here?'

He nodded. 'Yes. I love it here. So did Jack Murphy. He loved the mountains. He was as sure-footed as Maisy on the hills. That's why I know he couldn't have just slipped like they're all saying.'

'You admired him?'

'He was my tutor. A lot of the boys leave Darjeeling during the vacation, back to the cities. I'm usually left alone here, more so since Independence. Jack would come down to the house and tutor me. Not the boring stuff, but things that mattered. About the mountains. About the world.'

'Who do you think might have wanted to harm him?'

He looked away. 'I have no proof.'

'Right now, we're simply making enquiries.'

'I think Jack was . . . was seeing someone. I don't think it was going well.'

'Who was he seeing?'

'I'm not certain. He wouldn't say.'

Persis paused, then took out the note and showed it to the boy. 'Have you any idea who could have written this?'

He scrutinized the note, then looked back up. 'You mean you can't read it?'

'What do you mean?'

'Well, the name's right there.'

She stared at him. 'I don't understand.'

He pointed at the strange symbols. 'There. That's a pigpen cipher. Jack used to show this to anyone at the school who'd listen. He runs – ran – an annual coding competition, for staff and students. Codes and ciphers were his hobby. Here, let me show you.' He picked up a pen and began scribbling on the rear of the paper. 'With the pigpen, you use symbols to represent the letters of the alphabet. Like so.'

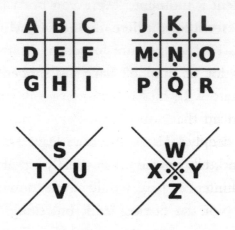

'So, take, for instance, *your* name – Persis. We'd write that as follows.' He wrote on the paper and showed her:

PERSIS

'And now . . . we decipher the name on the note . . .' Persis watched as he set each letter below the symbols:

AGNES

10

Persis waited until they were back at the school before broaching the matter, asking Agnes Sheehan to meet with her privately in

Byrne's office. Before stepping inside, she briefed Blackfinch on everything she had discovered and then sent him hurrying away on an errand.

Sheehan's eyes widened when she explained. 'What are you implying?'

'You spent a lot of time in Jack's company. Went down to the Maddox estate with him to tutor James during the vacation period. He noticed that you both seemed unusually close.'

She blushed deeply. 'That's— that's ludicrous.'

'Rector Byrne tells me he was a charismatic man.'

She said nothing.

'Where were you on the night of his death?'

'Asleep. In my room. Here at the school.'

'Do you own an ice pick?'

She blinked rapidly. 'Whatever you think was going on between me and Jack, you're wrong.'

Persis took out the note. 'This was found in Jack's pocket after his death. He was lured up to Tiger Hill.'

'I didn't write that note.'

'It has your name on it. That's what this code at the bottom says. Agnes.'

'I don't even know how to write in code!'

'James tells me that Jack Murphy ran a coding competition at the school. Apparently, you helped out this year.'

'I was curious. But that hardly means—'

A commotion turned their heads.

Blackfinch arrived, with Byrne in tow. He was holding something wrapped in a white cloth. He set it down on Byrne's desk, then looked at Sheehan. 'With the rector's permission, we searched your room. We found this hidden behind your wardrobe.'

He unwrapped the cloth, revealing an ice pick. Blond hairs

were visible on its dual-headed surface, matted to the metal by the residue of blood.

Sheehan stared at the pick, then slipped from her chair in a dead faint.

11

'I can't believe it,' said Byrne. His hand shook as he raised a glass to his lips and sipped at his whisky.

'Didn't you tell me that people are a mystery?' Persis was sitting with the rector on the veranda behind his office. The police had arrived just half an hour earlier and taken Agnes Sheehan away.

'Agnes insists that she and Jack Murphy had no improper relationship,' said Byrne. 'She swears by all that we hold holy that she didn't kill him.'

That was the one thing that troubled Persis. Even confronted with the note and the ice pick, Agnes Sheehan continued to protest her innocence. 'I thought Catholics were experts at confessing.'

'This is no joke, Persis,' said Byrne sharply. 'A young woman's life has been ruined.'

Persis stiffened. 'That young woman is a murderer.'

Byrne said nothing, returning to a fraught contemplation of his whisky glass. The doubt in his eyes was evident. That same doubt worked its way under Persis's skin, until finally she couldn't stand it.

•

Twenty minutes later she was standing inside a cell at the Darjeeling police station. Agnes Sheehan looked a sorry sight. She'd been weeping and her eyes were puffed. She'd taken off her cowl, and her long dark hair was dishevelled.

'I didn't kill him,' she said.

'But you *were* sleeping with him?'

'No!'

Persis leaned back, the stone of the cell wall cold between her shoulder blades. 'If you want me to help you, you need to tell me the truth.'

'I'm not lying. I had no relationship with Jack Murphy.'

'You're lying about *something*.'

Sheehan stared at her, then her shoulders seemed to collapse. 'If I tell you, it will cause a scandal. It will ruin lives. Not just my own.'

'Is that worse than going to the gallows?'

Sheehan sat slowly upright.

This is the moment, thought Persis. The dam was about to burst.

Agnes Sheehan began to speak.

12

The porch lanterns glowed in the darkness.

She was let in by a house servant.

Tom Maddox was with his son, taking a late supper. If he was surprised to see her back again so soon, he hid it well. 'What can I do for you, Inspector?'

'I just wanted to let you know we've arrested Agnes Sheehan for the murder of Jack Murphy.'

There was a moment of ringing silence, and then the fork fell from Maddox's hand. His chair scraped back and he was leaping towards her, eyes ablaze. She stepped back, hand instinctively moving towards the revolver she had left back in Bombay. It suddenly came to her that she had no jurisdiction here, no authority.

But Maddox stopped short. 'Have you lost your mind? Agnes couldn't hurt a fly. She's the most wonderful, sweet-natured girl you could hope to meet.'

'And how would you know that?'

His jaw worked silently.

'Agnes told me about your relationship. She was terrified that if it became public it would ruin you. A married man, carrying on with a woman almost three decades his junior, a nun no less. Your estranged wife owns this plantation. I don't doubt that she'd throw you off the estate. And then what? A life of penury, after decades of toil? And what happens to poor James? How does he fare, in the eye of the storm? Boys can be awfully vicious.'

Maddox looked horrified. 'What are you to trying to say?'

'I'm saying that the reason Jack Murphy was murdered was because of *your* affair with Agnes. He found out about it and tried to blackmail you. You told me that he wanted money from you – at least that part was true. Then again, you couldn't very well have lied – Mackenzie had already seen you arguing at the card game.'

'I didn't kill Jack Murphy, dammit!'

She took out the note, and laid it on the table. 'Someone lured Jack up to Tiger Hill that night. Someone who had access to his room at the school – I'm guessing this note was stuck under his door. Someone who knew the pigpen cipher and knew it would intrigue Jack. Someone keen to put Agnes into the frame. Someone who could have planted an ice pick in her room after it had been used to murder Jack. Someone who would have had no fear climbing up to the peak in the dark. Someone who knew that this note would lure Jack up there, possibly because he thought it might have come from *you*, via Agnes.'

He looked at her in mute incomprehension.

'You see, the note is signed by Agnes – using the cipher. Jack probably thought you had tasked Agnes to negotiate with him – given that they were working closely together – a quiet meeting away from the town to discuss the matter of his request for money. Perhaps even convince him to drop the whole thing. And yet . . .' She stepped backwards, away from the American. 'You're right when you say that neither you nor Agnes killed Jack Murphy.' She turned to James Maddox, sitting at the table with his head bowed. 'I understand why you did it, James. But it doesn't make it right.'

Tom Maddox turned in horror and looked down at his son.

James lifted his face to the light. His cheeks were streaked with silent tears. 'I knew Jack was blackmailing Father. I over-heard him when he came to see him the day before he died. I knew Father and Agnes were . . . carrying on. And I knew that while Jack and Agnes were around, Father and Mother would never be reconciled. I had to get rid of them both, don't you see? It was the only way.'

•

Later, the next morning, as the train steamed out of the station, Blackfinch furiously waving at the porters who had carried their bags down the hill, Persis would reflect on the boy's words. Had James Maddox really seen no alternative to murder? How diffi-cult human beings were to read. How capable of being misled, not just by others, but by their own faulty logic.

'I don't know about you,' beamed Blackfinch, 'but I've had a whale of a time.'

She turned to the window and looked out over the plantations as the mist curled up the slope and engulfed them.

A MURDER OF BRIDES

SULARI GENTILL

A murder of brides gathered like crows, preening, pecking, ready always to swoop. There were grooms too, but they receded against the spectacles of lace and beading and feathers they'd escorted to the cinema on Main Street. The dry summer air was heavy with lavender and talcum powder, charged with envy and triumph in equal measure as each new wife regarded and compared gowns and figures and husbands. The gentlemen had been asked not to smoke lest stray ash find its way onto a hand-embroidered train and begin a blaze of one sort or another. Brides were, after all, extremely combustible.

There'd been many spring weddings since the photographers had last come to town, and so, today, Jindymarra had turned out at least a score of newlyweds eager for a record of the day they'd last worn their nuptial finery. The occasional gown was already taut across the middle, betraying a premarital imprudence which might not have been evident at the wedding, but which would rely on the discretion of the photographer if it was not to be exposed in the photograph.

Gus adjusted the backdrop: a classical scene – painted marble columns, Delphi on the hill in the distance. They'd brought the garden backdrop, too – delphiniums, hydrangeas – in case anybody was particularly opposed to Antiquity. Regardless of which backdrop was selected, an urn on a pedestal integrated the fore- and backgrounds. More or less.

Gus handed the bouquet to the bride now perched on the stool. The groom stood proud in a diggers' uniform, though he'd probably been demobbed years ago when they'd all come home. The sleeve of his jacket was pinned up against the stump of what had been his left arm. Gus watched as Harriet positioned the man so the camera would not capture the disfigurement. In his wedding photograph, he would be whole.

From behind the camera, Harriet issued last-minute instructions – placement of hands and veils, adjustment of skirts, stance to highlight some beading or drape or cut to which Gus would be oblivious. Her eye for detail was extraordinary.

A flash, a count of three, and the moment was caught in colourless perpetuity.

Gus retrieved the bouquet and entered details, taking care to specify whether hand-colouring was required. Harriet changed the glass plates and readied the Eastman for the next happy couple. They had done several 'portrait days' now, working their way through the small towns of the Riverina, with the writer in tow since Cootamundra.

Gus glanced over at the bearded man, sitting in the front row making notes on God-only-knew-what in a leather-bound journal. He shook his head. Lawrence, a novelist, was, according to Harriet – and also Lawrence himself – famous, though Gus had never heard of him. An Englishman, he had come to Australia to write a book, and having done so, had decided to gather a little more inspiration before setting sail for New Zealand. Somehow, in a rush of blood and idiocy, Harriet had invited him to travel with them for a week or two. And so, they'd acquired a writer, who it seemed did little of use. But he was at least temporary. They'd return here in about two months to photograph the next batch of newlyweds, and he would, by then, be long gone.

'Miss!' A young woman pinned beneath a crown of silk roses trotted over to Harriet. 'I'd like to speak to Mr Johns or Mr Beasley?' she demanded, glancing at the sign which read Johns and Beasley Photographers.

'I'm Harriet Johns, Mrs . . .'

'Ellicot. I'd better speak to Mr Beasley then.'

'I'm sure I'll be able to help you,' Harriet said firmly.

Mrs Ellicot glanced at Gus, who pointedly ignored her. Eventually, she began to peck. 'I really must protest. I've been married for nearly two months and you've just photographed Mr and Mrs Jamison who have been wed barely a week.'

'We're taking everyone by their order in line, Mrs Ellicot.'

'Well that hardly seems fair!'

Gus kept his distance. At the moment Harriet's temper was in check. If that changed, he'd step in and save the Ellicot woman, albeit reluctantly. Harriet glanced back at him and pulled a face and he was reminded of Sturgeon.

Gus Beasley and Sturgeon Johns had joined up together – sixteen-year-old pretenders called to the Empire's cause, brave young hearts soon broken. Gus had called on his comrade's family when he returned. An act of respect and remembrance and guilt. He'd met Sturgeon's sister then. A strange, fierce girl who often wore trousers like a man, but who entranced him nonetheless. She'd seen through her own loss to recognize his, to care about his. Gus had no doubt that Harriet would insist that Mrs Ellicot return to the line and wait her turn. Hopefully she would do so in a way that did not end in the shedding of tears or blood.

The writer listened intently as Harriet negotiated with the squawking bride, lowering his eyes occasionally to make a note.

In time, the new Mrs Ellicot was persuaded to retreat, and Harriet reverted her attention to the next couple in line. She worked quickly, trying to get through as many portraits as possible before the day began to warm and the wilt set in. Even so, she took the time to pose each subject to best effect. To make every groom as dashing, and every bride as beautiful as the camera would allow them to be. When they were alone, Harriet would say that a good picture was as much about distraction as focus. Very occasionally she would admit that there was nothing to be done but accept that even God made mistakes.

It was mid-afternoon before they were able to leave the Jindymarra Grand Regent and reload the Ford TT.

The truck had been acquired by Gus's father while his son was at war, and was the only possession he'd not managed to gamble away by the Armistice. When Gus had finally got it going again, he set out for Sydney and called once more on the family of his old friend. He'd found Harriet struggling to make ends meet in a fledging photographic studio. He'd stayed – to help and because he had nowhere else to go. She'd taught him to take photographs, about lines and contrast, composition and light. She showed him how to find beautiful moments in the midst of chaos, and that ugliness was vulnerable to perspective. He'd taught her to drive.

Now the truck was emblazoned with Johns and Beasley Photographers in gold lettering, and fitted out to serve as a mobile studio for the weeks they were on the road. It held all the backdrops, cameras and plates they'd need for the towns en route, as well as swags, razors and changes of clothes. In some towns they'd stay in guest houses which could securely accommodate the truck and its irreplaceable contents while they slept in beds, but in small places like Jindymarra, they would camp just out of town. The novelist had been decidedly unhappy about the need to sleep on the ground – unaccustomed it seemed to the abundance of creatures that slithered and crawled through the Australian bush. Once all their appointments had been kept and the newlyweds of spring photographed, they would return to the studio in Sydney, retouch and hand-colour the plates as required, and mount the images onto card. They prided themselves on being able to deliver the finished product within six weeks of the sitting. More established and traditional studios would accuse Johns and Beasley of compromising quality for the sake of speed. The upstarts did, after all, advertise a pledge to deliver a wedding portrait while the couple was still in love.

The constable hailed them just as Gus was about the start the engine. They waited till the chubby policeman puffed his way down from the corner. Harriet climbed out of the cab and Gus stuck his head out of the open window.

'Miss Johns, Mr Beasley,' the constable wheezed. 'Inspector Brockleman has need of your services.'

Gus glanced at Harriet knowingly. They'd dealt with Brockleman before. A country policeman who fancied himself a champion of modern policing. Invariably, when they were in Jindymarra, he would summon them to photograph the scene of some petty theft or pub brawl. What use the images would be when they were finally delivered weeks after the incident, Gus did not know. Perhaps justice was slower than usual in Jindymarra. Even so, they humoured Brockleman, attending and photographing his crime scenes and dispatching the resultant prints back to him as soon as possible.

'Where?' Harriet asked.

The constable gave them directions to a property called

Mountainview. 'Just drive up to the homestead. The inspector will be waiting for you.'

Gus groaned. He'd been looking forward to lying under a tree beside the creek, throwing out a line to catch dinner.

Harriet's face was, to most, unreadable. Only Gus saw the slight flicker of vexation.

Perhaps it was Gus's groan, the lack of enthusiasm in Harriet's response, or perhaps the constable was simply bursting to tell someone. He puffed out his chest . . . or sucked in his stomach – the effect was the same. 'Miss Johns might like to sit this one out,' he confided. 'It's murder.'

•

Gus barely spoke in the truck on the way out to Mountainview, leaving Harriet to explain to Lawrence what they were about to do, and why. The writer was unashamedly excited. Quietly Harriet took Gus's hand, anchored him in now with the warmth of hers.

He was grateful. Gus had seen bodies before – twisted, bloodied corpses, some that were barely recognizable as human and others that seemed merely asleep on the battlefield. But not since the war. And here, under the broad Australian sky, in the warm light of an Australian summer, it seemed impossible, incomprehensible.

'It won't take two of us,' Harriet whispered. 'You could just wait—'

Gus shook his head as he pulled the Ford to a stop. 'This won't be about making people look good, Harry.' He forced a smile. 'We both know I'm better at the ugly truths.'

Harriet retrieved the hand-held cameras from amongst their equipment. 'Let's get it done then.' She warned Lawrence to wait in the truck.

They passed a man vomiting into the rose garden as they approached the house. A constable stood beside him, his eyes averted.

Brockleman met them at the door. He was flushed. 'Good, you're here!' He glanced out to the roses. 'Poor bloke found the body. Name of Ellicot.'

Harriet nodded. 'I know, I took his wedding portrait this morning.'

Brockleman's brow rose. 'Maybe you'd rather leave this to Mr Beasley.'

'I wouldn't.' Harriet waved away his advice as though it were a fly.

Sighing, Brockleman motioned them to follow him through the house to the drawing room.

Gus noticed the smell first . . . metallic, like rust. Too familiar though it had been years since he'd last encountered it in such volume. Blood.

The woman was on the floor, a pool of blood around her head which was turned to the side, and a trail from the window.

'She was trying to crawl away,' Gus murmured.

'This,' Brockleman announced importantly, 'is Mrs Marjorie Winslow, née Atkinson, formerly Carruthers.'

'What?'

'She was a remarried widow.' Brockleman was clearly pleased with his own cleverness. He pointed out what he wanted them to photograph, and they began.

'Do you know who did this?' Harriet asked as she framed up the bloody footprints on the drawing-room rug and the fact that they finished there, though the windows were locked. The murderer, it seemed, had flown out of the room.

'The gardener,' Brockleman replied. 'A Chinaman. Apparently, Mrs Winslow gave him a tongue-lashing yesterday – threatened to sack him if the roses didn't bloom . . . Take a picture of this.' He pointed to a broken rose beside the body.

'Did he confess?'

'Not yet, but he will once we find the wretch.' Brockleman folded his arms across his chest. 'The murder weapon was found in the garden shed, along with his bloodied shirt. Don't you worry,' he said, smiling. 'Once the jury sees your photographs, he's for the rope.'

'Was the shed locked?' Harriet asked.

'No . . . of course not.'

'Then anyone might have left the murder weapon and shirt in there?'

Brockleman scowled. 'It was the gardener. The knife was found in his barrow, and it was his shirt.'

'Which was in the unlocked shed,' Gus repeated Harriet's original point.

'I don't know that I care for your tone, son,' Brockleman snarled.

'Of course, you've already considered the implications of the unlocked shed, Inspector,' Harriet interrupted sweetly. 'You're clearly several steps ahead of us.'

Brockleman vacillated for a moment while he decided. 'Well, yes . . . of course one must consider all the possibilities.'

Harriet paused to look closely at the wedding photo on the mantel. The hand-coloured picture showed the bride in a pale blue gown with a ribboned and embroidered bodice, elegant and clearly happy. The groom stood beside her, beaming at the camera, confident and relaxed. Johns and Beasley had not taken the picture. It was only ordinary people who came to the cinema to sit for their wedding portraits weeks after the fact. People who lived in homesteads had private sittings.

A commotion at the door prompted Brockleman to leave the

photographers and investigate its cause. They heard a woman's voice in reply to Brockleman's, and then a gasp, followed by Brockleman cursing. Gus stuck his head into the vestibule. The inspector struggled to support a somewhat extravagantly dressed young woman who it seemed had swooned or fainted. He spotted Gus and summoned him to help.

Gus put down his camera and then lifted the insensible woman in his arms. She was barely any weight at all. He carried her to the chaise longue in the drawing room and gently laid her there. Pale and beautiful, in a gown of soft yellow silk, she seemed fine and fragile and he flinched at the necessity of placing her in this scene of horror.

'Who is she?' Harriet asked. There was something familiar about the woman, but she wasn't sure what.

'She called Mrs Winslow her sister. When I mentioned that the woman had been murdered, she fainted.' Brockleman shook his head, exasperated by the temerity of it. He patted her hand impatiently.

Long-lashed eyelids fluttered, opened, and then widened in alarm. 'Where am I?'

'You're in the drawing room at—'

'You're in my crime scene,' Brockleman declared loftily.

'I'm afraid Mrs Winslow has been killed,' Harriet said calmly.

'Miss Johns!' Brockleman snapped. 'May I have a word?'

As the policeman took Harriet aside to demand she not address the witness directly, Gus introduced himself and offered the now weeping woman his handkerchief.

She swallowed. 'I'm Mabel Winslow.'

'And you're Mrs Winslow's sister?'

'Well, I suppose, technically she's my sister-in-law. Jack Winslow is my brother . . . Marjorie and I were as close as any sisters ever were. I was just calling by because I know she gets lonely when Jack is away.'

'Mr Winslow is away?'

'He's in Wagga Wagga on business.' She clasped her hand to her mouth. 'Oh Lord, he won't know yet, will he?'

'Not unless Inspector Brockleman has managed to send word already.'

Mabel Winslow looked past him for the first time to the wall opposite, and followed the bloodstains to her sister-in-law's body. She sat up, staring, pressed her hand to her stomach as if the pain resided there. Sobs racked her body. Gus moved to block the line of her gaze and tried to comfort her, and suddenly she was clinging to him and crying into his chest.

'Mr Beasley!' Brockleman exploded. 'What are you doing? You are not authorized to—'

'For pity's sake, man, she's distraught.' Gus was fed up with Brockleman's posturing. 'Get her out of this house and have someone put the billy on. I'm sure she could use a cup of tea.'

'Inspector,' Harriet offered, 'perhaps you might speak with Miss Winslow on the verandah. I'll finish the photographs and Gus can make tea if he can't find someone else to do it.' It did strike Harriet as odd that there seemed to be no servants in a house this big, aside from the previously mentioned gardener.

Brockleman glowered at her.

'The house servants all have the day off,' Mabel volunteered. 'Marjorie always insisted that they have one full day every month. She was the kindest . . .' She buried her face in Gus's chest again. 'I can't bear it, I just can't bear it.'

Brockleman sighed. 'If you'll come this way, Miss Winslow.'

Mabel looked up and spoke to Gus. 'Will you come too, sir. Please. I don't need tea.'

'If it would help . . .'

'It wouldn't,' Brockleman snapped. 'May I remind you, Beasley, that you are not a policeman?'

'Perhaps Gus could accompany the young lady out, and then remove himself from earshot while you conducted your interrogation,' Harriet spoke before Gus could reply in a manner that was less civil.

'You're going to interrogate me?' Mabel exclaimed, clearly appalled.

'I'd just like to ask you a few questions, Miss Winslow,' Brockleman said wearily. 'It'll assist in the apprehension of your sister-in-law's killer.'

Mabel nodded tentatively, still clinging to Gus. He walked with her out of the house and settled her on the bench under the broad verandah, away from the horror within. As Brockleman took a seat, Gus turned to go. She beseeched him not to go too far. He assured her he would just be on the other end of the verandah with Lawrence, who had apparently tired of waiting in the truck and found his way to the house. After a couple of minutes, Harriet joined them there.

'Well, that's done at least,' Harriet said under her breath. 'They can cover the poor woman up before the flies get too thick.'

Gus leaned against the wall. 'What's the time – is it too early to drink?'

Harriet smiled, and checked her wristwatch. 'It's half past four. We'll wait till Brockleman's finished with Miss Winslow and then get out of here.'

Lawrence took out his notebook. 'What did she look like – the deceased woman? Can you describe the body?'

'No.' Gus was curt.

'This might not be the time, Mr Lawrence,' Harriet warned. Gus reached into his pocket for tobacco and papers and struggled for a minute before Harriet took them from him, rolling the cigarette with one hand before handing it back.

'Thanks.' Gus pressed the cigarette between his lips and lit it. He hadn't been smoking long enough to put one together with anything resembling efficiency. Ironically, Harriet didn't smoke at all. But she had rolled cigarettes for her father as a child. Clearly it was not something you forgot how to do. 'What do you think happened, Harry?'

'No idea. But I doubt the gardener had anything to do with it.'

'Why?' Gus did not particularly suspect the gardener, but he was curious that Harriet was so convinced of his innocence. After all, some blokes didn't like being put in their place by women, and according to Brockleman, Mrs Winslow had given the gardener a piece of her mind.

'Mrs Winslow was sitting down when her throat was cut.'

'How do you know that?'

'The blood on the wall is no higher than three feet and there's a pot of tea on the table in front of it. Two teacups.'

'You think she was having tea with her killer.'

Harriet nodded. 'I can't see her taking tea with the gardener, can you? I dare say he was never allowed inside the house . . . not beyond the kitchen in any case.'

'Perhaps she was having tea alone when the killer came in.'

'There were two cups, Gus.' Harriet frowned. 'Anyway, if someone broke into your house, surely the first thing you'd do is stand up. It seems odd that she would continue sipping tea, unless—'

'She was taking tea with her killer.' Gus wasn't entirely convinced, but he could see where Harriet was leading. 'And it's unlikely she was taking tea with her gardener.'

'Not impossible, but yes, highly unlikely,' Harriet replied. 'Even if they were carrying on some kind of clandestine affair, you'd expect them to have better things to do than take tea.'

'An affair with the gamekeeper, you say?' Lawrence's brow furrowed with sudden attention.

'Neither of us said that,' Gus corrected. 'There is no flaming gamekeeper!'

'Where's her husband?' Lawrence asked.

'He's in Wagga Wagga, apparently,' Harriet said quickly.

'Not able to fulfil his conjugal duties then?'

'Not while he's in Wagga, I expect.' Harriet's voice had an edge to it now, but Lawrence didn't seem to notice.

'Perhaps he was never able to fulfil them – some health problem, or perhaps some form of perversion which makes him unable to complete the marital contract—'

'Perhaps you'd be more comfortable in the truck,' Gus suggested.

'Not at all,' Lawrence said absently. 'I might just take a turn about the verandah.'

They watched him go.

'He's peering in the windows,' Gus observed.

'Hopefully, Brockleman will arrest him,' Harriet replied.

Gus's lips quirked. 'Ellicot is still here,' he said, nodding in that direction. Ellicot was no longer vomiting, but he looked wretched regardless. A constable remained a few steps away.

Noticing their attention, Ellicot walked over to the verandah. 'You're the photographers,' he said.

'And you're Mrs Ellicot's husband,' Harriet replied. 'What are you doing here?'

'Inspector Brockleman asked me to stay.'

'I mean, what were you doing here when you found Mrs Winslow?'

The pallor left Ellicot's face and a rose hue replaced it. 'I was delivering an invitation . . . from Mrs Ellicot.'

Gus drew on his cigarette. 'Who let you in?'

'I beg your pardon—'

'When you knocked, who let you in?'

Ellicot cleared his throat. 'Well, I didn't. I mean . . . in actual fact, the door was open.'

'The entrance door?'

'The kitchen door.'

'You used the kitchen door?' Harriet asked sharply.

'Yes . . .' Ellicot fixed his gaze on his feet. 'Tradesman's entrance. I thought I'd leave the invitation with the cook, but there was no one about.'

'So, you went in?'

'Yes. I thought I heard someone in the bedroom and so I went there first.' He turned red – embarrassed, though he tried to maintain a pretence that the intrusion was understandable. 'The room was in disarray and so I became immediately worried. I searched the house . . . and I found her.' He shook his head vigorously as if he were trying to dislodge the memory. 'I used the telephone to raise the alarm.'

Harriet nodded sympathetically. She glanced at her wristwatch. 'I expect Mrs Ellicot will be wondering where you are.'

'No . . . this is her afternoon at the Red Cross. She left me a supper of bread and cheese.'

Harriet's brow arched. 'You'll have a lot to tell her when she returns.'

Ellicot stared at her. 'I . . . I don't want to upset her . . . you know how women are.' He smiled nervously. 'I might just tell her I was at the pub.'

Gus glanced back at Brockleman and Mabel Winslow. The policeman was on his feet. The interview had obviously been concluded. 'We'd better go see if Brockleman requires our services for anything else.'

Harriet allowed him to go ahead, watching quietly as Mabel, sobbing, clung to Gus again. Harriet really didn't like the way she did that.

'You didn't see anyone when you came in, did you?' she asked Ellicot.

Ellicot's eyes narrowed. Harriet could almost hear him thinking. 'You know, I think I did. A Chinaman, but he didn't dress like one. Looked like an ordinary bloke from a distance.'

'Where did you see him?'

'Leaving the house. He came out of the kitchen just before I went in . . . is that who did it? Did that yellow heathen kill my . . . Mrs Winslow?'

'What yellow heathen?' The agitated rise of Ellicot's voice brought Brockleman over to them. He glared at Harriet. 'Have you been interfering with my witnesses again, Miss Johns?'

'I wouldn't dream of it, Inspector.'

'I think you and Mr Beasley should be on your way.'

'Of course, Inspector, there are just a couple more images I should take first — I know how thorough you are.' Harriet held up the Kodak. 'It won't take a minute.'

'What have you not yet photographed, Miss Johns?' Brockleman asked tersely.

'The bedroom,' Harriet replied, heading towards the door. 'Mr Ellicot will tell you why.'

•

Gus pulled the Model TT off the road near a creek-crossing, driving it a short way into the trees. They were a few miles from town, a couple from Mountainview, and it was as good a place as any to camp for the night. A riot of cockatoos startled into the air, screeching into a sudden beating cloud and announcing their presence to any who might have been watching the sky. Gus collected firewood and sheets of eucalypt bark to use as kindling while Harriet fetched swags and cooking implements from the truck. As the evening was clear, they moved the backdrops and a trunk of props out of the hold so that Lawrence could unroll his swag in their place. It was a consideration born out of Lawrence's tendency to wake them all with his paranoia about the encroachment of snakes and spiders upon their sleeping arrangements. And it was then that they found the gardener.

He was sitting behind the classical backdrop – a young man in a well-cut but ill-fitting three-piece suit. His glossy black hair was cut smartly short. His dark eyes were more defiant than scared.

'You know, mate,' Gus folded his arms as he looked down at the stowaway, 'you're not really dressed for gardening.'

'How should I be dressed?' the gardener asked coldly.

Gus shrugged.

'Aren't you going to ask what I'm doing here?'

'I expect you're trying to escape arrest.' Gus offered him a hand and pulled him to his feet. 'You can't stay here . . . it's where the writer sleeps.'

There was surprisingly little argument about what to do. The photographers had neither the authority nor the desire to arrest the gardener and Lawrence seemed utterly intrigued by the man. And so Long Zau, also called Bruce, joined them for a stew of potatoes, onions, and mutton, cooked over the coals.

Lawrence lit his pipe.

Gus was the first to broach the subject of the moment. 'So, tell me, mate, did you kill Marjorie Winslow?'

'Mrs Winslow was dead when I went into the drawing room.' Long Zau's inflection was local, his voice steady despite the circumstances.

'Why did you go into the drawing room in the first place?' Harriet asked.

A moment of hesitation.

Lawrence cleared his throat. 'Were you and Mrs Winslow engaged in that act which is the root of intuition and from which beauty flowers?'

They all stared at him bewildered. Lawrence sucked on his pipe.

'What the hell does that mean?' Gus spoke for them all.

Lawrence took the pipe out of his mouth and rephrased. 'Sex! Were you engaged in sex with Mrs Winslow, Mr Zau?'

'*Mr* Winslow asked me to teach his wife to play bridge,' Long Zau said finally. 'He gave me this suit so that I may be properly attired for the purpose of tutoring his wife.'

'And today was your first lesson.'

'No, I have been teaching Mrs Winslow every morning since November. She does not care for cards and so progress is difficult.'

'Is it that she does not care for it, or is it that she is distracted by you?' Lawrence suggested.

'Is that a snake?' Gus pointed at Lawrence's feet. Lawrence squealed, jumped up and leapt away.

'I didn't see anything—' Harriet said.

'No, I felt it slither past,' Lawrence insisted, jumping as if it were contact with the ground that put him in danger.

'Maybe climb into the truck for a while,' Gus suggested. 'Just until we can be sure it's gone. Where did I put that bloody snake stick, Harry?'

'Gus—'

'No, Harry, this man is an important writer. We can't be too careful.' There was a grin in his voice. 'We owe it to literature.'

Harriet exhaled. 'Maybe if you were to sit in the cabin while we searched for it . . .'

'Yes, yes, of course.' Lawrence was already on his way. 'I have a few notes to make in any case.' He climbed into the cabin of the Ford TT. 'Let me know when you've found the serpent.'

Gus stomped around the campfire in purported pursuit of the snake, swinging a stick at random.

'Right, then,' he whispered after a minute. 'Bruce, mate, what did you see when you went into the drawing room?'

'Mrs Winslow was dead.'

'Was there anyone else there?'

'No.'

'There was a pot of tea and two cups,' Harriet said. 'Was it your custom to take tea with Mrs Winslow while you tutored her in bridge.'

'No . . . never. She's never offered me tea.'

'Did you notice anyone come up to the house this morning?'

'Mr Ellicot was coming in as I left. He often called on Mrs Winslow.'

'What about before that? Before you entered the house. Did you see anything? Did anyone at all call at the house.'

'Not after Mr Winslow left for Wagga Wagga.'

Gus's eyes narrowed. 'Winslow left this morning?'

'At about ten o'clock. Why does that matter?'

Gus shrugged. 'Because it means he could have killed her himself.'

'Mr Winslow?' The gardener shook his head. 'Why would he do that?'

'Perhaps he had a lover, perhaps he found out about hers,' Harriet said.

'Her lover?' Long Zau pulled back. 'No . . .'

'Not you,' Gus said. 'She means Ellicot . . . though I reckon old mate was more hopeful than anything else.'

Harriet frowned. 'The shirt they found splattered with blood . . .'

'—was mine, but I was not wearing it,' Long Zau replied. 'I changed this morning – hung it in the shed for when the lesson was over.'

'What time?'

'Early . . . but the lesson was delayed because Mr Winslow wanted me to check a breakage in the fence on the far end of the property. There are new lambs in the adjoining paddock, so I did not pause to change.'

Gus turned to Harriet. 'So, what are we going to do?'

Harriet glanced at the truck's cabin. Lawrence was watching them through the window.

'We'd better tuck in our writer for the night – we can worry about murderers tomorrow.'

'And Bruce, here?'

Harriet turned to Long Zau. 'You can stop here for the night or carry on escaping, I suppose.'

Long Zau met her eye. 'And tomorrow? Will you turn me in?'

Harriet shrugged. 'Not unless you try to kill us in the night, in which case we'll return your remains to Inspector Brockleman.'

•

Gus was suddenly awake though he didn't know why. The stars still blazed overhead against a night sky that carried no hint of dawn. He rolled slowly onto his stomach.

'Harry?' he whispered.

'I heard.' Harriet was also ready to move. Why they knew there was something amiss, that the sound was not a bird or a wombat or the wind was hard to tell. But they both knew that something wasn't right.

Harriet signalled Gus to stay back and hidden until she could flush out what they were dealing with.

'Who's there?' she demanded, rising to her feet. 'What do you want?'

Before she could turn around, the cold pressure of a gun barrel pressed hard against the base of her skull. A voice, male and well-spoken. 'Don't move.'

'What do you want?'

'Shut up and I may not have to shoot you.'

A creak as someone stepped up into the back of the Ford TT.

'Wait—' Harriet started.

'What the dickens—' Lawrence woke now.

A scream. A woman's scream. Then Lawrence's.

Harriet wrenched away. The gun went off. She fell to her knees, ears ringing. A scuffle behind her and another gunshot, and bedlam in the truck. Still Harriet did not rise, and for a moment even she was confused as to why. And then pain informed her.

'Harry! Speak to me, mate.' Gus fumbled to light a hurricane lamp so that they could see how bad it was.

'It's all right, Gus.' Harriet grabbed his shoulder and used it to pull herself up. 'I'm not bleeding. I just twisted my knee when I fell.'

'Bloody hell!' Gus was weak with relief. 'I thought you'd been shot.'

'Did he get away?'

'No, Bruce has him pinned.'

'And the other—'

'Lawrence has her locked in the back of the truck.'

'Do you know what's going on?'

'No idea – can you stand?'

'Hand me the snake stick.'

Gus grabbed the sturdy branch he used previously. It had a small fork at one end, which made it a quite adequate crutch.

Once he was sure Harriet could remain upright without him, he turned to help Long Zau, and between them they managed to restrain and bind the intruder. Harriet limped over with the hurricane lamp so they could see what they were dealing with.

'Winslow?'

Gus pulled the man up so they could see his face clearly. 'You're Winslow, aren't you?'

'Yes, he is,' said Long Zau.

'What the hell are you doing here?' Harriet demanded.

Winslow glanced at the gardener. For a moment he said nothing and then, 'I'm looking for the yellow bastard who killed my wife.'

'I didn't touch her,' Long Zau said angrily.

'That's not what the police believe.'

'How did you know Mr Zau was here?' Gus asked.

Winslow said nothing now.

'Gentlemen, Miss Johns . . .' Lawrence called from the Ford TT, which he'd barricaded shut. 'I'm afraid the prisoner is . . . crying. Should I release her?'

'Crying.' Harriet's eyes narrowed. 'Is that your sister, Mr Winslow? Did you bring her to help you with whatever it is you're doing here?'

'Mabel?' said Gus, alarmed. 'We should let her out . . . see she's all right.'

'First,' Harriet spoke to Long Zau, 'remove your tie and gag Winslow. Stuff a handkerchief in his mouth so he can't make a sound.'

The gardener did as she asked, silencing his employer's protests or at least rendering them incomprehensible.

Once that was done, Harriet asked the writer to open the doors. It was, as they suspected, Mabel Winslow. After a pause in which she took in her situation, Mabel threw herself into Gus's arms.

Harriet looked from Mabel to the truck, contemplating. 'You were looking for the cameras, weren't you, the plates from today?'

She stared blankly.

'What is it in those photographs that will implicate you, or Jack Winslow, or both of you?' Harriet walked around Mabel. 'Was it the images taken in the drawing room, or the bedroom . . . or was it because I took a photograph of you?'

'You did?' Gus asked, surprised.

'She was in the background.' Harriet folded her arms. 'But I recall thinking that you seemed alarmed by it. What is it that you think I'll notice in a photograph that I didn't see in person?'

'How much the weary eye misses in the midst of horror that may be contemplated at leisure in black and white,' Lawrence said sombrely.

An irritated sideways glance and then Harriet's eyes grew wide with realization. 'The dress!' she said. 'You were wearing Mrs Winslow's wedding dress!'

'Don't be absurd!' Mabel snapped. 'Marjorie's dress was blue. I never wear blue.'

'It was coloured blue by the photographer . . . that doesn't mean it was blue. It's the same dress – all those ridiculous ribbons and embroidered roses. In monochrome I would have noticed immediately . . . actually, I probably wouldn't have noticed but you thought I might.' She stepped up to Mabel, who tried to retreat into Gus's chest. 'You couldn't take the chance that I'd put the dress together with the bedroom in disarray, could you?'

Mabel was silent now. For a moment Harriet seemed surprised that her tenuous deduction had found its mark.

'What happened? Did your own clothes get splattered with blood? It was OK for Jack Winslow – he was wearing the gardener's clothes, but you couldn't do that and not arouse Mrs Winslow's suspicions.' Harriet walked away from Mabel, piecing the event together in her mind. 'You called on Mrs Winslow – it was you she had to tea – and you killed her. Then you took off all your bloody clothes and shoes in the drawing room. Jack Winslow, wearing Bruce's clothes, picked up your soiled garments and disposed of them somehow while you went to the bedroom and put on one of Marjorie Winslow's gowns. Did you select the wedding dress by mistake or did you want to wear her best?'

Mabel drew back, looking around desperately for help or escape.

'But why would she kill her brother's wife?' Gus asked. 'She didn't seem to dislike the woman.'

It was Bruce who spoke up. 'I saw them together . . . in the woodshed.'

'Who?'

'Mr Winslow and his sister.' He shuddered. 'It was unnatural.'

Winslow spluttered furiously in his gag.

'How dare you, you filthy—' Mabel began.

'He's not your brother, is he?' Harriet asked, looking from Winslow to Mabel. 'This is not about an incestuous affair, but an affair nonetheless. Did you and Winslow always plan to kill that poor woman after he'd secured her fortune with marriage? Did he ask the gardener to teach her to play bridge so that he could be your scapegoat?'

Mabel hissed, and launched an invective of quite creative profanity at her captors. For a while they listened as the lady cursed. Lawrence took notes.

'So, what do we do now?' Gus asked.

'We take them to Brockleman, and we develop the photographs. They'll prove she was wearing Marjorie Winslow's wedding dress.' Harriet sighed as she realized they were going to be late to the next town. 'The brides of Batlow are going to be cross.'

THE TEN LESSONS OF BIG MATT SILVER

A NOIR HIP-HOP SCREENPLAY

NELSON GEORGE

EXT. SAG HARBOR, LONG ISLAND - MORNING

A large black man, 'Big Matt Silver,' early
40s, exits the back of a beautiful Long
Island home. He sits on a deck chair
overlooking an ocean view. On a small table
he places a cigar, a smartphone and a gun. He
lights the cigar. He types something in his
phone and presses 'send.' He picks the gun
up—a 9mm Glock—and aims it toward his head.

On a smartphone screen flash the words:
The Life Lessons of Big Matt Silver.

'The Sins of the Father
Can Be Transformed by the Son'

INT. BROOKLYN TENEMENT - NIGHT

Late '80s. A Brooklyn tenement. Night.

A black man in his 40s, SAMMY SILVER, dressed in wannabe hustler gear, enters the building with his son, MATT, a strapping college-aged man-child. It is Matt's 18th birthday and his father is giving him a peek into the adult world. Sammy knocks on a nondescript third-floor door. A peep hole opens. A stern, emotionless face looks out.

> Doorman: What?
>
> Sammy: It's Sammy. Sammy Silver.
>
> Doorman: That mean something to me?
>
> Sammy: T.J. I'm T.J.'s friend. I came here the other night.
>
> Doorman: Who's the duck?
>
> Sammy: This is my son.

The Doorman snorts derisively and closes the peep hole.

INT. AFTERHOURS CLUB - NIGHT

For a long moment Sammy and Matt stand there. Suddenly the door opens. Music and bright,

120

reddish light flow out. It is an afterhours club, not a crack house. The players and playettes snort coke from tabletops along with their alcohol.

Sammy sits Matt at a bar and buys him a glass of Hennessey to celebrate his birthday. Then Matt's father goes off in search of his man T.J. somewhere in a back room. A DJ with a young MC perform an early '80s hip-hop set in the corner. The duo is rocking old school party rhymes. Matt sips his Hen Rock and nods his head, feeling very adult.

A man sits next to Matt and introduces himself as T.J. He has a dusty voice and a face as hard and unforgiving as concrete.

> T.J.: You gonna have to go home alone,
>   son. Your father is already gone. He
>   said he was a coke dealer. But he was
>   really a mailman, right?

> Matt: Where is he?

> T.J.: I told you he was gone. Your father
>   wasn't who he said he was and couldn't
>   do what he said he could. Sorry it had
>   to go down like this, but it did.

Matt pulls away from T.J. and rushes toward the door his father disappeared behind. The doorman tries to block him but Matt hits him solidly in the gut and the big man doubles over. Matt marches past his prone body and opens the door.

Sammy lies face down on a card table, looking
like a drunk who's had three too many. Matt
is momentarily relieved, thinking his father
is just asleep or drunk. When Matt gets
closer he notices blood oozing from the back
of his head. Sitting Sammy up, Matt is
confronted with the awful truth: there is a
bullet hole in his father's forehead. Sammy
Silver is stone-cold dead.

From the doorway T.J.'s gravelly voice can be
heard:

> T.J.: (OS) Boy, I told you your father
> was gone.

INT. FUNERAL HOME - DAY

Two weeks later, at a funeral home, Matt sits
in the front row with his mother RUTHIE and
sister KHADJA, who are both overwhelmed with
grief. Matt sits impassive. There was no real
investigation. Matt tried to get the police to
come with him to the afterhours spot, but
they were reluctant. When they arrived only
the doorman was there.

His father's body was found a few days later
on a rooftop twenty blocks away. No witnesses.
Only Matt, who told his story to unsympathetic
eyes.

INT. SILVER HOME - MORNING

A few months after the funeral Matt is
heading to a construction job when Ruthie
chides him, saying, 'Your father would have
wanted you to go college.'

> Matt: Yeah. Well he should have taken out
>   a life insurance policy if that really
>   mattered to him.
>
> Ruthie: Don't you dare disrespect him.
>
> Matt: I'm sorry, Ma, but that's the way
>   it is. You need the money. Khadija can
>   go to nursing school, but I'm gonna help
>   you. And don't worry, I ain't getting
>   shot up in some damn bar.

EXT. DOWNTOWN MANHATTAN - DAY

High up at a Manhattan construction site, Matt
pushes a wheelbarrow of concrete. From the
high-rise Matt can look down at a brownstone
rooftop where a group of white kids are
dancing and getting high to a rap jam. His
co-worker Malcolm walks over and looks down.

> Matt: There's money in that rap shit.
>
> Malcolm: No doubt. My cousin Blue Streak
>   DJs at the Latin Quarters Friday nights.
>
> Matt: I've seen him there a couple of
>   times. That's a rough spot. He should
>   get some security.

Malcolm: I hear you. You know someone?

Matt: Yeah.

INT. LATIN QUARTERS, MIDTOWN MANHATTAN –
NIGHT

The Latin Quarters, the legendary and
dangerous hip-hop hot spot, is packed with
hard rocks and screw faces. Matt, doing
security, stands looking tough by the DJ booth
as BLUE STREAK plays for the hardcore hip-hop
crowd. GARY TEE, a record promoter for Dark
Nite records, tries to approach the DJ and
Matt intercepts him. Gary Tee is offended but
Matt doesn't move until Blue Streak gives the
OK. Matt watches as Gary Tee slips the DJ
some new 12-inch vinyls and a bag of coke.
Blue Streak immediately plays the latest Dark
Nite jam and big ups the record on the mic.

Matt notices two THUGS looking toward the
booth. Gary Tee tries to hand Matt some coke
as he exits, but Matt declines. He watches,
however, as the two thugs follow Gary Tee
out. Matt thinks a moment and then follows
them.

EXT. LATIN QUARTERS – NIGHT

He comes around the corner where the thugs
are robbing Gary Tee at knifepoint. Matt runs
up and wails on them. 'I won't forget your
ass!' the smaller thug says and Matt laughs.

Gary Tee is grateful. Calls him 'Big Matt' and offers him a job at Dark Nite records.

'Silence Is for Suckers'

INT. DARK NITE RECORDS - DAY

It's not much of a job. Basically, Matt's getting coffee and fast food and drops off mail. Mostly he sits by the receptionist NIECY WILLIAMS and keeps would-be MCs from bum's-rushing the offices. Gary Tee comes out and says Dark Nite label head DOUGIE BAILEY wants a cassette with a new track taken to the studio where CTC (aka COAST TO COAST), a promising young MC, is working on his first LP.

INT. RECORDING STUDIO, MANHATTAN - EVENING

When Big Matt arrives at the studio with the cassette, CTC is sitting with his engineer and some friends smoking trees. They offer Big Matt a hit. They listen to the beat on the cassette. Big Matt suggests CTC use a different sample than what Dark Nite suggested. CTC likes Big Matt's idea. Instead of rhyming over the track Dougie sends over, CTC uses Big Matt's idea. A couple of hours later an angry Gary calls the studio wondering where Big Matt is.

INT. DARK NITE RECORDS - NIGHT

Matt arrives back at Dark Nite's offices.
Niecy looks at him shaking her head.

    Niecy: Dougie wants to see you.

    Gary stops him on the way to the
      president's office.

    Gary: You just listen and maybe he'll give
      you some cash before he fires you.
      Whatever you do, leave my name out of
      it.

INT. DOUGIE'S OFFICE - NIGHT

Dougie, a bearded black man with a taste for
cigars, sits behind his desk in a tracksuit.

    Dougie: I understand that you suggested
      CTC change the track I sent over for him
      to record. A track that I approved.

    Matt: I did. I was at Latin Quarters and
      saw how people reacted to that other
      beat. I don't think anybody's used it
      yet in a record.

    Dougie: Normally I would fire you. I don't
      like being contradicted. But I do like
      having my work improved upon. You know
      what A&R means?

    Matt: No.

    Dougie: It means it bring me hits.

INT. MATT'S OFFICE - DAY

Matt gets a little broom closet of an office
and a stack of cassettes. He listens. Beat
after beat after beat. It's tedious. Finally,
he finds a beat he likes and brings it to
CTC, who already has confidence in his taste.
With Big Matt's input, CTC builds a rhyme
around the track.

INT. DOUGIE'S OFFICE - DAY

At a staff meeting Big Matt plays the track
he worked on with CTC.

> Dougie: OK. Put it out.

> Gary: Thanks for making me look good.

As everyone else leaves the meeting Dougie
calls Matt over.

> Dougie: This is a good start. Now what
>   did I first ask you?

> Matt: What does A&R mean? And the answer
>   was 'Bring me hits.'

> Dougie: It is a multi-part answer
>   situation. The other part is 'Bring me
>   artists.' You heard about Deuce?

> Matt: Yeah. I see him out. I like his
>   voice. His rhymes are just OK.

Dougie smiles and lights a cigar.

Dougie: I've been hearing Deuce's deal is
up at Strictly Biz and he's trying to
get out of his option. He'd be a good
fit at Dark Nite.

Matt waits for more, but Dougie just puffs
and walks away.

Matt: I hear you.

'Chinese Food Can Heal Old Wounds'

INT. MR. CHOW'S - NIGHT

Matt and Deuce sit at Mr. Chow's negotiating.
Deuce, who's been a big star at a small
label, is reluctant to sign with Dark Nite,
afraid of getting lost there. He's heard you
gotta give Gary Tee points on your releases
to get a push there. This is news to Matt.

Matt: If I sign you, I protect you.

Things get more complex when TEENIE, one of
the thugs Matt beat down at Latin Quarters,
walks in Mr. Chow's and over to their table.
Deuce introduces him as his manager. There is
a tense moment. Matt calls the waiter over
and orders the squab for Teenie with a bottle
of Dom to wash it down. Teenie sits down.

Teenie: You know why I was beating that
scumbag Gary Tee? I'd been supplying
that nigga with product and he kept
jerking me. He was owed a beating.

Aside from making a deal and making two new
friends, Matt gets insight into his benefactor
Gary Tee.

'Sometimes It Ain't About Business'

INT. DOWNTOWN CLUB - NIGHT

A Dark Nite party for the release of Deuce's
first CD on the label. Rap moguls, major and
mini, are all there. Matt sits with Dougie,
Deuce and Teenie, talking in a booth. An NBA
player walks up with a woman named RUBY
STAPLES, a stunner with style for days. The
player stops to say what's up to Dougie. The
others in the booth all stare at Ruby, but
she seems to have eyes for Big Matt. When
they walk away, Dougie gives the table the
low-down: Ruby is a stylist with high-level
clientele.

Dougie: She's wanted by many and had by
few.

Deuce heads to the stage where he's gonna
perform his new single. Matt, who seems to
have an instinct for sensing trouble, notices

THREE GUYS at the bar not looking at women.
He points them out to Teenie.

> Teenie: They down with Strictly Biz. Keep
> eyes on them, my dude.

When Deuce takes the stage, the Three Guys
begin throwing bottles at him. One pulls a
razor blade from under his tongue and heads
for the stage. Before the razor man can reach
Deuce, Big Matt blocks his way and clocks him
with a devastating right cross. The man hits
the floor. Out cold.

When the police arrive Big Matt goes quietly.
As they take him to the patrol car Ruby
catches his eye. He can't tell if she likes
him or is just judging him. He smiles at her.
She looks away.

EXT. POLICE PRECINCT - MORNING

The next morning Big Matt leaves jail with
Dougie and a lawyer. He's facing a civil
lawsuit and possible criminal charges for
assault. The brawl has made the cover of the
Daily News and the *Post*. Dougie is overjoyed!

> Dougie: You are a legend, kid. Niggas
> really gonna wanna fuck with you.

'Success Is the Mother of Change'

Montage of success. Big Matt gets a bigger office. Lots of women on him. His assistant Niecy gets a promotion too. He buys a sexy condo in Tribeca. At a party he sees Ruby with another high-profile man. They make eye contact but she walks away. She is a vision still a bit out of Matt's reach. Trade articles about Dark Nite's new golden age highlight Matt. Gary Tee reads that Big Matt is #2 in *The Source* magazine's power list right behind Dougie. He seethes.

INT. DARK NITE OFFICES - DAY

Matt comes in late to Dark Nite's office and is intercepted by Niecy, who tells him Dougie and Gary went through his files and his office computer. Matt heads right into Dougie's office, where he and Gary sit talking. Gary accuses Matt of using cash from his A&R budgets to enhance his lifestyle. Matt comes back with similar accusations about Gary's use of promotional budgets. Dougie laughs at them both.

> Dougie: I know both you guys are shaving the budgets. That's the game. Besides, you are really stealing from our distributor, not me, so as long as it doesn't get out of hand, I'm cool.

> However, I'm gonna sell this label
> outright real soon, so you guys are
> gonna have to get it together.

He asks to speak to Big Matt alone. After
Gary Tee exits, Dougie holds up a magazine.

> Dougie: Sometimes I read these articles
>   and you act like Dark Nite didn't exist
>   before you walked through these doors.

> Matt: I've always respected you.

> Dougie: Just cause you can knock a nigga
>   out don't make you no hero to me. You
>   work for me until I decide you don't.

> Matt: You can't fire me, Dougie.

> Dougie: How's that?

> Matt: I'm already gone.

Matt walks out of the office, tells Niecy to
come with him and they exit Dark Nite's
offices.

> Niecy: What took you so long?

'Survival Is 90% of Victory'

INT. POWERHOUSE OFFICES - AFTERNOON

Armed with his two-way pager and the support
of Niecy, Big Matt opens a small Soho office.

He calls his company POWERHOUSE Production &
Management, then buys a gang of mix tapes in
Harlem and sits in his office listening to
beat after beat after beat. The music has
changed since Matt first started at Dark Nite,
but the way you find stars hasn't. He gets
obsessed with TRUTH, an MC from the Boogie
Down.

In *The Source* magazine he sees a profile of
Ruby. He calls up the writer to get her
digits.

INT. RUBY'S APT HALLWAY - EVENING

Ruby comes home to find her hallway filled
with a rainbow of balloons. There's a card
from Matt: 'I find you colorful' with his
number. She tears the card up. The next day
her apartment hallway is again filled with
balloons - this time all red. This card
reads, 'Roses are red and so are balloons'
with his number. On the third day the
balloons are all blue and the card reads 'Why
you wanna give me the blues?'

NEIGHBOR sticks her head out of her apartment
and says, 'Would you please go out with him?'

INT. NOBU - NIGHT

Big Matt and Ruby have a mellow dinner at
Nobu, getting to know each other before

heading to Moomba, an industry hangout, for drinks.

INT. MOOMBA - NIGHT

The two are getting cozy at the table when ASIA, an up & coming singer, comes up wearing some beautiful diamonds. Ruby had styled her last video. Matt thinks they are friends, but then Ruby slaps the MC and rips a diamond ring out of her ear. Apparently, the singer kept the earrings from the shoot and Ruby had to repay the jeweler for their loss. Matt is impressed by Ruby's swag. Kindred spirits.

At the end of the night Ruby tells Big Matt she likes him but she's still seeing that NBA player.

    Matt: We'll see.

INT. POWERHOUSE OFFICES - NIGHT

CTC shows up at his office and tells Matt and Niecy that they have been blackballed by Gary Tee. He wants no one at Dark Nite to help or deal with them. But CTC, though signed to Dark Nite, is loyal to Big Matt.

    CTC: You are my new manager, so everyone
      at Dark Nite will have to deal with
      you.

Matt: You know this Truth kid from the
    Bronx?

CTC: Truth? Yeah, I know where he be at.

EXT. BRONX STREET CORNER - NIGHT

Matt and CTC roll out to the Bronx where
Truth runs a small crew of clockers. Truth
walks up to the car to sell some rocks but he
recognizes CTC, who introduces him to Matt.

Matt: Get in. I wanna talk to you. You
    need to sign with my label.

Truth: That's hot and shit, but I can't
    leave my crew right about now.

Matt: It's time to get off the corner and
    get some legal money.

As they talk a jeep rolls up and sprays the
corner and Matt's car. Truth is wounded in
the drive-by. Matt hustles the bleeding MC to
the hospital.

INT. BRONX HOSPITAL - NIGHT

At the hospital Matt meets Truth's mother and
promises to pay all his hospital bills - even
if he doesn't sign with him. Truth's crew
roll up to the hospital, they are packing and
ready for revenge.

Matt and CTC go and speak to Truth.

Matt: Let me tell you something. If you
   roll with your crew and do what you
   really feel like doing, you'll never
   hear from me again. I'll pay these bills
   for your mother but that's it. We can
   never do business. If you come with me
   to the studio right now, CTC and I will
   get you working with his producers. I
   can make you a legend. You wanna be a
   legend?

'Winning Is Good. Loving Is Better'

INT. JAMAICAN RESORT - DAY

CTC and the Truth collaborate on a hot track
that puts Powerhouse Records on the map. The
video is shot in Kingston, Jamaica, and Ruby
is the stylist. Matt is there and, after the
shoot, the two head to a private resort where
they reveal more of themselves, much more than
at their Nobu dinner. They have a pointed
conversation about the importance of family.

Ruby: You are already like a father/older
   brother to a lot of people.

Matt: But I need a son of my own to be a
   real father. I learned a lot from my
   father. A lot of shit really. But I
   wanna do a better job.

Ruby: So, having a boy is about your ego?

Matt: No. It's about doing something good for someone I love.

Ruby: You are a busy man. I love that about you. But pay attention to me. Always keep me in your thoughts and I'll always be there for you.

They make love. The next morning his cell rings. It's Niecy.

Niecy: You ever hear of Napster? Turn on your computer and call me back.

Matt searches for Napster online and watches the site, seeing the downloads and the files shared. He sees the names of several of his artists and they are too popular on the site for his own good. He calls Niecy.

Matt: This is a problem.

'Steal the Kids and the Parents Will Follow'

INT. WEST VILLAGE RESTAURANT – NIGHT

The launch of Deuce's LP goes well, selling multi-platinum numbers. But as Matt analyzes the numbers he sees sales are down 30% to 50% in markets where hip-hop LPs do well. He has lunch with Blue Streak, who does a radio mix show in Hot 97, who tells him he's starting to download his mix tapes instead of selling them on the street.

INT. MATT'S CONDO - NIGHT

Matt has dinner at his condo with Ruby and his mother, who isn't keen on his new girlfriend, feeling she's shallow. After his mother leaves, Ruby and Matt argue over when they can take a vacation. While they talk Matt notices that Ruby has the Home Shopping Network on. He sees a soap opera actress on TV selling jewelry and making cash.

INT. ADVERTISING AGENCY, NYC - DAY

Matt meets with an ad agency about developing more mainstream endorsement deals for his clients.

> Matt: There's got to be bigger deals out there than for sneakers and malt liquor.

Jeff, the ad executive, is sympathetic but skeptical.

INT. OHIO FACTORY - DAY

Big Matt walks through the rural Ohio factory of HONEST JOE'S, a leading clothing retailer where watches, designer jeans and jackets are manufactured. It is heartland USA. Matt, Niecy and Jeff meet with the CEO MICHAEL DAVIDSON. He's not convinced that rappers, no matter how many records they sell, can impact his consumers. He offers Matt an 'ethnic' market deal but Matt isn't satisfied. Jeff argues, producing a bunch of marketing and research papers. Matt takes a different tack.

> Matt: You have a son in college, right? Can you call him on speakerphone for me?

Davidson wonders where this stunt is going, but agrees. His son, Joseph, is attending Columbia. When asked what music he listens to, Joseph mentions a few safe white pop/rock acts. But when Matt presses him and mentions acts on his label, Joseph gets enthused and endorses CTC and Deuce. Joseph even offers his rap name – Joey D, something his dad knew nothing about. Matt offers Joey a summer internship and a still skeptical Davidson is impressed.

CTC is featured in a TV spot rhyming about the wonders of Honest Joe's retail outlets. The ad plays in a hospital room where Ruby has given birth to Trey Silver. Matt is in heaven, handing out cigars to all his old friends and family. He's got a new business model and a son. He's on top of the world.

Big Matt and Ruby become one of New York's 'It' couples, attending fashion shows, basketball games and charity balls. All the while spending money like water. Matt, encouraged by Ruby, purchases his and her Maybachs. He knows it's over the top but can't help it.

INT. SOHO GALLERY - NIGHT

At a Soho art show a fashion designer accuses Ruby of not returning clothes from her last video shoot. Matt intervenes and pulls the designer aside and squashes the beef. In the car home Matt asks if what the designer said was true. Ruby doesn't deny it. Matt is confused since she has money.

> Ruby: But it's your money. I took care of myself before I met you and I could do it again. Don't feel like you need to babysit me - I can handle my business.

INT. REHEARSAL SPACE - AFTERNOON

The Truth is out of the street, but the street isn't out of Truth. Matt goes to see a run-through of his show before the young MC is about to head out on a national tour. Matt notices some of the Truth's block boys are acting as bodyguards/roadies. Matt decides to take a look at the tour bus—something about Truth's posse bothers him. He looks inside the baggage compartment under the bus and, inside, Matt finds a couple of big bags of marijuana. When he sits down with the Truth it turns out the MC knew that his posse was gonna deal

while on the road. That way he doesn't have
to pay them as much. Matt gets angry with the
Truth for endangering himself. But Truth won't
stop it.

> Truth: Niggas need to eat. You livin'
> well. You should just respect the game.

Truth implies that Matt is now too removed
from the street to understand, which irritates
him.

'It Doesn't Matter What's in the Bottle – a Salesman Sells'

INT. DIDDY'S WHITE PARTY – EVENING

Big Matt and Ruby hang at Diddy's white party
in the Hamptons, looking like the rap royalty
that they are. He and Dougie see each other
and embrace. Dougie expresses his pride in how
Big Matt has developed Powerhouse. They talk
warily about the Internet and how it's
changing the game.

> Dougie: Would you come back and run Dark
> Nite? It's still the best brand in the
> game.

> Matt: So, I could fire Gary Tee? I'd just
> do it for one day so I could let that
> fool go. But otherwise it has no appeal
> to me. I'm building my own family. You

see how much Niecy has developed. She's
my partner now.

A concerned Niecy walks over and tells Matt
he needs to come see about his woman. Matt
walks over to his worst nightmare - his
baby's mother and Gary Tee are looking a
little too cozy sitting in a back room with
champagne and cocaine. Gary Tee knows he's
irritating Matt and milks it, goading Big Matt
while high. Ruby resists being calmed down.

    Ruby: You don't own me.

Matt almost hits her but is held back by
Niecy. Ruby drives off in her Maybach with
Gary Tee. Matt is humiliated. He attempts to
find his car and, when the valets are slow,
Matt socks one in the jaw.

EXT. EAST HAMPTON JAIL - DAY

Next day Matt is bailed out of jail by Deuce,
who finds the whole situation amusing.

    Deuce: Ain't this some shit. The artist
    bailing out his manager.

INT. MATT'S CONDO - AFTERNOON

Back at his Manhattan condo Matt finds Ruby
and his son both gone.

Matt spirals into a depression, feeling he overreacted and alienated the people he loves. He plays video games. He smokes chronic. He won't answer the phone. Days later Niecy lets herself in. Niecy doesn't like Ruby but knows Matt is no angel either.

> Niecy: If it's gonna work you'll need to give her and your son more. You are always giving artists good advice. Now you need to take some of it yourself. You always say don't put yourself above the game. Now don't put yourself above your family.

Big Matt meets Ruby at her girlfriend's apartment. He and his son immediately fall into each other's arms. Then Matt and Ruby walk hand in hand through Central Park, each promising to be better partners. The next day they get married at City Hall.

INT. CANCUN RESORT, MEXICO - DAY

The family goes on a honeymoon in Mexico. Big Matt is happy, but still distracted and checking his BlackBerry whenever possible. Too many clients. Too much money to make. One night Ruby and Matt are about to make love when Deuce calls. Matt takes the call. Deuce plays him his new banger over the phone. On a balcony overlooking the ocean Matt listens to his new jam and is sure it's a massive hit.

At the end of the record Deuce lays down a demand:

> Deuce: I'm ready to endorse a product. I want to endorse something healthy like cranberry juice. Shit keeps your dick working good.

Big Matt hangs up, happy about the track and confused by the endorsement request. When he goes back into the bedroom he finds Ruby asleep. Instead of waking her, Big Matt turns on his computer and begins researching cranberry juice companies. Ruby, who was not asleep, watches resentfully.

EXT. CRANBERRY FARM - DAY

Big Matt and Deuce walk through a field of cranberries with a white man named CARLSON, owner of Cranberry Beverages. Carlson gives them the lore of cranberry care and they check the crop like farmers. Carlson knows the deals that Matt's clients have gotten from other brands and he can't afford it.

> CARLSON: We hope to be purchased by a bigger concern one day, but that won't be tomorrow.

> MATT: You give us equity in exchange for Deuce's endorsement and we'll make you a multi-millionaire. First what do you know about bubble gum?

When the first billboards appear around the country people think the Deuce/cranberry juice hook-up is crazy, but people are buzzing about it. Deuce promotes a bubble-gum-flavored cranberry juice that people are loving and mixing with their gin and vodka.

INT. POWERHOUSE OFFICES - DAY

An FBI agent comes to visit Matt and asserts that Truth is under investigation for interstate drug trafficking and that Matt is implicated as well. Matt is contemptuous. When the agent leaves, Matt and Niecy discuss the fact that any indictment could torpedo his deals with mainstream brands.

As Matt masterminds the cranberry campaign and worries about the FBI investigation, his relationship with Ruby deteriorates. He starts sleeping with a young advertising executive, Sara, and is sloppy about it.

He takes his young son to a store to buy some clothes and gets served with divorce papers.

'Your Words Can't Hide Your Heart'

INT. COURTROOM - DAY

At the custody hearing all Big Matt's faults are documented by Ruby's attorney: his women, his travel, his arrests. Matt has made money but is he really a good man? Is he any better than his father?

Outside the custody hearing Matt receives a call from Niecy. A huge food company is buying the cranberry juice company. Between Deuce's share and Powerhouse's fee, their cut could top $100 million. Matt goes back in the room and reluctantly agrees to Ruby's terms, knowing that he's agreeing to an amount he can now afford.

INT. RECORDING STUDIO - NIGHT

Big Matt visits the Truth in the studio and the meeting is edgy. Jealous of the deals that CTC and Deuce have, the Truth says he's been speaking to the FBI and suggests he'll implicate Matt in his drug deals if he isn't rewarded with a huge endorsement deal. It's a petty, dangerously childish argument. It makes Big Matt wonder what he's doing with his life.

INT. RUBY'S NEW JERSEY HOME - MORNING

Big Matt goes to see his son, but when he arrives his son isn't there. Even worse he learns that Gary Tee and Ruby are about to leave for a vacation in St. Barth's with Dougie.

INT. CEMETERY – DAY

Matt visits his father's grave, contemplating his past and his future.

EXT. SAG HARBOR, LONG ISLAND – MORNING

Matt sits in his backyard. He pushes 'send' on his smartphone. He's sending his ten lessons to Niecy, his last will and testament.

He pulls out the gun, places it against his temple and pulls the trigger.

JUMPING SHIP

OYINKAN BRAITHWAITE

There is a lag in their chat. She puts the phone down and picks it up again. She sent the last three messages, so she has to wait. Eventually, she sees that he is typing:

I want pro pics of my baby.

Not what she was expecting, but she will allow him to pivot. In another life, he could have been a ballerina, spinning away from responsibility on his tippy toes. She imagines him wearing tights and a tutu. She smiles.

No worries. I know a couple great guys.

No. I wnt *u* to tk the pics.

LOL

Y u laughing? I'm serious.

You can't be serious.

Ur the best photogrphr I no. The best person I no . . .

Stop. Pls. It wouldn't be right.

I'll pay u ur asking price.

She blinks at the screen. It has been a long time since a client paid what she asked. Too long. She could certainly use the money. But . . . it is Kaeto. And Kaeto's baby. He is always doing this – pushing the envelope; pushing her.

It is only 11 a.m., but she opens a bottle of vodka and pours it into freshly squeezed orange juice. She sticks a multicoloured straw into the glass and sips. The straws were a gift from Kaeto; as part of a series of presents that were odd, mismatched, bright and inexpensive. It was how he saw her, he said. Her phone buzzes on the counter.

Well . . . what say u?

I'm thinking.

Wat r u tnkng bout?

How low I am willing to go . . .

Come off it Ida. It is jst a couple photos.

She takes another long sip and closes her eyes. Her throat burns and her mind is in disarray. Just a couple of photos . . . It shouldn't take more than a few hours to get the shots she will need, taking into account outfit changes, feeding breaks . . .

Will Mina be there?

What kind of question is that?

Just answer it. Pls.

Yes, the baby's mother will be there. To be honest, this was her idea.

Mina asked for me? Why?

Ur reputation precedes u. No need to make it weird.

She composes four replies; she deletes four replies. In the end, she sends him the amount she intends to charge and adds an extra hundred thousand naira; just because. Moments later, the full amount is in her account, even though she had stated that he need only pay the deposit.

Does Tuesday wrk for u?

This Tuesday?

Ya.

Sure. Tuesday.

He gives her a thumbs up.

•

Tuesday swings by and Ida stands before her wardrobe, sipping fresh mimosa and trying to decide what to wear. She is sweating from the effort of putting on and taking off outfits. She has gained weight – her dresses are snug where they should be loose and her jeans are digging into her belly. Eventually she settles on grey slacks and a black tee.

She sends Kaeto a message before she leaves her apartment, but he doesn't reply.

The Uber driver rattles on about Buhari, SARS, the ballooning cost of fuel, light, food; she provides him with little sounds to keep him sated but her eyes are looking through the window, tracing the familiar route to Kaeto's house. When they arrive she knocks on the gate, waits and knocks again. She can imagine Baba G sitting in his security post, folding his arms and refusing to budge, having satisfied himself that it is her on the other side of the gate. The man is the bane of her life. She sees him in her nightmares sometimes.

'Baba G doesn't like me.'

'You're being paranoid. Baba G likes everybody.'

'Everybody, but me.' He was being wilfully ignorant, if he did not realize that his gateman treated her like she was shit beneath his raggedy sandals. How many more times would she have to tell Kaeto this, before he did something about her concerns?

'He is just old, Ida.'

'There is nothing wrong with his sight or hearing . . .'

'Ida, come off it.' And that had been the end of that.

It has only been a few weeks since that conversation; if she complains about Baba G today, she will sound like a shrew. She looks around at her surroundings, helplessly. The Uber is gone. The driver helped her carry the tripod, soft box, lighting equipment and rest them against the widely spaced bars of the gate. The rest of her gear is in the rucksack strapped across her back. But the rucksack is heavy and the sun relentless. He is taking longer than usual to answer her persistent knocks. Between the wide gaps, she can see the quaint house, but she can no more access it than if it were a mirage.

'Baba G. It's me. It's Ida.'

She transfers her body weight from one foot to the other and then back again. With her eyes, she traces the path a line of ants are taking across the sand and rubble. She sips the mimosa from her flask. She takes out her phone to message Kaeto, but just then she glimpses Mina walking towards her, a vision in an Ankara blazer dress, her hair fanning out above and behind her in a glorious 'fro. Ida slips her phone back into her pocket and tries to smile. Mina waves to her and then slips into Baba G's alcove. Moments later, the gate slides open.

She grabs her equipment, managing to drop the tripod twice before deciding it would be easier to use two trips to bring her things to the front door.

'Do you need help?' asks Mina in the voice that sounds like gravel, but somehow also like honey. The scent she wears is heady – there are hints of cinnamon and cedar but it is mostly floral. The wind is blowing the perfume right into her soul. Ida turns away slightly.

'No, no. I can manage.'

'Are you sure?'

'Yup. They are fragile . . . so I prefer to handle it myself.'

'OK-o.'

She grabs the soft box and her rucksack first and places them on the steps of the front door. Then she returns for the tripod and the lighting equipment. She hears the gate sliding shut behind her.

The front door has been left open for her and she walks in. She drops her things by the door before following Mina into the living room. Mina's influence is everywhere – it is in the daffodil bouquet atop the coffee table, in the scented candles littered all around the room, in the mural on the wall. In the centre of the room, Mina lifts her baby and rocks it to music only they can hear. She is saying something to the newborn, but the words are unintelligible from where Ida stands.

Ida forces herself to get close to them and peers at the baby.

'She is beautiful,' Ida tells Mina. It is the exact same thing she told Kaeto. It is the thing you are supposed to say. 'Congratulations. I haven't . . . I haven't had a chance to tell you that.'

'Thank you. It's good of you to do this, Ida,' says Mina. 'I know it was last minute . . .'

'No, no need to thank me. It's not like . . . it's free or anything . . .' She can't help but stare at Mina's tummy. You would never guess that Mina had given birth a mere three weeks ago. She suspects, were they to measure both their waists, Mina's would be smaller. She continues to rock her baby, oblivious to Ida's scrutiny. The newborn is mewing and whining. It has Kaeto's mouth. 'Maybe we should get started. Is Kaeto here?'

'Kaeto?' Mina laughs, 'Kaeto here? Now, that's a good one,' she wipes a fake tear from her eye. 'No, he isn't here. He is at work.'

'I . . . I thought . . .'

'That he would be here for the shoot? Nope. He opted out.'

'Can I use your guest toilet?'

'Sure. You know the way, right?'

'Yea . . . I think I remember.'

She scurries away and shuts herself in the small room, taking a breath free from Mina's sickly sweet floral scent. When she thumbs her phone, there is no message from him. She chews on her lip and then she messages him.

I thought you were going to be here . . .

Did I say I would be?

She scrolls up through their conversations. No, he didn't say he would be. It wasn't expressly stated. But she thought it was a fair assumption to make. Why would he think it was OK to leave her alone with Mina?

I can't do this.

Relax. Mina won't bite.

She waits for him to say something more comforting, but her silence is met with his own. She flushes the toilet, in case Mina is monitoring her. When she enters the living room, Mina is breastfeeding her child. She looks away from them. Hopefully, the baby will fall asleep once it has had its fill and the work can begin.

'Is this where we will be taking the pictures?' She hopes it is. There is a good amount of natural light coming in from the French windows.

'Yes,' Mina replies. Ida walks towards the windows and drags the heavy curtains to their extremes to get as much light into the room as she can. She tries to picture where the baby could be placed. There is a pouffe ottoman that attracts her attention. 'I checked out some of your stuff on Instagram,' Mina is saying. 'There was a picture where the baby was dressed as a flower. I'd like that.'

'Of course you would.'

'What?'

'Nothing. I have a lot of props we can play with. And of course we can use any items or clothing you may have bought.'

'Sounds good.' Mina pulls her breast out of the mouth of the newborn. Her breast is large and swollen, and Ida is conscious that hers are like pebbles in comparison. 'Will you burp her? I've got to use the loo.'

'Uhm . . . can't you do it when you get back?' Mina is already handing over the baby. Ida holds it away from her.

'Just pat and rub her back gently.'

'Look, Mina . . . I . . .'

Mina is already at the door and then she is gone; leaving Ida with the newborn. She wonders if her hold is tight enough. What would happen were the baby to wiggle out of her grip? She closes her eyes and rests the baby against her shoulder, patting and rubbing as instructed. She feels something cold and wet against her skin and when she twists her neck, she can see traces of the spit-up the baby has deposited. It is cream, white, yellow and all the more visible against her dark T-shirt.

She holds the baby away from her once more. It stares at her with Kaeto's eyes. Mina walks in and sighs.

'Let me get something to clean that.' She goes to the kitchen and returns with a wet cloth. As Ida is holding the baby, Mina rubs her T-shirt for her. But the tee is starting to feel as though it were drenched in water. 'Oh dear. OK, look. I think you're going to have to wear one of my tops till this one dries.'

The blouse Mina turns up with is a neon pink crop top. Nothing like anything Ida owns in her wardrobe. She slips off her blouse and puts on Mina's top. It smells like Mina – potent, strong. She sucks in her stomach.

'Pink suits you,' she fidgets under Mina's gaze. Mina has always been generous with her compliments, with her kindness, with her love. It is why they could never truly be friends. She could not be comfortable around someone so sugary sweet.

'OK . . . I'm just gonna get my stuff and bring them here.'

She hurries out. Mina's scent pursues her. She gulps in as much fresh air as she can and takes her phone out to message Kaeto; but what she wants to do is complain, and he hates that, so she puts her phone back in her pocket. She carries her equipment into the living room in two batches as she did before, and she sets it up while Mina sings to her child.

Ida unfolds the bassinet she brought with her and stuffs it with blankets before reaching out for the now sleeping newborn. She has done this a thousand times before. Mina is just a client and the newborn is her client's baby. She can get through this.

'It's not going to hurt her, is it? Putting her in that position?'

'Babies are super flexible. And they also let us know when they are in pain. So, you needn't worry. But if you are uncomfortable with anything, anything at all, just let me know and we will try something else.' Mina hands over her baby. Ida places it deftly into the bassinet, without taking the time to focus on its softness and malleability. If Kaeto had an ounce of honesty in his system, this baby wouldn't even be here. But you weren't allowed to think such things about a baby, you certainly couldn't say them out loud. She wonders if this baby shoot was his way of helping her to bridge the gap. Mina hands her one of the large artificial flowers she had spread on the floor and she places them around the newborn.

She takes a series of photographs kneeling over the baby. Through the lens she can see the newborn has a birthmark on its cheek, not dissimilar from Kaeto's. What else does it have that belongs to Kaeto? How much claim will it have on Kaeto's time?

'So how have you been?' asks Mina.

'Good, good.'

'Anything new going on with you?'

'No, not really.'

'Seeing anyone?' There is an age you get to that all anyone wants to know is if you have someone special in your life; as though your singleness is a blemish that has to be fixed.

She shakes her head. 'There's no one new in my life.' That much is true. She stands up and shows Mina some of the pictures she has taken. She watches as a smile spreads on Mina's face. The pictures are good, but it helps when the client recognizes their worth.

'You're good at what you do.'

'Thanks.'

'She looks ethereal.'

'She has your good looks.'

'A lot of people say she looks like her dad.'

'She looks like you,' Ida tells her firmly. 'You should probably change her outfit now.'

'Mmm. The outfit is over there. Can you do it? I've gotta pee again. My bladder has not been the same since labour.'

'We'll wait for you.'

'No need. Just change her.'

Mina is gone and Ida is left with the baby. She sinks into the sofa and stares at it in the bassinet. She thinks of how tender and breakable babies are. She knows someone whose baby died because it was shaken too hard, too long. That's all it took, shaking. Her phone vibrates. It is Kaeto.

How is it going?

Fine.

You sure?

How'd you expect it to go?

Someone's in a bad mood.

No, she writes. Then she erases. I'm, she writes and then she erases that too.

She is a beautiful baby.

Isn't she?

She tucks her phone back in her pocket and kneels before the newborn. She carefully takes her out of the bassinet and begins to unbutton the onesie. It doesn't have Mina's sickly scent on it, it is all baby powder and that natural gummy smell that babies have. The newborn's next outfit is a white 'Aunty give me cake' dress. It is almost drowning in the fluffy fabric, but there is no denying how angelic it looks.

She returns the newborn to the bassinet and walks over to the stereo. She turns it on. The song that plays is Amaarae's 'Jumping Ship', so she knows Kaeto was the last one to fiddle with the stereo. Once he discovered a song, he would play it over and over, until they were both sick of it. She has heard this track a million times already. She turns the stereo off and continues to take photos. When Mina returns she will include her in the shots. She positions the newborn on the ottoman and places a miniature crown of flowers on her tiny skull. She plays with the curtains to adjust the lighting and tries to find efficient ways to place the reflector, reminding herself that she needs to hire an assistant.

Time passes and she starts to fidget. She needs Mina's input in order to move forward and she wants to leave. She takes another sip from her flask. The house is quiet. She returns the baby to the bassinet; it seems like the safest place to leave the baby. She leaves the living room to go in search of Mina.

'Mina?'

There is no answer. She knocks on the door of the guest toilet and then she opens it. No Mina. She heads to the staircase and looks up.

'Mina, you all right?'

Ida climbs a few of the steps. The first time she had taken the steps of this house, Kaeto had been leading her by the hand. When she is halfway, she calls out again.

'Mina?'

The house is modest in size – there is no reason why Mina wouldn't be able to hear her. She wonders if something has happened to the new mother. Who would be responsible for the baby then? How would Kaeto feel?

She enters the master bedroom. Mina's clothes are scattered on the bed. She spies a navy-blue blouse that would have been far more appropriate than the candy-coloured top she was forced to wear. She knocks on the door of the en suite bathroom. She turns the handle and the door opens. Mina is not inside.

She goes to the other rooms and bathrooms to check for Mina, but to no avail. She freezes for a second, did she hear the creak of a door? The newborn belts a shrill cry and Ida runs back into the living room, scooping it up and rocking it as she has seen Mina do. Its eyes are not even open but it continues to cry. It is as though it knows something isn't quite right. There is a smell emanating from the baby. She lifts its bum to her nose and then draws back. She had noticed nappies on the drawer in the master bedroom. This time she takes the baby with her and undresses it on the bed. She changes the nappy, possibly using too many baby wipes in the process; then she puts the baby in a nondescript onesie. They can resume the fancy clothing when Mina makes her appearance.

But there is no avoiding the fact that, despite all the noise the newborn made, the baby's mother has not presented herself.

Dude, I don't know where Mina is.

It is too long before Kaeto finally responds. The newborn is asleep again and she is kneeling on the floor beside the messy bed.

What are you talking about?

I don't think she is in the house.

You don't think? Have you checked?

I've checked.

Is my daughter with you?

Yes.

Then she is in the house. Mina wouldn't leave her. She is a fantastic mum.

Ida pauses. It is not like Kaeto to be so effusive. Especially not when it came to Mina. Was he trying to upset her?

I didn't say she wasn't. But I haven't seen her in like 40 mins. And she didn't say anything.

You have her number, call her. I'm in a meeting. Just handle it.

What does he expect from her?
She dials Mina's number, and she hears Rema's 'Woman' in

response. She follows the sound to the bathroom. Mina's phone vibrates on the sink. She picks it up and stares at it.

She carries the baby and gives the house another search. She goes upstairs and looks in all the rooms again. This time, she checks the rooms downstairs too. The guest toilet, the guest bedroom; the door of the kitchen is swinging when she enters the living room; but the kitchen itself is empty, though Mina's floral cloying scent is thick there. There is another door in the kitchen leading to the backyard, but when she tries to open it, it resists her. She presses her face to the glass panes of the door – there is nothing to see, except grass, trees, tarp and an empty washing line.

Perhaps Mina decided to go get something for the baby and forgot her phone. Maybe she thought it would be quick and got stuck in traffic. She leaves the house and knocks on the gate-man's alcove. There is no answer.

'Baba G?' She calls his name thrice more; after all, the man likes to pretend he's deaf. But there is no answer from him and she doesn't want to keep the newborn under the sun for too long. So she goes ahead and opens the door to the alcove. Baba G is not asleep within it. She hurries back to the house and closes the door behind her, locking it. Then she heads to the living room to grab her phone and message Kaeto, but she cannot find it.

She returns to the master bedroom to search for the phone. She removes all the clothing from the bed and then searches under the bed. She checks the bathroom, she even looks in the toilet bowl. She begins to suspect she is losing her mind. Her arms are becoming tired, unused as they are to carrying a baby for a long period of time. She goes back to the living room. Mina's phone is where Ida left it on the dining table. Fortunately, Mina hasn't locked her phone. She calls Kaeto, but he doesn't pick up, so she is forced to message him.

Kaeto, it's Ida.

What are you doing with Mina's phone?

I found her phone. But I can't find her.

Why are you using her phone though?

I can't find my phone. I don't know what the heck is going on. Baba G isn't here.

Baba G? Today is his day off.

Can you call me, pls.

I'm in a meeting. I shouldn't even be messaging you.

Kaeto, I have no idea where Mina is. I've looked everywhere for her.

OK. OK. I will send someone to check up on you guys. Is that OK?

Sure . . . I guess.

She paces. The newborn has fallen asleep again. She places the baby in the bassinet. Someone will be here soon and she will use that as an opportunity to leave. She is frazzled. It is clear to her now that she shouldn't have taken this job. She will send Kaeto his money back and suggest other professionals he can use.

There is a loud banging coming from the gate. She considers

taking the baby out with her, but she is loath to disturb the child now that it is quiet again. She uses the ottoman to keep the front door ajar and heads to the gate.

On the other side of the gate are two policemen. Her feet slow, but she approaches them nonetheless.

'Open the gate,' demands the man with the shiny bald head. She notices his tone is unfriendly.

'I'm not sure I know how, but I'll try.' She enters the alcove. She locates the remote that is used to open the gate, and she wonders why on earth Kaeto would send police. When he said he would send someone, she thought he meant a neighbour or a sibling. The gate slides open.

'Are you Ida?'

Yes . . .'

'Where is the madam of the house?'

'I don't know. That is what I am trying to find out.'

One of them walks by her. She turns to follow, but the other one stops her with his hand on her wrist.

'We need you to stay here, ma.'

'There is a baby in there.'

'We are aware.'

Their hostility is putting her on edge. She has done nothing wrong. If anything, she has kept her head in a scenario that others would find intolerable. She tries to stay calm as she waits for the younger policeman to come out and announce that he was unsuccessful and Mina is nowhere to be seen. But a few minutes later, Mina is walking out of the house with the newborn in her arms. There is an ugly grey blanket draped around Mina's shoulders that could only have come from the policeman. She is shivering and she does not answer when Ida calls out to her.

'What's going on here?' Ida asks no one in particular. There is suddenly a lot of activity around her. More policemen. A stretcher is rolled into the house, and when they bring it out, there is a concealed body on it. 'Is that Baba G?' she asks, but nobody answers her. It is as though she isn't even there, but when she tries to move, the policeman grabs her wrist again.

'You are under arrest.'

'For what?'

'For the death of Mr Kaeto Bardi.'

•

They have left her to her thoughts for hours. At this point, even a policeman would be welcome company. The room she is in is dim and bare. There is nothing to do but sit, wait and stew in the heat. So she mutters, trying to make it make sense. No one is watching her. There are no cameras in the corners of the room and no glass window through which a crowd of interested professionals can view her.

The door opens and she looks up to see the hostile policeman walk into the room with a tall broad woman in plain clothes. They both sit at the table across from her. They introduce themselves but Ida forgets their names as soon as they are done squeezing the hard sounding monikers and she does not think asking them to repeat themselves will endear her to them. The man records her name on a piece of paper. Her name will forever be a part of this place.

The Amazonian woman leans forward. She is the one who will be controlling the interview. She is the one Ida must convince.

'So why did you kill Mr Kaeto?'

'I didn't!' she cries. 'I told the other policemen that. There has been a mistake! All you people have to do is call him. Please just call him.'

'Did you not see them bring out his body?'

'I saw them bring out someone's body. But it wasn't Kaeto's. Kaeto is at work. Just call him.'

The woman sighs but she brings out her mobile phone.

'Oya, what is his number?' Ida calls out each digit. His is the only number she knows off by heart. And the Amazonian puts the phone on loudspeaker. It rings, and rings, and rings.

'Try him again.' The Amazonian obliges, but still the phone just rings and Ida can feel a well opening up inside of her.

'Do you know why he is not picking up? It is because he is dead.'

'Call his office.'

'Ida, let's stop playing these games. We know everything. We know you were having an affair with Mr Kaeto.'

The sweat runs from her forehead and into her eyes, burning them. She rubs her eyes and gets dust in them. The table is caked with dust. She uses the crop top to wipe her eyes.

'Who told you that?'

'We know things were starting to unravel when his wife gave birth to a beautiful baby girl.' She can feel a headache forming at the back of her skull. The woman with the giant head is wrong – nothing was unravelling. Kaeto had reassured her that nothing would change between them. But then, he had also sworn he was no longer sleeping with Mina. All we do is fight, he had said.

'Kaeto wasn't home when I came to the house. He was at work. I have been messaging him all day.'

'OK, tell me what happened from the moment you got to the house.'

'Mina opened the gate for me.'

'Mrs Bardi?'

'Yes.'

'Why were you at the house if your lover was at work?'

'I . . . he . . .' she clears her throat. She wants to ask for a bottle of water, or for her flask. 'I was there to take pictures of his daughter.'

'Why would he ask—'

'I don't know! Kaeto liked to push people's boundaries. My boundaries. Besides, he said it was Mina's idea.'

'Why would she invite her husband's mistress to take pictures of her baby?'

'She doesn't know . . . about the two of us.'

'So he asked you to come but then he left you, his lover, alone with his wife . . . that doesn't seem very smart. I heard Mr Kaeto was a smart guy.'

'He was. Is.' She takes a breath. 'He likes risks.'

'And you agreed to this risk?'

'Yes. Well, no . . . I didn't know he wouldn't be there.'

'That must have made you angry . . .'

'It was annoying, but that was all. Just a little annoying.' Not even the most annoying thing he had done. The baby was proof of that.

'OK. So you were in your lover's house, with his wife and his baby, taking pictures of said baby. And then what happened?'

'I couldn't find Mina.'

'Mrs Bardi.'

'Yes.'

'You looked for her.'

'Yes.'

'So you turned the house upside down.' Had she? She remembers being a little frantic, especially when she couldn't find her phone. But it wasn't as though the house had been tidy. Or is the woman with the hulk arms suggesting that if she had searched hard enough, the house *would* be in a tip? She can't tell what the right answer is.

'I was worried. I thought something might have happened to her.'

'Like what?'

'Like maybe she collapsed or something.'

'Why not alert a neighbour?'

'I . . . It hadn't crossed my mind and I had the newborn with me.'

'Hmmm.'

'It can't be Kaeto, you found . . .'

'His wife has identified him, and his brother is on the way.' Her body is trembling and she is finding it hard to centre herself. It doesn't make sense. None of it makes sense. 'Ms Ida . . . this is a serious matter.' The Amazonian has light brown eyes, uncommon eyes. If she had her camera, she would take a picture. 'I want you to think on it hard. It will be better that you come out with the truth now.'

'If you find my phone, I can show you—'

'We have your phone and Mr Bardi's. The last conversation between the two of you was on Saturday.' Saturday – a day before he procured her services. They had spent the afternoon together in a hotel. He had messaged her to let her know he had a good time. Her heart is pounding outside of her body. And there is a gushing sound in her ears.

'That doesn't . . . Ask Mina! She will tell you. Kaeto was at work. At least we thought—' but the Amazonian makes no attempt to move and beside her the silent policeman is scribbling away . . . 'What is Mina saying?'

'According to Mrs Bardi, you showed up at the house, threatened and stabbed Kaeto, and then attempted to kill her, forcing her to lock herself in the storage room without her child.' The storage room, in the kitchen, the one place she hadn't checked; and why should she?

'That . . . that isn't true . . . he wasn't even home . . .'

'We found his body under the tarp in their backyard.'

'Please! Listen to me. I didn't kill anyone. Wouldn't I have blood on me if I killed him?'

'Aren't those Mrs Bardi's clothes that you are wearing?'

'No! I mean, yes. Well, it's her top. The slacks are mine. The baby had spit up on my top, so . . .'

The policewoman takes out a clear bag. Inside the bag is a scrunched up black tee, and she can tell the T-shirt has been stained with blood. She can also tell that the bloodstained T-shirt is hers.

'Mina, she . . . she must have . . .' she lets her words trail off into the void. Mina. Mina who didn't know that she had been sleeping with Kaeto for almost as long as they had been husband and wife. Mina who had invited her over to photograph her newborn.

'Mina trusts everything I tell her,' Kaeto had said, a faint smile on his lips. 'And she has no reason to question me, we are discreet, aren't we?' he had asked as he rained kisses on her throat and breasts. 'Besides, you know Mina. The moment she finds out, we will know. She will burn the house down. She does not know how to hide her emotions; she isn't devious.'

'Not like you and me?'

'Not like you and me.'

PARADISE LOST

ABIR MUKHERJEE

It's always the little things.

The shitty wee stuff you don't even think about, but damn d'you miss it when it's gone.

For me it was the milk. Plain old pasteurized, and semi-skimmed, on account of doctor's orders. You'd think that wouldn't be a problem. You find it in the hotels, the five-star ones at least, and they're about the only kind on the island; but good luck to you trying to find it at the supermarket. All you get is that UHT rubbish that tastes like pish on your cornflakes, and frankly that's no way to start your day.

There's no fresh milk, you see, on account of there being no cows. Not a single one anywhere on the island. That's the sort of thing they don't mention in the brochures, or on the website that tells you which countries don't have an extradition agreement with the UK. The swanky hotels fly the stuff in (milk, that is, not cows), but for the ordinary folk, the half a million natives descended from slaves and slave owners mainly, it's UHT or nothin'.

There are other things of course: the beer for one. They do

a couple of local brews which are passable, but Jeez, I miss a pint of heavy. And then there's the football. It's amazin' how you can sit here, halfway round the world and watch a live match from the English Premiership, but try finding a channel showing the Celtic-Rangers match and you'll be searchin' till the cows come home . . . which, on this island, they actually never will.

•

Don't get me wrong; it's no' a bad wee place, especially if you like putting greens and pina coladas. But there's a limit to the number of rounds you can play, or drink, before you think, *with a coupla million in the bank, surely there has to be more to life*?

And that's the problem. Most people come out here for a fortnight's all-inclusive and fall in love wi' the place. Two weeks of soft towels, chocolates on your pillow and frangipani on the breeze. I mean, who wouldn't?

And that's what happened wi' me and Brenda. *A second honeymoon*, I told her, *an island paradise*, I said, *a wee bit different from the first one*, which, fair dos, was a wet weekend in Milport, so it wasn't as though the bar was very high. Course I didn't mention I might be doing a bit of reconnaissance on the side; just seein' if the place might suit us for a bit of a longer stay, so to speak. A few meetings with estate agents and bankers and extradition lawyers . . . and the odd politician.

That's the thing, you see. It's not the sixties any more. You can't just pull a Ronnie Biggs and toddle off to the Costa Brava to avoid the police. There's very few places these days which are beyond the reach of the long arm of the law. I mean, I suppose you could go to Russia, but you'd freeze your arse off, and who wants to do that?

This place is different though; just a wee dot in the middle of the ocean that Interpol and the rest of the world seems to have forgotten about. But, and here's the wonderful thing, it's a country nonetheless, a sovereign nation like any other, with the same rights and obligations as the bigger boys. I know this because I looked it up; and because the Prime Minister told me himself, over a bottle of thirty-year-old single malt which I gave him. The man's not exactly Barack Obama, but last year, he was up in New York addressing the general assembly of the United Nations. I mean, how mental is that? He's head of a speck of a place with a population the size of Dundee, but because it's a sovereign nation, he's treated like any other head of state. It's like the head of Aberdeen city council being invited to a summit of world leaders.

•

Anyway, at the end of our two weeks, while we were eatin' peach melba and bein' serenaded by a cut-price Demis Roussos, I convinced Brenda that we should move out here, permanent-like, and after some hesitation, she said *yes*, which came as a shock, to be honest.

'*If it gets you away from those bampots, then I'm all for it,*' she said, and by 'bampots' she meant Big Al McCurdy an' his team. Not the smartest apples in the barrel, it's true, but then the town of Hamilton is not a particularly deep barrel; and what McCurdy and his boys lack in brains, they more than make up for in violence. A psychiatrist would say they were overcompensating, but he'd be wise not to say it within earshot of McCurdy, not unless he wanted a new smile carved into his face.

McCurdy's pretty catholic with the use of a razor; more than happy to use it if he even suspected you might be grassing on him. Not that I would ever do somethin' like that. I mean, I'm not mental. And it's true, I haven't said a word, not to anyone. Not even to Brenda, but still, I think she worked it out. Women tend to, don't they? Sixth sense an' all that – about the job they pulled . . . that last one over in Edinburgh. Fair haul it was too, enough to set them up for life if they could find a buyer for the stuff, and they were careful about who they told about it.

An' that was the trouble. That was where things started to go a bit Pete Tong. See McCurdy *wasn't* careful. He just went an' touted the stones to some pal of his down in Shettlestone. I mean, *Shettlestone*? Seriously? Even if you'd never been to the place, one look at it on Google Earth would tell ye it's not exactly the sort of neighbourhood where discerning international purchasers of antique jewellery tend to congregate. But then, as I say, McCurdy's not exactly known for his smarts. No. He had me for that.

But I'm digressing; tellin' you about a bunch of *bampots* when I should be tellin' you about me and Brenda.

So we moved out here. I wanted to buy a boat. I was going to call it *Dignity*, but Brenda said that wasn't funny, and I didn't know how to explain to her that I wasn't trying to make a joke. She told me not to be silly, and at our age, what were we going to do with a boat anyway? Instead we bought a shiny white villa up in the north, where it doesn't rain so much.

Yeah, that's another thing they don't tell you in the brochures. Outside of tourist season, it tends to rain a lot, which is to say it pure buckets down, like Argyll in . . . well any month, really. Honestly, there have been days when I felt like I should have been building an ark and collecting all the animals, two by two.

The rain doesn't bother me too much, though. I'm conditioned to take it in my stride; water off a duck's back, et cetera, but Brenda's borderline allergic to the stuff. She might have been born in Glasgow, but she moved away as soon as she could, all the way down to Kent, the Garden of England, as they call it, though I can't see how it's much of a garden, not when April to September is basically just one long hosepipe ban.

But she put up with the rain, bless her; she put up with it, and with the mosquitoes, and with all the other wee creatures with altogether too many legs and wings and antennae. She even put up with the crappy TV. Aye, we have a satellite dish, but ye still can't get Ant and Dec on a Saturday night, and she missed that.

But what really did for her was the loneliness. She missed her pals, and while she made new ones, it wasn't the same. Island folk everywhere have a tendency to take their time warming to newcomers, but this place is different. There are two tribes on this rock: the natives and the ex-pats. The natives are, by and large, pretty pleasant, but their whole world is this island and it's difficult to find much in common with them. The ex-pats are far worse. There's something about a tax-free existence, augmented by an easy supply of maids and cooks and menial staff they'd never be able to afford back home, that drags the worst sort of Europeans to far-flung places, lording it over most of the locals as though they're some sort of inferior species. I say, *most*, because there is one type of local whom the ex-pats are in thrall to, and that's the politicians.

Brenda lasted six months. The arguments got so bad that, by the end, I was actually thinking of claiming asylum on another island altogether, but it was she who got on the plane first, back to Kent, and I miss her now.

I stayed on, rattling around in a villa that's suddenly got far more rooms than I need, with only Anju, the maid for company. She comes in three times a week to change the sheets on beds I haven't slept in and dust the furniture in rooms I haven't entered. She also cooks me a meal or two, putting casseroles and curries into Tupperware and transferring them to the fridge, where they'll generally stay till she comes back the next time and takes them home with her because I've not touched them; because I've spent all my time at the Fisherman, that's the local pub – if you can call a bunch of tables under thatched umbrellas, a *pub* – drinking their overpriced, piss-weak local brew.

And it's not just the beer that's overpriced. Everything out here costs a fortune. They say it's cos it all has to be shipped in from somewhere else; everything from the milk and the margarine to the mosquito nets and the ex-pat hotel managers.

You're probably wondering how the locals can afford to live here, and the honest answer is, they can't. A lot of them are dirt poor. Their kids look like the wee urchins you see in black-and-white photos of Govan from a hundred years ago, all runnin' about wi' bare feet and black necks. Many of them live in two-room shacks with corrugated roofs and brightly coloured walls, all painted by the government to make the place look cheery for the tourists. I know cos the minister for housing told me so over a curry one night, which I paid for.

I've paid for a lot of things. A lot of money to a lot of people, the usual leeches of course: estate agents and accountants, but politicians too, and no' just the government guys; a fair smattering of the opposition as well. My lawyer says ye never know when the other mob is gonnae get in, an' it's better to be safe than sorry, seeing how my resident's visa can be terminated with a month's notice. That's democracy for you; and while I might have cash in the bank, it's *their* bank – the state bank – which means the Prime Minister can freeze my account whenever he wants.

And *I'm* supposed to be the criminal?

But honesty is a concept that has little currency anywhere these days, and certainly not here, because it doesn't much matter whether you're honest or bent when you're stuck on this rock, this open prison in the middle of nowhere.

Still, it's better than a room at Her Majesty's pleasure, in Barlinnie say, with a single bed and an en suite bucket. Or worse, sharing a cell with McCurdy at HMP Sauchton.

They traced him, you see. One of the folks he went to, one of those Shettlestone fences, must've grassed him up to the police, cos three weeks after the job, the bastards raided his gaff at five a.m., which was a shame for McCurdy. If they'd arrived an hour earlier, he might still have been awake and had a sporting chance to get his pants on and try to jump out of the bathroom window. As it was, they caught him in bed in his birthday suit and dragged him out into the arctic embrace of a February morning in deepest, darkest Lanarkshire.

Well, I did my best to get him out. I hired wee Bobby Semple. He's the best lawyer in Hamilton, which is to say he's a regular down the masonic lodge and plays golf most weeks with the judges at the Sherriff Court. He's a local lad too, but not from Meikle Earnock like me and McCurdy. Bobby hails from Silvertonhill, the posh bit of town; *Spam Valley* as we used to call it, on account that the folks who lived there spent so much of their money on their houses that all they could afford to eat for dinner was Spam. Bobby was confident he could get McCurdy off.

'*Allegation and hearsay,*' he'd said. '*That's all they've got; and we've a strong case; a watertight case. Trust me, no judge in Hamilton or Glasgow is gonnae deny us.*'

And he was right. No judge in Hamilton or Glasgow *did* deny us, because the trial was moved to Edinburgh at the last moment and, due to Bobby not having as many friends there, McCurdy got sent down for twelve years.

'*A terrible miscarriage of justice,*' wee Bobby had branded it, and he was right. The police couldn't produce the stolen goods or even show any proceeds of the crime, mainly cos I had them.

But the jury didn't seem to mind too much. Twelve good women and men, overlooking the evidence and going with allegation and hearsay, almost as if they'd been bribed. McCurdy certainly thought so, swearing at them from the dock, claimin' a stitch-up and vowing his own brand of justice on all of them.

Now you might be wondering how the goods came to be in my possession, and all I can tell you is that I had no choice. I've never had a choice. Not since we were seven years old, growing up next door to each other on either side of a partition wall in a block of council flats. See, I'm McCurdy's oldest pal. I'm also his accountant and, ever since he watched the Godfather movies, his *consigliere*.

I should point out that I'm an honest man, on the whole at least. I've got half a dozen letters after my name and, before all this business, had a nice wee detached house over the river in Bothwell. Yes, I've looked the other way when certain clients put through hotel bills from dirty weekends with their mistresses as business expenses, or helped set up tax avoidance schemes that were 'exotic' to say the least, but giving racy tax advice to the Pringle jumpers and loafers set is a world away from doing the bidding of a man who's stabbed more people than I've got contacts on LinkedIn. But you don't say no to a bampot like McCurdy, especially when you go back as far as we do.

I was only going to look after it for him. Hold on to it till he got out, having served his sentence. I should have dug a hole in the ground and buried it, like the lazy servant from that parable in the Bible – the one who didn't quite understand the concept of investment and compound interest – but then, it seemed a poor use of my talents, and neither McCurdy, or Jesus, apparently, would thank me. So I found a fence – a proper one – a jeweller down in Soho, not some arsehole working out of the back room of the Thistle Bar in Shettlestone. The guy reckoned he could break up the sets and sell the individual stones. It seemed a shame to destroy such beautiful jewellery, but I was doing it for McCurdy.

After commissions and ancillaries and pay-offs, there was still the best part of three million left. Not a bad bit of work for a bampot. I washed the money, of course. Laundered it through half a dozen shell companies from Dubai to the Dutch Antilles, before finally finding it a home here, in an offshore account in the state bank. And that should have been the end of it. Unfortunately, some disgruntled wee bank teller, passed over for promotion no doubt, wrapped himself in the cloak of self-righteousness and sold a list of all offshore accounts to the *Guardian*, and before I knew it, I had forensic accountants from the National Crime Agency breathin' down my neck.

That's when I realized I had no choice.

I did my homework. If you invest a million dollars in the island, they give you residency, and they're pretty vague about what constitutes investment. In the end, buying a house and making a few political contributions was enough. Me and Brenda had a shiny white villa and nice green residency permits.

•

McCurdy's been in prison for almost three years now, and in a way, I've done my time too; put up with solitary for about as long as I can manage. I've paid Anju four weeks wages in lieu, put the house on the market and now, *right now*, I'm driving to the airport in the rain.

It was Brenda's idea, really. On one of our increasingly infrequent Zoom calls. She was the one who suggested doing a Reggie Perrin. Not that she called it that. She's not big on TV comedy from the seventies.

Why don't we just disappear? We can change our names, move to America and start again.

Course I just laughed at first, told her she was bein' mental, but afterwards, when I was lying there in the dark, listening to the raindrops splashing into the swimming pool, I began to think about it properly.

Maybe there was a way?

I went to see my pal the Prime Minister the next day, bought him lunch at Maxim's – it's a pretentious place overlooking the ocean, with a Michelin star and minuscule portions. The PM, bless him, has been in love with everything American ever since he came back from the UN last year. They say he's even taken to wearing cowboy boots on the campaign trail, though under his suit trousers. Over dessert, and coffees, and cigars and finally an extortionately priced bottle of Macallan, I laid out my suggestion.

'You've got an embassy in Washington, but America's a big place. What about the west coast? You've got no one looking after this proud nation's interests in California. How about you let me do it?'

He'd hummed and hawed and claimed poverty for the island, but in the end agreed, on the proviso that I pay for it all, including a small donation to his re-election fund, which became a rather larger donation once I mentioned the requirement for two new passports under false names: one for me and one for Brenda.

And so here I am, parking up outside the terminal, at the international airport named after the Prime Minister's father. Politics, like everything else here, is a family business. The car's a rental, and there's a wee chap from the company waiting for me, sheltering from the rain under an awning. I hand him the keys and, rescuing my suitcase from the boot, roll it quickly inside.

It's the off-season and the terminal has the air of a place after the party's finished; *like Memphis after Elvis*, as the Blue Nile once put it.

I pull out my passport. The new one. It's green, like the residency permit, but this has a coat of arms embossed upon it in gold. It's not a diplomatic passport, though. That would have required another fifty grand, and I don't have that much to spare, not till I sell the villa. I'm pretty much down to the last million at the moment, but at least most of that is no longer in the state bank. It's in an account on another island tax haven, registered to Alan and Brenda Murgatroyd. That's our new names. I open the passport to the back page, with a picture of my face staring out from behind laminated plastic. It too says Alan Murgatroyd, Honorary Consul. I guess I should get used to that. This is his life now.

•

There's no queue at the check-in desk, at least not for first class. I just walk along the faded red carpet to a check-in assistant who brightens on seeing me and gives me a smile through overly red painted lips that's the due of the premium passenger.

She barely glances at the documents, then offers me seat 2A. I ask her if she can change it to row four, or better still five. It might be nothing, but the front row, when it's booked, is often taken up by politicians jetting off on the nation's business, and tonight I've no real wish to be seated anywhere near one.

We settle on seat 4K and then I'm walking down the corridor with the sound of her words echoing in my brain.

'*Have a pleasant flight, Monsieur Murgatroyd.*'

I'm going to miss that island accent. They all speak French here, or at least some Creole version of it, and their English is tinged with an intonation that makes you feel like you're living on a giant set of '*Allo* '*Allo*.

Security is a breeze. A separate VIP queue and little time for me to look nervous. In any case, the guy manning the metal detector just yawns and waves me through, and why wouldn't he? People the world over are always less suspicious of those travelling first class, which is odd because in my experience, the most successful criminals are millionaires.

A few minutes later I'm through a set of doors and into the hush of the first-class lounge with its sofas and subdued lighting, its starched waiters bringing round complimentary buffet snacks. CNN is playing silently on a screen, the ticker tape scrolling along the bottom spells out an uninterrupted tale of international woe: of fires in Australia and floods in Europe; of riots and plagues and famines everywhere else, and it makes you realize, maybe this wee place isn't so bad after all.

Rather than watch it, I grab a complimentary gin and tonic and a copy of last Tuesday's *New York Times* and head for a quiet bit of the room. It's not the sort of paper I'd normally read. Believe me, I'd much rather it was a copy of the *Daily Record*, but you don't find many of them in airport lounges this far from Scotland.

I've hardly had time to digest the front page and down my G&T when the flight's called, the gentle tone of a tannoy announcement reinforced by a soft tap on the shoulder and a smile from the wee lounge hostess.

'Your flight, Monsieur Murgatroyd.'

I take my time getting to my feet and lifting my carry-on bag. Suddenly my bones feel a hundred years old and even pushing through the doors takes as much strength as I can muster. I walk down the corridor, my shoes squeaking on the linoleum, and I realize I'm almost shuffling. I force myself to pick up the pace. What am I scared of? In a few hours I'll be with Brenda, in the transit lounge at Heathrow, waiting for our connecting flight to LA and a new life, far from here and from Lanarkshire, and McCurdy, and everything else. This is hardly a moment for reticence, and yet . . .

I'm on the air bridge now. The plane is up ahead, two uniformed flight attendants flanking its entrance like prison guards around a cell door. I get a smile from both of them though, which widens further when they check my boarding pass.

'Second on the left, monsieur.'

I give them a nod, find my seat and make myself comfortable, just in time to see the foreign minister come on and head for seat 1A. He's a corpulent gentleman, to say the least, and I'm thinking I definitely made the right decision switching to the other side of the plane, if only to help with the weight distribution. The flight attendant comes over with my complimentary glass of champagne and I take it from her. I've never liked the stuff. It makes my throat feel funny, but I always drink it because, you know, it's champagne and it's supposed to mean something.

I take a sip and look out the window at the rain falling on the floodlit tarmac and the palm trees in the distance being blown horizontal by a south-easterly.

Five minutes later we're airborne, passing through the clouds and being thrown about like a rag doll in a dog's maw. I grip the armrest and say a prayer to a god I don't talk to these days, save for in emergencies. But he must be listening, cos we're through the clouds and things are calmer. I down the champagne and recline my seat and think of Brenda.

She's a good woman, that one, despite the shouting. And there must still be something there, some emotional attachment between us, after twenty-five years and two useless kids, and a year apart, she's still looking forward to starting again.

The flight attendant comes along and hands me a menu card,

as though this is some exclusive restaurant for me and the foreign minister in seat 1A, but tonight I'm not hungry. I hand it back and ask for a whisky, a Scotch, in international parlance, on the rocks. It arrives soon after and I nurse it for a good thirty minutes before falling asleep.

•

I wake to blinding light through a cabin window and the voice of the attendant asking me if I'd like breakfast. I say yes and ask her how long to London. She points to a graphic on the screen in front of my pod, showing the plane somewhere over blue water, approaching the outline of the UK.

'*An hour or so.*'

I spend it washing down plastic croissants with lukewarm coffee and then heading to the bathroom to splash water on my face and run a comb through my hair. I'm seeing Brenda for the first time in a year and I'd like to look presentable. Instead I have the haunted look of a refugee, but there's no time to think about it, cos the captain's just announced we've started our descent and switched on the seatbelt sign.

I make it back to 4K just as the plane starts to wobble, strapping myself in as we descend through the turbulence of the clouds and suddenly there's England, stretchin' out below in all its washed-out, monochrome glory, with even the green of the fields contriving to appear as just another shade of grey.

The descent is rapid and the touchdown like velvet, not even a bump as the tyres hit the runway. Brenda will already be in the airport somewhere; probably already checked in; probably wandering around the duty-free, trying the perfume samples.

The plane taxis to its berth which, judging by the time it's taking, might well be at another airport entirely, but finally we get there and the thing pulls to a stop. There's another delay as the crew go about their business. Every second now feels elastic, stretching and simultaneously constricting. Finally the doors open. I rush to the exit before the foreign minister has had time to unwedge himself from his seat, and then I'm rushing down the gangway. The cold of a winter's morning feels like a slap in the face, but it's energizing.

I pull out my phone and switch it on, hoping there'll be a message from Brenda, telling me where to meet, but there's nothing. No matter. She's probably still going round the shops. I walk and text, firing off a quick one-liner from the new phone that only she has the number for.

Just landed. Where R U?

I pass a couple of airport police, machine guns at the ready. I've seen it many times before, but there's still something jarring about seeing British bobbies carrying guns. Maybe it's a reality check. Whatever it is, I give them a wide berth and follow the signs for transit passengers, turning corners and riding escalators till all of a sudden, doors open and in front of me stretches the departures hall like the promised land in front of Moses.

I check my phone. Still nothing from Bren, and the beginnings of a sweat starts to prickle at my collar. I walk past the shops: WH Smith and Curry's and all the other high street names I haven't seen for two years; past shops selling tourist tat: *Welcome to London* mugs and *Keep Calm and Carry On* tees, and for once I appreciate the advice.

And then, there she is. Walking towards me through a crowd like she's the only person in the world. She looks good. I mean, she always has, but there's something more this time: a freshness to her; a spring in her step; and then she's in my arms and it's like the last three years never happened.

'Good flight?' she asks, and leads me to a row of seats.

'Absolutely, Mrs Murgatroyd,' I say. She's travelling under her real name, of course. I didn't want to risk couriering her the new passport, but still, it's nice to make the joke.

She laughs. 'I still don't know why you chose such a godawful surname.'

'It was in a story I read once,' I tell her.

'Well let's have a look at it then?' she says. 'Let me see Mrs Murgatroyd's passport.'

I fish it out of my bag and hand it to her. I watch as she runs her fingers over the green and gold cover; as she flicks through the pages and alights on the final one before digging me in the ribs.

'That's a terrible picture!'

I tell her it was the best one I could find, and anyway it's a passport. If your photo in that looks good, then you're probably doing somethin' wrong.

'How long have we got till the flight?' she asks.

I look up at the screen. 'Probably twenty minutes till they call it.'

She gives me a nod. 'I better go freshen up, then,' she says, rising to her feet, and before I can say anything, she's making down the concourse in the direction of the ladies' room.

Twenty minutes.

Twenty minutes till we get on a plane to LA. I've always wanted to go but never had the chance. An old mate of mine from school went out there hoping to become a film star. Imagine that, a boy from Hamilton, thinkin' he could make it in Hollywood. The funny thing is, he managed it. Against all the odds. Maybe I'll look him up when we're out there.

I lose myself in thoughts of LA, and the next thing I know, they're announcing the flight on the tannoy. I check my watch.

Christ, it's been almost twenty minutes. Brenda's fair taking her time. I look around, hoping to spot her, but all I see is an anonymous crowd. I'm getting nervous now; getting to my feet. There's no first class this time. Just regular economy. Brenda thought it safer. If she's not quick, we'll end up at the back of the boarding queue.

I scan the horizon; the shopfronts; the concourse. The crowd parts and then I see them. They're hard to miss. A guy in a suit with an entourage of two machine-gun-wielding cops. I try to keep calm, tell myself they're just doing their rounds; but I know. I know they're here for me. My throat's dry as I watch them approach. I know I should get up; try to lose myself in the crowd, but my legs have turned to jelly and Brenda might never find me.

Brenda.

Shit.

I check my bag and realize what's missing. She's kept a hold of the passport.

Brenda's not coming back. Brenda's never coming back. She's Mrs Murgatroyd now. With access to a bank account in the Caymans with a million quid in it.

The man in the suit is standing over me. He looks like a bulldog in a suit.

'Mr Murgatroyd?'

'Yes,' I say.

'Would you mind coming with us?'

CLOUT CHASER

RACHEL HOWZELL HALL

1

Imagine the wondrous discoveries found in the pockets of great explorers on Sunday laundry day!

Gold coins and stone beads in Vasco da Gama's pantaloons.

Penguin feathers and seal skin in Matthew Henson's fur-lined pants.

Moon rocks and star beams in Neil Armstrong's space suit.

Lucas is no great discoverer. He just maintains the highways that crisscross California. That means he sees all kinds of strange things. He keeps some of it, sticking random oddities into his pockets and forgetting them—until Sunday laundry day!

Once, I found a library card and a pewter rock in his pockets. Another time, a silver-and-teal letter opener.

Today's discoveries: a Zippo lighter and a plastic baggie of crushed Benadryl caplets.

I always present my finds to Lucas. The first time, he snatched the chess piece and jade earring from my hands. Then he screamed, 'Why are you snooping through my shit, Andi?'

Because I work as an office manager at a carpet store that no one visits, and you and your pockets are the most exciting things in my life? I didn't say that. No, I said, 'It's laundry day. Didn't want it gunking up the washing machine or melting in the dryer.'

His face softened then.

And my thundering pulse slowed.

He thanked me for being so thoughtful, then slipped out of the kitchen like a puff of air.

Later, I watched him place the chess piece and jade earring into a battered Adidas shoe box along with the library card and fancy letter opener.

2

<LUCAS MY LOVE>

Today 1:03 p.m.
Hey, sweetbaby!

Hiya, toots!

Read
Laundry day

Hooray!

You being careful in the rain?

Always

Found a baggie of crushed Benadryl
in your pants pocket.

Oh good
I was looking for those
Embarrassed
You've learned my big secret!!!

That you snort Benadryl lol

Don't you lol

> *Seriously tho*
> *I can't swallow pills*
> *I have to crush them and put them in my food*
> *Yes I'm grown man*
> *But I can't do it*

Makes sense
Now you know what I mean
About my gag reflex hahaha

> *Ha*
> *Find anything else?*

Nope

> *Awesome*

ILY

> *ILYMORE!!!!!!!*

3

Now that the clothes are in the washing machine, I glance at my True Crime desk calendar. On today's page, the unidentified murder victim is an American girl named Peaches. Everything about her is unknown: her name, race, age and hair color. Found on the shores of Long Island, she had no head, no arms, no legs beneath the knee. She had a tattoo of a peach above her left breast. Investigators believe she may have been one of the earliest victims of the Long Island Serial Killer.

We have another serial killer in Los Angeles. Every month over the last four months, a woman has been found dead in her home. There are similarities between victims that make detectives think 'serial killer' instead of homicide by a lover: each victim was strangled by the dog leash left around her neck. And they're always murdered on the third of the month.

Today is the third of February.

I should be freaked out since every victim has been found in my zip code. To be honest, I *am* freaked out, but then, I'm also vigilant. I keep my doors locked, my windows closed. There's a security camera doorbell on my front door, and I don't answer the knocks or rings of people I don't know. I don't even wear earbuds if I'm out walking Coco without Lucas by my side.

'Avoid being in the presence of someone who might do you harm.' That's what that 'Gift of Fear' guy wrote.

Aye, aye, Captain deBecker!

Still, I wonder . . . who will the Great Pretender choose next? That's what the newspapers have dubbed him.

There are nearly four million people in the city of Los Angeles, and there are almost 47,000 people living in the 90043 zip code, a significant percentage being Black people. The Great Pretender picks short and thin Black women who live alone. According to the only survivor of an attack, the Great Pretender claimed to have lost his puppy Gypsy. Near tears, this handsome stranger wearing blue medical scrubs had clutched a dog leash. The victim helped him search the neighborhood, but they never found Gypsy. She invited the distraught man in for a glass of wine, and shortly thereafter, he tried to strangle her with Gypsy's leash.

Some say she asked for it.

4

Rain falls hard and I wanna climb into bed and watch new puddles form. I wanna watch the clouds darken and push so close to Earth that I can skim my fingers along their bellies.

Lot of work to do, though.

I log on to Facebook and find the page of Alicia Goode, the second victim of the Great Pretender. She had soft brown eyes and maybe weighed 100 pounds soaking wet. Family and friends still post messages to this now-online memorial.

Gone too soon.

We love you, baby girl!

I miss you so much it hurts.

We'll find him.

A veterinary assistant, Alicia wore a lot of puppy-print scrubs and cuddled dogs, cats and even rabbits in most of these photos. Roses, tequila sunrises and custom VW Bugs—these were a few of her favorite things.

Someone has shared on the timeline the newest article about Alicia's case.

'. . . she made a friend out of everyone she met,' her mother Bess said Tuesday in a telephone interview with *Los Angeles Times*.

'She would've never turned away someone who needed help. He tricked her. He's the worst kind of evil.'

Unlike the unnamed survivor who had helped the Great Pretender search for Gypsy, Alicia Goode didn't leave her house alive.

On the left-hand side of Alicia's page, there's something I missed on my previous visit. In the 'Friends' panel . . . Alicia and I have four mutual acquaintances.

Jolly Steinman, a friend of mine from college. He's a veterinarian now.

Stacy Delgado—she used to work at Carpetorium with me.

Dan Jackson—I don't even remember how I know Dan. Do I *know*-know him, or did we simply find each other on the social media sea?

And the fourth mutual friend . . . Lucas Benedict.

My Lucas?

I don't visit Lucas's Facebook page that often. I don't wanna know that he's loved other women before me, that he had this entire life before he swooped into mine. I don't wanna see pictures of him snuggling, cuddling or canoodling with anyone other than me. But I'm here now on his page because he was Alicia Goode's friend.

He's never told me that they'd been Facebook friends.

I scroll—*doomscroll*—but I don't find any pictures of Lucas and Alicia together. Maybe they were like me and Dan What's-His-Face. With that possibility, the knot in my belly loosens, and I push out a breath I didn't even know I'd been holding.

Coco hops onto my lap and whines. She wants to go for a walk.

'Not yet,' I say, nuzzling her Aussie Shepherd head.

I need to finish the laundry and then I need to start packing. I also need to grab Coco's kennel from the garage and wash it out. 'Because you, young lady, are going to the doggie hotel.' I drop her back to the carpet.

Back to Lucas and his Facebook page.

He posted about good, affordable Italian wines.

I click 'Like.'

He posted about the standoff between a Native American tribe and pipeline operators.

He likes politics? He's never told me that. *I* like politics, too!

I hold my click until 'Love' appears—and that's the truth!

I continue to doomscroll, but the more I look, the more doom turns to hope. I find no random naked pictures, no bathroom-mirror selfies. Just posts about Italian wines and Native American protests. There aren't even pictures of him with Alicia Goode. Wonderful! I don't wanna be jealous of a dead woman.

And I'm not snooping—I just wanna get to know my man, not just what he tells me or through those tchotkes I find in his pockets on laundry day.

I want to know which Disney Princess he is.

Is he a glazed donut or a jelly-filled?

What smoothie flavor is he, based on his taste in music?

I hope he doesn't mind me 'liking' his posts.

Coco's whining makes me look away from my laptop. She's scratching at the heap of laundry piled on the floor. She snarls, then backs away with her butt in the air.

What has she found this time? A cricket? A roach?

Something is bothering her. Yet there's nothing in that pile except my leggings, Lucas's jeans, his socks, my T-shirts, his boxers . . .

Yeah, something is bothering her, but she's an Australian Shepherd. *Everything* bothers Australian Shepherds.

6

WATCH-IT!/A Place for Everyone
Andi Andrews • View Park • Feb. 3
POSSIBLE MURDER SUSPECT
We know what time of the month it is today! Just wanted to let everybody know that there is supposed to be a press conference by the Sheriff's Department about the Great Pretender (GP). I heard they may have footage from someone's doorbell camera. I've been doing some research and a woman posted here on WATCH-IT! that she was sad that she'd lost her dog Maverick. Because of that, she'd promised God that she'd help people find their missing pets if He brought Maverick back to her. And now she's dead. The GP may have a scratch on his face that's

healing because the last victim put up a fight! Watch out, WATCH-IT!

Leslie Kennick • View Park • Feb. 3
@AndiAndrews thanks for letting us know!

Shante Gibbons • Windsor Knoll • Feb. 3
They need to catch this monster! Be careful out there ladies!!

Caroline Bissett • Angeles Mesa • Feb. 3
The pros also disguise themselves as Good Samaritans. My cousin was jumped by someone wearing one of those orange safety vests.

Leslie Kennick • View Park • Feb. 3
Oh wow @CarolineBissett! How scary!!

Andi Andrews • View Park • Feb. 3
He's like the Black Ted Bundy! If the press conference is recorded, I will post the link here later tonight.

Andi Andrews • View Park • Feb. 3
Let's remember that it's also about taking personal responsibility, too! Not to blame the victim, but WHY DID SHE GO WITH A MAN WHO JUST RANDOMLY CAME TO HER HOUSE???? Just because he's gorgeous doesn't mean that he's not evil. 'For Satan himself masquerades as an angel of light.' That's from Two Corinthians (haha get it?).

Leslie Kennick • View Park • Feb. 3
PREACH @Andi Andrews.!!!

7

I read the thread of comments beneath my 'POSSIBLE MURDER SUSPECT!!' post.

Shante Gibbons • Windsor Knoll • Feb. 3
You should track him down @AndiAndrews. You're good at it!!

I blush and type, 'That was luck.'

It hadn't been luck—I'd been obsessed with the Kitty Killer case, and since I had no distractions—no job, no lovers, no life—I joined the hunt and dedicated my entire day to finding the sicko posting videos of him drowning cats. My band of internet sleuths helped crack the case the moment I recognized the Carpetorium—*my place of employment*—in the background as the sleazo filled a kiddie pool with water. The reward was only ten grand and was split between ten people, and well . . . The respect and esteem afterward have been worth more than the money.

Shante really thinks I can solve this case?

And now I post:

He could be more terrifying than the Grim Sleeper.

Though he's dead now, the Grim Sleeper terrorized Black Los Angeles for over twenty years. Murder and rape—that's what he did to at least twenty-five people. The one known survivor took the stand during his trial and told it all. He died on San Quentin's Death Row. Not because of the needle but because . . . who knows? I can't find the autopsy report online. It's like they want us to forget that he was found unresponsive in his cell.

Weird how his friends and neighbors only saw those qualities they wanted to see. His buddy said that he was 'pushy,' but 'normal.' Sure, he had caches of photos of partially nude and dead-looking women, but his very religious wife said nothing and *still* hasn't talked about her life with him. Was she caught off-guard? Was she charmed by him and swept off her feet and woke up one day and said, 'Shit, what the hell have I done?'

That must've happened with the Great Pretender's victims.

A beautiful man just *happens* to show up at your house in search of his dog? Were they lonely before he rang? Did they whisper a prayer of thanks as they searched beside him?

I understand: before Lucas, I'd been lonely and unlucky in love, too. I've never had a boyfriend, not one in all of my forty-four years. I'd thrown my hands to the sky, and said, 'Screw it. I'll be celibate for the rest of my life.'

Why risk pregnancy and STDs at this age? It wasn't like I had events to attend that required a plus-one. No hot parties at the Carpetorium. Besides, I had Coco and she's such a good cuddler. I told myself, 'You'll be OK, girl,' and then, *boom!*

There was Lucas, a tall glass of cool water during my trek through the desert. An oasis who became something more than a simple resting place.

My phone chimes with a text from my beloved.

I'm going to be late
Truck spilled tomatoes on the 210
Blame the rain

That's a-OK. He'll give me all the time in the world once we reach Oakland.

8

Guess I'm saying this: not every man who comes to your door is a serial killer. But sometimes, one man comes to your door and he is.

I didn't immediately open the door for Lucas the first time he knocked even though his square jaw and dreamy eyes made my pulse race. Door closed, I'd shouted, 'Yes??'

He'd lifted a bank card to the peephole, and said, 'I found this in your driveway.'

I gasped—that was *my* debit card. Without thinking, I threw open the door and plucked my card from his fingers. 'Ohmigod, thank you!'

He smiled, and the dimple in his left cheek went, *Ding!*

I offered him an orange Shasta and a baggie of chocolate chip cookies fresh from the oven.

We've been together ever since, and we do almost everything together.

Three months and I'm still here.

But we are the exception, not the rule.

9

Maybe I *will* announce that I'm gonna hunt down the Great Pretender.

How many 'likes' would I get for that? Can you 'go viral' on neighborhood watch sites? Would it be a waste? Should I post it there *and* on regular socials? Maybe I should do a 'live' post and drive past Alicia Goode's house.

What's the worst that can happen?

10

I shove clothes into the washing machine. I take more clothes out of the dryer.

How do women with children do this?

Between all of Lucas's clothes and the millions of drinking glasses he uses and leaves on the bookcase, the TV stand, at the foot of the couch . . . It's like it's Thanksgiving in our house every day with all the glasses he uses.

I peek out the service porch window to check on Coco in the backyard.

She's digging by the lemon tree near the back wall that separates my property from my neighbor's. In the dirt, I spot the bone I gave her last week. The battered rib looks . . . *longer*. Like being buried and rained upon all week has made it grow like the tree above it.

11

As soon as I grab the leash, Coco jams up the stairs and into the house. She spins and hops, excited for the walk. The rain has stopped and the clouds over Los Angeles are the color of bruises and battleships. The mountains that ring the city— wrecked by fall forest fires—are now dusted with snow.

Not many people have come out for a walk. Because of the weather? Or because it's the third of the month and the Great Pretender is on the prowl for his next victim?

On the other side of the street, there's a short and thin Black woman walking alone. She's wearing headphones.

In front of me, there's another woman. She's not as thin as the first, and she walks fast but she's texting faster on her phone. She's not paying attention to her surroundings. I'm following her now just to see how long it takes for her to look back over her shoulder.

Ten yards.

Thirty yards.

Fifty yards.

She *still* hasn't turned around, and now I know that she lives in the cornflower-blue house on the corner. There are no visible security cameras and there's a yellow PT Cruiser in the driveway.

If there are reports that a young Black woman between the ages of twenty and twenty-five disappeared on her walk along Angeles Vista Boulevard, I will call the police and tell them, 'She wore cut-out black leggings, fuchsia Nikes and a Bruno Marks sweatshirt. I worried that she was walking alone, and so I tried to walk with her for as long as I could, but it started to rain.'

She's brought this fate on herself.

12

A strange, rust-colored Honda is parked in front of my house. A man sits behind the steering wheel, staring ahead and frozen in his seat.

I've never seen this car before.

What does he want?

A tall man wearing a camouflage sweatsuit jogs past Coco and me. His dark eyes are sunken and glazed. Who jogs in the rain?

Coco barks at him.

He barks back.

I startle and hurry away from him.

Sicko.

A black Crown Victoria sedan cruises past me. The plates are government-issued. Are they detectives? Are they searching for the Great Pretender?

The wet air around me feels too tight.

The wet air around me feels too full.

The door of the rust-colored Honda creaks open. The driver spots me walking toward my driveway and he reaches back into the car and . . . pulls out two pizza boxes. He rushes across the street to the butter-colored Spanish-style.

I still hold my breath. Just because he's successfully delivered dinner doesn't mean that I, a single woman walking her dog, can't be his true target.

Right now, it's three thirty-eight. He wears jeans with a brown wash. There's a bulldog tattoo on his left forearm. He's between the ages of twenty and twenty-five. Short twists in his hair.

I commit this description to memory.

Just in case.

13

I log on to WATCH-IT! to see if anyone else has interacted with my post. My stomach turns—Zach Alexander, the mansplainer, has commented. He's an ex-military police officer who moved to this part of town because it's cheaper than Santa Monica or West Hollywood. He knows everything. He knows everyone.

Zach Alexander • Park Heights • Feb. 3
My buddy on the force told me that witnesses reported seeing a black Ford Explorer parked near Alicia Goode's house that day. They have footage from neighbors' security cameras and may have a plate number.

Leslie Kennick • View Park • Feb. 3
I'm so glad we have a real LEO on this board!!! It's about FACTS!!

Duke Morris • Windsor Knoll • Feb. 3
@Zach Alexander Year? Any distinguishing features? Dents? Rims? Etc.

Zach Alexander • Park Heights • Feb. 3
@Duke Morris I'll ask my buddy. See if he'll let me post the picture.

Leslie Kennick • View Park • Feb. 3
You have a picture??!! You are connected.

Whatever. I hate Zach Alexander. He won't '@' me, Leslie or any other woman on the posts. He'll take over my thread and he'll talk to Duke just like they did back when the first victim had been found.

This post is now dead to me.

A black Explorer.

I drive a blue Explorer.

Maybe the police will knock on my door and ask me where I was on the night of January 3.

Then, I could post about it, offer a first-hand account of this manhunt for the Great Pretender. I will talk about how scared I felt, how my heart pounded hard in my chest. No one will be able to take that away from me.

Maybe I should pull the Explorer out of the driveway and park it at the curb . . .

14

The aroma of homemade chili wafts through the house. Lucas likes to eat chili on rainy days.

The doorbell rings.

I peek through the peephole.

Two men the size of sequoias are standing on my porch. They're wearing trench coats and neckties.

Goosebumps run along my arms.

'Yes?' I shout through the door.

'Los Angeles Sheriff's Department,' the Black man says.

I tamp back my smile, then open the door. I furrow my eyebrows to show concern.

The two men smile at me and hold up their gold shields.

The Black detective says, 'I'm Detective Halsey and this—' He nods at his Latino partner.

'I'm Detective Morales.' He swivels to my Explorer, now parked in front of the house. 'Is that your Explorer?'

It's happening! It's finally happening!

I peek out to make sure they're talking about my *blue,* not *black*, SUV. 'Yes, it is.'

'Has it been in your sight over the last . . . two months?' Halsey asks.

I nod. 'I drive it to work.'

'And where do you work, if you don't mind me asking?' Both cops open their little steno pads.

'At Carpetorium in Culver City, over on Sepulveda Boulevard.'

They scribble into their pads.

'Does anyone else drive it?' Morales asks.

'No, sir,' I say.

'You live here alone?' Halsey asks.

'My dog, Coco,' I say. 'Sometimes, my boyfriend stays over.' The two cops look at each other.

Halsey asks me, 'Does he drive your Explorer?'

'Umm . . .' I squint as I think. 'Not really. Once a month, *maybe.*'

'Is he here?' Morales asks.

I shake my head. 'He's at work.'

'And what does he do?'

I smile. 'He's a forensic tech at the Sheriff's Department.'

Is that disappointment in their eyes? If they call me out on my lie, I have another prepared just in case.

But Halsey closes his notepad.

'Is this about the Great Pretender?' I ask, eyes big. They're about to leave, but I don't want them to go. Not yet.

Halsey pauses at the bottom of the porch. 'It is. What was your name? Should've asked earlier.'

'Vanessa Lewis,' I say. 'E-w, not o-u.'

'And your boyfriend, the forensic tech?' Morales asks.

'Lucas Benedict.' According to one of his driver's licenses.

In the backyard, Coco howls.

I chuckle. 'And that's my dog.'

Both men smile at me, then tromp down the slick walkway.

Before they climb into their car, they take pictures of my Explorer's plates, tires, the hood. *Pop, pop, pop.* The flash on the camera brightens the street and lights up my life.

And I take pictures of them taking pictures to prove that it all happened. I don't want to be called a liar like before. *She doesn't have any connections to cops. She doesn't know anything more about the victims and the GP than the rest of us. The woman who helped in the hunt isn't named Andi Andrews. WAKE UP PEOPLE!!*

As soon as the detectives drive away, I rush to my laptop and log on to WATCH-IT!

Andi Andrews • View Heights • Feb. 3
Guess who just got a visit from the Sheriff's Department?

15

'Coco!'

I call the dog to come inside. The rain falls too hard now for her to be frolicking in the yard and I'm not trying to bathe her before we drop her at the doggie hotel.

She circles her digging spot, chomps at the rain, circles again, then grabs her bone from the hole she's dug.

'Coco, dude! C'mon!' My stomach growls—it's time to eat. And I must finish packing. We're leaving as soon as Lucas eats.

Coco trots up the porch stairs and darts into the kitchen. She drops her bone on the tile floor and dances around it.

The bone *has* grown since I gave it to Coco two weeks ago.

Did the pit master at Phillip's BBQ butcher a cow-a-saurus? Did I transport it home in a *dino* bag instead of a *doggie* bag?

Ha.

16

All packed. Nothing here will tell anyone where we're headed. The Adidas box with Lucas's finds are tucked in the biggest suitcase beneath my bras and panties. Lucas is stopping at a pet store somewhere in the South Bay fifteen miles away, and then, he'll be home.

Outside, the rain has turned into a storm. Gusts of wind make the windows rattle. Rain hits like bullets against the roof.

Coco is mad at me for tossing her bone in the garbage bin outside. To be honest, it creeps me the hell out. She's asleep on the kitchen floor after whining to be let out, but I won't let her out because *there is a storm raging out there, you stupid dog!*

I grab a blanket from the closet and my pen and pad from

the desk. I aim my phone at the television, ready to record the police press conference airing now on the public access channel. I do a Boomerang post of my face beside the computer, and then, I send a Snap to my 3,000 followers.

Who is the Great Pretender?!

Sheriff Riojas steps in front of the bank of microphones and waits as cameras snap and flash. Finally, he starts, leading with the boring stuff—his name, his gratitude, who cares. He clears his throat, then says, 'We're now seeking the public's help to identify the driver of a vehicle that was parked on Buckler Avenue and 67th Street between the hours of four and seven on January 3.'

Buckler and 67th Street—just a mile away from me!

Sheriff Riojas continues. 'We now have a clearer picture of our suspect drawn by police artists after interviews with the suspect's surviving witness.'

The moment of truth.

The front door alarm sensor chimes.

Lucas is home. 'Vanessa?' he shouts.

'Down here.' I wince at the sound of my government name booming from his mouth.

His footsteps echo against the hardwood floors.

'You get a new leash?' I shout.

'Yep,' he shouts back.

There's a technical issue at the press conference and the drawing of the suspect still isn't up on the screen.

'What are you watching?' Lucas enters the den just as the picture fills the screen. 'Oh.'

'I made chili.' I tilt my head to look up at his perfect smile and that dimple.

'You posted a Snap,' he says. 'And you've been on my Facebook page.'

My nerves pluck beneath my skin. It's his tone. It's accusatory, and I don't like it.

His smile dims. 'You shouldn't have done that.'

And now, he's telling me, a grown-ass woman, what I shouldn't do.

He isn't looking down at me anymore—he's focused on the television screen.

'We should get going,' I say, irritated.

He cants his perfect head. 'Who says that *you're* going?'

I squint at him. 'I found a woman for tonight—she lives around the corner in that blue house with the yellow car. You can't do this without me. I've helped you—'

'For *clout*,' he says. 'For *likes*. Not because you love me or love what I do.' He snorts and waves his hand at the press conference. 'You're just like the others. I knew that, but I didn't wanna believe it. You're just like them.'

Them . . . Katelyn and Jeanna. I don't know *them,* but Coco and I *have* met . . . *parts* of Jeanna. I should've never let Lucas use my yard and my shovel.

Now, my love squints at the television. 'The police artist did a good job. Look at that.'

The eyes are a little too close. The cheeks too gaunt. The nose . . . almost there.

Otherwise, that police sketch looks . . .

Just like . . . me.

Lucas holds up the new leash and smiles. 'Don't worry. I'll be sure to post on your page. Something like . . . *Gone too soon.*'

My throat tightens and a flare shoots through my heart.

Wonder how many 'likes' I'll get.

EITHER WAY I LOSE

JOHN VERCHER

Omaha, Nebraska
September 1919

I'm used to people looking at me sideways, but the way that policeman stared at me made me think he knew. I'm a tall drink of water, so folks tossing a double-take my way when I walk down the sidewalk ain't a new occurrence.

That wasn't how this officer eyeballed me. At all. He strolled out the back room of the Budweiser Saloon, thumbing a stack of greenbacks the size of which I ain't never seen. When he looked up and saw me sitting, waiting to go in the same back room he just came from, he caught a quick hitch in his step. He shoved his payoff into a canvas sack and kept walking my way, giving me the once-over the whole way. I had to do that thing where I maintained enough eye contact not to seem guilty of nothing, while at the same time looking away enough not to seem like some kind of tough guy. I must've failed at one of those ideas, because he stopped right in front of me. I took a keen interest in the laces of my shoes, but when I saw his feet weren't moving from in front of mine, I looked up. He tipped up the bill of his uniform hat and peered down at me, resting his palm on the knob of his billy club.

'You White?' he said.

My throat tightened up. I took a breath to keep from stammering. 'I'm sorry?'

He narrowed his eyes. 'Nesselhous says there's supposed to be a tall fella out here waiting to see him. Last name of White. You look to be a tall fella waiting to see somebody. So, I'm going to ask you again: you White?'

My heart went from a sprint to a light jog. My name — leastways the name I went by now — of course, that's what he meant. He didn't know nothing. If he did know something, he wasn't letting on. Not enough to say so anyways. 'Yes, sir. I'm White.'

He kept his eyes narrowed. 'Then get off your ass. Billy says he's ready for you. Don't keep the man waiting.'

I stood and made for the back room. A little voice, one that often screamed at me not to be a fool (but one I hardly paid no never mind), told me to keep on straight and not look back at the patrolman. I was one step from the back room when I ignored that little voice. I knew the way that officer looked at me that he hadn't quite been satisfied by my answer. That he was watching me, his eyes giving my back the once-over. Seeing was I as pale as I looked in the sunlight. Was my hair straight enough for his liking or was there a wave to it that was a bit too wavy? I turned.

But he was gone.

I let out the breath I'd been holding and went on to see the man.

Billy Nesselhous, right hand to Pickhandle Dennison, sat behind a curtain of cigar smoke in the back room of the saloon. Nesselhous owned the joint, and being he was lieutenant to

Dennison, the bar doubled as headquarters for the Sporting District. Lined before him on a table were stacks of cash, the spoils of the gambling, drinking, and prostitution games Nesselhous ran throughout the district. When he put eyes on me, he leaned back in the burgundy cushioned booth and spread his arms across the back.

Two good old boys my height stepped forward as I ambled to the table hoping I didn't look as nervous as I felt. Neither of them boys looked like they'd ever missed a meal, the both of them as wide as they was tall, and they had faces that said they was fitting to scrap. I wasn't sure if it would take both of them to lay me out, but I figured they'd both take great pleasure in making it a team effort. I kept my eyes down, not keen to engage them in that particular mathematical equation. Billy waved them over to the other side of the room like they were a pair of hunting hounds. He gestured to a chair opposite him. I sat.

'So, you're *the* White, huh?'

'Not sure what you mean by "the," but, yeah. I'm White.' He leaned forward, put his elbow on the table, and cocked his head. He gave me an expectant look over the rim of his reading spectacles. 'Sir,' I said.

He sat back again and reassumed his regal pose, satisfied I'd given him his respect. I wondered if he'd assume the same posture if the Old Gray Wolf Dennison had been sitting there next to him. Didn't matter, though. I was hanging on by a finger's grip to the bottom rung of that particular ladder. He wouldn't but have to sneeze to see me fall to my death.

'The way I hear it, White, you've done some excellent work at Anna Wilson's sporting house over on Douglas Street. They used to have their fair share of troubles with some ne'er do wells trying to skip out on paying the ladies after they had a taste.'

211

'Folks got to pay. One way or the other.'

'Indeed, they do, White. Indeed, they do. But it's the way you went about collecting a few of those payments that caught my special attention. These gentlemen to your right and left are often content to simply beat a man to a pulp. But you?'

'Can't touch the product if their fingers are broke.'

He barked out a laugh. 'Once again, I cannot argue, White. How much are we paying you to guard those lovely bodies at the mansion on Douglas?'

I ran a hand through my greased locks. 'I'm eating most nights.'

'How'd you like to eat every night?'

'That's an appealing proposition. I'm in.'

'Just like that?'

'Just like that.'

'You're certain?'

'Yes, sir.'

He smacked the table. 'Well, all right. Here's the score. You follow politics, White?'

'I never had much use for them.'

'A smart lad, you are. Well, Mr. Dennison's got a keen interest in them. The right man in office keeps money on the tables, booze in the bottles, and the whores in their beds. You following me so far?' I nodded. 'Right now, the wrong man is in the mayor's office if we expect to live the lives to which we've grown accustomed. Pickhandle's got no love lost for the honorable Edward Parson Smith. I don't believe I have to tell you what happens when Mr. Dennison is unhappy, do I?'

'I reckon that's why you called me here, sir.'

'Yes it is, White. Do you read the newspaper?'

'Don't care much for the news, sir.'

Nesselhous rolled his eyes. 'But you are aware there are such a thing as newspapers and that this particular region of Omaha has its own, am I right?' I nodded again. 'We've got a reporter over there at the *Daily Bee* willing to write up tales of these violent and savage niggers accosting and assaulting our lovely white women – with a bit of necessary embellishment, of course, should some form of said accosting occur.'

I sat up straight. Though it was one of the hottest days of the summer, the back room went cold as a cooler. 'Is that true? I ain't heard nothing about that.'

Nesselhous leaned forward again and glowered at me. 'The truth is what we say it is, boy.'

It felt like I had a knot in my neck. I swallowed around it. 'Yes, sir.'

He relaxed. 'Now, thing is, we need some good old-fashioned eyewitness accounts of these acts to really get folks riled up. Get people thinking Mayor Smith isn't the successful progressive reformer that he makes himself out to be. That he's failing the upstanding, hard-working white folks of our fair city. Of course, it's not like we can go about asking the niggers to incriminate themselves in something that would likely get them killed, can we? That, White, is where you come in.'

Nesselhous reached down into the booth and produced a can of shoe polish. He slid it across the table, along with two stacks of cash that doubled the wad I saw the officer counting.

'What is it you want me to do with that?'

'Not so bright after all,' Nesselhous said loudly to his cronies across the room. They laughed a little too hard. He knew it, as he looked to be more annoyed with them than me. I chuckled in spite of myself. That was a mistake. Nesselhous's face darkened such that I thought someone had actually turned the lights down in the room. He lifted the shoe polish and waggled it back and forth. 'You're going to smear this shit all over your face. Then you're going to wait outside the movie theater just down the street. Pick a white woman, I don't care much who, and scare the ever-loving shit out of her. Rob her. Rough her up, if it suits your fancy. Just make it good.'

He set the tin of polish on the table with a soft clink. I stared at it, along with the money. I hadn't ever seen that much money in my entire life. Money like that solved a lot of problems for me. Might could get me out of that dump I was living in so I could get myself a decent place to hang my hat and rest my head. It sure would be nice not to wonder where my next meal was coming from, or if it was even coming. That kind of money, spent right, brought comforts I ain't never had. But what I had to trade for it? Turning on my own? Just cause I ain't never owned up to who I was didn't mean I was fitting to make someone else pay that price.

'I don't know, Mr. Nesselhous. Sir.'

'What don't you know, White?'

'I mean, I don't think anybody's gonna buy me being any kind of colored fella just because I paint up my face.'

'Now, White, I was led to believe you weren't the thinking type. Don't make a liar out of me.'

'Wouldn't do that, sir. I just think – I just don't believe I'm the man for this particular job.'

Nesselhous leaned on the table. When I didn't follow suit, he rolled his eyes and flicked his fingers at me, beckoning me to come in close. I obliged. His breath reeked of bourbon and tobacco. He ran a tongue across his yellowed teeth. It took a great deal not to grimace.

'Here's the thing . . . White,' he said with a smirk. The way he did made the back of my knees go wet. 'This isn't really something you say no to. I mean, now that you know what I want you to do, how do I know you won't go to the authorities and tell them what we've got brewing here? That's if you can find one of them that isn't on our bankroll. Used to be a time when that wasn't the case, when they were all ours. Right shame what this town has come to, isn't it?' I nodded. 'But that's besides the point. You're going to do this because I know what you think I don't.'

'Sir?'

He waved me in closer and, loath as I was to do so, I brought my face inches from his. 'I'll be honest, I only just now figured it out. Most people probably don't give you so much as a second glance. Hell, some of them would need a stepladder to look you in the eye. But that nose, those dark eyes . . . a less educated man might not see it, but then I'm not less educated, am I?'

I was glad we were talking in hushed tones, because when I went to answer, my words damn near choked me. 'I'm sure I don't know what you're talking about, sir.'

He looked to the boys on either side of the booth. 'How about them? You think they'd know if I asked them? And a few more just like them out back? You think they'd know what I'm talking about?'

That little voice screamed at me not to say one more Goddamned word. This time I listened. I nodded. He eased back into his seat with a smile fit for a cat stuffed full of canary. 'I don't know why it is you choose to get by the way you do – well, scratch that. Course I do. And I won't lie, engaging in your deceits *and* working for me and the Wolf? That takes stones you don't see every day. Normally, I'd handle things in a bit more permanent manner, but you doing this particular task for me? Betraying your own?' He slapped the table again and laughed. I flinched and cursed myself for letting him see that. 'Boy, White, that tickles me even more than killing you would. Be honest with me – you never thought your little subterfuge would land you in this particular sort of pickle, now did you?'

'No, sir, I did not.' As I said it, I thought about sliding the table so hard it'd crack his ribs and crush his spine. But his old boys were right between me and the door, and no telling how many others he had lurking around the saloon. Maybe I'd make it outside and taste the fresh evening air before they beat it all out of me. Nesselhous looked at me like my skull was made of glass – like he could see every thought the minute it came to be.

'That hard look you're giving me is making me nervous, White. You don't want me nervous, do you? If I'm nervous, then maybe I should just exercise other options, if you get my meaning?'

I did. 'When do I have to do this?'

He spread his arms across the booth once more. 'If you had plans this evening, they just changed.'

•

I scrambled up the steps to my apartment. Out of breath, hands shaking, I stabbed repeatedly at the lock until the key slid home. I shouldered open the door, kicked it shut behind me and hurried to the bathroom. I turned the hot faucet on full and leaned my hands on the edges of the sink, trying to get my breathing under control. Then I turned to the side, dropped to my knees, and vomited in the toilet. I wiped at my face with the back of my hand. When I pulled my hand away from my mouth, the skin there was streaked with black polish. I threw up again.

Stomach emptied, I stood at the sink again. Steam rose and fogged the mirror. The water from the faucet was damn near scalding. I splashed my face and hissed at the pain. Then I did it again. And again. The heat stung my skin, over and over, until I thought maybe I wouldn't have to scrub at the polish to get it off, that maybe my skin would just peel from my skull. A swipe through the steam of the mirror proved otherwise. What I saw staring back at me sent the bile bubbling up again. A washrag sat on the back of the sink. I soaked it, lathered it up with the sliver of soap I had left, and scrubbed hard at my cheeks and forehead. I twisted it in my ears to drown out the recollection of that poor girl's screams.

•

When I'd seen her leave the theater with her boyfriend, I damn near lost my nerve. Taking off and running wasn't an option, though. Nesselhous sent his boys along to make sure of that. They walked the block, watching the theater as much as they were watching me. Every time some white folks came out of the show, I told myself, 'They're the ones.' But I couldn't do it. I had never been so scared in all my life.

The girl and her frail little fella were the last to come out. I was out of options. I ducked down in my spot among the weeds in the park across from the theater. And I waited.

Sure enough, they came down the path, arm in arm. Her man was a rail, a head shorter than his sweetheart. His steps were short and shuffled, and she looked to be helping him along a bit. A bead of sweat rolled down my painted forehead and hung at the tip of my nose. I blew at it until it dropped away, knowing if I wiped my face and messed up my disguise, Nesselhous's boys would report back to him. I'd be as good as done for.

As the young couple got closer, I heard the girl call her fella Milton. That name was the last coherent thing I heard her say.

I jumped out my hiding place, hand shoved in jacket pocket

like a pistol, and yelled for them to give me their money. The little bit of color Milton had in his face made its way to his feet as his missus screamed fit to wake the dead. And I panicked.

Before I knew what I was doing, my hand flew up and covered the girl's mouth. She stepped back, letting go of Milton. The boy dropped to the ground like the sack of skin and bones he was. The girl's screams made their way through my fingers and into my ears. I hadn't never heard a sound like that in my life. I would have been content to never hear it again. On the ground, Milton fumbled for his wallet. I never saw if he got it out his pocket, because that girl's shrieking did me in. I ran as fast and as far as I could, and I never turned to look back.

Back in the apartment, I laid on my bed and stared at the cracks in the plaster ceiling. My cheeks throbbed and my face felt swollen, what with all the scrubbing. Any minute now, someone on the other side of my door would be knocking. There was no two ways about it. Might be the law. Might be Nesselhous's boys. Might be someone who saw me stick up those two kids come to drag me out and string me up, only to find what they thought was a white boy with some lingering streaks of shoe polish on his face.

Funny thing was, I was OK with all the anticipating. I didn't have to lay there and think about what I'd done. What Mama would have thought of me. If she was twirling underneath the grass in that potter's field over how I'd managed to let her down even after she'd passed on.

What choice did I have? Nesselhous had me dead to rights, and if I said no, wasn't no way I made it out of there alive. Yeah, things was rough for colored folks who couldn't get by like me. But the way he made it sound, they just wanted some rabblerousing to put that new mayor in hot water. What the hell did I care about politics? Things would calm down. Hopefully wouldn't nobody get hurt too bad. Then I could take my money and go about my business. Sure, that's what would happen. I told myself that enough times that I almost bought it. At least enough to close my eyes for a spell.

•

I woke up to that very rabblerousing just as dawn broke. All types of hollering coming from what sounded like right across the street. I peered out my window to see officers load some fella, couldn't quite make out who, into the back of one of their cars and hightail it out of there. There was all manner of white folks on the street, yelling at the police, tossing bricks and bottles that fell just short of their bumper. Some of them—hell, a lot of them, took off running after the police. I hadn't never seen nothing like it. I went to the bathroom and made sure I'd washed off the polish, then hustled on down the stairs to see what the hell was going on.

Across the street, a few people lingered in front of the home where the police had just been. They milled about, cursing under their breath, muttering about how whoever it was didn't deserve to go to jail. I came up on one of them.

'What's everybody all up in arms about?' I asked.

The fella shoved a paper in my hands. Morning edition of the *Daily Bee*. The headline read:

'Black Beast.'

'The most daring attack on a white woman ever perpetrated in Omaha.'

My guts twisted themselves into knots. I read on. The girl, Agnes, said she got grabbed up by her hair and dragged into the bushes while her feeble boyfriend, Milton got pushed around. I didn't know if that was her storytelling or the paper's, but I knew it didn't matter none because it was what that mob believed.

I cleared my throat of all the guilt piling up in it. 'So they took away the fella what done it?'

'Yeah, some nigger renting a room in this here woman's house. Somebody said they saw him coming back here around the time he would have done the deed.'

Not old Will.

I'd seen Will some nights coming home from work at the packing houses. Anytime we crossed paths, he'd always tip his cap at me, the bill pinched between those gnarled-up fingers of his. Never understood how he managed packing work knobbed up by that rheumatism. Though we hadn't exchanged but ten words, I knew the man had a quiet, gentle nature about him. He wasn't fit to rob no one, and he certainly wasn't no beast— especially when I knew I was the beast in question.

'They take him straight to jail?' I asked.

'Naw, over to the girl's house to see if she says he's the one what did it.' He looked around at the bottles and mess everywhere, then lifted his chin at the people off in the distance still running after the police car. 'If they make it that far.'

I looked down the road. The car had disappeared from sight. I handed the paper to the fella and stumbled back to my apartment feeling like I'd done one too many rounds with Dempsey himself.

•

Two days later, the courthouse was on fire.

There must have been thousands of white folks, some of them teenaged boys, far younger than me, standing outside the building while it burned. They screamed and hollered until their neck muscles strained and veins popped from their forehead. They gripped bricks and sticks. They looked possessed, and I suppose they was—by bloodlust and hate, feelings that had been brewing far longer than the two days since that headline ran. Not content to leave what they called justice in anybody's hands but their own, they called for Will Brown's blood.

A policeman got shoved through a glass door while the mob beat on the others. People got pulled from their cars and whupped up on. Gunshots cracked all around me. Some of the mob screamed like they were speaking in tongues about how they were going to teach these niggers a lesson.

That's when I heard it.

The hollowed-out clip-clop of a horse's hooves, somehow louder than all the chaos around me. A white boy no older than twenty atop the nag. A noose slung over its back.

Something in me broke.

Every time I shunned another Negro in public, every time I listened as white folks complained about this nigger and the next one, about the jobs they were stealing from them even though they were jobs they'd never deign to do themselves, every time I told myself I was smarter for passing myself off as one of these white folks, every indignity I'd both witnessed and perpetrated in the name of self-preservation, all of it became a match and set fire to the gasoline that replaced my blood, torching me in flames like the building in front of me, the building where Will Brown was praying for his life.

I added my voice to the shouts. But my words were not theirs. In fact, I didn't say no words at all. I roared from someplace deeper than my throat, like I'd pulled the sound from the ground beneath my feet. I charged at that old boy on the horse, grabbed him by the waist, and pulled him off that mule. The minute he hit the ground, I commenced to pummeling. On my knees, sitting on his chest, I wanted to punch through his face until I hit the concrete underneath. Felt like I was going to do just that, until I felt greedy hands and fingers grab my shoulders and wrap around my wrists. A sweaty, hairy forearm wrapped around my neck. Somebody's knuckles tried to touch my spine by way of my breadbasket, and all my air left me in a hurry. The bones of that forearm dug into my windpipe.

I lifted my head, hoping to let in more air. Though the air was filled with thick black smoke, there wasn't a cloud in the sky. Stars peeked through the plumes, twinkled, then faded, as everything went dark.

•

When I came to, the mob was gone.

I can only figure the boys who beat me down thought they'd killed me, too, else they wouldn't have stopped. A young fella helped me up off the ground. Said his name was Hank, said he'd been watching from his window across the way. When I seen he was white, I snatched my arm from him and stood on my own. I seen the hurt and confusion in his eyes, but I didn't care a lick. I looked around, surveyed all those white folks had wrought. Broken glass everywhere. The courthouse still burning. Bodies, black and white, that weren't getting up with any kind of help. My head throbbed and it pained me to breathe, but I felt that same fighting fire in my muscles light up again. Still, it hurt to stand. I took steps back toward the man what helped me up and spoke through swollen lips.

'Is he alive?'

His eyes went wet at the question. 'No.'

'What happened?'

His voice trembled. 'They beat him. Strung him up. That snap—' He seized up, then emptied his stomach at my feet. He came up wiping his mouth with the back of his hand. 'I ain't never heard nothing like that. And then they shot him. He was already dead, and they shot him.'

My eyes stung, then leaked. I looked around at the trees and lampposts surrounding the area. 'Where?'

The fella seized up again and covered his mouth. He pointed down the road. 'They tied him to a truck and dragged him away. Some of them was shouting about burning him.' I turned on my heel toward the direction he pointed and shuffled off. 'Don't. Those boys see they didn't kill you before, they're not going to stop until they do.'

I stopped. Dying was no less than I deserved. My cowardice had killed that poor man. Why should I live? But in my state, there was no way I could walk ten feet, let alone to wherever it was they'd taken poor Will Brown's body. I pictured those weathered hands tipping his cap to me once more and dropped to my knees. I sobbed harder than I'd ever cried, harder even than when Mama died, because I knew if she'd been here to see what I'd done, it might have killed her all the same. If I died on the spot, she'd have been on the other side of those pearly gates, holding them shut while she told me to turn around and go back the other way.

Tears ran into the cuts and gashes on my face, mixed with the blood already there, and slapped the asphalt in front of me. Hank placed two gentle hands on my shoulders. I shrugged them off, screaming for him not to touch me. That had been enough for the youngster. He took off running for wherever he'd come from. I pushed up off the ground and limped to the streetcar stop.

Back at my building, I walked past my apartment and took the stairs to the roof. The night was warm, but I wrapped my arms around myself as though I hadn't a drop of blood left in me. The sky was lit up with stars, except for a line in the sky where a pillar of smoke still rose from the courthouse. I stepped up onto the ledge of the roof and looked down. High up enough to do the job if I landed right. I picked up my foot.

Then I stepped back onto the roof behind me.

I was going to die. I deserved to die. But one more act of cowardice wasn't going to do nothing for the memory of Will Brown.

•

The next day, troops from Fort Omaha and Fort Crook came in and took over the town. The streets had an eerie quiet to them. I made my way into town where I picked up a copy of the *Morning World Herald*.

'Frenzied Thousands Join in Orgy of Blood and Fire,' the headline read.

They burned Will Brown's body on a woodpile, standing around him like a Goddamned bonfire.

I threw the paper in the trash and made for the police station.

The precinct was humming. I approached the desk. As I did, I saw the same policeman from Nesselhous's saloon milling around in the background. He saw me, too. The corner of his lip lifted in a sneer. I kept the stare, and right then, I knew, given the chance, he'd be the one to kill me. I was going to give him all the reason in the world. The officer behind the desk snapped his fingers in front of my bruised face.

'The hell happened to you, son?'

'Officer, I'd like to report an assault.'

'I'm assuming you mean yours? Jesus, must have been a real beast that laid that beating on you.'

I looked over at the officer from the saloon once more. Though he maintained his hard stare, there was fear behind his eyes.

'No, sir. I committed the most daring attack ever perpetrated on a white woman in Omaha.

'The beast is me.'

THE BEAUTIFUL GAME

SANJIDA KAY

She first became aware of him when Phoebe's face contorted into a strange combination of shock and seductiveness.

'Phoebes,' she started to say into the round red oh of her sister's mouth, and then he was there, standing a little too close.

She could feel the heat radiating from his chest against her bare shoulder. She noticed his equally famous friends, craning their heads over their pints to see how he was getting on, and a small pack of girls with fiercely straightened hair staring poisonously at her.

'All right, love?' he said, smiling. 'Can I get you a drink?'

Thalia and Phoebe were nodding in unison, but she couldn't speak. It wasn't only that he was good-looking, in a movie star kind of a way, but she'd literally just been looking at pictures of him on Thalia's Instagram. She wanted to touch him to check he was real.

'Yeah, course she does,' said Phoebe. 'Vodka diet tonic. And we'll have a couple of J2Os.'

Her sisters elbowed each other and giggled and reapplied their lipstick while they waited for him to return from the bar.

'Luke,' he said, passing her a glass and holding out his hand to shake hers. 'Luke Allard.'

'Aw,' said Phoebe, delighted that he was polite enough to introduce himself.

'And what's your name?' he asked.

'Selene,' she managed to say. 'Selene Jackson,' and his smile widened.

She already knew the most important facts about him: height: six foot two; weight: 86 kg; age: twenty-two; status: single; nationality: British; ethnicity: half-French; vocation: striker for Manchester United and England; net worth: undisclosed but bought from Man City for £100 million.

Thalia managed to pull Phoebe away. Luke was surprisingly easy to talk to. They spent a long time chatting about their common heritage – he'd also grown up in Wythenshawe, a stone's throw from the Northern Moor Road, with a single mum. She couldn't imagine what it must have been like: to go from their level to his when he was still a teenager.

'How old are you, by the way?' he asked.

'Eighteen,' she said quickly, although, of course, she wasn't.

'Want to come back to mine for a drink? My flat's round the corner.'

'Na, you're all right. I need to get home.'

He looked taken aback and then gave her one of his long, slow smiles. The Instagrammers were right: he was magnetic. He looked at her like he really saw her, like there was no one else in the club.

'All right then. Give me your number. I'll call you.'

'Are you fucking kidding me?' Phoebe said when she told her.

Her sister ranted at the wasted opportunity all the way back on the bus, Thalia interjecting every so often to tell her to shut up and leave her alone. Selene stared out of the window, holding her heels in one hand and shivering in her thin body con dress, as Manchester city centre receded.

She doubted he'd ring.

•

He called her in the morning and said he was heading back to his house in the country. Did she want to come and see it?

Her sisters were nodding in unison, their hands pressed together as if they were praying.

'OK,' she said.

Luke told her he'd send his car. He'd text her when Jammie was on the way.

'Jammie?'

'Jamal. My driver. Can't wait to see you, babes.'

The black Range Rover pulled up outside their house in the early evening. Her sisters had spent the day doing her hair and make-up and talking endlessly about him. They packed a small bag for her that had everything she might need, but wouldn't look as if she expected to stay over. Her mum, who was doing a double-shift at Tesco's, FaceTimed, breathless with excitement. Just before Selene got in the car, Thalia seized her hand and gave it a squeeze.

'Just be real, you know? Be yourself. He won't have anyone like that round him.'

By the time they'd reached the outskirts of the city, it was dark.

'Where are we going?' she asked Jamal.

'Luke's house, love. Hollow Hill.'

'Yeah, but where is it? This is taking forever.'

'On the moor. Near Hathersage, well, near enough.'

He interrupted her next question and said, 'Listen, love, no offence, but I'm not supposed to talk to you.'

She googled Luke Allard instead. He'd been married to his childhood sweetheart, Nicole Jones. The marriage was annulled after her death; according to the *Daily Mail* he'd wanted a divorce and Nicole had spiralled into depression and killed herself. His fiancée, Kelly Thomas, had taken an overdose, and since then, he'd been single, although there were numerous rumours in the *Mail* about all the girls he was 'allegedly' seeing.

An hour and a half later, Jamal said, 'Home sweet home,' as they turned off the narrow country lane.

They started to drive through two huge iron gates when something large and black ran out in front of the car and Jamal braked sharply and swore under his breath. It was an Alsatian, as big as a wolf, its teeth bared, eyes glowing amber in the headlights, barking ferociously.

'Don't fret, love, it's only Drac, Stefan's dog.'

A man, silhouetted in the light from the Lodge House, whistled and the creature bounded towards him.

'Means devil in Romanian,' Jamal said, shaking his head. 'Those boys have a sense of humour.'

The long drive, the darkness and the dog had made her extremely nervous. What if he'd changed his mind? What if they had nothing to talk about? What if he thought she was ugly? She fidgeted, pulling her dress a little further over her thighs.

She couldn't see much – there were no streetlights out here – but the house was enormous, like something out of *Bridgerton*. Jamal opened the car door, and she carefully climbed the steep stone steps to the front door, which was flanked by stone columns.

And then Luke was there, grinning, and he was so good-looking, her stomach turned over.

'Feels like it takes forever when you're in a rush, don't it? Want a brew?'

He was totally normal, like one of the boys from her college given the run of some millionaire's mansion. They drank tea and lounged on the biggest sofa she'd ever seen and watched a film on a giant TV screen. He kissed her once, after the movie had finished, and then led her upstairs to his bedroom.

•

In the morning she had to pinch herself. Luke Allard, the man with the golden boots, who'd been featured on the cover of *GQ* and *Vogue*, was lying next to her, his normally carefully styled hair rumpled, his clothes strewn across the carpet. She put one of his shirts on and went downstairs to find the kitchen.

'Here,' she said, elbowing him as she climbed back into bed, balancing the tray. 'Thought you had to be up early, you know, for training.'

'It's Sunday,' he said, yawning. 'Day off. What's this?'

'Tea. Toast.'

He didn't say anything for a moment and she said anxiously, 'Don't you like butter? Or did I toast it too much? I'm always forgetting and leaving it too long.'

'You could have asked Sammy to make it. Thanks. Perfect, babes.' He smiled. 'Can't remember the last time anyone made me breakfast in bed.'

He'd rolled back on top of her when the bedroom door opened and a woman walked in. She had long, wavy blond hair, and was immaculately dressed in designer jeans, heels and a low-cut top. Selene pulled the sheet round her and expected Luke to tell this member of staff to get out. Instead, the woman smiled and kissed him on the cheek and sat on the bed.

'What movie did you watch, love?'

Selene froze, unsure where to look while they talked. After

a few moments, the woman turned to her and smiled. She had perfect white teeth and large blue eyes; her skin was unnaturally smooth.

'And this is her? She's a pearl.' She held out her hand to shake Selene's, who fumbled, trying to keep the sheet tight against her chest. 'Colette. Pleased to meet you.'

'Your mum?'

'Yeah,' said Luke. 'She always wanted to live in the country, so I bought this house for her.'

'For us, love, for us,' said Colette, patting him on the knee. She looked at her watch and Selene imagined a tiny frown line would normally have appeared on her forehead. 'Rest and recovery day. When you're ready, sweetheart, we'll have a chat and I'll show you around while Luke does his stretches.'

•

Colette beamed at her when she walked into the kitchen. She'd laid out croissants and a plate of beautifully arranged strawberries and kiwis; coffee in a gilt cafetière. Selene didn't dare tell her she only drank tea.

'I'm so pleased you're here, love. It can get a bit lonely.'

Selene wasn't sure how, with so many people around: Sammy, who turned out to be a wiry Irishman and their chef, hustled round behind them, making Luke and his personal trainer, Bobbie, a green smoothie, and out of one of the windows, she could see Jamal polishing the cars.

'A lot to learn, being in the public eye so much,' Colette continued, 'but first things first, sign this, and then I'll give a proper tour.'

'What is it?' she asked, glancing at the sheaf of paper with a fountain pen on the top.

'NDA, love. Non-disclosure agreement. Nothing to worry

about. You know what the media is like, we can't have anyone telling anything to the press.'

'I wouldn't,' she said.

'Here and here.' Colette indicated where she could sign.

'There's no mobile signal,' Selene said, holding up her phone.

'It's a bloody nuisance,' Colette agreed. 'I'll airdrop you the Internet password and then you can make calls using the Wi-Fi. Blimey, treasure, that's an old phone. I'll give you one of mine instead. Let me show you your room.'

'My room?'

'Well, a girl needs her own space, doesn't she? Luke has some early mornings. He won't always want company.'

She followed Colette round the house trying not to look overwhelmed. Luke even had his own gym.

'I'm in the attic,' said Colette, clopping past the guest bedrooms on the third floor. She threw open the balcony doors and a bracing September breeze whipped through the room, which seemed to run the entire length of the house.

'I love this view. Don't you?'

The house really was in the middle of nowhere. There was a high wall round the garden. The drive, as Colette told her with satisfaction, was five miles long. Behind Hollow Hill was a tennis court, a football pitch, and a walled vegetable garden. The green of hills blurred into one another. Somewhere, in the distance, was Manchester. She'd never seen this much space before. It made her nervous.

'Is there a basement?' Anything to get away from all the emptiness. 'Big houses – don't they always have a cellar?'

'Sharp as a tack, you are. Follow me, love.'

The basement held a large pantry, which Colette jokingly called her wine cellar, adding, 'I drink too much, me, to keep any wine in it.'

Selene wandered down the corridor. There were two doors on her right – one was wooden with a small window and smelt of warm cedar. She peered inside and realized it was a sauna. The next one was made of metal and glass. An icy chill seeped out. She took a step closer.

A hand smashed against the glass and she screamed and backed away. The door swung open with a hiss, as if air was being released, and Luke and Bobbie, wearing only pants, socks, hats and gloves emerged. They laughed at her expression.

'Recovery rooms,' said Bobbie. 'Cold – minus 140 degrees in this one. We only stay for a couple of minutes.'

'It's ball-breaking,' Luke said, shivering. He grabbed a towel from Bobbie and they headed for the shower at the other end of the basement.

Colette turned to lead her upstairs, but Selene stopped and wheeled round.

'Where does that go?'

She'd almost missed it. There was one last door, right at the end of the corridor. It was a normal door – no metal, glass or funny dials on the outside – and she put out her hand to open it.

'Don't,' said Colette sharply. 'Sorry, love, didn't mean to snap. It's locked anyhow. That one you can't go in. It's where Luke keeps his valuables. Temperature controlled and what not. He'd not be best pleased if you upset his system.'

Colette found her a Barbour jacket and wellies and marched her round the grounds. Her bare legs froze in the stiff wind.

'I'm like a bloody lady farmer, me,' Colette said, smiling as she showed her the llamas, the duck pond, the mini orchard and waved at a burly man digging for potatoes.

'Vi,' she said. 'It's short for Viorel. It means bluebell in Romanian. Hilarious, isn't it? I don't think you've met his brothers yet, have you? We call them the Brothers Grimm, but that's just between you and me, love. Stefan is security, and Carol is our housekeeper. Better with the Dyson than I ever was.' She squeezed Selene's arm. 'So hard to take in. I brought Luke up on me tod in Wythenshawe. We didn't have a pot to piss in. But I worked two jobs so I could buy Luke's kit and pay for all the coaching. He's been training since he was a nipper. And now, well, this is what hard work and talent gets you.' She steered Selene round the apple trees: 'Come and see the pigs.'

There were five of them, large and deathly pale. They came running over, squealing and slipping in the mud in their haste. They regarded Selene with tiny pink eyes. She took a step back and folded her arms across her chest.

'They say you shouldn't name anything you're going to eat, but I can't help it. They're adorable. We've got Doris, Eris, Hebe, Iris and this one is Rhea.'

'After Greek goddesses?' said Selene. They'd covered the Greeks for two years running at school. Some mix-up with the National Curriculum.

'Oh, aren't you the smart one. Between you and me, most of the girls he brings back are thick as pig shit, pardon my French.'

The animals were so fat, with brawny backsides, she thought they'd be able to break down the pen with ease. The stench was overwhelming.

'You've been so kind, Colette, but I need to get home soon,' she said. 'My mum—'

'He wants you to stay,' Colette said. 'Didn't he tell you? And don't fret, love, we phoned your mum already. Didn't want her to worry.'

Selene wasn't sure what to say. She should be pleased, shouldn't she?

'What's that?' she asked, noticing a door set in the high wall.

'I'll show you,' Colette said, taking a large bunch of keys out of her pocket. She pushed the ivy back to reach the keyhole. The door was stiff and she had to put her shoulder against it. She stepped back to let Selene see.

On the other side was the moor. Miles and miles of it. The heather had started to wither to a dull shade of decaying purple. She shivered and backed away.

'I should go and find Luke,' she said.

'Oh pet, you're frozen. Come on, let's get you inside,' Colette said. As they walked back to the house, she said softly, 'Word of advice. My boy's got a heart of gold, but a quick temper and he gets bored easily. Stay out of his way unless he wants you – he's got a lot riding on those shoulders. It's the start of the season, and the team needs to win. He's their most expensive player – I'm sure you've heard, but the pressure isn't easy to handle. How about you and me take a ride into town later? Girls day out, eh? We can get our hair done, and pop in and see your mum on the way.'

•

'They want me to move in with him!' she told her mum and sisters.

Jamal and Colette were in the car; the engine still running.

'Baby girl, play your cards right and it could be your ticket out of here,' her mum said. 'Look what came this morning!' She pointed to a handwritten card from Colette stuck in the middle of a cellophane-wrapped basket filled with white orchids in moss.

'I hardly know him,' Selene said.

'You need to get a ring on your finger. Girlfriends are dispensable,' said Phoebe, who was bending over the kitchen table, sticking false nails on.

'Don't you like him?' asked Thalia.

'Yeah, I do. He's dead nice and good-looking . . .'

'Obvs.'

'But . . .'

Her mum bundled her back outside and put her head through the car window to talk to Colette as if she were trying to suck up to her.

'Hey, our kid,' said Thalia softly, 'text me, any time, day or night, if you're worried. I'll come and get you.'

'On your white horse?'

'Like a lady knight, me,' she said as she hugged Selene.

•

One evening, two weeks later, she and Luke were sprawled on his continent-sized sofa watching a reality TV show about footballers. The past fortnight had been strangely busy yet boring. Luke had been training at United most days, leaving early, coming home late and exhausted, and he'd only wanted to slump in front of the telly or his X-Box. Colette had been drilling her in how to behave: what she had to eat, wear and post on Instagram, as if Selene were her pet project. She even had Selene working out with Bobbie after he'd finished training her and Luke. Selene missed her friends from college, even the lessons themselves, though she'd hated it when she'd been there.

Seeing the WAGs in the documentary with their stacks of bracelets, reminded her of her own. It was a silver heart on a black thread that Thalia had given her on her sixteenth birthday. She wore it all the time, but it must have fallen off somewhere in this huge house. She ran her hand round her wrist. It felt odd, like she was naked without it. She'd had Carol and even Sammy helping her hunt for it.

'I still can't find my bracelet,' she said to Luke.

'For fuck's sake,' Luke snapped. He hated it when she interrupted him when he was watching TV. 'Stop going on about it. It's not like it's worth anything. I'll buy you a new one.'

She froze; she felt as if he'd physically winded her. He glanced over at her, and then hugged her.

'Sorry, babes, I didn't mean it. Just, you know, a bit, like, on edge. I'm heading to St George's tomorrow for the England training camp. I'll be there for the week – I'm going to stay at a hotel up there. Can't be doing with any distractions, you know what I mean?' he said, his hand drifting lower. 'Plus, it's a ninety-minute drive – can't be doing with that twice a day. Jammie's driving us there.'

'Us?'

'Colette's coming and so's Bobbie and Sammy. Stefan, Vi and Carol will be here, if you need anything.'

'What, you're leaving me? Why's your mum going then?'

'She won't be in St George's, you idiot. She's set up a few meetings with TV companies and agents. She wants to raise my profile in the media, maybe get a Netflix show.'

'I could go home.'

'This is your home, babe. And I want you here, waiting for me when I get back,' he said, sliding his tongue around the edge of her ear. 'I'll be up early tomorrow, so I'll say bye now. I've left a set of keys for you. They're on the kitchen counter. You've got the run of the place. You'll be like the Duchess of Hastings,' he said, pulling her astride his lap. 'Can do what you like,' he said, kissing the tip of her nose. 'Only thing is, don't go in that room in the basement. Mum said you were asking about it. Like she says, our valuables are in there. And probably best not to play about with the cryotherapy chamber either. Don't want to come back and find you stuck in there like a popsicle,' he added, licking her neck.

•

After a day, she was completely bored. She occasionally saw the three Romanian brothers on the Lodge House CCTV screen, smoking, or bench-pressing weights they'd laid out on the drive by the iron gates, or both. By the second day, the novelty of being able to eat ice cream instead of salad had worn off. She'd tried all her new clothes on, and followed a YouTube tutorial on contouring. She did a half-hearted workout in the gym, and sat in the sauna until she thought she might blister. She scrolled endlessly through her Instagram feed and then, when even that was dull, she looked at Facebook to see what her mum was up to. Apparently she'd bought a car. A car! And the new sofa and curtains were arriving this week.

'Going up in the world!!!' her mum had posted.

A sponsored link popped up about a missing girl. She was about to swipe it away when she noticed the name – Hebe White. She read on. Hebe was stunning – long blond hair, golden skin the same sort of colour as hers. Maybe she was half Nigerian too, Selene thought, scrutinising the bow shape of the girl's lips. Hebe lived in Hathersage, and had been missing for six months. The post was by her parents; they claimed Hebe had been Luke Allard's girlfriend.

She googled Hebe White, and then Hebe White and Luke Allard, but nothing came up. Not a single photo or a quote or even a denial that they'd been an item. Odd. She forwarded the link to Thalia.

She decided to open a bottle of champagne and drink it by herself, maybe offer a glass to the Brothers Grimm if they bothered to stop by. There was none in the fridge, so she went to look in the wine cellar. As she was returning with the bottle, she noticed a huge chest freezer that ran along one wall. It was locked – but after all, she thought, she had the keys. She wondered if Luke really had given her every single one. She grabbed the bunch from the kitchen counter, where they'd been lying untouched since Luke had left. Some of them were small, as if to open padlocks, and she eventually found the one that fitted. She eased the padlock out and lifted the lid of the freezer.

A pair of eyes were staring right at her. She screamed. The freezer was full of hefty joints. In the centre was a pig's head; the delicate hairs in its ears were coated with ice crystals, its small beady eyes clouded with frost. She slammed the lid back down. On second thoughts, she opened it again and took a picture of the pig. She sent it to Thalia for a joke.

It gave her an idea, though. If Luke really had left her a complete set of keys, there might be one to the room at the end of the corridor. It was the only part of the house she hadn't seen, and she wondered what was so valuable they had to keep it there. Colette had diamonds and rubies in her bedroom; Luke had some watches worth more than a normal person's house – what could they possibly have that had to be kept in a locked room in the basement? It wasn't like it was an easy house to rob, she thought, what with Stefan and Drac at the gates, the five-mile-long drive and the fact that Hollow Hill was in the middle of a moor on the edge of the Peak District.

Surely they wouldn't mind if she just had a quick look? After all, she was his girlfriend.

The light in the low-ceilinged corridor was dim and she couldn't see the keys properly. Finally, just as she was on the point of giving up and going to open the champagne, she found the right one.

She opened the door.

She wasn't sure what she was expecting – maybe shelves with trophies, perhaps a safe. She turned on the light. At first, it felt as if she'd stepped into a small art gallery. The walls and the floor were white. There were spotlights, each one centred on a plinth with a glass display cube on the top. The one in the middle of the room housed something that glittered. As she walked towards it, she realized it was a skull. It was completely covered with diamonds. It must be an original sculpture, she thought, or why have it locked in here? There was a silver plaque beneath the skull with a signature etched into the metal, and next to it, a small box lined with black velvet. Inside was a necklace with a gold-plated snitch – the ball in Quidditch, the game Harry Potter played.

Weird combo.

She looked at the signature and with a start, saw that it wasn't the name of the artist. It said *Nicole James*. Luke's ex-wife.

She turned to the plinth next to it. The skull inside this cabinet was not as lavishly decorated. There were tiny emeralds inlaid round the outside of the empty sockets, and one on the cheekbone, as if it had been pierced. It too had a trinket next to the plaque, a charm bracelet, this time, with silver and enamel unicorns and rainbows. The signature was *Kelly Thomas*. Luke's fiancée.

Selene felt sweat prickle on her palms, and her heart started to beat faster.

There were another four plinths. Three of them also held skulls: the bone a dull ivory and decorated with a different gem: opals, rubies, sapphires. She read the names: *Doris Elliot, Eris Cartwright, Hebe White*.

The box on the last plinth was empty. It too had a silver plaque and a velvet-lined jewellery box. Inside was her missing bracelet, the silver heart on a black cord. She picked it up, and pushed it back on her wrist. The name on the plaque was in her own handwriting.

Selene Jackson.

She wheeled round and saw the glint of a camera lens in the corner of the ceiling. The room was L-shaped and windowless, yet light was seeping in from somewhere. She put her hand over her pounding heart to try to calm herself. She walked slowly towards the far end. A plastic curtain separated the two areas. She yanked it back. This section was not quite as pristine white as the rest and there was a strange smell: cloying, metallic, slightly sweet overlaid with the astringency of bleach. There was a long wooden table and fastened on the wall behind it, a series of metal instruments, including a hack saw. There were two runnels carved in the concrete floor. The light filtering in was coming from a hatch in the wall that must, she thought, lead outside.

She backed away, getting tangled in the curtain, and ran down the corridor and up the stairs. By the time she reached the kitchen, her phone was ringing.

It was Luke.

She thought about not answering, but that would make him suspicious. He was on a pitch at St George's, for fuck's sake, she told herself. He would have no idea that she knew.

'Hey, babes, how's it going?' she said, trying to keep the tremor out of her voice.

'Selene, you idiot,' he hissed.

'What? What's up?'

'My mum's livid. She's on her way home now. Why the fuck did you have to open that door?'

'What? How did you—'

'Fuck's sake, Selene, get a grip. There's a sensor in every room in the house. Most of them have security cameras. Colette has the whole system on her mobile. Bloody hell, Selene, the one room she didn't want you to go in—'

'She? You told me—'

'I don't have a fucking clue what she keeps in there, but it's important to her. Got to respect her privacy, right? My last girlfriend unlocked the door – and Mum literally chucked her out that day. I never saw her again.'

Hebe White, she thought.

She suddenly realized that Luke wasn't angry with her, he was worried, maybe even scared.

'Don't worry. I'll calm her down,' she said soothingly.

'I fucking hope so. I like having you around, Selene. I thought, you know, it could go somewhere, you and me. I've got to go – my physio is waiting for me.'

She looked at her watch. She had less than an hour if Colette had left shortly after she'd unlocked the door in the basement.

She FaceTimed her mum, who was at the conveyor belt, chatting to a customer.

'Mum. Mum! You've got to come and pick me up.'

'Can't you ask that driver of Luke's?'

'He's not here. Mum—'

'The Terry's chocolate oranges are three for two. You want to get another one?'

'Mum, listen—'

'Selene, baby girl, what have you done?'

'Luke's mum's dead annoyed. You have to get me now!'

'I can wait while you get another one,' she said to her customer. 'Honey, I can't drive.'

'You bought a car!'

'And now I need driving lessons. Girl, you apologise for whatever you've done.'

Selene looked at her phone in disbelief. Her mother had hung up on her.

She tried to book an Uber, but none of the drivers picked up her request. She called Dad's Cabs, her local company, and the lady who answered, snapping gum, said it was too far, and there'd be no one available for at least a couple of hours. As she hung up, she realized that she didn't have enough for the fare. She'd arrived with virtually nothing, and Colette had bought her everything on her own credit card.

She started sending a text to Thalia, when the Wi-Fi dropped out. It dawned on her that if Colette had access to the room sensors and cameras, then not only did she know exactly where Selene was and what she was doing, but she could probably control other aspects of the house remotely too – like the Internet. Selene grabbed the keys and the coat Colette had lent her and let herself out the back door.

There was no point running down the drive. Five miles? Fuck, she couldn't run one. Plus the Brothers Grimm would be at the Lodge House by the locked gates. The wall was too high to climb.

What the hell was she going to do?

She ran past the flower garden and the walled vegetable plot, the ornamental pond, the llama pasture, the tennis court, the football pitch, an outdoor pool with a hot tub and a jacuzzi that she and Luke had once swum in late at night. She swallowed hard; she had a stitch and couldn't breathe. She doubled over, sucking in air. At the far end of the garden was the door in the wall.

She shivered, thinking of the vast expanse of moorland on the other side. It was dusk. She would get lost in the dark, she knew it. But what else could she do? Stay here and wait for Stefan to hunt her down with his black Alsatian?

She'd reached the pigs. As soon as they smelt her, they came running over on their tiny trotters, as if tottering on stilettos, their vast saggy behinds wobbling. She took out the keys, and started to search feverishly through the bunch for the one she needed.

'Oh Selene, treasure, why did you have to do it? I told you. Luke told you. I was starting to, well, not like you, obviously, but warm to you.'

Colette was standing at the other end of the pigpen. Her hair was beautifully styled, and she was wearing white jeans, a cashmere jumper and quilted gilet, black patent high-heeled boots and a long silk scarf in a pale cerulean blue.

'How did you—'

'Shortcut, love,' Colette said. 'Or did you mean, how did I get rid of the others?'

Selene leaned against the door of the pigpen, propping herself against it. Her legs were shaking. She wondered if she could sprint to the door leading to the moor before Colette – surely she couldn't run in those ridiculous heels? But no, Selene thought, she'd probably whistle for Drac.

'Yes,' she said in a hoarse whisper. She needed to keep her talking.

'I've learned so much, living out here in the country. You wouldn't believe how poisonous some of our native plants are. And no one thinks to check for them in a post-mortem. Nicole *was* depressed. Kelly *was* a little junkie. So it wasn't hard to get rid of them. Did you like the skulls? Thought so, my homage to Damien Hirst. Heard of him, love? We're friends, you know. Amazing how interesting people find you when you have money. Of course, they're not *real* skulls. I had to get their heads scanned and make plastic replicas. A little disappointing, but there we are.'

243

'But the other girls—'

'Oh, no, I didn't poison them. Where would be the fun in that?'

'The cryotherapy chamber,' said Selene slowly.

'Indeed, love. And it's handy having a window so I could watch.'

'So *their* skulls—'

'Are real. Bingo. I put their heads out on the moor. The wasps eat the flesh and leave the bone nice and clean. And there's no one out there to see but the sheep.'

'And then you put their bodies in the freezer.'

Colette laughed. 'You really aren't all that clever, are you? Course not. Can't leave any evidence. Where do you think their bodies might be? Come on now. Use that pretty little head of yours.'

'But didn't anyone miss them? Doris, Eris and Hebe?'

The pigs snorted at the mention of their names, and Selene shouted their names again, so that the pigs went into a wild frenzy of squeals, expecting to be fed. She needed to distract Colette from what she was about to do.

'Calm down, love. Listen, those girls and their families were desperate. Literally threw themselves – threw their girls – at Luke. Looked the other way. They thought it was easy money. A quick way to the top. Luke had to earn that money. He's worked hard to be where he is, unlike those lazy, entitled little bitches.'

'But, Colette, someone must know, someone must have seen them with him.'

She was thinking back to who had noticed her with Luke. A handful of people in a club? She hadn't even gone home with him that night. Only her family and his staff knew where she was. Surely they'd call the police?

As if Colette knew what she was thinking, she said, 'Luke is the lad with the golden boots. Worth £100 million to Man United. You think anyone with a vested interest in football is going to allow a manky chav to claim they saw him with some trashy girl, if we say he never slept with her – wasn't with her when she went missing? We're lawyered up to our armpits, love,' she said. 'Now then, that's enough chat. Don't be difficult, treasure. There's nowhere to run, but I expect you've clocked that,' Colette added, striding towards her.

The padlock finally slid off the bolt to the pigpen. Selene kicked open the door and screamed the names of the pigs, the names of all the lost girls, as she sprinted for the nearest apple tree and swung up into the boughs.

The pigs, for such enormous fat creatures, were surprisingly fast, and Colette, in spite of all the personal training, was not quite quick enough. Selene climbed as high as she could. From the top of the apple tree, she could see over the garden walls, and out across the moorland beyond, where the sun was starting to sink, blood-red, behind the heather.

QUIET NIGHT IN

AMER ANWAR

Southall, London, 2018

With his wife away, Tej was enjoying a rare weekend on his own. So far, his Saturday had consisted of a long lie-in, afternoon at the pub watching football – with a tandoori mixed-grill and a few pints thrown in for good measure – then back home and a nap on the sofa. Now it was evening and he was up again, pouring himself a beer, the local news on the TV, as he contemplated a quiet night in, with some dinner and maybe a movie.

The news was the usual stuff, apart from two items that caught his attention. One was about the proposed third runway at Heathrow Airport, where he worked, and the other concerned some human remains that had been found on a building site in Uxbridge, not far from Southall, where he lived.

His mind had already drifted from the news back to the lamb curry and pilau rice Sonia had left in the fridge for him when the doorbell rang.

Tej frowned. Who the hell was that? He wasn't expecting anyone and people didn't usually turn up unannounced, not these days when everyone had a mobile phone. Maybe it was someone trying to flog something or a grifter collecting for a fake charity. If he ignored it, they were bound to go away.

The bell sounded again, followed by an insistent knocking on the door.

What if it was someone he knew? Or perhaps a delivery? Had Sonia ordered something else? More than bloody likely. Clothes, make-up, books, gadgets – there was no end to it. He took a sip of the beer he'd finished pouring, put the glass and can down on the coffee table, and went to answer the door.

The man on the doorstep said, 'All right, Tej?'

It took Tej a moment to work out who he was. 'Bloody hell,' he said, as recognition dawned. 'Billy. Long time, no see. What're you doing here?'

'I was just in the old neighbourhood, visiting family, thought I'd pop by, see if you were home. Not disturbing you, am I?'

'Nah, not at all. Come in, it's bloody freezing out there.'

Baljeet 'Billy' Attwal stepped inside. He was dressed all in black: black jeans, and a black top, under a long black coat and with a black beanie on his head. It gave him a sombre appearance and, with his thick growth of stubble, even made him a little scruffy looking, which was a bit of a surprise, seeing as Billy was a very wealthy man.

'How long's it been?' Tej said, closing the door.

'I think last time we saw each other was when you guys came to Vijay's twenty-first.'

'Blimey, yeah, it must've been. How old is he now?'

'Twenty-four.'

'Three years . . .' Tej shook his head. 'Where's the time go?' Neither of them had an answer to that. 'Come on, man, come and sit down. You want a drink? I just poured a beer.'

'A drink would be great. You got anything a bit stronger though?'

'Sure. What d'you fancy?'

'Whisky or a brandy, if you've got it.'

'Pretty sure I have.' Tej went to the kitchen and returned with a tumbler of brandy in one hand and a bottle of Hennessy in the other. Billy had taken off his hat, revealing a balding pate with just a thin covering of hair, like the worn crease of a cricket pitch. Tej's own hair was much more salt than pepper these days, both men only a few years shy of their sixtieth birthdays. He handed Billy the glass and put the bottle on the coffee table in front of him. 'Take your coat off, make yourself comfortable. Get you anything to eat?'

'No, thanks,' Billy said. 'I wasn't planning on staying long.'

Tej sat on the other sofa, picked up his beer and raised his glass in salute. 'Cheers.' Billy did likewise and they had a drink together. 'So . . . how've you been?'

Billy shrugged. 'You know how it is, good one minute, shit the next.'

'Ain't that the truth.'

'I got divorced.'

Tej nodded. 'Yeah, I heard. I'm sorry.'

'Don't be.'

'How're the kids?'

'Hardly kids anymore, busy with their own lives. Kiran and me, we hardly see them, so it's just the two of us together on our own. We realized we don't really get on anymore.'

'And you decided to split?'

'I did. She would've hung on for the money but I didn't want to put up with her moaning, told her it was over and that she could sling her hook. She wanted half of everything I've got, said she was entitled to it. I told her if she tried it, I'd make sure she got nothing, not a fucking penny. She shut up after that . . . Why you looking at me like that? Ain't like I left her penniless or anything. I got her a house, a car, and she gets more than enough money to live on without ever needing to work. She's pretty fucking sorted. Don't know what more she'd want.'

Tej thought about his own domestic situation. He'd been married to Sonia for twenty-five, mostly happy, years. They'd had their ups and downs, like any couple, but he could never imagine just ending things like that after all they'd been through together. Money was never such a big issue with them because they had just about enough to get by, so there was no point arguing about it. Money couldn't buy you happiness, or so the saying went; though, if you didn't have it, you were certain it could. But those that did have it weren't always the happiest people in the world. You only had to watch the news to know that.

'Anyway,' Billy said, 'I didn't pop round to talk about all that. How've you been? You here on your own?'

'Yeah. Sonia's away at her sister's this weekend and the kids are still at uni. They'll be back in a few weeks, for Christmas.'

'Oh, I might've seen something about that on Facebook, now you mention it. Everything OK with you, family-wise?'

'Yeah, can't complain. Well, I could, but only about little things, nothing major.'

'Cool. How about work? You still at the airport?'

'Yeah, been almost thirty years now. Just holding on until I retire – bloody hell, even just saying that makes me feel old. I'm looking forward to taking it easy. Good job I started a pension early.'

'Pension? Just listen to you. Not like when we were younger, huh?' Billy said with a grin. 'No pensions or savings on our minds then – not unless it was other people's, that is.'

Tej didn't return the grin. 'That was a long time ago.'

'No scrimping and scraping just to get by, or relying on

benefits – we went out and took what we wanted.' There was a gleam in Billy's eye as he talked about it.

For Tej, it stoked bitter memories. 'That's all in the past. We were young and stupid, did things I ain't so proud of now – when I think about it, which I try not to. We would've got caught eventually and ended up either dead or in prison. Maybe it's just as well it all stopped when it did. I'm happy and comfortable enough now. You ain't done so bad, either.'

Billy had eventually gone into property development, starting with small flats then working up to larger and larger places. 'Yeah, I know . . . but still, we had some wild times back then, didn't we?'

Tej frowned. 'They were wild, all right.' Why was Billy dredging up the past? He'd had a nice relaxing day and wasn't in the mood to start going over old memories, especially ones he'd buried for so long.

But Billy carried on regardless. 'You remember the first time we got our hands on some shooters?'

It wasn't something Tej talked about these days. 'I remember you almost shooting me then almost blowing your own foot off.' Was Billy's divorce affecting him more than he was letting on, making him misty-eyed about the past? Or was he, perhaps, having some kind of late-stage mid-life crisis where he was feeling the need to relive his youth?

'I never did get on with guns,' Billy admitted.

'That was pretty obvious. It's why we gave you the sawn-off. You just had to pull the hammers back and fire it into the ceiling to get everyone's attention. Then you didn't have to worry about using it again – and we didn't have to worry about you shooting anyone, including us or yourself.'

'That shotgun was cool. Used to scare the shit out of everybody.'

'Us as well, with you holding it. We all felt safer when we knew it was empty.'

'Sometimes wish I still had it,' Billy said. He took a sip of his brandy. 'What about you? You were good at handling them. You ever tempted to keep one?'

Tej pursed his lips. He wasn't sure how to respond – but Billy was one of the old crew, the only one he was still friends with and who knew all about his past. In fact, he was probably the only person Tej could talk to about any of it. 'As a matter of fact,' he finally said, 'I've still got that 9mm from the last job.' *Before everything went to shit*, he didn't add. He didn't need to. They both knew it.

'What, here in the house?'

'Yeah, in the bottom of my bedside drawer, wrapped in a cloth.'

'Why'd you keep it?'

'After what happened, everything going sour the way it did, I thought I might need it. Everyone was convinced I had to have been involved, or even behind the whole thing.'

'I never did.'

'You were the only one. The others were out for blood. Things kicked off more than once. Threats were made. I wasn't sure if they'd follow through on them. I kept the piece handy, just in case.'

'What's Sonia think about you having it?'

'She thinks it's a replica. Probably forgotten all about it.' He hadn't thought about it himself for ages, either. The knowledge it was there was always in the back of his mind, a reassuring presence, protection if ever anyone came at him again, but he never really gave it any thought – until now. He realized he'd just got used to having it there.

'Shame things ended the way they did,' Billy said.

'That's the understatement of the century. Everyone thought I shafted them and wanted me dead. It's a fucking shame, all right, especially as I had nothing to do with it.' Remembering things he'd put behind him three decades ago only served to rake over the hot coals of an anger that had been dormant within him all that time. Tej found he needed something stronger than beer. He stood. 'I'm going to the kitchen to get a glass, join you in that brandy. Get you anything while I'm up?'

'Now you mention it, I wouldn't mind a little snack, some nuts or something to go with the drinks if you've got any?'

'Yeah, no problem.'

'OK if I use your bathroom?'

'Sure. Upstairs and to the right.'

Tej went into the kitchen and got himself a heavy tumbler, then rummaged around in the crisp cupboard and found a bag of salted peanuts, which he opened and poured into a bowl. When he returned to the lounge, Billy was still in the bathroom. Tej poured himself a shot of brandy and took a sip, the warm liquid seeming to catch fire as he swallowed it, burning its way down into his stomach then dissipating slowly, taking a little of his dark mood with it.

He grabbed some peanuts and popped them into his mouth. The toilet flushed upstairs, then he heard the boiler come on in the kitchen as the hot water was used. A minute later, Billy came down, still in his coat, and rejoined him.

'Cheers,' Tej said, raising his glass.

Billy raised his in return, drained it and put it down on the table. 'You been in touch with any of the others recently?'

'You're joking, right? We ain't been on friendly terms since . . . well, you know. I see them around now and again, but just to nod to, nothing else. You're the only one I'm really in touch with – and I ain't seen you in three years.'

'Things did end pretty badly. They shouldn't have blamed you, though − I mean, it wasn't as if you disappeared with it.'

'No, but my brother did.'

'Yeah . . .' Billy nodded.

They sat in silence for a moment, then Tej said, 'Even after all this time, I still find it hard to believe he'd do something like that.'

'Eight hundred grand would be enough to tempt anyone.'

'But we chose him because we all trusted him. He was always a straight arrow.'

'That's true. I mean, if we'd had any worries about him, we'd never have left the money with him. But how else do you explain it?'

'I've thought about it over the years . . . maybe someone else took it from him.'

'Who?'

'I don't know.'

It had been their most ambitious score, thirty years ago, when they'd all been young and full of the reckless bravado of youth, and when banks had been easier to rob. They'd watched that particular branch in Wembley for several weeks beforehand, working out staff routines and the comings and goings of the security vans. Then, they'd worked out a plan, armed themselves and, on the day of the robbery, taken up their positions.

When the security van arrived with the cash delivery, they'd moved fast and gone in hard. One of the gang members, Sukh, had cut the aerials on the van, leaving its radio and tracking devices useless. The rest of them went into the bank and Billy had fired both his barrels into the ceiling, shocking everyone, rooting them to the spot, making it easier for Tej and the others to round them all up.

They had to rough up the manager a little, and the guard

from the van, to make them do what they were told, but no one was shot or seriously injured. The manager opened the vault and the gang grabbed all the large denomination notes, along with the money from the cashiers' trays and the cash being delivered by the van guard.

By the time they got outside, Sukh was in the front of the van, with the driver at gunpoint. The third guard was still in the back of the van, inside the armoured section with the rest of the money.

Two getaway cars were waiting around the corner, the route planned in advance to make any potential pursuit as difficult as possible. The van driver was made to follow the cars to a small industrial area near railway lines, where he was dragged out of the van, blindfolded, gagged, and handcuffed to a metal fence. From the back of a Transit van the gang had parked there ahead of time, they took a heavy-duty industrial chainsaw and cut open the side of the security van. It took less than two minutes. The third guard was dragged out and bound and cuffed, beside his colleague.

The money was transferred from the security van to the Transit, along with everything they'd taken from the bank. They then poured bleach over both getaway cars, inside and out, to obliterate any prints and evidence, before driving away in the Transit and two other getaway cars they had waiting nearby.

The three vehicles took separate routes to a lock-up in Southall, where they repacked all the money into cardboard boxes and burnt the canvas bags it had been in, along with the clothes they'd worn on the raid.

It was at that point that Tej's younger brother, Jackie (so-called because his first name was Chan, short for Chandeep), turned up in a rented van. The boxes were loaded into it, and then Jackie drove to a flat, rented in someone else's name, in

Hillingdon, close to Brunel University, where he was due to start a degree course at the end of the summer. Under the guise of moving in, he took the boxes into the property. The idea was for him to stay there and look after them until the heat died down. The rest of the gang went about their day-to-day lives as if nothing had happened.

The plan was to wait at least six weeks and then, if all seemed safe, retrieve the money and split it. Jackie was meant to call daily, to check in and let them know everything was OK.

And that's exactly what happened for the first five weeks – and then he stopped calling.

'If it *was* someone else,' Billy said, 'then where's Jackie been all this time? What about the travel brochures we found at the flat? And the fact all his clothes were gone?'

'I know all that. I just . . .' Tej still couldn't bring himself to believe it – there had to be some other explanation. But anything else sounded too far-fetched, like the plot of a bad B-movie.

'It's always the people you least suspect,' Billy said.

When the money had disappeared, the others had immediately thought Tej and Jackie must have planned it together – all except Billy, who'd tried to defend his friend. Tej had told them if he'd wanted to double-cross them, he wouldn't have done something that fucking dumb, but they didn't believe him.

Then things had got nasty.

The other gang members had started following him. Then one night they broke into his house and attacked him, demanding to know where the money was and turning the place over, searching for clues to its whereabouts. Tej wasn't sure how far they'd take things next time – that was when he'd started keeping the gun close.

The mistrust caused the gang to split and go their separate

ways. Word spread quickly and no one wanted to work with Tej on any other scores.

Eventually, needing money, he'd had to search for straight work and managed to find a job at the airport. A couple of years later, he'd met Sonia and found himself settling into a normal life, his criminal past well and truly behind him.

Time went on and there was never anything to suggest he had access to a large amount of money. He had to scrimp and save to get by, same as everyone else. Over the years, the other gang members grudgingly began to accept he might not have had anything to do with Jackie taking the cash.

Now, his life was happy and uneventful, and he was perfectly content with that.

'Well, thanks for the drink,' Billy said, 'but now I better do what I came here to do.' And he stood up, pulled a gun from his coat pocket and aimed it at Tej.

'What the fuck, Billy?' Tej said, staring at the weapon. Then: 'That's my gun.'

'I know . . . it was exactly where you said it would be.'

Tej realized he needed to calm down. His heart was thumping like a techno bassline. 'What the hell are you doing?' Was this about the money? Had Billy somehow got it in his head that he *did* know something about it, *now*, after all this time? Is that why he'd been talking about the past? 'Look, I don't know what you think, but I really don't know anything about what happened to Jackie or the money.'

'Oh, I know that.'

There was something about the way he said it – the certainty in his tone – that struck Tej as odd. 'Then what's going on?'

Billy looked down the barrel of the gun at him. 'They just don't build houses like they used to.'

'What the hell are you on about?'

'Back when the Georgians, the Victorians and the Edwardians used to build them, they were built to last. Good solid construction. But your modern stuff – I'm talking Sixties, Seventies, and Eighties here – it's mostly cheap and flimsy. When people put houses up, you imagine those places will last a hundred years or more, like those older properties, or at least maybe seventy but that ain't the case. They built houses in the Eighties that they're tearing down now to make way for flats. I should've thought of doing it myself and bought them up.'

'What the fuck's any of this got to do with me?'

Billy considered a moment before answering. 'You been watching the news lately?'

Tej frowned. 'Yeah.'

'They knocked down some houses in Uxbridge, found a body on the site.'

Tej remembered watching the update on that story just a little earlier. 'So . . .?'

'So, it's only a matter of time before they identify it, what with DNA and all that stuff they got these days, and when they do, the shit'll really hit the fan.'

Something colder and harder than fear wrapped its tendrils around Tej's insides. 'Why's that?'

'Because then you'll finally know where Jackie's been the last thirty years.'

Tej's mind suddenly felt like it was trapped in treacle, his thoughts sluggish and confused, as he tried to process what he'd just heard. With comprehension came a punch of rage to his gut. His hands tightened into fists, jaw clamped, muscles bunched, wanting to fly at the newly unmasked killer standing in front of him.

Billy saw his reaction and stiffened the arm pointing the gun. 'Easy. Just stay right there.'

Tej looked at the gun and tried to calm himself. He needed to know more, hear the details, fill in the blanks. It took him a moment to swallow his hatred enough to speak. 'What did you do?' he said. There was no hiding the malice in his voice.

Billy gave a cold smile, confident behind the gun. 'You know, it's going to be a real weight off my mind to finally talk about it. Bit like the talkie bit at the end of a James Bond film, where the villain explains his big plan before Bond manages to escape and fuck it all up for him.' Billy chuckled to himself. 'Only, you won't be around to fuck anything up – I'm going to make sure of that. Besides, it's too late anyway. My plan already worked, thirty years ago. Now I'm just tying up loose ends.'

'Just fucking tell me.' Tej ground the words out, thick with hate.

'What do you think I did? I killed him.'

Tej moved, involuntarily, fuelled by a desire to snap Billy's neck.

'Uh, uh.' Billy stepped forward and shoved the gun in his face, stopping him before he was off the sofa. 'Sit back down if you want to hear it, or else I'll just shoot you now.'

Tej did as he was told and Billy backed off, keeping the gun trained on him. 'I liked your brother, he was a good kid.'

'Funny way of showing it.'

'I made it quick and painless for him.'

'How?'

'You really want to know?'

'Just tell me.'

'OK. A kitchen knife, here –' he put his free hand to his neck. 'Straight down, severing the artery. He went into shock but I managed to walk him to the bathroom before I pulled it out. He bled into the tub. Only took a few seconds. Made it a lot easier to clean up.'

If looks could kill, Tej's glare would have choked the life out of Billy. 'Then what?'

'I had to get rid of the body,' he said, matter-of-factly. 'Somewhere it wouldn't be found. You probably don't remember, but I was labouring where those houses were being built, in Uxbridge. I had access to the site and knew where I could pour concrete without it being a problem. I had to get the body over there, though – not an easy thing to do in the middle of a built-up area – but I knew that and went prepared.'

Tej was staring at Billy, breathing heavily, trying to keep a tight rein on his emotions.

'I cut him up in the bath.'

There was a guttural growling sound. It took Tej a moment to realize it was coming from him.

'I'd brought a hacksaw and a roll of black bags with me, in the van I'd rented,' Billy continued. 'Used the saw and the knife to cut through at the joints, like with a chicken. Head and torso were the worst bits to sort out. His insides were slippery as fuck, but it was OK once I got everything into bags.'

Tej couldn't believe what he was hearing. He felt his gorge rising.

'I double-bagged everything to be safe. It was late by then, so easy enough to carry the bags out to the van without anyone noticing. I took a load of his clothes and stuff too, and drove to the building site. Laid the bags out along a trench and covered them with concrete. Afterwards, I went back and cleaned the flat, planted the travel brochures and took the money. Pretty simple really.'

'But he left the country.'

Billy grinned. 'That was me. I found his passport in the flat and it gave me an idea. I booked a one-way flight to Spain and flew out using his name, with my photo stuck in his passport. I was always pretty good at faking documents, if you remember. I made it look as if Jackie had left the country. I had a separate one-way flight booked back. When I got there, I burned his passport and flew back on mine the same day. No one even knew I'd gone.'

Tej was silent for a moment, letting the words sink in. 'All these years you let everyone think Jackie fucked us over when it was you all along.'

'If they hadn't decided to pull those houses down, no one would ever be any the wiser and I wouldn't be here now, doing this. But I knew, soon as you found out that it's Jackie's body they've dug up, you'd know he never went anywhere with the money and you'd start looking for whoever did take it. Wouldn't have taken you long to figure out who it was and then—'

'I'd kill you.'

'That's why I'm here. Just doing to you what you'd do to me. I've worked too hard the last thirty years to let you fuck it all up for me now.'

'With our money.'

'I did more with it than any of you lot would have.'

'Because you had more to do it with – by screwing us over, stealing from your mates – and murdering Jackie.'

'We'd have got, what, about eighty grand each if we'd split it? What would we have done with that? Spunked it away, that's what. It wouldn't have lasted long and then we'd have had to pull another job and then another. I wanted more than that, wanted to set myself up properly . . . and I had an opportunity. But eighty grand wasn't enough to get me in. Property was booming back then – still is – that's where the real money was. I needed half a million to go into partnership on a housing project. You know what they say – you got to speculate to accumulate.'

'You should've told the rest of us about it, so we could all have made money.'

Billy laughed. 'You might have gone for it, I'll give you that, but the rest of them? They wouldn't have invested a penny. They'd have blown the lot, being careful maybe, but still living it up for six months, possibly a year, and then having to pull another job. After the money disappeared, that's what I figured you'd all do, just find another bank to hit.'

'Except there never was another one after that. You soured everything and split the gang apart.'

Billy shrugged, the gun still on Tej. 'Would've happened sooner or later anyway.'

'You killed Jackie, left me in the shit and then just stood by and watched as the others came after me. You're the reason I had to keep hold of that.' Tej nodded at the pistol.

'It's worked out well for me now, though, eh?'

'We'll see.'

It was Billy's turn to frown.

'What about the others?' Tej went on. 'When they hear about Jackie, they'll know that he didn't run off with the money. They'll want answers as well.'

Billy was nodding, his grin returning. 'I thought about that. I could probably just pay them off. A hundred grand each, maybe? I can afford it if I have to – and I bet they'd welcome it now, when they could probably use it, rather than having blown it all back then. Jackie wasn't their brother, so why should they give a shit about that now? But you, on the other hand . . . money won't do it for you.'

'You got that fucking right.'

'That's why I knew I'd have to put you out of the picture. I thought I'd have to do the same to the others, then I figured on maybe paying them off . . . but *then* I had an even better idea.' His grin widened.

'Yeah? What's that, then?'

Keeping the gun steady, Billy reached his other hand inside his coat and pulled out a piece of paper and waved it in the air.

'Am I supposed to know what that is?'

'It's your suicide note,' Billy said. 'And a confession. Says, with Jackie's body being discovered, you knew it would come out that you killed him and took the money. You couldn't face that and decided to end it. I've apologised to your family for you. I'll leave it close to your body for someone to find.'

'What if I don't make it easy for you? Nobody'll believe I shot myself more than once.'

'I didn't get where I am by not thinking of all the angles. If it gets messy, I'll trash the place, make it look like a burglary gone wrong.'

'What about neighbours hearing the shots?'

'This is Southall, there's racket all around. People slamming doors, dropping plates – who even knows what a gunshot really sounds like and, even if they do, what do you think they're going to do about it?'

'Good point,' Tej said and stood up. 'I think I've heard enough.'

'What're you doing?' Billy extended his gun arm. 'Stay right where you are.'

'And why the fuck would I do that?'

'Because, if you don't, I'll shoot you.'

'I thought that was your plan anyway. Though, I don't know how you're going to do it without any bullets in the gun.'

'What the fuck you talking about?'

'You didn't check it, did you, when you went up and grabbed it from the drawer? You think I'd keep a loaded pistol lying around the house? If you knew anything at all about guns and bothered to look properly, you'd have seen there's no magazine in it. Don't believe me? Take a look. It goes in the bottom of the handgrip.'

Billy twisted his hand slightly, just enough that he could see the empty space in the base of the gun, where the magazine should have been. 'Shit!'

'Not feeling so tough now, are you?' Tej said. 'You think you can make it up the stairs, find the bullets and load the gun before I get to you? Go ahead, give it a try.' He began advancing towards his former friend.

'Stay there,' Billy yelled at him and then threw the gun at his head.

Tej pivoted out of the way as the gun whizzed by and landed with a thump on the sofa behind him. He turned back in time to see Billy pull a large black object from inside his coat.

'Just as well I brought this with me,' Billy said, sliding the protective cover off a large kitchen knife. Light flashed along its wicked-looking blade. 'My original plan was to have a drink, put you at your ease then come up behind you and put this in your neck, just like I did to Jackie. But then I thought the gun would be a nice touch. Suicide by gunshot. Guess being stabbed during a burglary's just as believable.' There was a manic gleam in his eyes as he now came around the coffee table, the blade looking bigger the closer it got.

Tej retreated to the sofa behind him.

'You got nowhere to go,' Billy said. It was true, Tej was backed into a corner. 'If you don't fight, I'll make it quick and painless. Otherwise, I can't promise anything.'

Tej felt around behind him on the sofa until his fingers touched cold metal and found what he was looking for. He grabbed the gun, brought it up and aimed it at Billy's chest.

'What the fuck you going to do with that, scare me to death? I just seen there ain't any bullets in it.'

'There's no magazine in it, that's right,' Tej said, in a flat tone.

'But you never did pay attention to how a pistol works. You were happy just pulling the trigger on a shotgun, making a loud noise and scaring people. See, the thing is, I put a round in the chamber before I took the magazine out . . . an insurance policy, in case I ever needed it – like right now. If you knew how to look, you'd have pulled back the slide enough to check the chamber and seen the bullet in there . . . but you didn't.' He watched Billy weigh up what he'd told him.

'You're bluffing.'

'Am I? Make a move and find out.'

Their hard stares bore into each other, the tension between them so thick Billy could have cut it with the knife in his hand.

'No,' Billy said, shaking his head. 'You're bullshitting, trying to pull a fast one. You got no move left but to try and fake me out – only I ain't falling for it. Time to join your brother.' And with that, Billy came at Tej, raising the knife he intended to plunge in him.

One step.

Tej stayed where he was, the gun steady.

Another step.

Tej pulled the trigger and shot Billy through the heart, stopping him in his tracks. Eyes wide in surprise, the knife fell from his hand, his legs buckled and he collapsed to the floor, dead before he hit the carpet.

Tej stepped forward, the gunshot still ringing in his ears, the smell of cordite acrid in his nostrils, and looked down at him.

'That's for Jackie, you piece of shit.'

Then he grimaced.

So much for a quiet night in. Now he had a body to get rid of.

Ā-LI-EN

HENRY CHANG

Illegal

She lay crumpled, a broken doll with a pretty Asian face. One long leg twisted back; her red miniskirt hiked from the fall. One shoeless foot. The back of her head flat from the impact, dark blood flowing toward the rainy gutter of 40th Road. Her eyes open, staring up at the roof ledge of the four-story building shadowy with security lights. She wore a puzzled look. Did she fall? Did she jump? Or was she pushed?

Chinatown, Queens.

Legal

Kasey Lee leaned back from the ALDA desk at the Women's Center, took a breath. She wasn't from Queens but the Asian Legal Defense Associates had started an investigation into the death of a local massage worker.

Kasey sipped her take-out *nai cha*, a meditation period moment. As ALDA's lead activista lawyer, she considered a list of questions for her upcoming interview with NYPD Community Affairs Officer Anthony Kong.

It was 9 a.m.

She had an hour.

The local precinct was crowded and busy with all kinds of Asian ethnicities existing together in commerce and cultures. Chinese, Indo-Pakis, Koreans, Thai, Japanese, Pacific Islanders. Seventy thousand Chinese here, many of them Taiwanese.

There were 120,000 Chinese in Queens and Flushing alone, aka 'the Chinese Manhattan'. A great place to live, but with sketchy areas all around. *Visitors were warned to avoid the housing projects.*

In the overall police picture, how much of the precinct's crime was Chinese? And what about Chinese organized crime in the precinct?

She nursed the remaining *nai cha*.

Law and Disorder

Sergeant Tony Kong paused at the escalator rolling down to the food court of the New World Mall, stepped aside and scanned the assembly below. At 8:30 a.m. the Flushing breakfast crowd was prominent; Chinese seniors with a take-out tea and a bun, coffee and a rice roll, college students on the run – the courts' fast-food kitchens warming up for the noon-day lunch crunch.

He spotted them right away: two white guys, Lieutenant Dick, Sergeant Murphy, nursing coffees and croissants at an edge table.

They'd brought his pay, a cash-money envelope taped to the underside of their table. Clandestine police, undercover, internal affairs. Kong stepped onto the down escalator, immediately caught their eyes. *Two hours left in the shift.*

He casually strolled to their table, joined them, ready to spill on the overnight shift.

The lootenant started first with 'So whaddaya got, kid?'

'So,' Tony began, 'the On Loks got money in the karaoke clubs and they got the Dragons providing protection.'

'They're not just in Flushing?' Dick asked.

'The clubs are spread out,' Tony, acting nonchalant, 'some out of the precinct.'

'What about the bars?' from Murphy.

'And the gambling?' smirked Dick.

'It's connected to Chinatown stuff in Manhattan and Brooklyn,' continued Tony.

'What's membership like?' frowned Dick.

'I've seen like twenty guys, but feels like it could be a hundred, if you count other boroughs and chapters.'

Murphy, drinking his coffee: 'Where?'

'Sunset Park. Grand Concourse. Lower Eastside, Manhattan Chinatown.'

'What the fuck!' from Dick.

They exchanged looks.

'Everywhere,' from Murphy.

'Bars and restaurants,' said Tony, 'even a pharmacy chain.'

'And you've seen Fung? or Kam?'

Tony paused. 'Not yet, I'm working on it.'

'Badass,' noted Murphy. 'OK, what else you got?'

'I got an interview at nine, talking about precinct crimes and Asians.'

'Kasey Lee,' grinned Murphy. 'Some dumb guy.'

'It's a *she*, lady lawyer,' from Tony.

'Whatever.'

'And if she asks about the massage girl?' asked Tony.

'You read the report,' frowned Dick. 'She jumped. Trying to escape the raid.'

'Sad.' Murphy shrugged.

'Yeah, sad,' Tony agreed. 'But now there's allegations against the precinct.'

'Stay the fuck off it, right?' snapped Dick.

'But—'

'No buts! She *jumped*. That's it.'

'Yeah,' frowned Tony.

'No, *really*. Shut the fuck up about that girl. It's gonna be *resolved*.'

'Right, gonna be resolved,' added Dick.

'*Suicidal*, got it? Accidental at best,' sneered Murphy.

'Stay off it, right?' warned Dick.

'Right,' Tony shrugged.

Dick took a breath. 'Just give me the bad lootenant Fung. And Kam the sneaky sarge.'

'Fung and Kam, got it?'

They caught their collective breath, until Murphy exclaimed, 'HOW ABOUT THEM FUCKIN' RANGERS, HAH?'

They gave Tony the nod and a pat on the back before they disappeared up the escalator.

Tony reached under the table and ripped off his cash envelope. Pocketed it, his weekly pay.

He still had a half hour before his appointment at the lady lawyer's office.

Community Affairs

Sergeant Kong simply strolled up and showed his badge, an NYPD gold shield.

'Thanks for coming today,' Kasey said with a small smile.

'My pleasure,' Tony answered, taking a seat.

'How are you in involved in Community Affairs?' she asked.

'The department promotes local sports events, like basketball tournaments and softball games. We sponsor teenager's trips to Shea Stadium and tennis camps with youth groups. Also, cultural events like Chinese New Year, lion dances, the Moon Cake Festival. Stuff like that.'

'*Very* involved,' she said, impressed.

'We work with the local churches, which provide free tutoring in many instances.' He was happy to share and promote. 'The congregants also help keep an eye on community trends, promptly reporting crimes and suspicious behavior.'

'All noble, and *righteous* neighborhood services.' Quietly cheering him on.

'Builds connections within communities we serve.'

They take a collective breath as Tony watches Kasey jotting down notes.

'Let's talk about local crime,' she suggested.

'Sure.' *His territory.*

'What type of criminal activity do you face daily?'

'Well, we have everything from pickpocket teams working Main Street, to shoplifters and grifters. Occasionally victims get robbed, mugged. The usual street crime elements.'

'What about drugs, prostitution?' Her earnestness became more focused.

'Those activities occur in certain areas. We have special units dedicated to those.'

'Like the vice squad?' she quipped.

'Something like that.'

'What about *Chinese* organized crime?' she pressed.

The smile left his face. 'Well, the gang's all here. The Dragons, the Tigers, the Ghosts – you might have heard about those

271

– they got chapters throughout the City's Chinatowns.' *Rolling off his tongue like a poem.* 'Weapons come from down South, so they're selling street muscle.'

She shook her head at the information.

'There's illegal booze and cigarettes. And dealing with tribal nations folks too. Street soldiers *everywhere.*'

'What about *organizations*?' she went deeper. 'Like who owns and runs the karaoke bars and nightclubs? The mahjong clubs.'

'There are traditional crime groups, like Triads overseas. The Taipei group. The Chiu Chao Brotherhood. The On Leongs and the Hip Sings, old school, local and nationwide.'

'Yes, they run massage parlors,' she remembered, 'and oversee drugs and prostitution, right?'

Tony paused. 'Whoa. Not sure I can comment on some of those things.'

'OK, then let's talk about the massage parlor industry,' she challenged.

Tony hesitated but shrugged, *OK.*

'What crime group runs this area? And did a police raid recently cause the death of a masseuse?'

'You're referring to the lady,' Tony clarified, 'who jumped to her death recently?'

'From the Plaza building? She *fell.* Or was *pushed.*'

'The *official* report is she *jumped.*'

'Not she *fell* to her death?'

'No, she *leapt* to her death.'

'NOT she was *pushed* to her death?'

'No.' Kong took a breath.

'So the brother says,' Kasey presses, a surprise.

'The brother?'

'From China.'

'No, he's not in the report.' Playing it off.

'Yes, but he's made some statements.'

Tony shook his head slowly. 'I haven't heard any of them.'

'He was meeting her in eight days, coming from Shenzhen. She was happy, so why would she go out a window and jump to her death?'

'I can't comment on that,' said Tony.

'He said his sister told him she'd been sexually assaulted by a cop. A white cop. And that he was threatening her.'

Tony gritted his teeth and frowned.

'The brother thinks a cop pushed her to her death,' she continued.

'Can't comment,' he repeated. 'Sorry.'

'I'm going to need a copy of the NYPD's incident report. Like, who were the officers on duty during the raid? And what about the brother's assertion that she'd been sexually assaulted by a cop? Who was trying to turn her into an informant?'

'Sorry.' He knew the interview was over, tried to think of a gracious way out.

Kasey beat him to it. 'Don't be sorry: I *get* it. No, thanks for your help anyway.'

'Wasn't much help.' He stood up.

'Please call me if you think of anything,' as she handed him her ALDA business card.

'Sure,' he said. 'Take care.'

'Likewise.' She watched as Tony left the Women's Center as abruptly and as quietly as he'd arrived, never looking back. A cop at the end of his shift?

She checked her watch. *Her* work was just beginning.

Crime and Punishment

Kong strolled through the three-story plaza complex on 36th Avenue. Modern, neat, complex in more ways than one. This was clear even in the setting sun.

At one entrance a bright poster featured a young Eurasian couple getting a relaxing shoulder massage under a pagoda-motif Temple Garden SPA. *Heated stones, herbal treatments, the works.*

Tony knew the Garden SPA was part of a hot-sheet hotel and hooker-massage operation in Flushing; Hookers 'R' Us, 24/7.

There was another poster at the steps leading to the second floor. A pretty Asian face above a price list for foot rubs, body rubs, a combo rub. He could hear faint music from above.

He'd come clean. No gun, no weapons. No recording devices. Undercover, straight up, regular guy. He had a ready story: *Just dropped by after work for a drink, maybe some fun. Gambling later. Pussy? Who knows?*

•

The SPA bar lounge is crowded and noisy, mostly Asian male faces with drinks in hand, grooving with the low-key music driving the scene. *Maybe sixty people.*

Cute girls in skimpy outfits offer free shots of lesser liquor from Jameson bottles.

Tony takes a sip of his cheap liquor mix, scans the raucous gathering. *What's on the menu around here?* A crowd of business types and yuppies, office workers and local players.

It doesn't take long to spot them, the group of Asian cops, a couple of them still in uniform in the side section of the bar. Among them the White Shirt Commanders with Lieutenant Fung, and Sergeant Kam.

Tony takes another sip, grimaces, looks back to see the bad

lootenant fingering one of the bar girls wearing a regretful look on her face. The sick sarge Kam, sends a blowjob grin to someone in the background.

Tony grabs one of the Jameson girls, slips her a ten-dollar tip for a 'selfie,' capturing in background the crew of crooked cops led by Fung and Kam.

'Thanks, baby,' offers Tony. He remembers the words from Dick and Murphy:

Get me fuckin' Fung, and Kam.

He trades his mix for a shot of the fake Jameson, letting the girl dance away as he watches several of the cops disappear out a back door EXIT. When Fung and Kam follow, so does he, discovering it's a passageway to another section of the floor. Serviced by a separate bank of elevators. A separate section operating a multi-table massage business, backed up with cubicles for 'lap' dances and blowjobs. The cops gather outside the cubicles where another cute Jameson girl is explaining 'the hundred-dollar deal includes a twenty-dollar drink!'

'And a blowjob!' someone shouts. All the cops laugh, spreading out now.

Kam muscles one of the massage girls into a cubicle. Her muffled pleas and protests are heard below Fung's chortle. All the cops laugh, *men with guns.*

Fung throws a smirk in his direction, and Kong knows it's time to exit, turning for the elevators. On the way down, wishing he could spit out the cheap drinks he's swallowed, he pulls ALDA's business card. Remembering Kasey and a meeting that could have, *should* have, been better.

Clues

Kasey needed the police case file, which ALDA could request under the Freedom of Information Act. *Could take a while.* Meanwhile, she reviewed news footage from friends at Sino Cast News.

The victim's brother, in a video from Shenzen, stated:

'A *gwai lo, white* cop who was trying to turn her into an informant, sexually assaulted her as well. Yes, she had some pressures, sure, but not to jump off a building. I have no doubt that the police have a hand in it.'

She considered that for a long moment—*bad cops*—until her business number pinged. It was a text message from Sergeant Kong: 'NYPD CORRUPTION TAKE DOWN. Watch 6 p.m. news tomorrow.'

Intrigued, she texted him back. To no avail, no answer.

Kong on duty, she guessed. It's a shady shift.

And the police have a hand in it, the brother's words echoed . . .

Rat

He drove around the neighborhood, Francis Lewis Boulevard, and passed Cunningham Park. A short drive from Flushing, past the big Chinese supermarket, and down the avenues. An evasion route getting home, making sure no one was tailing him.

Almost there, he killed the headlights, parked across from his house. Number 127.

He waited a minute in the dark before exiting the car. When he got near the pathway, he'd expected the security strobe would light up his approach. There was a lumpish shape near the steps that looked like a wet sock, which upon a closer look was a dead rat. With a carpenter's nail driven thru its head. *A clear signal.*

He stepped around it, not looking back. He'd understood that the job came with risks, but he'd never expected that other cops might want him taken out bad enough to cross that blue line and blood lines.

He keyed home, secured all the windows.

The threat was clear; he'd have to move. They'd find him as long as he stayed in the city. He'd need his cop pension, so wherever he moved or fled to, he could still be found. Unless he changed his identity—the Feds were good at setting that up. He'd probably wind up running a take-out joint somewhere in Arizona or Iowa, wherever.

He wanted to laugh but then didn't think it was all that funny.

Video

Eyewitness News at 6 p.m. came to a crime report that featured corrupt NYPD cops, many Asian, under arrest for extorting Asian massage and sex operations in Flushing, Queens.

She saw Kong for a split second in a karaoke club bar photo. CRIME VICTIMS are urged to call 1-718-888-8080.

The news piece was a minute long. She'd recorded it, played it back twice.

Bad cops. Massage parlors. Sex. Mostly Asians. A lieutenant and a sergeant. *Busted.* Great for Internal Affairs victories, she guessed. But what about the dead massage girl? And others like her?

And Tony Kong not answering his phone.

Other voices from Yellow Canary, another women's activist group, challenged, 'This has been a systemic silencing of voices for the convenience of those who prey on them, and others who are uncomfortable to acknowledge them. No sex worker should have to fear law enforcement or our district attorney officers.

'We demand justice in her name.

'Arrests of Asian New Yorkers on prostitution-related charges have exploded during the last several years, from twelve to three hundred thirty-six. A coalition of sex workers and trafficking survivors are organizing to decriminalize the adult sex trade and demanding an end to police raids on massage establishments. The NYPD's Force Investigation Division, assigned to thefts in custody, should investigate, because the victim felt harassed and intimidated by police.'

Another coalition group, Asian Song, said: 'The victim's brother has called for an end to massage establishment raids,' adding, 'immigrant sex workers have so long been made invisible. Sex workers are forced to perform as either victim or criminal, to be pitied or punished and nothing in between. They are not allowed to speak for themselves. In the past, when workers were harassed or assaulted by others and went to the police for help, they never received it.'

In response the NYPD stated its goal to end prostitution conditions has 'shifted focus on enforcement operations to target pimps and johns primarily during anti-prostitution investigations and arrests, and on the closure of locations through civil actions taken against landlords who are complicit in the illegal business of prostitution.

'Whenever arrests for prostitution are made, they are delivered to a diversion court where they are offered help and services.

'The NYPD understands that some of the women involved in prostitution are being forced, coerced, or otherwise made to against their will, and the department offers services and assistance to victims of human trafficking.'

Only darkness beckoned outside her window and tomorrow would be another fight.

Justice

In Queens Court, Kasey rose before the judge and spoke earnestly.

'Your Honor, I'm here today to represent the dismissal of these two hundred cases, and instead focus on the health and safety needs of women workers in the sex industry. Many of these workers, these *women*, are victims themselves, forced into prostitution and drugs. The City should not be stressing precious resources to incarcerate and prosecute poor and victimized people. And, Your Honor, our good mayor *himself* is supportive of this same decriminalization.'

The judge paused, held on a few extra seconds, shook his head.

'In *spite* of that *last* remark,' he smiled, 'I actually concur.'

Kasey took a huge breath as the judge went on:

'Well said, madam. Yes, I concur. Those cases shall be dismissed.'

He hammered the gavel.

The sound made her think of Sergeant Anthony Kong.

•

She still needed inside information, a police point of view, that proved to be elusive. She called Kong's number but got no response.

After a week Kong's telephone went straight to tone, then completely dead. When she inquired at precinct level, the official response was 'he'd been reassigned' and there was 'no further information available.'

NYPD.

Not sure why, she worried about Kong in that shady cop world, where a Chinese woman had died, unjustly. In spite of legal action, she had yet to view the police case file of the deceased masseuse.

She awaited the trials of the arrested police officers, hoping they'd offer some clues. Until then the case remained in limbo.

The Queens DA's office stated, 'It's sad and tragic but the prosecutor found no misconduct in her death.

'Attempting to flee apprehension by law enforcement officers is a result of her unlawful conduct. Prosecutors recommend that the case be closed.'

•

ā-li-en

THE LONG CON

NADINE MATHESON

Now

I *thought* that I had blood on my hands. The crime was committed so long ago that I'd convinced myself that it didn't happen and was no more than the remnants of a nightmare. The woman that I was before had to disappear. I'd walked away, changed my name and left that part of my life in an opaque past, but I should have known better. There is no such thing as a perfect crime, and I don't know why I thought that my secrets would stay buried.

It was handled the old-fashioned way. Like a scene from a 1970s conspiracy movie starring Gene Hackman. I stood in the hallway and watched as a brown envelope made its way under the thin gap between the hardwood floor and the door. This was six hours after the postman had already delivered his post, in the letterbox, in the communal area four floors down. I could hear the ticking of the kitchen clock, which seemed to grow louder as I held my breath and watched the edges of the envelope bend and curl as it met the resistance of the dark green doormat. It was probably nothing. I prayed that it was nothing. Junk mail or maybe someone had made a mistake and delivered this envelope to the wrong flat.

I needed it to be nothing.

I took two steps forward and pressed my right ear against the door. I wasn't sure what I was expecting to hear. Perhaps the sound of someone breathing or an apologetic voice asking for the envelope back because they had the wrong address. I heard nothing. I'm not a woman who scares easily but fear gripped me as I slowly moved my head and looked through the peephole in the door. The hallway was empty. Only the distorted door of number 53 stared back at me, but I didn't experience a feeling of euphoria, only a growing sense of dread.

'Come on, Julia. Pull yourself together.'

My body reacted with an involuntary shiver as I spoke my old name out loud. What was it about that envelope that had triggered my brain to revert to the identity I'd long ago shredded? It was probably nothing. I *needed* it to be nothing, but it was as if I instinctively knew that the life I'd carefully curated for myself was about to be ripped apart. I took two deep breaths, bent down and picked up the envelope. The envelope was light in my hand as though it contained nothing.

'It's junk,' I said out loud, to no one. I ran my fingers over the back of the envelope, absent of finger marks, tea stains or smears of dirt. I turned it over and read the two words that had been written in black ink. I didn't recognize the handwriting, but I recognized the name.

Julia Carter.

It felt as though someone had placed a pair of firm, calloused hands around my neck and squeezed. I had run away from that name four years ago. No one who I now associated with knew me as Julia Carter.

Two thoughts ran on a loop through my brain as I ran my thumb over the black ink. Someone knew who I used to be, and that person knew where I lived. Two questions followed these thoughts: Who posted the envelope? What did they want?

•

There were two 5 x 7 photographs inside the envelope.

My pulse began to race and I began to hyperventilate as I sat on the hallway floor and stared at the first photograph of a man standing next to a blue BMW X5 in the middle of a petrol station forecourt. It was a man that I had known. A man that I'd once committed my life to.

I checked for signs that the photograph had been photoshopped or had been taken years ago, but that faint flicker of hope disappeared as soon as I looked at the second photograph.

'No, it can't be him.'

But it was *him*, standing next to the newspaper rack in front of the petrol station shop as he stared at his phone. The skin on the back of my neck prickled with heat as I brought the photograph closer to my face and squinted at the front pages of the newspapers. I couldn't see the date, but I could clearly see who was on the front page. A government minister who had been the talking point of every news bulletin for the past three days after she'd been caught accepting bribes. I don't know why I started laughing.

I've been a lot of things. A liar and a thief. Four years ago, I thought I'd added murderer to that list.

Then

'Julia. Don't just sit there. Say something.'

The urgency in David's voice was irritating. He'd spent the

past twelve minutes sitting anxiously on the edge of the sofa. He'd taken off his blue Hermes tie and wrapped and then unwrapped it around his hand as he told me what he'd done. Even though he was begging me for forgiveness, David wouldn't look at me.

I turned around to see what was grabbing his attention.

He'd been focusing his gaze on the section of wallpaper behind me that had started to peel away from the wall, as frayed as his nerves. That's when I knew that something had gone very, very wrong. David didn't do nerves. David did swagger and confidence that straddled the fine line into arrogance. He was good looks and eyes that sparkled with fake intelligence. He was quick to talk and even faster to act.

'You weren't supposed to touch that money,' I said as I picked up the wine bottle from the coffee table and emptied it into my glass.

'I know.' David's voice was muffled as he bent his head in what I hoped was shame.

'It didn't belong to you.' I could feel the tension gripping the muscles in my neck as I placed the empty wine bottle onto the table. I took a large mouthful of wine as though I was trying to swallow the unspoken truth that the money wasn't mine either.

'I know. I know. I just thought . . .'

'You just thought what?' I snapped. 'That you could take a million quid and turn it into three or four million?'

'I've done it before.'

'And you've lost it before.'

David raised his head but again he didn't look at me.

I took a deep breath as I tried to hold onto my rising temper. 'Do you have any idea the position you've placed me in?'

David didn't answer. Instead, he stood up, walked over to the fireplace that had never been lit, and picked up the bottle of single malt whisky that had been sitting on the mantelpiece untouched since Christmas. I watched as he pulled out the cork and drank straight from the bottle. 'I'm going to get the money back,' he said unconvincingly.

'Oh really?'

I didn't bother to stop myself from laughing at his declaration. I stood up and grabbed the whisky bottle from David's hand and placed it back on the mantelpiece next to a bronzed statuette of Rodin's *The Thinker*.

'I'll get it back,' David said as he wiped his mouth with the back of his hand.

He still wouldn't look at me and it was starting to piss me off.

'You're no more capable of getting that money back than a headless donkey,' I said.

'It's not as bad as you think.'

'Oh, I think that it's a lot worse than I think.'

The trouble with my marriage to David was that, despite the lows that often ended up with him in a pathetic heap at my feet, there were highs where he did win big at the casino or pulled off a con so elaborate I wanted to erect a shrine in his honour.

David always thought he was one step ahead of everyone else and that no one could pull off a better long con than him.

Of course, we'd first met *because* of a con.

We'd been chasing the same mark in Dublin, a self-made millionaire who'd made his money setting up discount sportswear shops and by investing in a second division Spanish football club. David was good, but I was better. It took David two days to realize that I'd made him part of the con and had walked away with over two and a half million euros.

Five days later I tracked him down and offered him fifty thousand euros as a thank you and an apology. He accepted the apology, told me that he was impressed and invited me to dinner. Six months later, David proposed. I ignored that little voice in my head telling me to walk away, because I thought that I was in love and that David was the one. We were honest about our deceptions, but we never deceived each other.

Not in a way that mattered.

The first engagement ring that he bought me was a fake, and the replacement was stolen. He won the ring that I'm wearing now in a card game that took place in the back of an Indian takeaway on Brick Lane. I'd lost count of the number of favours that I'd called in just to make sure that the next job David was involved in wouldn't be the one that led to his body being found in the middle of Epping Forest.

•

The sound of children screaming with excitement drifted through the open windows. A cool breeze was circulating through the room, but every item of clothing on my body felt tight and uncomfortable. The air in the room felt thinner and hotter as I waited for David to tell me that maybe, just maybe, he had a plan to get himself out of this mess. Instead, he said:

'This is not entirely my fault.'

'Excuse me?'

David walked around me with that annoying swagger of his, straightened his jacket and ran a hand over his beard. He had the look of a man who'd found a way to dig himself out of a hole. Probably, by throwing me in it.

'You know what I'm like.'

I didn't think that after six years of marriage he would have the audacity to think, let alone say out loud the thing that he said next.

'You should never have told me about the money.'

I bit the inside of my lower lip so hard that I could taste blood. He was right. I knew exactly what he was like. He was the man who'd gambled away the proceeds of a fraud that I'd spent months working on because he had a good feeling about the number 28 on the roulette table. I'd lost count of the number of times that I'd bailed him out of a debt.

'Are you seriously standing there telling me that this is *my* fault?'

'You know what I'm like,' he repeated.

It was then that I forced David to look at me as I picked up the glass, poured the dregs of wine over his head, then picked up the empty wine bottle and threw it at the wall behind him.

I didn't flinch as the glass exploded and tiny shards caught my cheek.

'What the hell do you think you're doing?' David shouted as he put his right hand to his neck and wiped away a trickle of blood that had already stained the collar of his shirt.

I felt as though I was being submerged under water as I struggled to regulate my breathing. I could almost see the anger leaving my body and surrounding me like a thick red mist. I don't know whether it was the arrogance in David's tone that had triggered me or the fact that he was more than happy to leave me in the shit.

I'd never been scared of David. I knew how to deal with his fluctuating moods, but the man who was now looking at me was almost unrecognizable. *This* David was looking at me with cold hatred, as if I meant nothing to him.

•

I wasn't expecting him to hit me. That's why I didn't scream. The impact of the slap shocked me. I knew, in that instant, that whatever David had done was a lot more serious than gambling away a million pounds of a gangster's money.

His face grew pale and his eyes widened with disbelief as he looked down at the hand that had struck me. He looked up at me with a pained expression. His lower lip trembled. I thought he was going to cry.

'I'm sorry. I don't know what—'

'Shut up.'

'I–I'm so sorry.'

I turned to walk away but David grabbed me, spun me around and squeezed me hard against his chest. The stench of wine, whisky and aftershave clung to the small hairs in my nose. Bile rose in my stomach. David squeezed tighter as I tried to wrestle myself out of his grip.

'You're hurting me,' I said.

David's hot breath whistled down my ear. 'Let me fix it. I can fix it. I can get the money back.'

'Let go of me.'

I'm not sure if David heard me or if he'd just got tired of holding onto me, but I felt the muscles in his arms relax as he let go and stepped back.

Then he turned his back to me.

•

It didn't happen the way that it did in the movies. David didn't fall in slow motion or let out a blood-curdling scream that alerted the neighbours. It was quick.

It was just once. I hit him once on the back of the head, with the statuette of *The Thinker*.

His knees didn't buckle, and he didn't collapse. Not right away.

His body grew rigid, and then he fell, like a tree that had been cut down. His head cracked against the edge of the coffee table, then hit the parquet flooring with a hard thud, and then he was still.

'David,' I said softly as the statuette fell from my hand and landed at my feet.

David didn't answer and he didn't move. There was nothing.

I sniffed the air with the expectation of breathing in the copper-infused odour of spilled blood but there was nothing. I knelt and placed my fingers against the spot where the statuette had struck David's head. I pressed my fingers gently against his hair until I felt his scalp. I pulled my hand away and peered at my fingers, but the only thing that I could see was the sheen of the hair oil that David religiously applied to hold back his impending baldness.

'David,' I said again. Louder this time as I crawled around David's body.

His face had paled, his mouth was closed but his eyes were open. I felt sick as I saw the thin veins of blood that had spread across the white of his eyes. I placed my shaking fingers against his neck. There was no pulse.

'You can't be dead,' I whispered as I shook him by the shoulders and waited for his eyes to flicker back to life, but there was nothing.

•

I closed the curtains and sat in the darkness with David's body and worked through my options.

One. I could call the police and tell them that David had attacked me and that I had defended myself. They would believe me, but that wouldn't stop them from arresting me and asking me questions. I did not need the police digging into my business. Second option. I had to clean up my own mess. I had to get rid of the body. And I had to do it myself.

One hour had turned into two and I knew, that on average,

rigor mortis appeared in a body within two to four hours. Pins and needles ran through my muscles as I painfully eased myself from the sofa and knelt next to David. I wanted to close his bloodshot eyes. It's not as easy as it looks. The thin skin of his eyelids kept springing back in defiance. It took five attempts before I managed to close those dead eyes.

I tried to move quickly but it was hard to move fifteen stones of dead weight. My body was drenched in a cold sweat. I stripped David of his clothes. I'd learnt the hard way that the best way to get rid of evidence was to burn it. I also needed to burn him.

•

I was only gone for four, five minutes at the most. I needed bin bags, plastic sheeting and latex gloves. Disposing of bodies was not something I did regularly. The roll of plastic sheeting had been left behind by the decorators and was in a cupboard in the utility room at the back of the kitchen.

I was pulling the latex gloves out of the box when I heard the sound of glass crashing against tiles and the front door slamming hard against the wall. My heart started to beat so fast that I thought I was having a heart attack. I ran out of the kitchen and into the hallway. Shattered green glass that had once formed a vase crunched under my feet. I braced myself against the wall as I slipped on the slimy stalks of the lucky bamboo now scattered on the floor.

I made my way towards the living room.

I gripped the edge of the door frame so tightly that it was surprising that the bones of my knuckles didn't pierce through my skin.

David's clothes were gone. The bronze statuette of *The Thinker* was gone. David was gone.

•

How?

Had I made a mistake? I honestly thought I'd killed David, but I couldn't ignore the fact that there was no body.

David had played me. That was the only thing that made sense.

I thought back to all the cons I'd planned over the years. There hadn't been one where I'd faked my own death, but could I say the same about David?

I closed the front door and made sure it was deadlocked. I didn't need any more surprises.

I went upstairs.

The day after we'd moved into this house, David had sat down with me and showed me a metal filing box where he kept his most important documents, just in case something happened to him. Well, something *had* happened to him and I needed answers.

I opened David's wardrobe, pulled out the box from the top shelf, sat down on the bed, and opened it.

The box was empty.

Passport, birth certificate, medical and financial documents. It was all gone and so was the fifty thousand pounds that I kept in my bedside table.

I got up and began a search of the house.

•

I found what I was looking for in the bottom of the bathroom bin.

A tablet blister pack.

I carefully pushed back the aluminium foil over the creased plastic capsules. It took me three attempts to pronounce the name written on the pack.

'What the fuck is Flunitrazepam?'

David was the sort of man who made a song and dance about

being ill with a simple cold. I would have remembered if he'd been ill enough to need tablets.

I took out my phone. Moments later, I had my answer.

Flunitrazepam was the medical name for Rohypnol.

My anger mounted as I scrolled through the information.

Apparently, it took twenty to thirty minutes to feel the effects of Rohypnol, but it was quicker if ingested with alcohol. I replayed the image of David drinking whisky straight from the bottle.

I swiped through the side effects.

Impaired mobility. Slow heart rate. Suppressed breathing and bloodshot eyes that often remained open.

'He roofied himself,' I said out loud.

I checked the time on my phone. It had been over four hours since I'd hit David on the head. It may have been David's plan to fake his own death, but you can't plan for everything. People are unpredictable. David knew that I had a temper, but he had no idea that I was going to hit him with *The Thinker*.

Then again, a good con artist needs to have the ability to adapt to a fast-moving situation.

Perhaps, it was his plan all along to engineer a fight with me, and for that to lead to a situation where I would strike him. Or perhaps he'd pretend to stumble, pretend to hit his head against the mantelpiece.

Either way, I'd watched David motionless on the floor and I'd believed that I'd killed him. But maybe I hadn't hit him as hard as I thought. I'd checked his pulse in a panic – perhaps, that's why I'd failed to register the fluttering heartbeat that must have been there, all but disguised by the effects of the Rohypnol.

I sat on the bed and tried to make sense of the million and one questions running through my head. A police siren sounded in the distance and my body reacted as though I'd been tasered. My senses were on high alert.

What now?

David had taken and lost a million pounds that didn't belong to me. I was supposed to hand that money over in five days, to the sort of people who would be less than understanding. That meant I now had to find a way to make a million pounds in next to no time.

I needed a short con.

I always had a list of potential marks ready, but my mind couldn't focus, not with so many questions unanswered.

Why would David want to fake his own death?

Why would he want to run away from me?

Why would he put me in a position where my life was at risk?

One word penetrated my brain like a surgeon's drill. Payback. Was this payback for when I'd stolen *his* con and walked away with two million euros in cash?

'No,' I murmured. 'No way. Not after all this time.'

I had a fleeting thought that maybe, just maybe, this was part of a bigger plan and that David would call and explain.

But I wasn't a fool.

David was on the move and I had no idea what his next steps would be.

But I knew mine.

•

Two days later I declared David missing. What else could I do? It was my only option. I couldn't just disappear; at least not yet. I told the police that David hadn't returned from a canoeing trip and that he'd last been seen on the River Avon in Bristol. Conveniently, I had a witness who gave a statement about the afternoon David's yellow canoe disappeared. The police had no idea that the witness had been bought and paid for by a woman who may have looked like me but was not me.

I dug into my emergency savings – money even David didn't know I had – paired it with a rushed short con that netted me three hundred thousand, and somehow managed to pay back the money that David had said he'd lost.

And then I disappeared and became someone new.

Two years later the court declared David dead and I received three large payouts from the life insurance policies that I'd taken out in David's name and with only one beneficiary.

Everything had worked out well, all things considered.

Now

James is speaking but I do not believe a word that is coming out of his mouth. I should believe him – after all, I have paid him for this information. I couldn't find the man in the photograph on my own.

A month ago, I paid £2,500 for the 'General Non-Criminal Investigation Package'. This included a tracing and people search, financial investigation and, because I was paying cash, a free counter-surveillance sweep of my home and office.

Six days ago, James called me at the office, something that I had specifically told him not to do. Recent revelations meant that my package had to be upgraded to the 'Spousal Criminal Investigation Package'. I didn't ask what those revelations were. I just needed to know where David was.

'Are you sure that you don't want a drink?' James says.

I shake my head and say no.

'Each to their own.'

There's a glass tumbler filled with whisky on the table. The glass hasn't been cleaned properly and I cannot take my eyes away from the greasy fingerprint on the side of the glass. James swirls the double measure of amber liquid around and raises the glass. I look away as his lips cover the fingerprint.

This is not my sort of place. I don't *do* old man pubs in the back end of Stepney. I should be at home on the sofa with a large glass of Pinot Noir watching *Newsnight* or catching up with the last two episodes of *The Walking Dead*. I should not be chasing the shadows of dead men. Instead, I am sitting in a corner booth where the cracked burgundy leather is peeling away from the cushions and splinters from the rough wooden table leg have laddered my tights; twice. I had dressed so that I would fit in and go unnoticed, but there is nothing that I could have worn that would have made me fit in. Even my cheapest clothes are too expensive for this place.

I cough as the smell of rotten eggs and burnt cabbage makes its way from the direction of the men's toilet and catches in my throat. The man who has left the toilets and re-joined the two other men standing by the bar, nursing their pints and watching the football highlights, doesn't turn around as I cough again. I cough a third time and catch the eye of a woman, wearing too much make-up, who has been talking and flirting with a man who looks at least thirty years older than her. If I had to guess, I would say that she was pushing thirty-five. She's wearing a purple fake-fur coat and a low-cut black top. She looks like a very cheap and haggard version of me. As she runs her fingers through her matted black hair and adjusts the front of her cheap wig, she gives me a look which I interpret as *you should not be here. This is my place.*

'I'm going to get another. Probably a packet of crisps too,' James says as he squeezes out of the booth and stands up. Tonight is the first time that I have met James, and he's not what I expected. When I was typing *private investigators* into Google, I imagined a middle-aged, overweight, white man with pock-marked skin, thinning hair and wearing a shiny, cheap, grey suit. I'd looked around the pub twice before I realized that the slender, good-looking, mixed race man in his early thirties, wearing a dark-blue Ralph Lauren jumper and black jeans was waiting for me.

Five minutes ago, he'd handed me a brown envelope.

•

'I take it that you haven't opened it yet.'

I look up and see James standing next to me. I shake my head as he places two glasses on the table. A double whisky for him and a double vodka for me. He's forgotten the crisps.

'The glass is clean,' he says as he sits back down.

'I didn't ask for a drink.'

My tone is harsh and condescending and I immediately regret my words even though he doesn't seem to be bothered. He's probably used to it. Clients not wanting to believe that the seed of doubt, planted months ago, has grown into a looming tree of truth.

'I don't believe that he's alive and has been living in Aberdeen,' I say as I pick up my glass and gulp down half of the vodka. The vodka is cheap and tastes like it was distilled in the men's toilet. It burns my chest. 'David hated Scotland. Said that it brought back bad memories of boarding school and hill walking with his dad.'

I'm rambling now but I can't help it. I'm on autopilot. Ready to explain why my late husband's parents were not at our wedding. Why he had no family. Why I have no family. It's a well-rehearsed story that is a lie but sounds more like the truth every time I repeat it.

'His dad died when he was sixteen and his mother walked out and moved to Canada when he was two,' I say. 'He didn't know her. He had no one until he met me.'

James raises an eyebrow but, to his credit, he doesn't laugh in my face. I can see the pity in his eyes though. He shifts in his seat and his knee brushes against mine.

'David's real name is Clayton.' James's eyes don't leave mine as his mobile phone starts to ring. He takes the phone from his coat pocket and mutes the call without looking at the screen. I divert my eyes away from him as he places the phone on the table next to the glass of whisky. I look at the phone to see *'Sabrina – missed call (4)'* before the screen goes black. I wonder briefly who Sabrina is and why he's avoiding her.

'Excuse me.' The shock in my voice is convincing because this is news to me. David has always been David. I never had any reason to believe that he had been someone else.

'You could have made a mistake.'

Even to my own ears, the words sound stupid and unconvincing. James smiles as he leans across the table. He's so close to me that I can smell the whisky on his breath and the spicy aftershave on his skin.

'No mistake.'

I clench my jaw and nod at James to continue.

'Three years ago, David or Clayton met and married a woman called Olivia. The poor thing thought that she'd finally found love again after her husband ran off with the nanny.'

'What did he do?' I ask.

'Cleared out . . . Sorry, *stole* nearly eight hundred grand from her savings account and sold her house without her realizing. Luckily, it wasn't the home they lived in but a second house that she rented out. It was in the nice bit of Wandsworth, near the common. He walked away with nearly two million.'

I'm angry, but not because of what he did to that woman. She was clearly an idiot. I'm angry because at no point did I realize that all I'd ever been to David was the mark in his own long con.

'Where did he go?'

I downed the remainder of the vodka.

James doesn't answer. The sound of the pub door being slammed open reverberates around the pub. The man who walks in, his coat covered with a dusting of snow, stops in the middle of the pub and looks straight at me. He's looking at me, but I can tell that he can't quite place me. He takes a step towards our table but stops when there's a collected groan from the men watching the football. West Ham have failed to score a penalty and have lost 3-1 to Brighton. Someone swears and their mate bangs their empty pint glass on the bar in frustration. The man turns away and heads towards the bar where his pint is already waiting for him.

I release the breath that I hadn't realized I was holding.

'Where did he go?' I ask again, aware that James is now watching the man who walked into the pub a moment ago.

'Melbourne,' he says quietly as he turns his attention back to me. 'He changed his name to Christopher Peake and married a woman, a widow, called Hannah Stenson.'

'He married again?'

'It was brief,' James says. 'Ten months, and then he disappeared with all of her savings. Left her with nothing. She was found dead seven weeks after he left. The report said suicide, but her family said that she was a strict Catholic and that she would never have taken her own life.'

There's a lump in my throat and a knot in my stomach. I want more vodka, but I can't react. Not here and not in front of that woman wearing the purple fake-fur coat, who has been watching me for the past fifteen minutes.

'Where is he now?' I ask as I shift my body away from the gaze of that woman. I wince as my leg brushes against the table leg and another splinter pierces my skin.

'I forgot to give you this.' James places a folded piece of paper underneath a creased beer mat and slides it over to me. It's the way we've been handling this business. Any information that he gives me can be burned. 'It's his new address.'

'Do you know who took the photographs that were sent to me?' I ask as I remove the piece of paper and place it in my blazer pocket.

'He paid a student a hundred quid to take the photos and to deliver them to you.'

I say nothing as I discreetly take a white envelope out of my bag and tap it against James' leg under the table. His fingers briefly touch mine as he takes his final payment from me.

'Thank you,' I say as I stand up and put on my coat. I bristle with irritation as I notice that the woman with the bad wig is still watching me.

'You know where I am if you need me again,' James says as he stands up, leaves the table and joins the men at the bar.

•

I'm sitting in a car that doesn't belong to me, outside the address that James wrote down for me. The man that I knew as David is at this address. Alone. I also know that David recently met a woman named Monica on a dating app and that he's waiting for her to arrive promptly at 8 p.m. Monica has offered to drive them both to her favourite restaurant, for their first date, not too far from Epping Forest.

I'm a few minutes late but I'm ready.

There's a box of latex gloves and a can of petrol in the boot. The front and rear seats are covered with plastic sheeting and

I'm holding a syringe filled with potassium chloride. I'm wearing a purple fake-fur coat and a cheap wig. In the darkness, I look like the woman who was watching me in the pub. In fact, this car belongs to her. What can I say? I didn't like her.

I can see David in the rear-view mirror. He's walking towards my car with that same over-confident swagger.

Do I feel guilt for what I'm about to do?

What would you do if you were me?

I have no guilt and I doubt that anyone will miss him.

After all, you can't kill a dead man twice.

A BREATH OF CHANGE

MIKE PHILLIPS

There was a deflated balloon in a branch of the tree opposite. The wind had twisted it round and round until it was a ragged strip of orange rubber fixed among the leaves. Watching it, I wondered how long it had been there and when it had arrived. I had no recollection of seeing the plump round shape float into the trees before its capture, and although I could remember looking through the clean and uninterrupted green of the foliage, I had no idea when the change had taken place. A gust of wind swept through the park and the remains of the balloon fluttered idly in response. I leaned forward on the park bench looking to see whether the rubber would fly away, and as I did so, someone sat down on my right.

'Why don't you answer your bloody phone?' the man said.

I took my time looking around. The last time we had met, we'd shaken hands and hugged, but that had been in a different world. On the other hand, the voice had been immediately recognizable. Simon Hudson.

'I've been trying to reach you for days,' Simon said. 'Then

someone told me they'd seen you here, sitting on an effing park bench all day.'

I'd heard the telephone ringing and I'd ignored the urge to answer it, but it was reassuring to know that it was only Simon on the other end. With my luck it could have been the taxman or a debtor or someone else with whom I no longer wanted to communicate.

'Sorry about that,' I said. 'Nice of you to take the trouble.'

He threw his head back and laughed. A familiar touch. This was how he'd been when we first met in a lecture hall in London all those years ago. Luxuriant black curls, jeans and an open-necked sweater, the scent of weed. Definitely a student. Nowadays the hair was more or less straight, decorated with streaks of white, and he was wearing a light grey suit and tinted glasses. He looked a bit too elegant for my spotty park bench.

'North London,' he said. 'I haven't been here for a while. It looks more or less the same. Remember the house?'

We used to share a house nearby, back in the days when it was bedsitter land.

'Couldn't afford to live there now.'

He laughed again.

'Speak for yourself, mate. I just moved to Folkestone. Raised the tone of the place.'

That was the last straw.

'OK,' I told him. 'You win. What can I do for you?'

He took his glasses off and leaned forward, hands clasped. His blue eyes stared straight at me for a moment before he looked away.

'I've got a little job for you,' he said. 'There's some money in it.'

I was halfway through a couple of reviews, and an advertising piece about the latest laptop, so I wasn't any more than usually desperate, but he knew which buttons to press. I nodded.

'You know what I do,' he said.

'Something in the civil service,' I told him. 'I've seen your name in the papers.'

I was downplaying it. Simon was a professor, and director of a well-funded think tank in Cambridge. His name had been in the papers because he had also been appointed head of a government commission reporting on some aspect or other of youth crime. We'd started our lives in the same neighbourhood, but now he was a player behind locked gates and impenetrable walls. Not bad for the youngest son of a postman in Tottenham.

'I live in a goldfish bowl,' he muttered.

On the path behind him, a couple pushing a pram were strolling past. They must have heard what he'd said, and the woman turned her head to look. She was wearing a hijab, and Simon shifted uneasily, leaning a couple of inches closer. Automatically I squeezed back against the metal rest behind me.

'This is a little bit awkward. I'm trying to find someone.'

'Begin at the beginning,' I said.

He looked around at the strip of tarmac behind him, and turned back, taking a deep breath. In almost the same movement, he reached into the breast pocket of his suit, and took out an envelope. Holding it between his thumb and fingers, he waggled it at me. I took it from him and opened it. Inside, there was a photograph of a couple, casually posed in what seemed to be an office. They were kissing. The photograph was printed on a sheet of A4 paper, and I guessed it had been reproduced from the screen of a mobile. The surface was dark and smudgy, but it was clear that the image was of a white man with a dark-skinned woman. It was also clear that the man was Simon. The woman looked much younger, but it was hard to tell. I turned it over. A piece of newsprint had been cut out and glued to the back of the photograph. It said one word – GOTCHA. I shrugged. In some circumstances the picture could seem casual and inoffensive. But there was something about their posture, the way his hands were placed on her body, the yielding shape of her thighs, the contrast presented by their skin colour, which made the whole thing flagrantly erotic.

'Nice,' I said. 'Who is she?'

He hesitated.

'My assistant.' He dragged the word out. 'Look. I've got three four jobs. Officially. I need someone to handle things. Answer the phone, write letters, make appointments. Do stuff.'

'Like I said. Nice.'

He swivelled his head round and stared directly at me.

'Hey. We're not young enough for moral judgements. I know what I've done. I'm here because I need you. We used to trust each other. What's changed?'

Weird. It was years since I'd seen him, and I'd almost forgotten about our friendship, but the question hit me with an almost physical force. I'd been trying not to think about it, but the tone of his voice, and the way his eyes were confronting mine, took me right back; a teenaged boy again, on a dark night, walking past the shops and pubs which lined the streets on the way home. It was a route I would have usually avoided, but on this night I was tired and anxious to get back to the house where I'd just moved in. It had been raining and the streets were deserted, so it was a shock when I heard the voices behind me. Later on, I couldn't remember what they were calling out. I could guess, but in my memory the event telescoped into a blur which ended with the first punch, three or four of them, men, boys, I was never quite certain. I was slumped on the pavement, taking a beating, when I heard a new voice, shouting and swearing. The next thing I knew Simon was holding me, his eyes searching mine.

I closed the envelope and handed it back.

'Why do you need me?'

I was still being difficult, but I wasn't sure how easy I wanted it to be for him. As if signalling his awareness of my mood, he sighed, sat up and puffed his breath out. Then he started filling in the details.

The photograph had arrived in his office a week earlier. His assistant, Claire, was on a day off. By the next day, she hadn't turned up so he had been forced to open his mail himself. In a state of shock he had tried to reach her on the telephone, but she didn't answer. Since that day he hadn't seen or spoken to her. When he visited her flat it was empty. Deserted. At first he had been worried. Now he was panicking. Only the day before this, another envelope had appeared, slipped under the door of the flat he occupied in Southwark. The photograph was the same, but this time a different word was written on the back. RESIGN.

'Have you been to the police? They'd love this.'

His face screwed up in irritation.

'I go to the police with this, next day it's all over social media. What I need to do is find her. Find out what's going on.'

'What do you expect me to do?'

I already knew. He looked round towards the park gates again. A couple of sweating middle-aged men were pounding towards us. When he looked round again he was smiling.

'I've been asking around,' he said, 'but there's something about being a middle-aged white man asking about a young black woman that puts people off. It's going to be easier for you. Could be her brother.' He paused. 'Or maybe her dad.'

He chuckled. I kept a straight face.

'I hope you're right.'

'Come off it,' he said. 'You'll do what you do, the way you always did.'

•

I had agreed to do what Simon wanted without thinking very much about it. He'd shown me another pic, where I could see her face clearly, and one look told me that she wasn't the sort who would simply disappear of her own volition. She had curly black hair, and she was looking straight at the camera, smiling a little. One of her parents, I guessed, was black and from the Caribbean, but when I asked Simon, he couldn't be certain. The truth was that, in spite of their relationship, he didn't know much about her. She'd worked for him during the last three years, and they had become lovers a year or so after she started. In her spare time she was working on starting a PR firm. She actually had a few clients, a couple of small charities and a rap group. They were good friends, he said, and he couldn't believe she had anything to do with the photographs. I was thinking about this while I flipped through the file he had given me. I didn't know whether or not his instinct was right, but, like it or not, I had to start somewhere.

I picked up the telephone and dialled the first name on the list of her friends with which he'd provided me. When the woman answered, she sounded puzzled. She hadn't seen Claire for a few weeks, she said, and what was my name again? This was how it went for the next hour. No one had anything to say that I wanted to hear. I put the phone on the floor and stretched out, wondering what to do next. The sun had gone down, and it had started raining. Late evening, the sky was dark and cloudy, light from the street lamps glittering on the pools of water on the pavement. Typical North London, I heard myself muttering. All of a sudden my mood seemed to be echoing the weather outside, the pattering of the rain a companion to the confusion in my head, rattling against the silence of the rooms around me. Somewhere inside me, during the time since I'd seen Simon, the conviction was growing that he hadn't told me everything. But then, that was the man I knew. He always used to hold back something. 'Need to know,' he'd say. 'Need to know.'

A few minutes later I pushed myself off the sofa and I was outside, running across the street to the pavement where I kept my car parked. I'd made the decision in a split second, checking Simon's file and throwing it back on the table, almost in one movement. The address of Claire's flat was off Holloway Road. Not too far away, and I would have to go there sooner or later.

•

It had stopped raining by the time I reached my goal. The flat was situated on the ground floor of a row of houses in a side street off the main road running down to Kings Cross. Most of the windows were dark, curtains drawn, except for the little attic window at the top of the house.

I took a mask and a pair of plastic gloves out of the glove compartment and put them on. Now I look like everyone else, I thought as I got out of the car. I walked through the tiny garden in front of the house and rang the bell. No answer. I tried again. After a little while, when there was no sound or movement in reply, I took out the keys Simon had given me, opened the door, and found myself in a narrow hallway, which ended in a white door with a brass numeral glinting from the centre of it: *1*. I tried the other key on the ring, and the door opened silently. I stood still for a moment, peering into the darkness in front of me. Up to this moment what I was doing had been a sort of game, in which I was involved because Simon had decided to call in a debt about which only the two of us knew anything. Crossing this threshold would commit me in ways I couldn't guess.

I stepped inside, feeling on the left for a light switch, then closing the door behind me. The corridor was neatly carpeted in grey. The doors were open, revealing a small nest of rooms, all of them equally neat and tidy. I prowled through them. A bathroom, small, but spectacularly clean, the usual scattering of tubes, bottles and brushes. A kitchen, larger than I expected, utensils mounted on an island in the middle of the room. A bedroom in neutral tones of pale grey and white stretched from the front to the back of the house. All the furnishings seemed clean and fresh, but somehow the airless silence of the flat felt oppressive. A space lonely and deserted. As if to provide a contradiction, there were lines of framed photographs fixed to walls and perched on the shelves dotted around the walls. A crowd of smiling young people. A few pictures of Claire, dressed in an academic gown at a graduation ceremony, arranged next to one of Simon, grinning happily.

The telephone rang, and when I located it, sitting on a table near the door, it turned out to be an old-fashioned handset. I watched, wondering what would happen if I picked it up, but before I could make up my mind, it switched itself over to deliver Claire's recorded message. There was no reply, only a buzz and a click as the caller shut the recording down.

I went over to the table and switched the messages on. They seemed to be mostly personal. A couple of the same women arranging meetings to go for walks. Several from Simon. Almost as many from another man who announced himself as Vincent and had a voice that sounded Caribbean. The voices seemed to echo round the space, tricking me from time to time into looking over my shoulder, and there were moments when I felt breath-less. Crushed.

I'd been listening for close to half an hour, and I was about to switch the messages off when a voice came on that I recog-nized. I was tired and bored, so I had nearly missed it, but when she said her name I was sure.

•

I rang Simon in the morning. I'd rung him the night before, on his mobile, then at his flat in town, but there was no reply, and I didn't know any of his other numbers, so I'd waited and called during office hours.

'Sam.' He sounded surprised. 'You found anything?'

'Yes,' I told him, 'but I need to see you now.'

After some hemming and hawing he told me to come to his office where we could talk. It was a building round behind Waterloo train station, and I was there within the hour. He was waiting for me in the lobby, wearing a black pinstriped suit, but when I opened the door, he held his hand up in a stop sign.

'Let's take a walk,' he said.

We walked through the courtyard outside, crossed the street into the square opposite, and sat on a bench.

'I thought you'd like this,' he said. 'Visiting a posh bench.' He could see I wasn't in the mood for his humour, so he continued. 'This time of the morning there'll be no one here. We can talk.'

Without preliminaries I told him that I'd been to the flat in Islington, and there was no one there.

'I could have told you that,' he said. He was frowning now.

'You could also have told me that Mel knew her.'

Mel was his wife and we'd both known her for almost the same length of time. They lived separately, but I couldn't be sure about the state of their relationship. His frown grew deeper.

'Of course Mel knew her. She worked for me. Christ's sake. It's not as if they were pals.'

In the phone message I'd heard Mel speak with a familiar tone, arranging a meeting, and referring to the last time they'd seen each other.

Simon looked away from me, gazing at the grand houses on the other side of the square's iron railings. He drummed his fingers on the back of the bench. Suddenly he got to his feet.

'Thank you, Sammy. I'll sort this lot out myself.'

His tone was abrupt, and he spun around, scattering a little gravel. Then he marched off quickly, heading back in the direction of his office.

•

I knew what my next step had to be. The alternative was to go home and lie down until I felt better, but I knew I wouldn't. Instead I went home and rang the college where Mel worked. The woman on the line said that she wasn't there. She couldn't tell me anything more. Professor Hudson was a very busy woman. That's why I needed a quote from her for the article I was writing in the *Times Higher Educational Supplement*, I told her. She asked me my name again, and when I replied she muttered amiably, then she told me that Professor Hudson might have gone somewhere on the coast for a meeting, but she would be around later on.

I dressed carefully. I wasn't sure why, except that, somewhere deep down, I wanted Mel to see me as a success instead of a shagged-out no-hoper, and, strangely, I felt a twinge of excitement at the thought of seeing and talking with her. After all this time.

I got to the gates of the college a couple of hours later, and called Mel's office again. This time no one answered. I hung around, loitering by the railings, reading the opinion column in the newspaper, and then when I had finished that, pretending to read the rest of it. It was going dark, the evening coming on fast, and a steady trickle of cars began to emerge. None of the drivers looked like Mel, though. An hour passed like this, and I had almost decided to leave when a black Skoda swung in off the road, and paused while the barrier creaked open. Mel was driving it, and I dashed the few steps to the side of the car and rapped on the window. She looked around and in that moment I saw that she recognized me.

I waited while she parked in a line of cars on the curve of paving stones in front of the ornate entrance. Then she got out, waved, and I pushed the pedestrian's gate and went in.

'Hey, Mel. Long time.'

She smiled. She must have been in her fifties now, but she was still sporting gleaming blond hair, which swung across her face when she moved. She wore spectacles now but when I got closer, she took them off, and I could see that she had the same deep-set hazel eyes. A little bit tired and narrower, but the same.

We sat in her office at a correct social distance. I congratulated her on her academic status and her promotions. She said she'd read something I'd written sometime, she couldn't remember where, and how much she'd enjoyed it. I didn't believe a word of it, and in any case the room was choking with our mutual insincerity.

'I came about Claire,' I said eventually.

'Who?'

'Simon's assistant. He must have told you.'

She nodded her head slowly. One of those teacher's tricks she'd picked up over the last twenty years.

'He mentioned there was some problem.'

Suddenly I was fed up with the elaborate game we were both

playing. Talking fast and refusing to be interrupted I told her about Claire's disappearance, and the difficulty it had created for Simon. I thought about telling her about the dodgy photographs, then I decided not to.

'What's all this got to do with me?'

'I thought you might say that,' I told her. 'But if Simon gets screwed over this. So will you.'

'I'm not sure that's true,' she said.

She was clearly unmoved, so I started again. I began with the photographs this time, and I could see that this was evoking some kind of emotion below the surface, but I couldn't work out what it was. I stopped. It was time to play my last card.

'We all make mistakes,' I said. 'Even you.'

She glared at me and I knew she was thinking about the times we had taken advantage of Simon's absence from the house we shared all those years ago. Neither of us had ever told him about those nights when she had slid into my bed, her naked body moist with arousal.

'I wondered when that would come up,' she said.

'Nothing's come up,' I told her. Unexpectedly, she grinned and shook her head.

'Don't lie,' she said. 'I'm not a child any more.' She paused, watching me, speculation in her eyes. 'If I tell you about this woman. Will you go away?'

'Of course.'

'I've known about her for ages. I was coming to meet him one night. Big surprise. Well, I was the one who got the surprise. They were sitting in a hotel lounge in the middle of town gazing adoringly at each other. He looked ridiculous. That was the first time we separated. He came back after a few months, swearing it was over, but she was working for him, and it all started again. So I left.'

That was bad enough, she said. What followed was worse. She bumped into Claire at a conference of some sort. They'd started chatting, and without wanting to, they'd become friendly.

That was all there was to it, she said. They'd more or less stopped seeing each other a few months ago when Claire got pregnant. That was too difficult, even when she knew the baby wasn't Simon's. Suddenly the room seemed to be crackling with tension, and I remembered that she and Simon had been trying for a long time to conceive, but they'd never succeeded in having children together.

'Of course,' she said, her voice taking on a deeper, slightly bitter tone. 'He knew nothing about her being pregnant until recently. Clever man.'

'He really didn't know?'

'He really didn't.'

In the end I knew that Mel, like Simon, was holding something back. It was nothing obvious, because once she started talking, she'd told me a lot I didn't know, and a lot that Simon must have been concealing. She told me, for instance, that the baby's father was a musician named Vincent Chambers, and she told me, also, that it had been Claire's intention for at least a year to break up with Simon. She'd had some nasty rows with Vincent about seeing Simon, and he'd hit her. Several times.

'I didn't want to know too much,' she said, 'but she was on her way out. I felt sorry for her. Vincent was bad news, but she couldn't cope with who Simon was. He was becoming part of the Establishment. He'd spent most of his life trying to creep up the ladder, to a place she didn't want to be. That wasn't going to change. Claire wanted to find herself as a black woman, and a radical. They were never compatible.'

And that was only the half of it, I thought.

•

The insistent music coming from my mobile woke me next morning. I'd gone to sleep on the sofa and the sun was shining straight into my eyes. I rolled over and hit the floor, then scrabbled around until my hand came to rest on the packet of noise. The voice was Simon's. He wanted to meet me in the park in about an hour. The usual place, he said.

He was dressed in dark blue this time. And white trainers. He still looked good, though.

'Look,' he said, plunging straight in. 'Sorry about yesterday. It was a lot to take on board. Some things I should have told you. I talked to Mel.'

I nodded. 'Yeah.'

We sat in silence for a few minutes.

'What are you going to do?' I asked him.

'I don't know yet,' he said. 'I might have been overreacting to those photos. You can't imagine how vicious public life is now. Insults, death threats, I've had them all.'

'What about Mel?'

'Mel? What about her?'

'You said you'd bought a house in Folkestone. You're separated. Are you going to live there?'

'No. No,' he said slowly. 'We're selling the place. It was a good idea, but it wouldn't work.'

He stood up, put his hand in his pocket and gave me a folded sheet of paper.

'A couple of addresses which might be useful.'

'You want me to keep on looking?'

He puffed out his cheeks and blew a gust of breath out.

'Till we know more. I might talk to the cops tomorrow. Carefully.' He gave a reflective chuckle. 'Just keep looking.'

He walked off, looking around him as if he didn't have a care in the world.

Back in the flat I looked at the sheet of paper he'd given me. The name Vincent Chambers was printed on top and below were a couple of addresses in West London.

That was how the day started. By the time the sun started to go down, and the streetlamps began to glow I had driven through a sizeable portion of West London, first visiting the addresses Simon had given me, then going through several caffs and pubs, asking around for Vincent. I don't know what I expected but gallons of petrol later I still had no results. The population of the city seemed to have thinned out substantially, and most people didn't want to talk or even get closer than a couple of yards. Eventually, tired of the streets and houses which seemed to be closing round me, I drove through the centre of the city and ended up parked on the inner ring of Regents Park, thinking about what to do next. Eventually I gave it up and started back home. The rain had started again, a fine drizzle this time. I found a parking space under the row of trees lining the street, got out of the car and prepared to run the short distance to my flat.

'Fadah,' a soft voice said. 'Fadah.'

There were three of them huddled round the tree. Young black men, all of them wearing masks and hoodies pulled up over their heads. I checked my run, but kept my distance.

'You're looking for me,' the same voice said. 'Why?'

He moved a little closer and pushed the hood back, his marmalade-coloured eyes boring into mine. I guessed who it was.

'I don't know you,' I said carefully. 'But I was hoping you could tell me where to find Claire Dupont.'

'You a relative?'

I shook my head and told him who I was, and that I was working for Simon.

'You can stop looking,' Vincent said. 'She's in Jamaica.'

'Jamaica? Where in Jamaica? When did she go? When is she back?'

'Cha,' he said. 'You don't hear about the virus? People can't get in a plane and fly like they used to. You can stop looking.'

He turned and began to walk away, followed by the other two, but he'd only gone a few paces before he turned around and stood still looking at me. Then he lifted his finger and pointed, saying one word.

'Stop.'

Back in the flat I thought it over. I couldn't believe Claire was in Jamaica. If she was anything like the other children of immigrants that I knew, she'd now be more English than anything else and she'd want her baby to be born a citizen, especially since the babyfather was close by. I couldn't believe, either, that Vincent would be remotely interested in bombarding Simon with messages demanding his resignation. I knew what I had to do, but I hoped I was wrong.

In the morning I called a friend who worked for a local paper on the South coast.

'I'm writing a piece for a website,' I told him. 'It's all about house values and prices in somewhere like Folkestone.'

This was the sort of barefaced lie I had given up a long time ago, but now I was desperate for some help checking out the local agents and real estate people. He took my request in his stride, however, and when I told him who the enquiry was about, his lack of interest was obvious. He rang me back in about an hour.

'Got it,' he said. 'Here's the address.'

•

The building looked a little dilapidated. Semi-detached, three storeys, faced with scaffolding, an overgrown garden. There was a gate by the side of it leading to the back garden. I pushed it and eventually something gave on the other side, and the door sprang open, revealing a concrete path which went to the back of the house. I walked in and made my way into the overgrown garden at the rear. Once there I looked around. It was completely fenced in, with high wooden boards that surrounded the patch of ground. I knew what I was looking for, and on the left, close to the fence, I found it. A patch of bare earth, recently dug, covered by weeds and twigs.

I turned around and went back through the path to the street, where I'd left the car. I got in, started the engine, grinding the gears, and drove blindly away.

·

I had found Claire, but that wasn't all there was to it. By the time I got back to London night had fallen, and I went into a sleep disturbed and haunted by dreadful dreams and visions of shapeless horror. Early in the morning I was sitting on my park bench, waiting for Simon and Mel. I had rung them separately, and as luck would have it, they'd each answered the telephone immediately. I told them I'd been in Folkestone and said I wanted to meet them on my park bench in the early morning.

'I've got a meeting,' Simon barked irritably. Mel merely said it was OK.

They turned up, walking in together, and they sat down on one end of the bench, leaving a space between us, which suited me fine. I told them what I'd seen in Folkestone, and they watched me with faces which might have been carved from stone.

'Didn't you dig it up or anything?' Mel asked me.

'No. I didn't want to know what happened. I still don't.'

She turned to look at Simon.

'That guy Vincent was there with her,' she said, 'a few weeks ago. Anything could have happened.'

She was squeezing his arm, and he pulled away from her.

'I'm so sorry to hear that, Sam,' she said. She leaned towards me, her hand flat on the surface of the bench.

'You sent the photos, didn't you?'

Simon stood up staring away towards the park gates. He sniffled and wiped his eyes with a snow-white handkerchief. Mel grimaced.

'Sanctimonious bitch. I went to see him that time, and before I knew it I'd taken the picture on my cell phone.' She clenched her fist and pounded on the armrest of the bench. Now she was crying too. 'It's funny. I didn't hate her until the baby. Funny. Funny. When it wasn't even his.'

She took the handkerchief out of his hand and blew her nose.

'What are you going to do, Sammy?'

'Nothing.'

She looked up at me, her eyes wide with surprise.

'I knew,' she said. 'I knew you'd help us.'

'I'm not,' I said. 'You've got till one o'clock. If you haven't gone to the cops by then I'll report it myself. Leave me out of it.' I got up, then I remembered. 'And don't drop that boy Vincent in it. He may be an evil little shit, but he doesn't deserve that.'

'OK.'

We got on our feet and she put a proprietorial arm around Simon.

'Let's go,' she told him. 'We've a lot to do.'

Walking home, I thought about what I had done. It was Mel, of course, who had done it, and presented Simon with a fait accompli. The look on her face when she realized I was letting them off the hook had told me everything. She was always the more clearheaded and decisive of the two, and she'd spent too many years of agony with Simon to see him vanish into happy fatherhood. My hope now was that I'd never see either of them again.

They met the deadline, of course. They were talking to the police by one o'clock.

I didn't want to know anything about the whole affair, so I avoided the newspaper for a while. I couldn't miss the TV or the stuff on my computer, but I survived it. So did Simon and Mel. By the time the police began digging up evidence, they'd muddied the waters successfully. Mel wrote a book about the experience and Simon spoke at Claire's memorial service. As for Vincent. I never heard his name again.

THE YELLOW LINE

AUSMA ZEHANAT KHAN

Haniya

He followed her home again. He wasn't ugly or frightening at first, but she knew that he could be cruel. Haniya noticed things like that about people. From a glance, from an interaction with a street vendor, from whether they held the door for a woman during the rush from the subway to the commuter trains.

She could tell who a man was if he was sprawled over three seats when a woman wearing a hijab was standing there in plain view. Did he meet her eyes or did he stare in disgust at her scarf? Did he pretend she didn't exist, or did a sneer curl the corner of his lips?

This man wasn't like the others, though his eyes said he was petty and vengeful well before he opened his mouth. He was tall and well-dressed with a Richard Spencer haircut, and he carried a black briefcase that matched his shiny shoes. Money must have been new to him, because he felt the need to show it off. He needed her to know that he made more during his lunch hour than Haniya did all week. She worked at a gallery, as a particular kind of restorer—a colorist in oils. She didn't make much money, but she loved her work and thought of herself as part artist and part historian.

There was beauty to be discovered under centuries of grime. If you were careful, and if you were curious about the past, you could find buried treasure beneath the murky greens and browns. But you had to be meticulous. Each stroke you laid down had to be precise. The colors had to match. You couldn't invent a palette that didn't already exist. All you could do was reveal the existing color—let people see what you saw. Until what you knew was there became what they expected to see. A con artist's trick, some might say.

The man who was threatening her didn't care. Not that she was an artist, and not that she dressed well, her dresses and her scarves coordinated with a vivid sense of color. Subtle, at times, bold at others. She wasn't short on self-confidence. She didn't avoid looking at people when she took the subway to Union. She smiled, she was pleasant, she wasn't impatient, and she didn't push through people for a seat on the train though her ride from Union station to the suburbs was an hour and a half.

She bumped into the man coming out of the gallery; he worked at the bank next door. She'd like to say he looked reptilian, low-browed and cunning, but the truth was that he didn't. He was handsome, fresh-faced and clean. He knew how to use cologne. He must have worked out because the jacket of his suit was snug around his broad shoulders. He wanted that, she could tell. He wanted women to notice. Not noticing meant she bumped into him, hurrying down the sidewalk to the subway. He was equally at fault, crowing about a deal he had closed to someone on his phone. He was planning to celebrate with friends, taking them out to a club to get drunk and spend the night 'hitting on bitches'.

She didn't think well-groomed men with high-paying jobs would call women bitches.

When she knocked his arm with her elbow, he cut off his phone call and said, 'What are you looking at, bitch?'

She was about to apologize for not watching where she was going, but hearing that, her temper flared. So instead of letting it go, she said sharply, 'A gentleman doesn't use language like that. A gentleman would apologize.'

'Apologize to what, a walking tent?'

His rudeness erased his good looks. She wasn't wearing a tent. She was wearing a blue summer dress that flowed down to her ankles, her scarf a contrasting pink. It was flattering, not tent-like. Haniya's vanity was pricked. A Muslim woman could be stylish. She could be anything she chose.

She could guess at what was coming next. A round of uninspired insults. A jolt to the ribs, or possibly a tug at her scarf. The man wasn't carrying a drink, so he couldn't throw it at her. But they were still close to the bank he worked at, so people he knew could be nearby. He should be smart, hurl his insults and go.

Haniya knew he wasn't going to. The kind of man he was, he wouldn't leave her alone until he'd broken her down. She wasn't the crying type, but neither was she stupid.

Though the truth of it was that her very presence provoked him.

He was in her face, now, shouting, 'Who the *fuck* do you think you are?'

Haniya had a line she used for encounters like these. She would trail the fringe of her scarf down her fingers and say, 'I am a daughter of Khadija, Mother of the Believers. Whole and worthy in myself.'

This wasn't the man for that line. He was the kind she mumbled an apology to as she darted into a busy street to avoid escalating the situation. And that was what she tried to do.

He blocked her, his black briefcase swinging around to hit her hard on the back.

A lot of people would tell her to take out her phone and start recording the attack, but you couldn't react that quickly when you were in the middle of it. Her only thought was to get away. She took the blow and the insults, then wheeled in the opposite direction. She ran away, sweating under her scarf.

People were rushing by, making sure not to *see* the encounter. No one stopped or cared. Big cities swallowed up kindness. No one wanted to draw the man's wrath by stepping up to confront him.

Haniya didn't blame them. She wouldn't have either.

Instead, she looked for the men, the six-footers with briefcases, with stature and heft.

'Chill out, bro,' they could say. Or, 'Dude, let it go, she's half your size.'

And white guy to white guy, the man would ease up, give an embarrassed little laugh and explain that he was sorry. Not to her, to them. They'd accept the apology on her behalf, relieved not to have to do more. They'd let him off, saying, 'It's this city, man. It makes everyone a little crazy.'

No one said anything like that, but at least the man didn't chase her.

That first time, he let her go.

•

The next time, she wasn't as lucky. He tracked her from the door of the gallery all the way to Bloor and Yonge. She was descending the stairs at the busy cross-section, her headphones on under her scarf, when a hard thump between her shoulder blades sent her flying through the air. She landed on her hands and knees, the wave of commuters parting around her, some clucking their tongues at the inconvenience, one hijab-wearing girl stopping to help her up. When she got to her feet again, she could see the tall man's back. He'd waited to make sure that she knew.

'Raghead.'

The whisper chased her up the stairs.

Coincidence, she told herself. It wouldn't happen again.

By the third time, he'd found out everything he could except her name. Where she worked, where she lunched, which train she took to the suburbs, how long the journey was, the stop she disembarked at to connect with the local bus. He followed in his car the next night, honking his horn in her driveway.

That was when she filed the first complaint, not knowing that more would follow, reports that ranged from racist bullying to sexual aggression. Haniya didn't feel safe. Not at work, not at home.

But through the terror and discomfort he inflicted, a moment came when things changed. A man could rip a scarf from your head, but after he'd taken his picture and posted it online, he was done with your humiliation. He would forget all about you.

This man didn't. This man was unrelenting.

His name was Blair Hegland and he came into the gallery, posing as a well-heeled client, telling her boss, Langdon Prentice, that he'd gotten to know his assistant. That was when Hegland learned her name. He insisted that Haniya help him choose a painting for his office. Langdon Prentice demurred. Haniya Mirza was an art restorer; perhaps Prentice could help him in her stead. Hegland wouldn't be denied. He convinced Prentice of Haniya's suitability. He knew she had an artist's eye from the way she dressed. Her sense of color was superb.

Haniya was called from the back room where she was working on a picture by a little known painter named D'Amboise, a master of line, the dull ochres in the painting flaring to life beneath her brush.

She stumbled when she saw Hegland, who put his hand under her elbow and guided her across the showroom. The hand on her elbow slipped to her waist where his fingers dug in. Frozen in fear, she couldn't speak.

'That's right, *Haniya*, be a good girl, and stay quiet.'

He uttered a series of threats, insinuations that played on her name, his meaning so foul that her whole body trembled. She had to get to safety. She should call for help, but her tongue was dry in her mouth.

Hegland bought a painting while she stood frozen, saying to Prentice, 'Haniya was so helpful. Sweet as honey, in fact.'

Your blood will run like honey, he'd said.

When she'd gotten herself together, she warned Langdon Prentice that Hegland was harassing her, but he said she was overreacting. Haniya must have misconstrued Hegland's artistic interests as personal. Prentice couldn't keep his gaze from her headscarf when he told her Hegland could have anyone he wanted.

•

Haniya changed her route home. She changed the locks on her doors. She paid for a security company she couldn't afford to monitor her house. She started keeping a log. She called the police and was referred to the Hate Crime Unit. She reported Hegland's threats. Patrol officers drove by her house, nothing was found to be amiss. Blair Hegland was interviewed and he'd been exceptionally cooperative. His colleagues vouched for his integrity. He had women friends to spare. No one else had filed a complaint.

Blair Hegland was a banker in a thousand-dollar suit, and Haniya was just another girl in a headscarf. Alien. Different. Other. The police took no action. No one believed her.

Hegland retaliated after the police came to see him. He found her again, and, when she was walking to her townhouse through an alley, he caught her and did things she *didn't* report.

She didn't want anyone to know. She could barely face it herself.

Her hands developed a tremor. She couldn't control her brush-strokes. D'Amboise's elegant line wavered before her vision, yellow bleeding through brown to drip down the edge of the canvas, until the painting was ruined.

Langdon Prentice fired her. She should have been angry, but what she felt was relief, free at last of the secrets Hegland had forced her to keep. She'd find work in the suburbs, where she'd never cross paths with a man who thought he owned her, from her headscarf to her hopes.

She was to find out she was wrong.

Hegland wasn't going away.

Esa

Esa Khattak sat at his desk. He'd just cleared the last of his paperwork and was contemplating a stack of blue aerograms, tied together with a thin green ribbon, faded at the corners with age. They represented the decades-long correspondence between his grandfather and his father, both long since deceased. The letters had passed into his care, and he'd promised himself that one day he would untie that ribbon, sift through the letters from Pakistan, and bring his father back to life. He was vulnerable when it came to grief. Years had passed, but his loss was still fresh, and though the letters were a gift, he'd left them untouched all this time. Perhaps the moment had come to change that. His fingers hovered above the parcel as Rachel came into the room.

Detective Sergeant Rachel Getty was his partner at Community Policing, a job that had less and less meaning when reform continued to be blocked by those in a position to change things. It was a wonder he and Rachel could hold their heads up in the communities they served. He let that thought go—he and Rachel had fought hard but would never come to terms with their superiors.

He was relieved to have an excuse to put off opening the letters. Rachel held a case file in her hand. She slapped it down in front of him, and perched on the edge of his desk, licking the traces of a Mars bar from her fingers. He could only be grateful that she'd used her clean hand to offer him the file.

She nudged the parcel of letters with her hip. 'Chickening out again? I thought you were going to read them this century.'

No one addressed Esa Khattak, Director of Community Policing, with Rachel's air of irreverence. From Rachel, Esa didn't mind it, so he teased her in turn.

'I was thinking deep thoughts, Rachel. I'd nearly made up my mind.'

'I'll bet.'

He opened the file and was confronted by a gruesome set of photographs. A body thoroughly dismembered by the weight of an underground train. A white man by the look of things, though with all that blood, it was hard to be sure.

'A jumper?' he asked. 'Why did it come to us?'

Community Policing dealt with Toronto's minority communities, specializing in cases where racial tensions were involved.

Rachel snatched a tissue from the box on his desk. 'Not necessarily a jumper; he could have been pushed.' She leaned forward, sorted through the photographs, and showed him a picture of a South Asian woman in a bright summer dress with a matching yellow headscarf. Her eyes looked wide and shocked, the pupils dazed by the flash of a camera.

'That's from the camera at the station. Her name is Haniya Mirza. She was there when our victim "fell".' Rachel made scare quotes with her fingers. 'Her name was on a witness statement. Someone in the Hate Crime Unit picked up on it and sent the file our way. Thought the whole thing looked suspicious.'

Now Esa was interested. 'Hate Crime Unit? These kinds of crimes are usually the other way around.' He meant that the victims of hate crimes were normally people of color.

'I know that, sir, but get this. The man on the tracks is Blair Hegland—he's a well-known investment banker. A mover and shaker in the city. And Haniya Mirza filed *nine* complaints against him in the past seven months. He'd been harassing her, threatening her. Then suddenly she's on a platform with him and he hits the tracks right before a train pulls up?' Rachel's expression was dubious.

'Which station?'

'Bloor and Yonge. Southbound to Union.'

'Rush hour?'

'I know what you're going to say. It's a crush there, maybe he was crowded to the edge. But she was standing right next to him. Would you do that if someone was harassing you?'

'He could have followed her onto the platform. A crush, like you said, so she couldn't get away.'

Rachel's brown eyes lit with enthusiasm. There was nothing she loved more than having a puzzle to solve.

'There's security footage. She's caught on camera speaking to our victim. She's on the wrong side of the yellow line.'

The yellow line designated the safe zone. Crossing it put commuters too close to the incoming trains.

'But the camera doesn't show her pushing him?'

'Not from the footage we have. But we're hunting down another angle. We're also looking to see if anyone else was using a cell phone to film. I've got Gaffney on that.'

Gaffney was their tech specialist. If there was video footage out there, he would find it.

'Good.' Khattak looked down at the file, disturbed. Haniya Mirza had been a victim of harassment. Nine complaints and Hegland had faced nothing other than a conversation with Hate Crimes.

'Oh no you don't.' Rachel jabbed a finger at him. 'Don't go soft on me. Did you see the body on the tracks?'

Khattak stifled a sigh. Rachel was going to insist on being lead in the interview, so he tried to redirect her.

'Why so many complaints? Weren't any of them followed up?'

Rachel looked a little abashed. 'Hate crimes, sir. You know how that goes. No proof to back up her claims, no evidence that he did the things he was accused of. She said he followed her wherever she went. Groped her on the subway, yanked off her scarf. Could be he was escalating, but her word against his, so either he was smart about how he targeted her, or she had an axe to grind.'

'Her testimony is evidence,' Khattak pointed out.

He studied the photographs in the file. Haniya Mirza looked to be about thirty, Hegland a few years older.

'No corroboration,' Rachel said absently. 'No witnesses to any of it.' She touched a finger to the image of the headscarf. 'You letting Mirza off because of this?'

Khattak didn't take the bait. Rachel knew he was devout, just as she knew that his faith may have heightened his empathy but it didn't get in the way of his commitment to his work.

'I'd like to hear her out, that's all.'

He spread the stack of complaints across his desk, covering up the photos of the body. Rachel pulled up a chair to join him.

They hadn't been reading long when Khattak raised his head, a fine rage in his eyes. No woman deserved what Hegland had put Haniya through.

'Hate Crimes let *all* of this pass?'

There had been no justice for Haniya when Hegland was alive. And now that he was dead, his shadow still hung over her. What could he possibly say to this woman whom his colleagues had failed? Why hadn't they referred Haniya's complaints to him?

She was owed something from him if only for her courage in continuing to report Hegland's harassment. But also because she was a Muslim sister to him, and as far as he could bridge that gap as a man, the torment she had suffered appalled him.

Rachel reached a different conclusion. Her ponytail bounced with excitement as she said, 'That's why I think he didn't jump.'

Haniya

The detective was beautiful in a way men weren't meant to be beautiful. So beautiful that she almost didn't realize he was treating her as a suspect, and not as a witness he'd invited to speak. He had sleek cheekbones, deeply green eyes, and thick black hair, in that way that South Asian hair was thick, lush and springy. Beautifully shaped lips with a delicate upper edging that was likely sensitive to touch. Not that she was thinking of touching him, but she wondered if she'd be able to paint such a strong yet delicate line. Looking at him, she wondered how people took him seriously.

Her glance must have lingered too long because his handsome face became shuttered, a hint of distaste in the lift of his chin.

He had to know he was attractive, yet he didn't altogether welcome it. Haniya found that interesting. The inner and outer man at odds—the detective wary and cool, the rest of him opposed. Those green eyes with tiny flames at the center, the mouth held tight—he could be a man who shared her rage. She knew from his reputation that he'd walked some distance in her shoes, censured for being who he was—a Pakistani Muslim in a white man's job, while claiming to speak for those he considered his own.

He was the face of Community Policing and that was not an easy thing to be. But Haniya would test him and see. She would know very quickly if he was brown or blue or some strange mix calibrated to suit the current politics. Her replies to him would be governed by whether or not he passed the test. *Are you like me or not?*

His partner was another matter. Detective Sergeant Rachel Getty had kind, sharp eyes that glinted with good humor. She wore a hockey jersey over slim black trousers, her lank brown hair in a ponytail. Not a look that Haniya envied. Not like the woman in the photograph on Khattak's desk, whom Haniya noticed at once. A photograph placed beside a stack of letters that looked well-thumbed, though the ribbon that tied them was new.

She took a closer look at the picture. The woman had russet hair that fell in soft waves; she was attractive in a way that Haniya resented. She *could* look like that if she chose, style her hair in long, loose curls. But she'd made a choice about how she expressed her faith, and no matter how dire the repercussions were, she stayed firm in that choice, though the cost of it was loneliness and fear.

When you wore the hijab, people looked through you when you passed them on the street, in the same way they ignored the homeless, as if it was a virus you could catch.

For others, she was *too* visible. They were the ones who expressed their hate, who brushed up against her body, who shoved their palms between her legs, or who grabbed her breast when no one was looking and squeezed hard enough to bruise. Misogynists *and* racists. They spit or punched and kicked, they pulled at her headscarf until her pins came loose to score a trail of blood across her cheeks.

She glanced from the photograph to Rachel. Hijab wasn't just about hair, and here she was, focused on hair. Hegland had wanted to see her hair, and in the end he'd succeeded. He'd pushed her to her knees. She shuddered at the memory. Yet here she was, still breathing and in one piece, a little humiliated maybe, but Hegland was dead, and she was here with Esa Khattak.

Funny, that. Hegland had been visited by the police only once. He'd denied the allegations, and ended up giving them a tour of his boardroom with its stunning views of the lake. The visit had ended in the kind of all-boys-together camaraderie that made Haniya want to throw up, her anger a burning ball in her gut.

Hegland should have been in her place, questioned by two detectives, on the hot seat for his actions. But no one had called him in.

Her eyes flicked to Esa Khattak. He was Muslim and South Asian too. So what was Khattak doing on the other side of that desk?

Whatever it was, he wouldn't arrest her for the part she'd played in Hegland's death.

He couldn't, without any proof.

Esa

Haniya Mirza didn't look like she could kill, which was probably a facile assumption. Killers came in all shapes and sizes, from all denominations of faith, or from none at all. He'd once considered arresting an imam. A headscarf didn't mean a woman was saintly; it simply ensured that Esa proceeded with a certain decorum.

He'd studied the security camera footage, and hadn't come up with answers. One minute a tall red-faced man was standing on the platform, the next he leapt at a woman in a yellow dress, and then he was on the tracks. Electrocuted then crushed by a train that weighed nearly eighty thousand pounds.

A mutilated body. An ugly death.

Was Haniya Mirza beautiful? No. But perhaps, without at all excusing it, there had been something about her that sparked Hegland's obsession. A generous nature, or a quick sense of humor, an underlying sexuality? He could see none of these things in the woman seated across from him, her ankles neatly crossed beneath her dress. She wore a white chador with her dress, its folds modestly draped over her torso.

He played the footage again.

'Did you push him?'

She denied it a second time. And then she said, as she hadn't done the first time, 'You're very concerned about this man who managed to fall from the platform.'

'It could be that he was pushed,' Khattak said. 'And I'm curious as to why your arms are raised, as the footage makes clear, if it wasn't to push him.'

One didn't necessarily establish the other, but Khattak wanted to see how she'd respond.

'Does it?' She tipped her head to one side. 'I'm not seeing what you see.'

'That isn't you in the yellow dress? The same one you're wearing now? Engaged in a conversation with Blair Hegland, moments before his death?'

She could have worn the dress to the interview to taunt them, or as proof of her innocence. Or maybe she was just confident that the footage wouldn't convict her. It was difficult to see what had transpired because Hegland's lunge at her at the crucial moment blocked her body from view. Khattak could only see the upraised arms, and the fitted yellow sleeves. The crowd surged ahead and Hegland fell.

'What was he saying to you?'

'The same vile things he always said. Racist insults followed by sexual threats.' She placed a small hand on his desk, pointing to a complaint. 'I did give your officers a thorough report. There seemed to be much less interest in Mr Hegland, then.'

She was angry, and she had every right to be if the reports were true, yet her response to Esa was impersonal. Candid, cool, and not at all anxious or frantic. He couldn't get a read on her. The contrast between the woman who sat before him unperturbed, and the one at the end of her tether in the complaints, was stark. Sending Hegland to his death would have taken a great deal of nerve. Did she possess that kind of nerve?

'What did you say to him before he lunged at you?'

Her fingers slid over the papers on his desk, soft and lightly caressing.

Her eyes slid away from his, and, with a complete change of manner, she said, 'You know that he assaulted me? On many occasions, he—groped me?'

'I've read every word of the complaints.' Voice grave, gaze respectfully turned from her.

'He was going to do the same again. I could see it in his eyes. He thought I was powerless, and that gave him some kind of high. He was an evil man,' she went on. 'But that doesn't mean I killed him.'

Esa wanted to believe her. Rachel was still skeptical. Her thick brows were raised, a nerve ticking in her jaw.

'You didn't answer the inspector's question. What did you say to Hegland that made him come at you like that?'

Haniya's lips firmed, a sign of temper at Rachel's accusation, but her answer was frank.

'I told him not to touch me. I told him to save himself.' She gestured at Khattak without looking at him. 'No woman should be touched without her consent. Inspector Khattak knows exactly how he was trying to degrade me.'

Rachel frowned. 'To save himself from what? Retaliation?'

Haniya's voice cracked. 'To save his own soul. As a daughter of Khadija, I wanted to warn him. He was so determined to abuse me that he didn't notice the train. He sprang at me and he fell.'

Still doubtful, Rachel pushed on. 'Daughter of Khadija? I don't know what that means.'

Esa Khattak did. Khadija, the first woman to accept Islam, was the beloved wife of the Prophet. A partner and mentor of unquestionable integrity. And he wondered if Haniya saw herself that way or if that self-knowledge had colored Hegland's treatment of her.

'Why didn't you report Hegland's threats to Community Policing?'

She should have lashed out at the question. She wasn't the one at fault. Her eyes came to rest on the little parcel of letters. As if she understood what he was grappling with, she said, 'It's hard to face the things that strip you raw. Or to bear up against the past.'

Empathy warmed the space between them. The tightness in

Khattak's chest eased because the truth in the end was simple. He wasn't ready. And he wouldn't touch the letters until he was.

Rachel said, 'Hegland was in your present, not your past.'

He gave Rachel a hard look before he followed up, 'Can you tell us why your arms were raised if you didn't push him?'

The moment between them lost, Haniya's hands worked in her lap.

'He was going to touch my body. I was guarding myself.'

•

As a last resort, Khattak called in an old friend, a reporter by the name of Vicky D'Souza, who excelled at analyzing film. Vicky was small, bright, lovely and persistent, a great favorite of Rachel's and Esa's, whom she'd met on another case. They'd asked her in to cast fresh eyes over the security footage.

No other record of Hegland's fall had turned up, no cell phone videos, no witnesses, no proof that he'd been pushed. Only that brief confrontation on the platform.

'I like her gloves,' Vicky said, nodding at the screen. 'They're a perfect match for her scarf.'

Esa had missed this. Haniya Mirza hadn't been wearing gloves in his office. He'd seen her small brown hands smoothing the papers on his desk. Keeping her hands concealed wasn't part of her dress code. So why had she been wearing gloves on a warm summer's day?

'Take another look at this, would you, Vicky?'

'Anything for you, Inspector.'

He smiled and she continued, 'Stop smiling at me like that. You know my heart can't take it.'

He shook his head in reproof. 'Stop flirting with me and pay attention.'

Vicky wasn't serious. She had married her college sweetheart earlier that summer, and Esa had given a toast at the wedding.

'Do you see anything I don't?'

They stared at the screen together, Khattak peering at the gloves.

He couldn't see anything to arouse suspicion.

Rachel was prepping the file to return to the Hate Crime Unit. Now she looked up. 'I did wonder why she came downtown. She'd lost her job, so why was she in the city?'

'I did a little digging,' Vicky said, still peering at the image on the screen. 'Haniya had a paycheck to collect.'

'It could have been mailed to her. Or deposited in her account. It must have been a major inconvenience to come into the city, and then return at rush hour.'

Vicky magnified a segment of the image, as she answered Rachel. 'Same rush hour every weekday, same crush, everyone shoving to get a spot on the train. After all her years at the gallery, no way Haniya wouldn't know that.' She clicked off the image, frustrated. 'It's no use. I don't know what I'm looking at. Yellow gloves, long sleeves, it feels like the glove on her right hand could be a little distorted, but the flow of the line is continuous. It's too hard to tell from a distance.' She gave a cavalier shrug. 'Hegland was a lowlife so I'm thinking, no loss there.'

'Lowlife or not, we have to investigate the possibility of homicide.'

Khattak fell quiet, thinking.

Haniya Mirza was an art restorer. She would know what they expected to see on camera—a continuous line. And no contact with the victim, unless he made contact first. Suppose Blair Hegland had. His mutilated remains wouldn't tell them a thing.

I told him to save himself.

If she'd pushed him, someone would have seen. Yet had Haniya given Hegland a warning? The thought was so absurd, he didn't voice it to the others.

'Anyway,' Vicky was saying, 'Hegland made her life a nightmare, I won't be losing sleep over him.'

Haniya

The ruined painting had given her the idea, colors flowing to the edge, bleeding together as one. Film took color in the same way that canvas took color: you noticed a broken line.

In the end, she'd left it up to Hegland. Harm had been done, and he meant her further harm, so she purchased a stun gun in Buffalo and smuggled it across the border. It was small enough to fit inside her palm. She painted it to match her glove and slipped the strap over her fingers. If Hegland didn't cross the safety barrier, he wouldn't suffer the penalty. It all depended on the kind of man he was, the kind of man she knew him to be.

If he did make contact, the surge of the crowd would do the rest.

•

He'd looked her in the eye afterward, bewildered that he couldn't command the movements of his own body.

Tugging her scarf to cover her face, she stared at him as he fell.

The train juddered to a halt.

The crowd screamed at the crunch of bone. Blood spurted up along the rails. Another iridescent color, burning bright against cold steel. She'd paint a red like that one day, a red as beautiful as blood.

•

What was left of Hegland's body meant the autopsy would yield nothing of value, and the stun gun was tucked safely in her purse. There was nothing to worry about.

As for guilt . . . the choice had been left to him.

Haniya was only guilty of crossing the yellow line.

GNOME MAN'S LAND

FELICIA YAP

Herbert Poole, the Deputy Commandant of the Royal Military Academy at Sandhurst, was not amused. There were three reasons for this. Firstly, the Commandant had vanished to Afghanistan for a couple of weeks, ostensibly to deal with several pressing engagements in Kandahar, leaving Herbert to attend to the bureaucracy left in his wake.

Secondly, the temporary absence of the Commandant meant that responsibility for the upcoming Sovereign's Parade was transferred to Herbert. Her Majesty the Queen was due to inspect the academy's cadets, flanked by an entourage of visiting dignitaries. If Herbert remembered correctly, this particular retinue would feature three luminaries, all ex-graduates of the institution: the King of Jordan, the Sultan of Brunei and the Crown Prince of Tonga. This meant that Sandhurst had to put on her best show; Herbert couldn't remember when the academy had last had so many royal guests visiting at the same time. It was now up to him to figure out what could go wrong on the day, potentially ruining his hitherto unblemished military career.

The third reason had appeared on Herbert's mahogany desk

twelve days before the Sovereign's Parade. Normally, his desk featured a writing pad (which he seldom used, preferring to think on his feet instead of on paper), a miniature Union Jack and a china bulldog with a nodding head that reminded him of Winston Churchill, a man he greatly admired. Yet when Herbert entered his office that morning, there was a new entity next to his nodding bulldog. It had a broad grin on its face, a smile both devilish and mocking.

This couldn't be, Herbert thought. This surely couldn't be. His eyesight had deteriorated quite a bit recently. It was probably playing tricks on him again. Yes, he was definitely imagining it.

Herbert blinked hard.

He was *not* imagining it.

He was staring at a green garden gnome that looked as if it would be more at home on a Camberley council estate than in the hallowed precincts of the Deputy Commandant's office. A gnome with a bright red coat and beanie hat to match, tilted at a rakish angle.

Stumped by the unprecedented sight, Herbert took a cautious step in the gnome's direction. Its grin seemed to widen as he did so. To his surprise, he saw that a note had been tacked to the gnome with Sellotape. Puzzled, he lowered his head to inspect the note. It said:

'*Please help me find my 277 brothers.*'

Herbert collapsed onto his chair. He had always prided himself on his ability to recall each of the 359 articles in Sandhurst's 'Handbook of Rules and Regulations', a fact that, no doubt, accounted for his meteoric rise to Deputy Commandant within twenty-nine years of joining the academy. Unfortunately, there were no clauses in the handbook that dealt specifically with garden gnomes. This meant that Herbert would have to improvise, an activity he seldom enjoyed.

Herbert had never liked garden gnomes. His aversion had begun at the age of nine, when a neighbour's dog had chased him for half a mile and he had cracked his head on a stone gnome after leaping a garden fence. His eyesight had never been as immaculate after that; he also became prone to ocular migraines that were preceded by blinding headaches and followed by bouts of bad temper. In fact, his vision had deteriorated quite a bit in recent years, though he dare not admit this to anyone.

With a shaking hand, he pushed a buzzer beside his desk.

A few minutes later, Major Adjutant Samuel Stopford marched into the office and snapped off a brisk salute.

'What's that?' Herbert said in a bellow, pointing a finger at the latest addition to his desk.

'It's a gnome, sir.'

'I can see that it's a gnome. What is it doing here?'

'Beats me, sir.'

'Remove it at once,' Herbert said, his voice turning shrill. 'The cadet responsible for this prank must be tracked down and punished.'

'What exactly is the crime, sir?'

'I can think of at least two Tier Three offences: Article 47(a) for breaking and entering, and Article 319(b) for indecorous speech and/or provoking a commanding officer.'

'Yes, sir,' Major Adjutant Stopford said, clicking his heels and saluting again.

Herbert continued to eye the gnome with suspicion as the Major Adjutant carried the figurine out of his office with gloved hands. The Deputy Commandant had a sneaking feeling that the gnome merely represented the beginning of his troubles. He was also uncertain why the gnome had '277 brothers', which in Herbert's estimation constituted a threateningly large number of comrades. It was also unclear which cadet had masterminded

343

the thing and how the guilty party could be pinned down with certainty. In fact, the whole affair was an unsettling mystery.

Herbert sighed. He had once read in *The Times* that a study of American prisoners had found that men on death row tend to be less miserable than those who are waiting to find out if they will be executed. Humans hate uncertainty even more than the prospect of death, the article concluded. Having stared death in the eye multiple times during his time in the field, Herbert agreed with the researchers. While he was a man who could deal with threat, he was not a man who liked uncertainty.

Neither was he a man who enjoyed unsettling mysteries.

•

Later that evening, Herbert found himself blinking with disbelief as he trudged down the front steps of Old College in the direction of his bungalow, located a half mile away in one of the wooded areas of the Sandhurst estate. A second gnome was perched on the barrel of one of the cannons captured at the battle of Waterloo. It had a fluffy white beard and a girth to match Napoleon's, a delirious grin that stretched from ear to ear. Herbert was reduced to staring at the gnome in silent consternation before he found his voice, prompting Sergeant Peters, who manned the front desk at Old College, to come pelting down the stairs.

'What on earth is riding that cannon?' Herbert said.

'It's a gnome, sir.'

'I can see that it's a gnome. What is it doing here?'

'Excellent question, sir.'

'Take that gnome away.'

'Yes, sir.'

'Tell the Major Adjutant that the cadet responsible for this must be tracked down and punished for committing a Tier Four offence, namely Article 256(a) for the unauthorized placement of a personal item in a public space within the academy.'

'Of course, sir.' The sergeant scurried forward to remove the gnome from its uncanonical position. 'By the way, sir, I saw four more gnomes earlier today.'

'What?'

'There were three gnomes inside the salt bin at the back of Old College when I looked in this morning. The fourth gnome was in the men's loo on the first floor. It was serving as a toilet paper dispenser.'

'A *toilet paper dispenser*?'

'Indeed, sir.' Sergeant Peters nodded. 'A loo roll was attached to its head. I must confess, sir, that the three gnomes are still enjoying their salt bath and the fourth is still dispensing toilet paper. I wasn't aware of the protocol for dealing with this invasion of gnomes.'

Herbert was about to issue another curt order for the removal of the gnomes when Sergeant Peters' final phrase struck him hard.

'Dear Lord,' said Herbert with a gulp, turning as white as the beard on the gnome in Sergeant Peters' hands.

'Are you all right, sir?' There was concern in the sergeant's voice.

'An *invasion of gnomes*,' said Herbert in a soft growl. 'I've just figured out what "*my 277 brothers*" means. If we include the gnome on my desk this morning, that makes two hundred and seventy-eight gnomes in total.'

'If you say so, sir.'

Herbert had the distinct impression that Sergeant Peters had no idea what he was talking about.

'How many cadets will be graduating next Saturday?' said Herbert, his brain now working overtime.

'Two hundred and seventy-eight cadets, sir . . . ah, I get it now.'

'One gnome per cadet, indeed,' said Herbert with a nod. 'They must have swept the shelves of the Camberley Garden Centre bare over the weekend . . . Sergeant Peters, please inform the Major Adjutant that he should expect a total of two hundred and seventy-eight garden gnomes to appear on the grounds of Sandhurst over the next few days. I have reason to believe that each graduating cadet has smuggled a gnome into the academy.'

'Yes, sir.'

'The gnomes are an affront to the dignity of our august institution and should be removed from sight. Tell Major Adjutant Stopford that the operation should be codenamed "Bucket Garden" and its execution should be both swift and decisive. The Queen will soon be visiting us for the Sovereign's Parade. We must ensure that Her Majesty will be inspecting cadets and not gnomes.'

'Very good, sir.'

'*Immediately*, Peters,' said Herbert.

Happy that he finally had a battle plan, Herbert turned his back on Sergeant Peters and began walking in the direction of his bungalow. After passing a lake, he decided to take a shortcut through a copse of birch trees to his bungalow. It was getting late and he had already wasted enough time. Unfortunately, he had only ventured a hundred yards down the path when he saw six grinning entities around the base of an oak tree. All of them wore pointy red caps and looked quite at ease. One gnome had a raised hand; it seemed to be waving cheerfully at Herbert. It even looked similar to the gnome that had given him a bloodied head at the age of nine.

Herbert groaned. He had just realized that if he was right and two hundred and seventy-eight gnomes were indeed lurking about the grounds of Sandhurst, Operation Bucket Garden was going to be a protracted engagement rather than a decisive skirmish.

•

By the end of the third day, between them the Deputy Commandant and the Major Adjutant had rounded up ninety-six gnomes. Most of the gnomes were discovered in unusual, if inventive, locations. One gnome had been riding the Centurion tank on display outside Churchill Hall, while another four were found propping up the Chaplain's bible inside the Royal Memorial Chapel. Seven gnomes in camouflage gear were spotted enjoying an afternoon siesta near Lower Lake, while a gnome with a pipe had waved impudently at Herbert from the window of Kashkets, the academy's kitting-out shop. Herbert had always prided himself on his ability to count. His able calculations indicated that one hundred and eighty-two gnomes still remained at large and Sandhurst remained infested to the extreme.

Irked by the situation, Herbert decided to attend the Adjutant's Practice that afternoon. It was the norm for cadets to undergo several march-past rehearsals before the Sovereign's Parade, the most notable of which were the Adjutant's Practice and the Commandant's Practice. It was not usual protocol for the Deputy Commandant to attend the Adjutant's Practice. But Herbert was keen to track down the mastermind behind the gnome affair and hoped that a scan of the parading faces might reveal the guilty party.

•

Major Adjutant Samuel Stopford was supervising the practice with a smile on his face when Herbert appeared at his side. Stopford had long known the cadets enjoyed the Adjutant's

Practice the most. It was their only opportunity to horse around a little, before the more serious practices began. On a previous occasion, one cadet had turned up as Darth Vader, much to the Major Adjutant's private delight. In Stopford's opinion, the appearance of Darth Vader with his light sabre was as memorable as the entire platoon of Elvis Presleys that had marched past him two years earlier.

'Fancy seeing you here, sir.' The Major Adjutant rose from his chair and greeted Herbert with a smart salute.

'I'm here to find the cadet behind the gnome affair,' Herbert said. 'In my experience, a guilty conscience is hard to hide.'

Stopford was tempted to make a remark or two about 'wishful thinking', but dared not voice his thoughts.

'Of course, sir,' he said, nodding as the first platoon of graduating cadets began marching into view. They seemed to be wearing banana skins on their heads, which in Stopford's opinion were neither original nor interesting.

'Does this happen often?' Herbert asked, presumably referring to the banana skins.

'Yes, sir,' said Stopford. 'No, sir.'

The Major Adjutant received an exasperated glance from Herbert, before he turned his gaze back to the passing cadets. Unfortunately, none of the young faces marching by seemed particularly guilty to Stopford. Which prompted him to ask:

'What does guilt look like, sir?'

The Major Adjutant saw consternation flit over Herbert's face. But the Deputy Commandant eventually pulled his shoulders back and said with a forced air of authority:

'Shifty eyes. A smile a little too wide for comfort.'

The Major Adjutant was tempted to say that Herbert had just described the multi-coloured gnome in his granny's back garden, but he bit his tongue again.

'Very good, sir,' he said, before adding. 'Do criminals usually look guilty?'

The Major Adjutant saw Herbert frowning, just before he pulled himself up again and said:

'Most of the time, yes.'

'What happens when they don't, sir?'

'They get away with it . . . bloody fucking hell.'

The Major Adjutant nearly fell off his chair; he had never heard Herbert swear before. He turned his head to realize that eighteen members of the Alamein Company were wearing curved red caps, thick buckled belts and fluffy white beards. One of them had a long pipe in his hand and even shot the Deputy Commandant a cheeky grin as he passed. Stopford was tempted to suggest to his superior officer that they should perhaps subtract eighteen from the remaining figure of one hundred and eighty-two. But the Major Adjutant wisely kept his mouth shut. He had realized that poor Herbert had suffered two heart attacks in the past year and that the gnome affair was fast-tracking his superior to a third prolonged stay at Camberley's Frimley Park Hospital.

•

Saturday, when it came, dawned bright, dry and sunny. As Herbert saw it, the conditions were perfect for the Sovereign's Parade, if not for the fact that sixty-seven gnomes had remained unaccounted for. Although he and Adjutant Stopford had undertaken a last-ditch sortie at gnome-culling the day before the parade, Herbert was aware that the operational objectives of 'Bucket Garden' had not been fully realized. He had a horrible feeling that a few gnomes would make inopportune appearances during the day, much to Her Majesty's displeasure. While Herbert had no idea what the King of Jordan, the Sultan of Brunei and the Crown Prince of Tonga thought about gnomes, the little voice in his head had remained adamant that the creatures would land him in a royal mess. For the umpteenth time that week, Herbert found himself cursing the fact that the Commandant had vanished to Afghanistan, leaving him behind in gnome man's land.

The first inkling Herbert had that something was amiss were the expressions of the cadets' faces as they marched past Old College. While all of them were turned out impeccably and did not place a single foot wrong, they seemed to be trying hard not to chuckle. As he strode up to the dais to deliver a congratulatory speech on the Commandant's behalf, he could have sworn that the cadets in the back row were doing their best not to smirk.

Yet to his astonishment, Sandhurst appeared gnome-free. He did not spot any gnomes when the Queen and Commander-in-Chief of the British Armed Forces, resplendent in her burgundy beret and matching coat, conducted her inspection. When the parade ended with the Major Adjutant riding his horse up the steps of Old College, the hallowed grounds of the Royal Military Academy remained surprisingly gnome-less.

Maybe it was his bad eyesight, he thought.

Or maybe it was good luck.

By the time the grand reception swung around at the end of the day, Herbert began to feel cautiously relieved. He accordingly decided to help himself to a large flute of champagne from a passing waiter.

'An excellent day, wasn't it?'

Herbert turned around to find the King of Jordan beaming at him.

'Indeed, Your Majesty,' Herbert agreed, permitting himself a rare smile before gulping down half of the champagne.

'I had a chat with one of your graduating cadets just now,' the King continued. 'He told me that the dais – the one you were standing on to give your speech earlier – was propped up by four garden gnomes.'

'I . . . I wasn't aware of this, Your Majesty,' said Herbert, sputtering.

'His friends had planted the gnomes under the dais just before your speech, to ensure your declarations were amply supported. What a delightful story. It reminded me of the pranks my fellow cadets had engaged in during my own days at Sandhurst. I'm glad the British Army hasn't lost its sense of humour.'

Herbert found himself turning a bright shade of red. He nodded in agonised silence before pouring the rest of the fizzy liquid down his throat.

'I thoroughly enjoyed your speech, Brigadier Poole.' The Crown Prince of Tonga appeared at Herbert's side. 'Inspiring stuff. It reminded me of the speech the Commandant gave when I graduated from Sandhurst a few years back. I was also enthralled by the latest addition to the Old College portico.'

'What do you mean, Your Majesty?' Herbert said, his voice beginning to shake. Just then, a waiter glided up to remove his empty flute. Herbert grabbed a glass of sherry from the waiter's tray and gulped most of it down.

'I could have sworn that a garden gnome was grinning down on us from the tympanum of Old College,' said the Crown Prince. 'It was sandwiched between the statues of Mars and Minerva.'

Herbert had a distinct feeling that even the tips of his ears had turned red.

'When I first arrived at Sandhurst, my CO explained to me that Mars is the Roman God of War and Minerva is the Roman Goddess of Wisdom,' continued the Crown Prince. 'He also said that the gnome is a descendant of the Greco-Roman fertility god Priapus, a god known for his oversized and permanent erection.'

By then, Herbert was beginning to feel that he had been reduced to a flaccid state. To spare himself a reply, he turned to another passing waiter to swap his empty glass of sherry for a full glass of port. Gasping for breath, he poured half of the liquid down his throat to fortify himself.

'I couldn't help but overhear what you just said, my dear friend,' said the Sultan of Brunei, striding up to join the group. 'I agree that gnomes can inspire us to much bigger things. By the way, I chatted on the phone to your Commandant this morning, Brigadier Poole. He's having quite the adventure in Afghanistan. He asked me to pass a message to the cadets, but I never got a chance to deliver it.'

'Did he?' said Herbert, swallowing the rest of the port. 'What did he say, Your Majesty?'

'He had heard about their recent adventures and could only hope they didn't get *too* carried away at the Garden Centre.'

Herbert felt faint. He also felt something painful rushing to his head and blurring his vision even further. Oh no, he thought. It was probably the start of yet another blinding migraine.

'Aha,' said the Sultan. 'I see Her Majesty coming in our direction. I've been itching to tell her how fetching she looks today, in that beret of hers.'

Herbert spun around to discover that the Queen was indeed making her way in their direction, flanked by her courtiers. But then, she stopped and turned her head, distracted by something. He squinted hard. Her Majesty was looking at what would have normally been the bust of General John Churchill, on a raised marble pedestal. Instead, the bust had vanished, to be replaced by a . . .

All that Herbert could think of was the necessity of removing the appalling object from Her Majesty's line of sight, the necessity of rescuing his precious institution from lasting opprobrium and his career from the prospect of prematurely enforced retirement. Unfortunately, it had been a while since he had dashed anywhere, particularly after drinking champagne, sherry and port in quick succession. By the time he got within striking range of the pedestal, he felt so light-headed, his knees were buckling.

'What a delightful . . .' he heard Her Majesty say.

The last thing Herbert remembered was collapsing to the floor, with the Queen's face looming across his vision. He recalled striking his head against something immobile as he went down, something that sent sharp pain thudding through the right side of his skull, agony as excruciating as the blades that had sliced across his forehead at the age of nine.

•

The first thing Herbert saw, when he came to, were bright fluorescent lights. He blinked hard, forcing the world into focus. He appeared to be lying on a hospital bed with lurid pale-green sheets and a matching duvet cover. The right side of his head felt sore, but there was no trace of his usual migraine. Someone was sitting by his bed. He blinked even harder, only to realize that the person was the Commandant himself, wearing a large smile on his face.

'Welcome back,' said the Commandant. 'I've just returned from Kandahar. Came over as soon as I heard.'

'I . . . I . . .'

'I'm assured you will make a full recovery,' said the Commandant, flashing Herbert another broad smile.

'What . . . *what* happened?' said Herbert in a faint voice.

'It wasn't a heart attack, don't you worry,' said the Commandant, in his most reassuring voice. 'You just collapsed, hit your head on the way down. You've been out a good long while, though.'

Just then, Herbert's brain cranked back to life, reliving his embarrassing exchanges with the Sultan, King, and Crown Prince. He gasped, recalling the precise sequence of events before he ended up flat on his nose.

'The Queen,' he said, wincing.

'Ah yes, the Queen,' said the Commandant. 'She sends her best wishes, hopes you'll be back on your feet in no time. I'm told she counted forty-five gnomes over the course of the day and was pretty impressed.'

'Forty-five?' said Herbert, his voice an incredulous whisper. 'Her Majesty spotted *forty-five gnomes*?'

'She did, indeed.'

Herbert was reduced to opening and closing his mouth.

'The powers above will be issuing my marching orders,' he said, eventually finding his voice again. 'If they haven't done so already.'

'Most certainly not,' said the Commandant. 'Her Majesty said she had never seen anything so delightful. Spot-a-gnome whack-a-mole. Truly, the best show Sandhurst has ever put on. She even suggested she might order a few placed around the cairns of Balmoral.'

'You must be joking,' said Herbert.

'I usually am,' said the Commandant.

Herbert paused to consider the Commandant's words.

'So, I'm off the hook?' he said.

'You were never on it,' said the Commandant. 'I always knew Her Majesty would see the funny side.'

Herbert took a deep breath. He felt as if a weight had lifted from his shoulders. In fact, his vision seemed much brighter than it had been in years. He blinked a few times to confirm his hypothesis. Everything around him had sharpened into focus, acquired a high-definition gloss. Even the hospital sheet which shrouded him wasn't just pale green, it was an unmistakable shade of Kermit green. In fact, Herbert had not seen the world this clearly since he had bumped his head at the age of nine. He felt rejuvenated, a better and brighter version of himself, a version more capable of dealing with mystery and uncertainty. More thoughts flashed across his head, insights bold and beautiful. Maybe skewed eyesight causes rigid and inflexible thoughts, he mused, an unhealthy obsession with rules and regulations. Maybe poor vision makes people poorer versions of themselves. Maybe that's why he had been such a stick in the mud all these years.

'What did I hit my head on?' he said, reaching up to rub the side of his skull.

'Number two hundred and seventy-eight,' said the Commandant. 'The last gnome standing.'

'I see,' said Herbert.

'I'm sorry to say you managed to smash your port glass along the way, but that was probably the only thing in the room you broke convincingly,' said the Commandant with a chuckle.

Herbert silently thanked Gnome Number 278 for contributing to his clearer vision. In fact, he couldn't wait to get out of the hospital, to test his restored eyesight and newfound appreciation of the world. How ironic, he thought. A gnome had sent him to no-man's-land for decades, a bleak humourless world of migraines and bad temper, and it was a gnome that had brought him back from the trenches of despair. He didn't know if he should feel happy or sad. Maybe he should try to feel happy, for a change. It had been a long time since he felt truly happy.

One thing, however, still niggled. It was not the question of Why-It-Happened (the universe, after all, works in mysteriously unfathomable ways). It was the question of Who-Did-It.

'Do you, by any chance, know who masterminded the affair?' said Herbert.

The Commandant winked.

'You said to me, a long time ago, that the academy was operated by a bunch of gnomes who stayed firmly in the back room and it would be nice to see them out in the open for once.'

CHINOOK

THOMAS KING

Chinook was an unpretentious prairie town, banked low against the weather that slid off the eastern face of the Rockies. Summers were hot. Winters were cold and long. People in Chinook tended to stay put. Unless you wanted to drive three hours on bad roads or catch a flight to somewhere else, there was nowhere else to go.

Then there was the wind.

Thumps DreadfulWater generally kept his mouth shut about the wind.

•

Al's café was sandwiched between Fjord Bakery and Sam's laundromat, with no sign to mark the spot except the turtle shell that Preston Wagamese had super-glued next to the front door with the word 'Food' written in black marker.

The café itself was unremarkable, a railroad car of a place that had once been a dead-end alley. A long, narrow aisle with plywood booths huddled against one wall. A run of scruffy chrome and red Naugahyde stools wedged tight to a lime-green Formica counter.

There was nothing foreboding about the place, but it was dark. The only light came in through the window next to the grill. And it was muggy, with the damp smells of grease, burnt toast, strong coffee, and sweat swirling through the café in currents and eddies.

Thumps DreadfulWater was a regular, and yet, each time he came into the café, the first sensation was that of being shoved underwater.

Alvera Couteau was standing by the grill with a spatula in her hand.

'Looks like someone took your favorite toy. You depressed again?'

'Nope.'

'Wind will do that to you,' said Al. 'Did you know that depression can be linked to the weather?'

'Nope,' said Thumps.

'Sheriff was looking for you,' said Al. 'You want to know why?'

'Nope.'

'You know, denial is another sign of depression.'

'Breakfast,' Thumps repeated. 'The usual.'

•

Duke Hockney had been the sheriff in Chinook for longer than Thumps had been in town. He was a solid man, a sack of boulders in a long-sleeved shirt, a whip-cord jacket, and a cowboy hat.

Thumps liked Duke well enough, but the man had a bad habit of dragging him into adventures which, more often as not, involved dead bodies.

'You used to be a cop,' said Al. 'So, you know one end of the bull from the other.'

'And now I'm a landscape photographer,' said Thumps. 'A hungry photographer.'

'How's the diabetes?' said Al.

'Don't hold back on the potatoes.'

'You check your blood sugars this morning?'

'I don't see anything cooking.'

'Wow.' Al ambled back to the grill. 'You ex-cops don't miss a thing.'

Thumps settled on the stool and reminded himself how he should have started the day. He should have been up at dawn, his photographic gear packed. He should have driven out to Red Tail Lake or up to Glory or to the high ground above the Ironstone. He should have set up his field camera and waited for the perfect moment of light and shadow to come together in a stunning landscape.

Instead, he had stayed in bed, had spent the better part of the morning on the edge of depression. And for no good reason. He and Claire were on again. His one-man show at Shadow Ranch had been a success, and Vernon Rockland wanted to do another one in the late fall.

All in all, life was good.

Al appeared with the coffee pot, stood there and waited.

'OK,' said Thumps, 'what did Duke want?'

'You know what makes life worth living?'

Thumps pointed at the grill. 'A hot breakfast.'

'Surprises,' said Al. 'There's nothing like a surprise.'

'How about surprising me with food.'

•

Thumps was halfway through his meal when Sheriff Duke Hockney banged in through the door and sat himself down on an adjacent stool.

'Been looking for you.' Hockney picked up a fork. 'That garlic sausage?'

Thumps used his forearm to protect the plate.

'Macy has me on a diet,' said the sheriff. 'Oatmeal. Who the hell eats oatmeal?'

'Evidently,' said Thumps. 'You do.'

'Know what happens when you eat too many carbs?' Duke helped himself to the hash browns. 'You get sluggish.'

'I like sluggish.'

'Finish up,' said Duke. 'We got ourselves a rodeo.'

'There is no "we."'

'You're going to like this one,' said the sheriff.

'No, I won't.'

'Sonny Martell is dead.' Duke waited for the news to sink in. 'Out at the Mustang.'

Thumps watched his eggs glaze over and his toast go cold.

'If it's murder,' said Duke, 'the suspect list is going to be impressive.'

'Who's in first place?'

'Besides myself?' said the sheriff.

•

The Mustang had been a Texaco gas station, until Delroy 'Hack' Chubby bought the property at auction and turned it into a western saloon and biker bar. He dragged in a double-wide, cut out one wall, and spliced the trailer up against the station's service bays, so the place had enough room for a couple of pool tables and a dance floor.

And in a moment of decorator madness, Delroy hung the original Texaco sign from the ceiling and nailed the grille from a 1965 Mustang to the wall behind the bar.

The saloon was famous for fist fights and arm-wrestling

contests, with the occasional range war between the pickups and the motorcycles.

Delroy was killed on his '47 Knucklehead, trying to pass a semi on the long grade north of Chinook. There was a huge and noisy wake that lasted the weekend, and, when Monday rolled around, his daughter moved the Texaco sign and the Mustang grille and the pool tables into the parking lot and burned the place to the ground.

•

'You know much about Sonny Martell?'

'Just the rumors,' said Thumps.

'All true,' said Duke. 'Man was a mean son of a bitch. Practical joker. You know that game where you spread your fingers on a table and the other guy takes a knife and jabs between the fingers as fast as he can?'

'The one where you stab as fast as you can, try to miss the fingers? If you draw blood, you lose?'

'That's the one.' Duke held up a hand. Thumps could see the faint line of a scar. 'Sonny liked to lose.'

'You?'

'When I was young and stupid.'

'What's Martell doing now?'

'Construction mostly,' said the sheriff. 'Rip-offs and real estate scams.'

Thumps leaned against the door and watched the land fly by.

'Build Your Western Dreamhome.' Hockney yawned. 'Sonny would put a company together, take up-front money from half a dozen hedge-fund hamsters, company would fold, and he'd disappear with the money. After a while, he'd pop back up with excuses about the economy and bad loans and start another company.'

'Nobody ever nail him?'

'A few tried,' said Duke. 'Appears that losing money and going out of business isn't illegal.'

'Charming.'

'He and Lorraine used to be an item.'

•

Lorraine Chubby had her mother's brains. Before the ashes of the old Mustang had gone cold, she brought in a bulldozer, leveled the site, and started work on the new Mustang, a high-tech, red prefab building with a herd of wild horses painted across the front, and a satellite-receiver array on the roof.

And in anticipation of boys having a good time while drunk and stupid, Lorraine built a sandpit with a rope ring behind the Mustang, complete with lights, a sound system, and benches for spectators.

Along with a remarkably well-stocked first-aid station.

Any disagreement in the Mustang was quickly adjourned to the sandpit where combatants could beat on each other to the theme song from *Rocky*.

•

'We know how Martell died?'

Duke pulled the cruiser into the Mustang parking lot. 'We do not.'

'Just that he's dead?'

'Could be someone shot him with a silver bullet,' said Duke.

'That's for werewolves,' said Thumps.

The sheriff set the parking brake and opened the door. 'Or put a stake through his heart.'

'That's for vampires.'

Duke nodded. 'With Sonny, it would be best to cover all the bases.'

·

All the action was at the rear of the Mustang. Lance Packard and Deanna Heavy Runner had cordoned off the area and were standing guard. Lorraine Chubby and her husband Big Fish Patek were off to one side in a huddle. Beth Mooney, the county's coroner and medical officer, was in the sandpit kneeling next to Sonny Martell.

Martell didn't have a stake through his heart, and neither was he going to turn into a bat and fly away any time soon.

'Beth,' said Duke, touching the brim of his hat the way John Wayne might have done in *Rio Bravo*. 'What do we have?'

'One dead Sonny Martell,' said Beth, without looking up. 'Some days I love my job.'

Thumps had seen more than his fair share of bodies and didn't need to see another.

'Can't wait to get him on my table and cut him open.'

'Supposed to be impartial,' said Duke.

'I'm betting I won't find a heart.'

Duke walked around the body. 'Don't see any wounds.'

'What big eyes you have,' said Beth.

'So, it could be a natural death?'

Beth stood up. 'Too soon to tell,' she said. 'For the time being, let's just savor the moment together.'

Duke walked over to Deanna and Lance.

'Deputies,' said the sheriff. 'What are we looking at?'

'Not sure,' said Lance.

'We got a ladder,' said Deanna. 'And a bag of tools.'

'Window on the second floor is busted,' said Lance.

'So, you think Mr Martell climbed up a ladder, smashed a window, started to climb back down, ladder slipped, and he fell to his death?'

'Maybe,' said Deanna.

'Because the ladder's on the ground,' said Duke, 'and we got tools scattered about?'

'One way to read it,' said Lance.

Duke looked at Deanna and then at Lance. 'But?'

'As far as we can tell,' said Lance. 'Nothing's been taken.'

'Not that far a fall,' said Deanna. 'And the sand's soft.'

'Bag up everything,' said the sheriff. 'You know the routine.'

•

Thumps followed the sheriff to where Lorraine and Big Fish were standing.

'No easy way to ask this,' said the sheriff.

'Then don't try,' said Lorraine.

'You and Sonny . . .' Duke let the question hang in the air.

'I was seventeen,' said Lorraine. 'We were together for about a year. He was an asshole. I threw him out. End of story.'

'You two married?'

'One of Sonny's fantasies. Never happened,' said Lorraine. 'I was stupid, not brain dead.'

'He come around much?'

'I haven't had anything to do with the man for well over twenty years,' said Lorraine. 'He came sniffing around a couple of years back, figured I owed him part of the Mustang 'cause he was friends with my father.'

'And?'

'And nothing,' said Lorraine. 'Wasn't about to give him the time of day.'

'Last time he came by,' said Big Fish, 'me and the boys threw him and Crusty the Clown out on their asses. Told them not to come back.'

'Crusty the Clown?'

'Stu Cruster,' said Big Fish. 'Sonny's weasel sidekick. Maybe he can tell you why his pal is lying dead in our sandpit.'

'Can I go?' said Lorraine. 'Got a baby to feed.'

Thumps nodded. 'Who found the body?'

'I did,' said Big Fish. 'When I came to open up this morning.'

'We've been closed for the last couple of days,' said Lorraine. 'We're renovating the stage.'

'Tonight was going to be a sort of grand opening,' said Big Fish. 'And now this.'

Duke looked at the eaves of the building. 'You ever get those security cameras installed?'

Big Fish shrugged. 'Top of list, Sheriff. Then the baby came along.'

'How is little Hack?' said Thumps.

'Sweetest boy in the world,' said Lorraine.

'Takes after me,' said Big Fish.

'Hell he does,' said Lorraine.

•

Deanna and Lance helped to load the body into Beth's station wagon. Thumps stood off to one side with the sheriff.

'So, we got options,' said Duke. 'Sonny hikes out here from town with a bag of tools, climbs up looking to break into the bar, falls off the roof.'

'That's one,' said Thumps.

'Or someone drives him here, whereupon he climbs onto the roof and falls off. Whereupon, the same someone who drove him out leaves him here and drives away.'

'Whereupon?'

'And three,' said Duke, holding up fingers. 'There's the chance that Sonny died somewhere else and was dumped here to confuse us.'

'Sounds like you got most of the bases covered,' said Thumps. 'How about you take me home?'

'Sure,' said Duke. 'But how about we vote first.'

'Maybe we should wait for Beth to tell us why Sonny died before we go jumping to conclusions.'

Duke took off his hat and wiped the sweatband. 'Be nice and tidy if he did something stupid and killed himself.'

•

Thumps spent the next few days in the darkroom, away from the world at large, sorting through negatives, listening to NPR, and rearranging his kitchen.

He was at the sink when he saw the sheriff's car pull up to the curb and Duke get out.

'You ready?' Sheriff Hockney waited on the sidewalk. 'Beth's got the autopsy results.'

'Busy,' said Thumps.

'Don't be like that,' said Duke. 'You're dying to know.'

'I haven't had breakfast.'

The sheriff held up a bag and shook it. 'Law-enforcement special.'

'A donut?'

'Donut *and* a coffee,' said Duke. 'Nothing too good for a cowboy.'

'That's not breakfast.'

'You want to go to the morgue on a full stomach?'

•

Beth Mooney had her offices in the old land-titles building. Beth's apartment was on the second floor. The first floor was reserved for her medical practice. The county morgue was in the basement, a dank tarn of a room with creepy shadows and frightening smells, a stainless-steel table and a set of morgue drawers for storing bodies.

Duke pressed the button for the basement. 'You're not going to pass out on me again, are you?'

'I don't pass out.'

'You get woozy.'

'You know much about Native culture and dead bodies?'

'This that Navajo thing again?'

'It is,' said Thumps.

'You're not Navajo, Dreadful Water,' said Duke. 'You're Cherokee.'

'I have Navajo sensibilities.'

Beth was at her desk, shifting papers in a folder.

'You brought Thumps?'

'De-sensitivity training,' said Duke.

'He pukes this time,' said Beth, 'and you clean it up.'

The smells were more alarming than usual. Thumps switched to breathing through his mouth.

'The air exchanger is broken,' said Beth, 'so it's a little ripe.'

'We've smelled worse,' said the sheriff.

'No, we haven't,' said Thumps.

Beth was dressed in jeans and a blue work shirt. Her hair was pulled back tight to her head. More than anything, she reminded Thumps of the nineteenth-century photographs of pioneer women. Fierce, with no time for maternal indulgences.

'Our Sonny Martell is an interesting case,' said Beth. 'Why don't I bring him out so I can show you what I mean.'

'No need,' said Thumps. 'We're good with words.'

'I have photographs,' said Beth.

'Great,' said Duke. 'Thumps loves photographs.'

'Either one of you want to guess as to cause of death?'

'Suicide?' asked Duke. 'Self-inflicted accident?'

'Do I detect a hopeful tone?'

'You do.'

Beth handed the sheriff the file. 'Not your lucky day.'

'Murder?'

'It appears that our Mr Martell was stun-gunned.'

'Stun-gunned?'

'I assume you two know the difference between a stun gun and a taser?'

'We do,' said Duke.

'Stun gun shouldn't kill anyone,' said Thumps.

'Quite right,' said Beth. 'Unless you happen to have a pace-maker.'

'And Sonny Martell had a pacemaker.'

'He did.'

'Shit.'

Beth put a photograph out on the stainless-steel table. It showed two small burn marks on Martell's chest.

'It gets better,' said Beth. 'In addition to being zapped, it appears that our Mr Sonny was also frozen.'

'Frozen?'

'Fully defrosted when we found him,' said Beth, 'but there's evidence of ice-crystal damage in the cells.'

Thumps took a deep breath in through his mouth.

Beth put a second photo on the table. 'As well as what is known as skin slippage.'

'Charming,' said the sheriff.

'You two are the "who done it" guys,' said Beth. 'But I'd say you're looking for a killer with a stun gun and a large freezer.'

•

368

There was no one in Al's. The sheriff waited until the two of them were settled on stools.

'About fifteen years back, I hired Sonny to build me a sunroom.'

'And he ran off with the money?'

'Nope,' said Duke. 'He built the room. But he used untreated lumber for the posts and joists. Three years later, the whole thing rotted away and I had to tear it down.'

'Don't suppose he stood behind his work?'

'Said I should have specified treated lumber if I had wanted treated lumber.'

'Were you sheriff then?'

'Deputy,' said Duke. 'Spent a fair amount of time researching liability and construction law.'

'Didn't know there was such a thing,' said Thumps.

'Turns out,' said Duke, 'there isn't.'

Al appeared with the coffee pot. 'Hear you boys had a busy morning.' Al poured two cups without asking. 'Sonny Martell really dead?'

'He is,' said Duke. 'You wouldn't have done the deed?'

'Last time that man was in the café,' said Al, 'I had thoughts of parking my cleaver in his head.'

'Looks like we got ourselves a suspect,' said Duke.

Al held out her wrists. 'You'll never take me alive, you dirty copper.'

'What do you know about Stu Cruster?'

'Martell and Cruster?' Al slapped her towel on the counter. 'You keep talking like that, I'm going to shove your mouth in my dishwasher.'

'You know if Stu has been hanging with Sonny?'

'Set the cycle on sanitize.'

'Breakfast,' said Thumps. 'The usual.'

'You might want to give him extra potatoes,' said Duke.

'Order your own breakfast,' said Thumps.

'I'm on a damn diet,' said Duke. 'Have a little sympathy.'

Al headed back to the grill, mumbling as she went. Thumps settled in behind his coffee.

'Who do we know has a stun gun?'

'Yeah,' said Duke. 'I was thinking about that.'

'And a walk-in freezer.'

•

Thumps ate his breakfast in silence. The sheriff busied himself making lightning raids on the hash browns and the sausages, and letting Al catch him up on the gossip.

'So, the tribal council is teaming up with some arts organization in Canada to bring in a Blackfoot artist from someplace called Standoff.'

Duke set his hat on the stool next to him. 'We got plenty of Indians in our own back yard.'

'Evidently, this one is special,' said Al. 'Going to do an installation out on Antelope Flats.'

'A what?'

'Word is she's going to build scale models of the major religious sites in the world.'

'Like the Vatican?'

'Right,' said Al. 'And then she's going to blow them up.'

The sheriff sat back on his stool. 'That might upset a few folks.'

Al nodded. 'Supposed to be a statement on the oppressive nature of religion.'

'As in residential schools,' added Thumps.

'And Wutty Youngbeaver,' Al continued, 'is considering life as a Crime and Trauma Scene Cleaner.'

Thumps stopped eating.

Duke stole another piece of sausage. 'What happened to that electro-shock thingie for drunks he was so hot about?'

'Small problem with liability.'

'So, now he wants to clean up crime scenes?'

'Evidently, there's a course out at the community college,' said Al.

Thumps moved his plate out of the reach of the sheriff. 'How about we eat in silence.'

'Figure as soon as Wutty has to deal with his first pile of brain tissue,' said Al, 'he'll rethink his career options.'

'Silence,' said Thumps. 'Silence.'

●

When the sheriff pulled in around the back of the Mustang, Big Fish Patek was unloading boxes from a panel van.

'Didn't you guys just leave?'

'We did,' said Duke. 'But then we remembered a few more questions.'

Big Fish carried the boxes inside and began unpacking. 'Potato chips, pretzels. You wouldn't believe how many we go through of a night.'

Duke rocked on his heels. 'As I recall, the Mustang has a walk-in freezer.'

'We do.'

'Mind if I take a look?'

'At the freezer?'

'That a problem?'

'Not much to look at.'

'Maybe not,' said the sheriff, 'but I bet it's big enough to hold a body.'

Big Fish stopped what he was doing.

'And as I recall,' said Duke, 'you keep a stun gun behind the bar.'

Big Fish wiped his hands. 'She didn't do it,' he said. 'I did.'

Duke took off his hat. 'Why don't we sit down and see if the cuffs and collars match.'

•

It took a while for Big Fish to explain how and why he had killed Sonny Martell.

'If Sonny was trying to rob the place and you killed him in self defense,' said Duke, 'why didn't you call me?'

'I wasn't thinking straight.'

'And you weren't thinking straight when you put his body in the freezer?'

'That's right.'

'Or when you dumped his body in the sandpit.'

'That too,' said Big Fish. 'Look, I'd really appreciate it if you didn't say anything to Lorraine.'

'And just what is it we aren't going to tell Lorraine?'

Lorraine was standing in the shadows at the far side of the stage. She had the baby in her arms.

'Hi, honey.'

'Don't "hi honey," me.' Lorraine bounced little Hack against her chest. 'What's going on?'

'Well,' said Duke, 'Big Fish was just telling us how he killed Sonny Martell.'

Lorraine tried to keep a straight face. 'What?'

'He thinks you killed Sonny,' said Thumps, 'so he's trying to take the blame.'

'But he's not doing a very good job,' said Duke.

'Jesus,' said Lorraine. 'I thought we agreed that if there was any serious thinking to be done then I would do it.'

'I take it that you didn't kill Sonny either.'

'Can't say it never crossed my mind,' said Lorraine.

'Just don't say anything, honey.'

'Hell's bells,' said Lorraine, 'I didn't kill Sonny.'

'You didn't?'

'No.'

'OK,' said Big Fish. 'Then I didn't either.'

'All right,' said the sheriff. 'How about we slow down and start at the beginning.'

•

Duke put the word out, and the next day Stu Cruster walked into the sheriff's office on his own bat. He was a pear-shaped guy with eyes that didn't quite focus and curly hair that tended to turn up at the sides of his head. Thumps could see where the man got his nickname.

'Hear you wanted to see me.'

'Trying to find out what happened to Sonny Martell,' said Duke. 'You two being friends, I figured you'd want to help.'

'Damn straight,' Stu told Duke. 'Anything I can do.'

'Appreciate that,' said Duke.

'Good citizens do that sort of thing,' said Stu.

'Yes, they do,' said the sheriff.

Stu turned to Thumps. 'Did you know Sonny?'

'Can't say I did,' said Thumps.

'Heart of gold,' said Stu. 'Heart of gold.'

'Bit of a mean streak, though,' said Duke.

Stu waved it off. 'Sonny was a joker. Always joking around.'

'Like that knife game,' said Duke.

'Five-Finger Fillet?' Stu held up a hand and waggled his fingers. 'Oh, yeah. Got the scars to prove it.'

'What about stun guns,' said the sheriff. 'You two like to play around with stun guns?'

Stu's face went flat. 'Naw, that's stuff's dangerous.'

Duke nodded. 'Thumps here didn't know Sonny the way you did, and he was curious about Sonny and Lorraine.'

'Lorraine?'

'I hear that she and Sonny were an item,' said Thumps.

'I guess,' said Stu.

'He ever talk about the two of them getting back together?'

'You think Lorraine did him?' said Stu. 'You know, that makes sense.'

'No, it doesn't,' said the sheriff. 'I figure that you killed Sonny.'

Stu tried laughing. 'That's bullshit.'

'Bear with me,' said Duke. 'Couple of years back, Sonny tried to hustle Lorraine for a part of the Mustang.'

'Hey,' said Stu, 'Sonny was entitled. They were married. He had a share coming.'

'They were never married,' said Duke.

'Close enough.'

'So, I think that when Sonny heard about the stage renovations at the Mustang, he decided to teach Lorraine a lesson. How am I doing?'

'Your guess is as good as mine.'

'What do you think, Mr DreadfulWater,' said the sheriff. 'You think Sonny was vindictive?'

'Heart of gold,' said Thumps.

'I think the two of you broke into the Mustang looking to sabotage the renovations,' said Duke. 'Maybe the supports for the stage. Maybe the electrical.'

'Naw,' said Stu. 'Wasn't us.'

'But when you guys got there,' said Duke. 'Sonny found the stun gun.'

'Don't know nothing about no stun gun.'

'I'm thinking that Sonny zapped you with the gun,' said Duke.

'That would be like him. Stun gun would be a lot more fun than a knife.'

'Me and Sonny were friends.'

'Would have pissed me off,' said Thumps. 'Getting zapped like that.'

'So, you zapped Sonny,' said Duke. 'Imagine you didn't know he had a pacemaker.'

'Pacemaker?'

'And you killed him,' said Duke.

'You crazy?' Cruster's eyes were blinking rapidly. 'Why would I kill my best friend?'

'Don't think you meant to,' said Duke. 'I think you were angry.'

Stud was on his feet. 'Have a hell of a time proving any of this.'

Duke took his gun from the holster and laid it on his desk. 'Easy enough for you to prove your innocence.'

'And how's that?'

Duke was out of his chair, handcuffs in hand. 'Take off your shirt.'

•

The opening for the Mustang's new stage was a success. Thumps sat around afterwards over coffee with Lorraine and Big Fish.

'Hell of a turnout,' said Big Fish.

'Sorry the sheriff wasn't able to come,' said Lorraine.

'You guys really saved my ass.'

'It was the sheriff,' said Thumps. 'As soon as Stu took off his shirt and we saw the burn marks, it was all over.'

'So, Sonny was going to sabotage the electrical system?'

'That's what Stu says,' said Thumps. 'Sonny was going to rig it so when you turned on the spots, it would have started an electrical fire.'

'That could have been bad.'

'But he found the stun gun first and zapped Stu. One of his jokes.'

'And Stu got pissed and zapped Sonny?'

Thumps nodded. 'Screwed up his pacemaker, and that was that.'

'When I found Sonny and the stun gun,' said Big Fish, 'I thought Lorraine had done it.'

'And that's why you stuffed him in my freezer?' Lorraine shook her head.

'*Our* freezer, honey,' said Big Fish. 'At the time, I couldn't think of anything else to do.'

'Then you staged a robbery,' said Thumps.

'I thought *that* was a pretty good idea.'

'Broken window,' said Thumps. 'Ladder on the ground. Tools all over the place. And Sonny in the sandpit. As though he'd fallen off the roof or missed a rung on the ladder.'

'It could have worked.'

'Maybe you should lock him up,' said Lorraine, 'just on principle.'

'She's kidding,' said Big Fish. 'Who would run the place?'

Lorraine stood, put on her coat. 'Not a question you want me to answer.'

•

Thumps got to Al's early the next morning. Jimmy Monroe, Russell Plunkett, and Wutty Youngbeaver were on their usual stools across from the grill deep in an argument about *Star Trek*.

Thumps found his favorite stool. Al took her time walking the coffee pot down.

'Don't you want to add your voice to the discussion?'

'*Star Trek?*'

'They're trying to decide if Seven of Nine's boobs are real.' Al filled his cup. 'Should keep those three chuckleheads out of trouble for most of the day.'

'What's happening with Mr Crime Scene Cleaner?'

'Class hasn't started yet,' said Al, 'so he still has his illusions.'

Thumps closed his eyes for a moment. 'Nothing wrong with a few illusions.'

'Yep,' said Al. 'Definitely depression.'

Through the plate-glass window, Thumps could see the sun stretch out on the street. With any luck, Chinook might enjoy a day of warm sun and high skies. With any luck, the wind might stay in the mountains.

'So, how we going to cheer you up?'

'Breakfast,' said Thumps. 'The usual.'

BUTTONS

IMRAN MAHMOOD

Buttons.

I like buttons. There's something about the way that they feel in the hand, insignificant, unremarkable. Neither hot nor cold. There's nothing demanding about a button, nothing conspicuous. That's why it's the perfect choice. Who would even notice?

I took my first one ten years ago. First the life, then the button. It was an afterthought. But an immediate one. My mind was vibrating with power. So much power that I could feel it right in the fingertips. And the decision was fast. Making all those connections so quickly that I felt the world turning at half-speed.

It had been hanging by a single, almost stray, cotton thread. A plum for the picking. So, I picked. And then I ran. 1, 2, 3, 4, 5. Then the corner. 6, 7, 8, 9. Stop. Then check. Then check. Then bike. Then home. Then. Then.

Then I took the button from my pocket and placed it perfectly on the mantelpiece. Then I stared at myself in the mirror. This house. This room. This same mirror. And there, just for a second, I caught it. A glow just around the whites of my eyes and behind the ears.

Life. Yes! You could call it life. I could see my life. Glowing.

That was ten years ago. And now I have more buttons. A button a life. Always there. Crying to be picked. So I pick.

•

Today I have a date.

I don't like dates, but this one seems interesting. I met her at the bakery. 1, 2, 3, 4, 5, 6, 7, 8 croissants I buy. One for each morning. And one extra. In case. If you store them in the dark and dry, they keep well enough. I don't like the fridge for baked goods. It dries them.

•

She was at the counter and when she looked at me I looked at the floor. Her gaze was like sunlight. A lot of gazes feel like sunlight to me. I can't stand what they do to my eyes. She mistook that for shyness and it wasn't long before she nudged me into conversation.

'That's a lot of croissants,' she said. Northern. That accent. Leeds? Manchester?

I held up my bag and nodded. 'Eight,' I said and put the bag back down to my side.

'Eight is a weird number of croissants to buy.' She leaned across the counter to pay for a sourdough loaf she had chosen.

'I like to keep a spare,' I said, and took the chance to look her up and down. Early thirties? Eight stone? Good calves. Nice shoes. I don't care about hair colour but it was blond, if it matters to you.

She laughed and turned her body towards me. 'A spare! I'm going to use that. I like to keep a lot of spare chocolate at home.'

She wore a shirt. I like shirts — not enough women wear them. The buttons on hers, tiny. She caught me looking at what she thought was her chest. I was about to compliment her on the colour of her shirt and how it brought out her cheeks. People like compliments — I have never understood why they fall for them. But then she looked at me and smiled.

'I've just moved into East Dulwich. Maybe you could recommend some good places to eat?'

I was about to tell her that I don't eat out much but then I thought that she was trying to *hit on me* as the Americans say. 'There's a great gastro pub on Peckham Road,' I said, and I remembered to hold her gaze, although it hurt. And to smile.

She coloured slightly and began to pull at her hair. 'OK,' she said, and then stood uncertainly as if she didn't know whether to leave.

'Saturday,' I said, still smiling.

'What?'

'Saturday. If you're free? Around seven?' I could see her wondering whether she could say yes. She *was* free. She had just moved to the area. That accent was too — fresh? She'd just arrived in London. All that make-up for a loaf of bread? In the morning? And talking to strangers? She'd grow out of that in a week. My guess was that she was fresh off the bus.

'Erm, I am as it happens,' she said. Cheeks pinking up again.

'Great I'll see you outside. Just google it,' I said, and smiled before leaving. I had to leave. If I stay too long, sometimes they can tell something's a bit off with me. They're never sure exactly what it is. But they feel it.

•

I made my way home and pre-heated the oven. One croissant in. 2, 3, 4, 5, 6, 7 in the cupboard. Wrapped tight.

•

I stand in front of the mirror for my exercises. Corners high in the face to make full cheeks. A tiny flash of teeth. The trick is in the eyes though. A real smile is all in the eye. Just a crinkle does it. Hold it for 1, 2, 3 and 4.

The 'oh!' is the hard one. Mouth slightly open. Eyebrows lifted. Raised for a count and then a hand to the open mouth. Then add something like: 'No way.' It's difficult but in many ways this is the most useful one. The one I will use most.

I bore of these exercises but I know the importance of getting these things right. Only for social occasions. No need for this at work. At Court. One seat down from the judge's desk. A computer screen as a screen when needed – a shield. The rest of the time I can relax. Leave my face alone. This is what is expected of me any way. No emotional response to any of it. The evidence as it comes pouring out in steady streams from all directions. From the projectors. The documents. The photographs. The charts. The expert reports. The witnesses. The victims. The complainants. The defendants. It comes all of it in a tangled mess of truth and lie and half-lie. And I sit there letting it wash through me. My brain filtering, separating and sifting until there are only neat towers of truth and lie sitting on either side of those scales. Until the end, I sit and I sift. And then. And then. At the end.

They tip.

I didn't ask her name but I must ask it. That is an expectation too. So many of these untidy, unruly rules that do not stack. No sense to any of them. No rhyme. No weft or weave. No logic. Just – conventions.

So many of these crimes are lazy. I'm sorry. There's another rule here, I know it. Segue into these, gently. Feather yourself in so that it happens without notice, these changes of subject. In any case, the crimes – they're lazy. It's all just a question of planning. And sequence. Get those steps into proper order and then follow them. Always. Each and every step to the end.

My steps are in order. Everything is where it must be. In. Out. Vanish without a trace. And when they look they will see what they see, but they will not see me. It's an impossibility.

For my purposes, there is only one scalpel, the no.12 blade. A graduated 3 long handle. Re-usable. I would prefer disposable but that involves more risk. And risk must not be unnecessarily courted. Disposable means having to purchase again. And anything more than once creates a pattern and patterns can always be followed. I cannot.

•

It's simple really, pattern theory. Ulf Grenander posits that one can describe the world as a series of patterns whose—

I am doing it again. My date. I must leave in 6, 5, 4 minutes.

I look again in the mirror and my smile comes more quickly this time.

'Hi. I didn't introduce myself properly last time. I'm Daniel,' I practise. The scalpel is in the top pocket of my navy blazer with the pearl buttons. I have latex gloves in the right front pocket of my jeans and there are latex socks in the left. The size 11 Caterpillar boots, the paper overalls, the cigarette lighter, are all in the boot.

The gastro pub is a four-minute walk from my house. My penny loafers look just the right side of casual. I want to insert shiny two pence pieces into the slit but I don't have the time to do it properly. Aligned, centred, polished. I slam the front door shut and double-lock the Banhams. Five steps down to the bottom and then straight to the end of the road and then left. And then walk. Then meet. Then dinner. Then. Then. That.

She is there. Already. All ready.

The hair is freshly blown. I can scent tuberose in the air as I near her. I smile. Hold her gaze. Hold out my hand. Freeze my smile for the count of five. 'Hi. I didn't introduce myself properly last time. I'm Daniel.'

She smiles. 'Hiyya. Holly. Weren't sure you were going to turn up,' she says, and laughs nervously.

Holly. Probably a Christmas baby. Her coat is long, rust-coloured – cashmere maybe. Buttoned up so that I can't see what lies beneath.

I decide not to answer. The lack of validation shifts the power in my favour a little. Not that I need it. I just – prefer it.

'I've booked a table in a quiet corner. Hope you don't mind,' I say, raising an eyebrow that I know looks cheeky but do not know why. I push the door open. Noise and warm air blankets us as we walk in.

A man shadows us to a table in the corner and I remain standing while Holly peels away her coat. And I see it at last. A blouse – Broderie Anglaise. Buttons translucent.

When she sits, I do too.

She looks around and smiles. 'Great place. I love all this,' she says, pointing to the black-and-white framed photographs on the wall.

'What do you love about them?' I ask, knowing that it is in the process of being made to talk about herself that she will be drawn to me. She talks. I look. She feels interesting. I look. She glows. I stare. She feels luminous. She has become her own aphrodisiac.

'Oh,' she says, 'I don't know. They're just so evocative.' The 'o's all stretched. *Ooh I dohn't knoh.*

I smile at her and look into her eyes. They are brown, flecked with green. It's possible they are pretty by themselves. But I can't tell. I can only see the whole. She's definitely attractive, as the whole. And the buttons. Well.

'Evocative? Tell me. What do they evoke in you?' I say, looking at her again. I stroke my jaw and smile at her.

'Oh. God. You're intense, aren't you? I like this one. Ha,' she says. 'Well let me see. They evoke a feeling of loss, I suppose. But not sad loss. More like a loss of a bygone era. You know. When life was simpler.' *You knoh*.

I stare into her eyes. I like this one too. I modify the smile. Nod slightly. Pat the scalpel in my top pocket – still there –sharp.

'I like your blouse,' I say. It's out before I can stop it. Stupid. I make a mental note. The shifts need to be smoother.

'Oh. This? Thank you. A guy who notices. Like hen's teeth.' I have lost her and my face has given something away.

'You know. Rare. Ha,' she adds, before looking up to take a menu from the man who has appeared at her side. 'Thank you.'

Rare. You could say that. I'm rare like good beef – pink in the middle. Bloody. I am rare. One in a million maybe. And whatever you do, ignore the stats and those lazy patterns they make. No room for the individual – for the unique. I'm more than just a 'Skin Job'. *I've seen things you people wouldn't believe.*

'I *am* rare,' I say and wink. Then I pick up my menu and pretend to study it. Just as people do.

Rare. I'm fifteen years old and studying Human Biology – something about the cardiovascular system. I remember it.

'Right, boys. OK settle down now. Settle. I need one volunteer. Good. Good lad. Come up here. Right put the sticky pad on your wrist. Here on the pulse. Good. Now everybody, watch the screen. Here we go, 58, 59, 60, 61. Great. 61 beats a minute. Make a note.'

There are scribbles, some bored, others frantic.

'Now who wants to see something fun? Settle down, lads. OK. Quiet now. Right, in ten seconds I am going to give Daniel here a small electric shock—'

'You going to kill him like electric chair, sir?' Laughter – boys simulating shocked American death-row convicts.

'Don't be daft. I'm not going to kill him. It's just the tiniest shock. Couldn't stun a fly with it. Right now, count backwards from ten. Out loud and watch what happens to that pulse as we get closer to one. 10, 9, 8 – closer, watch that pulse: 61 still. But keep watching. 4, 3, 2.'

Then silence. The pulse still beating 61. 61. 61. Then the promised shock like static. Then there it is. 61. 61. 61. Still. Then silence descends. No more laughing now. Then. Then.

'What are you having?' Holly says, looking at me over the top of her card.

'The steak,' I say, not meeting her eye.

'Mmm, nice choice. Was going to go for that myself.' *Goh for that.*

The man comes to our side and I tell him we are ready to order. She looks across at me smiling, half-laughing – jaw dropped open.

'Wait! I haven't even decided yet!' she says, and mock slaps my hand with her menu.

'I'll have the steak. Rare. And my guest is having the sea bass with mango and chilli salsa,' I say, looking her in the eye. 'With a glass of the Sémillon.'

'Oi,' she says. Eyes wide. 'Cheeky. I'm not one of them girls you know.'

I give her a low chuckle and raise an eyebrow. 'I tell you what. If you don't like it. You can have my steak.'

She relents and leans back in her chair.

'And for you, sir? Wine?'

I shake my head. 'Coke. Full-fat.' This gets a giggle. It always does but I am not sure why.

'No wine? You are intriguing, aren't you? So,' she says. 'Tell me about you, Daniel. What do you do?' She leans forward, her arms steepled at the elbow. I recognize these signs of interest.

'I'm a court clerk in the Crown Court.'

'Ooh! Exciting. All that drama. You must have loads of stories to tell. So interesting.'

'Not interesting. Just verdicts. Some good some bad.'

'Oh'. She seems disappointed. The shoulders drop and then a moment or two later she picks up again and her eyes flash. 'Tell me about a bad verdict then.'

So many to tell.

I tell her the story of the current one. I shouldn't. It creates risk. But I change enough of the details to make it safe.

•

Two years ago. Two old tramps, fighting. Drunk. A tiff over nothing. And then in an alcoholic rage this one goes at the other with everything. Fists. Kicks. Bottles. His eyes and brain groping about in red mist. On he goes until there is nothing left inside his body.

'And when he wakes up, his friend is lying next to him. Dead. A hot bloody mess.'

Her eyes are wide. She is making that 'oh!' face and I study every line. And then she even says it. 'Oh.' She whispers it. 'Shit. What happened then?'

'Nothing. That's the point. He was acquitted.'

'What?' she says, and just then the man returns with food and interrupts her indignance.

He sets down the food and I pick up my steak knife. I cut through the flesh to check that it's right. Bloody. I look up, smiling at her.

'What?' she says again. 'Got off? How?'

'Happens sometimes,' I say. 'More than you think. Just a bad verdict.'

She picks up her fork and touches her fish which flakes steamily in front of her. 'But how? How can he just get off that when he's lying next to him covered in blood?'

'Oh. That? Well, his barrister argued that he was so drunk that he couldn't form what they call the requisite intent.'

She takes a mouthful of fish and chews thoughtfully. Then a thumb out in appreciation of my menu choice. Then the brows together again as she swallows. 'What so he was too drunk to be guilty?'

'Something like that.' I take a sliver of meat and hold it between my teeth.

'What, even though he probably only did it because he was drunk in the first place?'

I nod as I finish chewing. 'Ironic. Isn't it?'

This seems to occupy her thoughts for a while, since she falls silent. I am nearly through my meal by the time I remember that I have not DONE THE THING. I am supposed to ask her questions about herself.

I push my cleaned plate back and lie the cutlery in a neat pair. 'That accent. It's – delicious,' I say, setting the question up with a compliment. 'Where is it from and what brings you from there to me?'

She looks up and giggles a little. 'What this? You like it? Most people don't. Manchester. Or just outside but you wouldn't know it.'

I nod. Two questions there, but only one answered. I wait. She looks at me and colours a little as the pause descends over her. 'Oh, and what brings me here?' she says, remembering suddenly. 'Work. And boyfriend trouble. Mainly work though.'

'What do you do?'

'I was a pattern cutter,' she says and leans back as the man approaches to clear away her plate.

Patterns – where mathematics on the page and in life intersect. Fibonacci. That sequence. All those spirals and curls. Shells. Leaves. A curling fern. All those golden ratios.

'What's that? Never heard of it,' I say.

She sits back suddenly and pops her eyes open a fraction. I have done something but not sure what. I do what I usually do in these situations. I smile.

She smiles.

'You know, like making templates for cutting clothes. I used to freelance for small to medium size boutiques. Ones that still hand-make stuff. Anyway, I want to get into leather now.'

'Really?' I say, because no alternatives spring to mind.

'Yeah. Leather is the next thing. Again. I mean. It's cyclical. Fashion is. Sorry I'm boring you.'

I am looking at my watch and that's enough to have made me look bored. I apologise and wave the man over to bring the bill.

'No. It's on me,' I say, and pay with wads of cash. This is another thing I know to be true but am unable to fathom why. Having even just a couple of hundred pounds in cash makes them swoon.

'A real gentleman!' she says. 'But really, I can pay my own way.'

'I tell you what,' I say, standing. 'Let me walk you back and I will consider that payment enough.'

I pat at the scalpel. Still there.

She keeps her eyes on me as she squeezes her arms into her coat. Studying me. Assessing me. Getting me wrong.

'Why do I think I'm going to regret this?' she says, laughing, and then follows me through the pub and out into the February night.

It was a February night when I first found out. About me.

He repeated the experiment. Of course he did. *Must be a gremlin. Let's try someone else. Jack. You next. Come on. Up you come. Make it lively now.'*

First with Jack. And then the Aspinall twins. *'There we are. Works perfectly. See her climb? 68, 71, 75, 82.'* And then me again. And there it was. Blinking at him. At me. 61. 61. 61.

Then there were all the letters. Father tore up the first. I intercepted the second. But then there were the calls. A test, they all said, is considered necessary.

•

Before I have become aware of it, Holly has tucked her arm into mine as we are walking.

'So, Daniel. Is this a ruse of yours?' She turns her face to me a quarter-turn.

'Is what a ruse?' I ask. There is the slightest breeze but it is enough to funnel the scent of tuberose into my nose.

'Getting the bill before coffee,' she says, chuckling. 'Mine is just round this corner,' she adds, pointing needlessly in the air with her loose hand.

I don't understand exactly what she means so I just smile and ask her a question.

'How do you like it here?'

'Yeah. It's nice. I guess. But if I told my mum how much I was paying for a one-bedroom, she'd think I'd lost my mind.'

I laugh and suddenly she stops. Red ankle-boots planted. Black door. She spins on a boot heel and turns to face me. She leans in as she speaks, as if we might be overheard.

'So? Do you fancy coming in for a coffee?'

I slide a hand into my top pocket. Pull the scalpel out as she turns to her door. 'Oh look,' I say, 'You're losing a button.' I lift up a large silver decorative button screwed tight into the back of her coat. 'Here. Let me,' I add, and with a quick flick of the scalpel, the button is free. She turns to look and I open my palm. There it sits. Fat. Beautiful. Perfection.

•

I walk from Holly's red door along the road until I reach the streetlights. Left at the top, then around the corner to where the car still sits. I check my watch. This is an Omega Speedmaster. 1969. Calibre 861. The watch they took to the Moon.

I look at it. I am on time.

The engine starts. First time. Diesel engines like these always start. No black cabs or white vans run on petrol.

I flick on the headlamps and make my way to the church. It's so close I could walk there in fifteen minutes. But I need the car for this.

The traffic is light. The streets are dark though, just as I like it for these nights. The comfort of shadow all around me, absorbing me and the car into its enormous self.

The lights go red. When I stop someone tries to get into my car and reaches at the rear door. I quickly pull away and then lock the doors. Stupid mistake to have left the TAXI light burning. But not, you know, fatal.

Finally, I stop. I choose the space carefully. No light pouring in from an overhead lamp. No houses with windows looking at me. Just a wall. Some garage doors. It's desolate.

•

I retrieve the items from the boot and get back into the car. The internal light has been switched off. First, I remove the penny loafers and then I pull on the paper suit. Then the latex gloves. Then the socks. Then finally the Caterpillars. Size 11. I wait until I step out onto the tarmac before zipping up. Just as the zip reaches my chest, I stop. I slide the scalpel out of the top pocket. Hold it tight in my left hand. The right holds the lighter. Then I walk.

These shoes clump.

But no matter. I can clump tonight.

Clump. Clump. Clump.

In 19, 20, 21 steps I am there.

I pass nobody along the way. But even if I had, it wouldn't matter. I look up at the huge stone structure behind the gates. This old church. Massive. Square. Bathed in quiet darkness. Beautiful. I push the gate. It swings open silently. Recently oiled. By me.

Clump clump. I walk through. The pale moonlight just the right shade of bright to see by. The air is still. There are almost no sounds contaminating this space, as if somehow the Church sanctifies it.

I walk on the overgrown ground to the back. This place, once so used, so gloriously communal. So binding. Salutary. Welcoming. Reduced now to shut gates and cold loneliness. And memories of a significant past.

Weeds crushed under Caterpillars, clump clump clump, I go. And then. And then. I see him. Sleeping. So peacefully. With 3, 4, 5 beer cans around his head. Perfect. There's a tent next to him but he hasn't had the sense to crawl into it before passing out near the wall.

I lean down over his face until I am close enough to smell the alcohol on his breath. It comes at me in waves. He's wearing a cheap hooded coat, the fur around the head twisted with filth. I pull down the front zip so that the body beneath spills out. The sound does not wake him. Under the coat, a shirt. Red and black checked. The smell from his body disgusts me but I master the revulsion. At the point where his stomach crests to its highest point. That point at which the shirt begs to separate itself from itself. At that precise point I lay the curved edge of my number 12 blade. And I slice.

The button comes away and I pick it between a latex finger and thumb and turn it in the moonlight. Yes. Mine.

I lay it carefully on a bare patch of ground. Steps. First this then that. The button always follows. Never precedes.

I step back towards the sleeping drunk and then I am there, in position, a foot either side of his head. When I look down his face is framed by Caterpillars.

•

The first diagnosis, the official one, that was a stroke of luck. Not that we asked for one. Father was too caught up in his own idiotic web to bother about me. Credit cards. Borrowing. CCJs. Passing off false notes. No, this came because the Youth Court insisted on a psychiatric report. *Traits of Narcissistic Personality Disorder . . . positive affect . . . exhibits features of grandiosity . . . tendency to deflect responsibility for his crimes onto others. Could not understand what was wrong with exploiting what he saw as the stupidity of others. May in the alternative meet the Hare's PCL-R threshold . . .* In any case, they were wrong. The psychotherapy was wrong also – but interesting at least.

I'm not a narcissist. Or one of *them*.

I raise my right foot high and position it so that it hovers over the man's face. The heel is aimed so that the edge of the boot aligns with his temple. And then I bring it down hard. And again. There is a muffled yelp so I take to the air – in full flight – both feet high and I jump. Up and down. And up and down. Clump. Clump. Clump.

He dies much quicker than I had expected. Hoped? Perhaps. I don't really have any sort of hunger for the violence. Don't misunderstand me though, I don't mind it either. It's all just a part of the larger design. I don't dislike or like the violence any more than I like or dislike a particular jigsaw piece.

The Omega tells me I must move quickly now. I remove the Caterpillars and place them neatly on either side of the man's collapsed head. And stand back to look. So perfect.

Then the paper suit is off and I walk on latex soles towards the small patch where my button sits, patiently. I pocket it and roll the suit into a small bundle and lay it on the ground. The lighter catches it straight away and I walk quickly away towards the gate and push through without a backward glance. I don't ever look back. That's a weakness that other people possess. If you have certainty, you need never do it.

Within a minute or so I am at the car. I slip into the driver's seat and peel off the latex socks and ball them into a neat inside-out package with my gloves. You shouldn't burn latex. It smokes. I will drop these off to my safe place to be hidden in plain sight. At the hospital – any of the medical waste bins they have will do.

For now, I concentrate on getting back smoothly. I slip on my penny loafers. Size 9. I turn the engine on and drive away. I keep it at low revs the whole time and glide the car through the streets just as taxi drivers do – in no particular hurry. The lights are on but mine is off. I weave in and out of lanes, slowly but efficiently. Within fifteen minutes I am parked and then I check. And then I step out. And then I walk. 2, 3, 4, 5 steps. Then the corner. 11, 12, 13. Stop. Then check. Then check. Then home. Then.

Button eleven.

Of course after the Psych report and all that talk of narcissism, I had to check. But it seemed like hoopla to me. What did I do anyway? The tuck shop was badly managed, that was the real crime. And anyway, the place had been abused for years – to the point of tradition. But I gave it some class.

I was a fool though for undercutting the tuck shop. People became suspicious when they saw me, an ex-tucky, selling chocolate buttons for 10p a bag. And boys don't like it when other boys come good.

So I checked.

Number 1. *Glib and Superficial charm.* Well of course I object to that. It's not exactly scientific, is it? How is one to measure that exactly except subjectively. Your glib and superficial charm may be another person's oily Eton boy. And in a sense is not all charm, whatever that is, superficial? Just another handful of social grease. Superficial is what all charm is. Nobody has ever been comprehensively charming.

Besides, I am charmless. Born without luck or allure. So I must manufacture it. Practise it until it is there in perfect simulation. So, I object. Of course, I do. Even a shallow thing of substance is more 'thing' than any glaring simulacrum. And my charm, all of it is fake.

So no to number 1. No glib charm.

I stand now before the mirror. Eleven buttons. Spaced out. One inch apart. I look at my eyes. The blue has been called piercing. But I have other methods of piercing. I stare hard and narrow the eyes a touch. Then one raised cheek in a demi-smile. '*Soh. Do you fancy coming in for a coffeh?*'

'*Maybe later. There's an errand I need to run first.*'

'*Okaay. See ya later then.*'

I hold the fat silver button to decide how much I like it. If I like it enough, then I know what has to be done. But two buttons in one night feels greedy.

But then. But then. It's such a pretty button.

HOOCH

DAVID HESKA WANBLI WEIDEN

I looked in the refrigerator to see if I had anything to eat. A bottle of hot sauce, half a loaf of moldy bread, and some dried-out chicken wings from the Gus Stop, the Rosebud Indian Reservation's gas station and convenience store. Those would have to do.

After zapping the wings in the microwave and giving them a liberal dose of Tabasco, I turned on the television and stretched out on my couch. I picked up the first wing and was about to take a bite when my cell phone buzzed. I didn't recognize the number, but that wasn't unusual. I wiped the sauce off my hand and pressed the button.

'Yo, is this Pudge?'

I knew it was a customer because he called me Pudge. My friends knew me as Sam, but to the rest of the reservation, I was Pudge Iron Shell, former high school football player. Back then, I'd weighed over 300 pounds, but no matter how much weight I lost, people remembered me as the oversize guy who'd terrorized other teams on the field twenty years ago.

'This is him,' I said. 'What's up?'

'You got any Joose? Need some vodka, too.'

Yeah, I had Joose. It was my bread and butter—the horrid-tasting malt liquor beloved by the drunks around here. It came in flavors like Blue Lemonade, Black Cherry, and Mango, each one sickly sweet and carrying a fourteen-percent alcohol punch.

'What kind you want? I think I got Fruit Punch and Green Apple.'

'Don't matter. Any one's good. What about vodka?'

'What size?' I had over 300 travel-size bottles of 100-proof Tvarscki vodka—called T-Var by the locals—and a couple dozen of the 750 ml bottles of the 80 proof.

'Biggest you got. And ten of the Joose. You come out to Norris?'

Shit. I hated driving out there and I'd been looking forward to staying in and watching a movie. Norris was a 45-minute drive each way, and it was already dark outside.

'This late, it's a twenty-dollar delivery charge,' I said.

I heard him shout to some people in the background. 'Yeah, that's cool. If you get here right away.'

The guy's shitty attitude pissed me off, but I decided to ignore it. 'All right, I can head out now. Six dollars each for the Joose and twenty for the vodka. Plus the delivery. That's a hundred total. Text me your address and come out when I honk.'

'Will do, homes. But step on it.'

I decided that the asshole could wait for me to finish my chicken wings, so I sat down and finished every bite. I knew they'd wait. Everyone knew I was the best on the rez.

I was a bootlegger. No, I didn't make my own liquor in a still, I simply sold alcohol to people on the reservation. I bought large quantities of booze off the reservation and sold it here to thirsty people for a profit. Simple as that.

You could say I was part of a tradition. For decades, the

reservation was dry, so ambitious folks made the drive to Nebraska to get liquor to supply Natives who wanted to drink and forget about their problems for a few hours. Now, you could buy spirits on our reservation at a couple of spots, but that hadn't lessened my business. The off-sale spots closed early, and no one wanted to drive for hours at night just to get some hooch. Not to mention, the Rosebud reservation was huge, and many people didn't have cars. I'd deliver the booze to them for a small delivery fee. My mark-up on the bottles was about double what I paid for them, so I ended up making at least twenty dollars on each sale, sometimes more. On a good night, I cleared over a thousand dollars. But some days, I barely broke even.

I sold individual cans of beer, six-packs, and cases, mainly Bud and Bud Light. I kept plenty of Joose and Hurricane High Gravity malt liquor on hand, as well as vodka and sweet fortified wines. I stocked some bottles of gin, Everclear, and cheap whiskey, as well as a few bottles of decent red wine for an older gentleman out in Two Strike. He'd always invite me in for a glass after I delivered the bottle, but I didn't drink on the job.

I knew the stereotype that Indians had a problem with liquor. You just had to turn on the TV to see that crap. I'd had some elders cuss me out for supposedly contributing to the reservation's problems and not supporting Lakota culture. But that was horseshit. Natives were no more likely to be alcoholics than any other group of people, and that was a fact. People liked alcohol, and that's been true since the first person fermented some grape juice back in ancient times. Better to get drunk than hooked on meth. That crap was the real poison that was ruining lives around here.

The way I saw it, I was providing a community service. Not only was I assisting people who didn't own a vehicle, I was helping to reduce drunk driving. When folks ran out of booze during a party, they called me rather than try to drive themselves across the state line and possibly get into an accident. Yes, bootlegging was against the law, and there was a five-hundred-dollar fine if I got caught by the tribal police. But they had bigger issues to worry about, and the laws against bootlegging were rarely enforced. The only real threat was the possibility of selling to an undercover BIA agent. If that happened, I'd be subject to federal law and looking at serious prison time.

I wasn't the only bootlegger on the rez, for sure. There were at least two dozen others, and more were trying to get in the game every day. They thought it was easy money, but they didn't realize that a top-notch bootlegger had to keep his vehicle in good repair, maintain a good stock of booze, and always be willing to hop in the car. If you turned down a delivery, you might lose a customer for good. The younger bootleggers didn't want to give up their Friday and Saturday nights for deliveries, but I was happy to have the business. Good customer service, that was the secret.

I made good money bootlegging because I treated people fairly and didn't try to rip them off. I was known as the ethical bootlegger because I wouldn't sell to teenagers or kids, and I didn't raise prices when the other bootleggers ran dry. And I absolutely refused to sell Purell. Some of the shitbag bootleggers would sell the little bottles of hand sanitizer for five bucks, which the truly desperate would mix with water and drink. Disgusting. Not to mention, some of those same shitbags would trade liquor for sexual favors, which I found to be repugnant. But my biggest selling point was that I only sold full-strength booze. Most of the others would buy giant bottles of cheap vodka, water it down, and sell 500 ml bottles for a massive mark-up. My customers knew they were getting the real thing.

It was time to make the delivery to the guy in Norris. I put my plate in the sink, then loaded up the ten cans of Joose and the bottle of vodka into a plastic bag. The vodka was in a heavy glass bottle, so I added another bag for safety. I grabbed my keys and a Coke for the road. It was a long drive out there, and I'd need the caffeine.

While I drove, I turned my radio to KOYA, the rez radio station. DJ Jackie was on, playing her usual blend of country music and classic rock. I heard 'Eye of the Tiger,' 'Spirit in the Sky,' and then she played 'These Boots are Made for Walkin'' by Nancy Sinatra. The cheerful melody and jaunty beat immediately reminded me of my daughter, Jamie. When she was a little girl, she'd loved to dance to that song, waving her arms around with a big smile. It was hard to believe that she'd been gone for ten years.

My girlfriend Brenda and I had loved that child more than the stars, but Jamie had drowned when she was just five. She'd been at the swimming pool with Brenda's mother, who'd left the child alone for a few minutes to talk on the phone. When she came back, it was too late. Brenda and I entered into a cavern of grief from which we'd never emerged. I stayed in the house, barely speaking, not showering, and eating just a handful of nuts a day. I lost a staggering amount of weight, my skin turned sallow, and Brenda accused me of trying to kill myself.

Finally, Brenda left for California, unable to deal with me or the memory of Jamie. When I ran out of money, I tried working at the tribal college library, but they let me go when I failed to show up for a few weeks. A friend of mine suggested that I start bootlegging, and he was right. The schedule suited me, as I didn't have to go to an office or get up early in the morning. I was able to be alone with my thoughts while I delivered temporary relief to others. The years passed, but I stayed the same, delivering hooch to the thirsty while I tried to forget what I'd lost. After the Nancy Sinatra song finished, I turned off the radio and just watched the road go by.

Half an hour later, I arrived in Norris and located the address the guy had texted to me. The place was one of the shabby Sioux 400 manufactured homes that were common in this community. There was an old Chevy sedan parked next to a rusty Ford Ranger truck in front of the place. The house next door was boarded up, which meant it had been used as a meth lab and was no longer fit for people to live in.

I honked my horn and waited. No one came out, so I honked again, twice. The front porch light was on and I could see lights inside, so I knew they were there. I waited another few minutes and gave up. Irritated, I grabbed the bag with the bottles and got out of the car.

I pounded on the door a few times. After a moment, it opened a few inches.

'Hey,' I said, 'I got the stuff.'

The door swung open. A younger guy was standing there, maybe around twenty, with dark skin and long black hair. His arms were all tatted up and he wore an oversized white hoodie.

'Bring it in,' he said, and motioned for me to come inside.

I hesitated. 'You got the money?'

'Uh huh. You want your paper, you gotta bring that shit in.'

I wondered what I should do. I never went inside anyone's shack with the liquor—that was just stupid, and bad business. After a moment, I sighed and followed the guy inside. He led me past a tiny kitchen into the living room.

The television was blaring, and I saw there were three men sitting on a dirty couch and another guy slumped in a plastic lawn chair, staring at his phone. The guy who'd opened the door pointed to the coffee table. 'Yo, set it down there.'

I kept holding the bag. 'I need the cash. One hundred even.'

The guy sitting on the couch farthest from me stood up.

'You're Pudge, right?' he said. 'We heard about you.'

He was a little older than the other guys; he was stocky, with short hair and a tattoo on his arm that said OGLALA PRIDE. So, these guys were from the Pine Ridge reservation, one hundred miles west from our rez. No wonder they didn't know me—they were Oglalas.

'Yeah. Just need to get the cash and I'll let you guys party.'

He nodded. 'That's cool. You wanna drink? We can give you one of them Joose.'

'No, I'm good. I got to head on back, catch some shut eye.'

The guy nodded again. 'I hear you. Get some z's, right? Wake up feelin' all refreshed and shit.' Now he shook his head. 'Dang, I been rude. I know who you are, but you don't know us. I'm Bear—Mato, right? Keepin' it real in Lakota. And that's Jay Jay, Gabe, Stacks, and Shorty.'

I glanced over at them, but they sat motionless, just looking at me.

'All right, you all have a good time,' I said. 'If I can get the cash, I'll—'

'Hold up,' the guy called Bear said. 'Need to talk with you about some shit. Grab a seat.'

He motioned to the guy in the lawn chair, who got up and moved behind me. Two of the other guys stood up and moved behind me, blocking my exit. I stared at them for a second, then sat down in the chair, the sack of liquor at my side.

'Yo, break out the hooch,' Bear said, 'I'm fucking thirsty.'

I took all eleven bottles out of the bag and put them on the filthy coffee table. They each grabbed a bottle of the Joose and opened them, leaving the big glass vodka bottle unopened.

I didn't say anything. I wondered what these guys were after. I wasn't stupid enough to carry large amounts of cash, so the worst that could happen is I'd lose forty bucks of alcohol and the twelve dollars in my wallet.

'You sure you don't want one?' Bear said. 'The Fruit Punch be bangin'.' He took a drink.

I shook my head.

He shrugged. 'Suit yourself. Anyway, we been wantin' to talk with you. We hear you the top boot around. That right?'

It took me a second to understand what he meant. 'I sell a little. Plenty of other bootleggers around here.'

'Yeah, but you the OG, right? Been slinging hooch the longest.'

I glanced around the room. 'I guess. Been doing this about ten years, I think. Just getting by.'

'Well, damn!' he said. 'Today's your lucky day! Because we gonna up your sales like a mofo. What you think of that?'

I didn't understand. 'You want to buy more booze?'

'Sheeit, no! We gonna help you sell more to the skins here, a lot more. See, we from Pine Ridge.'

'I figured that.' I pointed with my lips to his OGLALA tattoo.

He smiled. 'Good eye. You see this one?' He pulled the sleeve on his other arm back. An image was inked on his skin in an ornate style; it proclaimed A705.

I shook my head, but I knew what it meant. That was one of the dozens of Native gangs that existed on Pine Ridge and Rosebud. He was trying to show me how hard he was.

He smirked. 'We like you Sicangus. Like you so much, we decide to come over here and show y'all how it's done.' He took a long swig from the Joose. 'Deal is, you gonna start working with us on the hooch sales. We gonna be your muscle, and Shorty over there help you with deliveries.'

'Hey,' I said, 'that's cool, but—'

'I ain't finished! Don't be cutting in on me.' Another swig of the Joose. 'Thing is, we gonna take care of the competition for you. We find the other boots and they gonna stop doin' deliveries. Unless they wanna partner with us. You feelin' me? In six months, we gonna control all hooch round here—be like damn Amazon. You know, doing business like the wasicus.'

This caused laughter from the other guys, and they all took big drinks from their Joose cans.

'We gonna be the kings. Split the dollars 50-50, that fair, right? Doin' it Lakota style. So what you say?'

I paused for a moment and thought about how to respond. 'I'm kind of a lone wolf. Been doing this a long time on my own. You know, I got my own way of doing things. So, thanks, but I'm gonna pass.'

Bear smiled. 'Lone wolf, I respect that. Goin' solo.' Another drink. 'But maybe I didn't say shit the right way. We ain't asking you, we tellin' you. You gonna partner with us or we bring some Pine Ridge thunder down on your ass. Hear me?'

I grabbed my bag and stood up. 'I need my hundred bucks. Then I'm getting out of here. You guys want to sell booze on the Rosebud, I got no objection. But give me my fucking money. Now.'

Bear signaled to the guys standing behind me. I turned around and one of them punched me in the stomach. Hard. I dropped down to the floor, doubled over in pain. I hadn't had time to brace myself, and it felt like my stomach and intestines had ruptured. I couldn't breathe and started gasping.

'That's what I thought,' I heard Bear say. I was still wheezing, and I felt like I was going to throw up. I'd been hit in the solar plexus and it felt like something was trying to crawl out of my midsection. I focused on the dirty tan carpet to deal with the pain. Up close, I could see each individual carpet fiber shimmering in the dim light. They looked like the ribbons worn by dancers at powwows.

'Like I said, we ain't asking you,' he said. 'We taking over the bootlegging here. Gonna happen with you or without you. So, you ready to join the 705 now?'

I was starting to get my breath back, but couldn't stand up yet. After a bit, my head cleared, and I was able to move to a sitting position. I thought about my options for a moment, and realized that my only play was to join these guys and partner with them. They were going to take over the liquor deliveries on the rez no matter what I did. In time, they'd strongarm the other bootleggers and force them out of business as well. I might as well get on the winning side now. Not to mention, it made sense to let them help with the deliveries. Maybe I could even take a day off once in a while.

The five of them stood above me, waiting for me to say something. I started to speak, but then I thought about my daughter Jamie. The image of her little warrior face flashed in my head, and I remembered when she wore her first regalia at the Rosebud Wacipi years ago. She'd been wearing a little ribbon skirt and had been so excited to get out and dance for the first time. She'd had no fear or shyness, but had rushed out into the circle and danced her little heart out. When she was finished, she dragged me to the lemonade stand, telling me all about it. Usually, her memory sent me into a day-long grief spiral, but it was different this time. Her image comforted me, gave me strength, and I imagined her looking down on me. I thought about what she'd say if she could see the situation I was in.

I slowly lifted myself up while the five of them watched me. 'OK,' I said. 'You got a point. Working together makes sense, right?'

Bear smiled. 'Now you talkin'—knew you'd see it the right way.'

'How about some shots, to celebrate?' I said. 'Let's break out that vodka.'

A couple of the guys nodded. I could tell they wanted something stronger after drinking cans of Joose.

'You got any shot glasses?' I asked.

Bear laughed. 'You don't need no shot glasses, homes. Just open that mofo and take a drink.'

I picked up the Tvarscki bottle and unscrewed the plastic cap.

'I know we got off on the wrong foot,' I said. 'But I get it now. You guys just want to make some money. I'm good with that. So, let me make a little toast. You speak Lakota?'

Bear shook his head. 'Naw, just a few words. Only the old people speak Indian at Pine Ridge.'

'That's cool,' I said. 'I'm not fluent; I just remember a few words my mom used to say.' I held the vodka bottle in front of me in order to make a toast. 'So here it is: *ayustan yo!*'

I raised the bottle up.

'Hold on,' Bear said. 'What does it mean?'

'It's not an exact translation,' I said, and looked over at him and the other gang members. 'Essentially, it means FUCK YOU!'

I smashed the full bottle on Bear's head, glass and vodka flying everywhere. He stumbled and fell, his hands going to his head. The bottle had shattered, but the neck stayed intact, with several jagged pieces of glass sticking out like a double-edged knife. The room reeked of vodka, and I realized I was drenched.

Two of the guys bent down to assist Bear, and the other two started moving towards me. I backed up a few steps while watching them.

'Just don't move, all right?' I said, while holding the bottle in front of me. I looked down the hall to see if the front door was open.

All of a sudden, the one called Shorty rushed toward me. I

remembered one of my old football moves. I faked like I was moving left, but went to the other side. He missed me and ran into the wall. I tried to get past him, but he came at me with his fist raised.

I took the vodka bottle and swiped the jagged edges across his face. The sharp glass went straight to the bone of his cheek, just under his eye. I could see the flesh and subcutaneous fat gleaming in the wound I'd opened. He screamed and raised both hands to his face.

The other guys looked stunned, and I saw my opening. Still holding the bottle, I ran for the door, opened it, and took off running. I looked behind and saw that no one was chasing me. My hands shaking, I dropped the broken bottle and fumbled for my keys. After a few seconds, I was able to fish them out of my pocket and unlock the door. I jumped inside and started the engine.

I looked back one last time. Still no one there. I put the car in drive, and hit the accelerator. Within minutes, I was on the road past the Norris cemetery, driving as fast as I could. After a while, I realized that no one was behind me and I relaxed. I opened the window to let some fresh air in.

It was a beautiful night, and I watched the road and the trees and the bushes glide by me as if I were in a dream. I realized that I felt better than I had in years. I knew the gang would come for revenge, but that didn't bother me. After a long time, I was finally ready.

BRING ME YOUR PAIN

WALTER MOSLEY

Acme Green sat erect on the baby-blue, vinyl-covered, foam-padded chair set before the reception desk at Pamela's Patents of Santa Monica. Pamela's was situated in the hinge angle of an L-shaped strip mall at the far eastern side of town; as distant from the ocean as the beach city could offer. This was the fourteenth patent service Acme had visited in the past sixteen months. Traveling mainly by bus, he had been to New Electrix in Silicon Valley, Northrop Inventors' Service in Montclair, New Jersey, Questions Answered in Miami, and Heartland Inventions in Chicago – to name a few. Because of the nature of his projector all companies so far had refused to submit to a demonstration of the little white box – mostly because it was *just too weird*.

They had asked for blueprints, detailed descriptions of parts, energy sources, and those patentable aspects of any new machine. But Acme knew better than to expose the elements of his inventions before people saw what the white box could do.

•

'Can I get you some water?' the receptionist asked Acme.

'No, ma'am,' the brown-skinned son of Detroit replied.

The young white woman gave the patent applicant a friendly smile and then returned her concentration to the computer screen before her.

The storefront office of Pamela's Patents was definitely a step down from other larger copyright firms. But that didn't matter, Acme told himself, as long as he could register the amazing invention in his name. His years of research, experimentation and design would be worthwhile if in the end the appellation Acme's Tactile Projector could be affixed to his white-box progeny.

•

For years Acme worked in the basement of his parents' home in Southwest Detroit. Pernell Green died of heart attack when Acme was fourteen and his father only thirty-two. Already in his junior year, the boy decided that there was no more time to waste on high school. He might die at any moment and all the brilliance of his mind would be doused by the sands of mortality.

•

'Mr. Green?'

Acme was wondering about his life just below the surface of the world. His mother, Maddie Lusk-Green, would come down into the musty cellar filled with books and electronic equipment, and ask, 'Ace, why'ont you get up and go out sometimes?'

'Because, Mama, I might have inherited heart attack from daddy and if I die 'fore I finish then everything I done here'll be lost.'

•

'Mr. Green,' the voice said again, tugging Acme out of that long-ago basement listening to the concern in his now-dead mother's voice.

'Yes?'

The woman standing there was tall and generally straw-colored. She had dark gold hair and naturally tan skin with maple syrup eyes. Even her skirt was light brown with a blouse the color of wheat chaff.

'My name is Normandie Frisk. I'm what they call the clearance officer here at Pamela's. Would you like to come in?'

•

The office was small and windowless. Ms Frisk's desk was metal, painted light brown. The six four-drawer filing cabinets were also metal, and dark green in color. The floor was covered in pitted linoleum decorated with tiny little flecks of blue, pink, metallic gold, and red in a confetti motif. The room reminded him of the trailer his father's brother George lived and died in.

'Have a seat,' Normandie Frisk offered.

The chair set before the desk was painted lacquer-black. It was spindly but felt somehow equal to the task of any weight when the middle-aged inventor sat. Acme leaned his large art folder against the chair and set the toaster-sized white box on his lap. Normandie Frisk lowered into her office chair and smiled at the short and yet burly dark brown man.

For a moment they sized each other up.

'Normandie,' Acme said at last. 'That's an unusual name for a woman.'

'It is,' she agreed. 'Acme is also uncommon.'

'Yeah. Kinda like the company titles Wile E. Coyote used for products in the old Roadrunner cartoons.'

'I'm not familiar with them,' Normandie said, crinkling her nose in a way that was disarming.

'My mother named me for her favorite grandfather – Acme Harder from Tupelo, Mississippi. They named him that because it meant that he was the best. It meant that just to say his name was to honor him.'

Normandie Frisk exhaled and seemed to relax even though Acme hadn't thought that she was in any way uptight.

'My great grandfather was part of the D–Day invasion in World War Two. He fought at Normandy – died there.'

'But your nameplate spells it with an "ie", not a "y".'

'Both spellings are acceptable and my father thought that way was more girly.'

•

Remembering this brief conversation years later, Acme Green regretted ever showing his empathy projector to anyone.

•

'So,' Normandie Frisk said. 'Tell me about your machine.'

Acme's mind went blank for a moment. Not his whole mind, just the part that was concerned with the empathy projector. It was Normandie's choice of words that confused him. If she had asked him to *explain* the invention or maybe to describe its function he would have been prepared to answer immediately. But asking him to *tell* her *about* the machine seemed to be a much more fundamental interrogative.

He breathed in deeply and then exhaled before saying, 'I guess you'd have to say that it all starts with gospel music out of the Mississippi Delta. Back then it was call and response, praise for the Lord, and prayer for deliverance. But most of all it was that deep aching desire to be understood. Because when you're in pain, when your brethren are in pain you believe that if only your tormentors knew how you felt . . . well, then the goodness of humanity would take over and make them stand back and ask, why?'

There were heartfelt tears in Acme's voice. These words, he felt, had been bottled up in his soul since a time back before he was born.

Normandie brought a hand to her throat and uttered, 'Oh.'

'My people have suffered and died, been murdered and denigrated, ignored and, worst of all, we have been misunderstood,' Acme continued. 'Many things are better today. As a rule we don't carry the physical loads or suffer the unearned blows that our ancestors had to bear. But other problems and memory of the pain our people have endured live on inside us like tapeworms or viruses.'

Acme could see that there was something Normandie wanted to say but she kept the words behind clenched teeth.

'What?' he asked.

'My father called me Norma after mother died.'

Acme nodded and said, 'My mother called me Ace when we were alone.'

•

'The machine projects pain from one person and causes it to manifest in another,' Ace told Norma.

'How can that be possible?' asked the woman reminiscent of a windblown field of grain.

Standing up, Acme lifted the large art folder and laid it flat upon the metal desk. He ran the zipper down three sides and flipped it open to reveal what looked like a loom. Stretched across this device were many thousands of incredibly thin interwoven wires which were anchored in a black metal frame that seemed to come from some older time. The silk-like knitted wires glimmered now and again. These flashes of radiance gave the illusion that the cloth of metal wires was moving, as if gently on a breeze.

'It's beautiful,' Normandie Frisk exclaimed. 'What's it made of?'

'Ultra-thin graphene wires strung across and anchored in a frame made from black silver, the most conductive naturally occurring metal on earth. First, I connect my white box to the loom and the Source, you know, the pained individual. The wires pinpoint the location and the intensity of the greatest neuronal disturbance – pain. Then I hook up the Target, the person who will receive the information. When I initiate the power source, that pain is immediately transferred.'

'How can that be?' Normandie asked, not for a moment doubting this awkward Black man's words.

'Are you in any pain, Miss Frisk?'

'Um,' the young woman hummed. 'Is it necessary for me to answer that question?'

'No. Not at all. If you'll allow it, I can attach you as the Source and I will be the Target, the receiver of your discomfort.'

'Does the connection break the skin?'

'In the early experiments it did. I needed the silver shawl, that's what I called the graphene netting, I needed the shawl attached directly to the individuals' neuronal networks. But now my finger pads read the faintest electrical impulses and transmit the data.'

'Does it hurt?'

'In this case I will experience your pain.'

Normandie looked into Acme's eyes. From therein she could almost feel the preternatural calm he emanated. For some reason this peacefulness frightened her.

'Oh, OK,' she said, thinking of the grandfather she never knew and how brave he had been.

•

The high school dropout attached a conductive cap to the tip of the forefinger of the clearance officer's left hand. She could see a blue glow coming from under the fitted cap, which fitted the fingertip like a tiny hardhat designed for a construction site. Immediately the loom of fine metal threads became agitated, shimmering, she thought, like a pond brushed over by a whimsical draft. Colors rose into these shifting lights; mostly blues with hints of green. After a while a dull red spot occurred near the corner closest to Acme. When this spot stopped growing, the Detroiter took another conductive cap, attached to his white box, and placed it on the point-finger of his right hand.

A moment passed.

'Mmm,' he mused. 'Your left shoulder. It aches in there. Doesn't feel too bad though.'

Normandie noticed a bright yellow knob on the side of the tactile projector. For some reason this prompted her to raise her left arm up above her head.

The red splotch on the sparkling loom brightened until it took on the aspect of a setting sun in a crystal-clear sky.

'Oh my God!' Acme exclaimed. He bent over in the chair putting his right hand on his left shoulder.

'A severely torn rotator cuff,' Normandie explained. 'I got it playing tennis in Culver City. This is the first time I've put up my hand like this in over a year.'

'You could put it down now.'

Normandie brought her arm down but then raised it again, causing Acme to groan while bringing a quizzical look to the patent supplier's face.

She put the arm down again and asked, 'Why doesn't it hurt me now?'

Panting slightly, Acme said, 'I can't explain it but somehow the machine draws the experience out of the Source when broadcasting it to the Target.'

'Do you feel any pain right now?' Normandie asked.

'You mean the shoulder? No.'

'But anything else? Something you could pass to me?'

Acme reached over and tapped the yellow knob twice. Instantly Normandie felt an intense ache in the joints of six fingers and a sharp, stabbing pain in her left knee. She tried to stand in an instinctive attempt to escape what was hurting her.

'Don't sever the connection to your finger!' Acme shouted. 'If you do the echo of my arthritis will stay in your system for days.'

The young woman sat and asked, 'Can you turn it off?'

The patent applicant reached out again and slowly turned the yellow knob. Normandie heard two clicks and suddenly the pain in her hands and leg were gone.

'Thank, God,' she whimpered.

For long moments the two sat there.

'How long have you had that pain?' Normandie asked.

'For years. My line has never been very healthy.'

Normandie's light brown eyes settled on Acme's face.

'It's amazing,' she said.

'And as far as I can tell the transmission of the Source's pain to the Target is nearly equivalent.'

'But it's more than that. I felt, I don't know, I felt close to you. It's like I knew you, I know you.'

'The yellow knob,' he said, nodding.

'What about it?'

'It has five focus points. First is the on position. The second identifies greater or lesser pain on a scale of one to a thousand. The third is a loop of the second setting. It registers all pains above or below a standard setting; also between one and a thousand. The fourth creates a document listing the pains and their location in the body. And the fifth, the fifth scans neuronal data not affiliated with pain, at least not exactly.'

'So the fifth setting allows the Target to somehow identify with the Source?'

Acme nodded. 'But I haven't been able define those emanations. I feel them but can't locate them on the tapestry—you know, the loom. All that occurs is an emotional response of one type or another and a kind of rippling across the weave.'

'So, the fifth setting on the machine is emotional?'

'Maybe. It can't be registered on the fourth setting's reporting system and the experiential affect is subjective.'

'How do you mean . . . subjective?'

'To begin with, the fifth setting works both ways,' Acme said. 'You and I will respond to each other's non-specific neuronal emanations. Like right now, when I look at you or think of you I feel a deep patience. It calms me somewhat and makes me feel comradeship. You know?'

'I think so,' Normandie said. 'But you didn't turn the knob to five, did you?'

'No, I didn't. The setting orients the focus of the reader to one of the five points, but they are all engaged whenever the power is turned on. That's why you felt the emotional side of the Source.'

'Is it the same with all of your experiments?'

In Acme's cover letter making the appointment with all the patent companies he reported that he had conducted over a thousand experiments with twelve consenting persons. Normandie's question made him rue that admission.

'There were nine women and three men I used,' he said. 'They were paid and I brought them to my mother's home to conduct the trials. Mama was already dead. I made a hollow table to contain the box and loom and so they only saw small needles, and, later, the finger-caps attached to the table.'

'What is it about the light under the caps, Mr Green?'

'You can call me Ace . . . Norma.'

'OK. What is it about the light, Ace?'

'It's based on Einstein's photoelectric effect theory. Basically, it helps my white box read electron emissions from the Source and then transfer them. Through trial-and-error I found that these emissions, under certain conditions, contain numerous readings from the Source – including neuronal responses.'

'Why hide the box and loom?'

Acme smiled for the first time since Normandie had met him.

'I guess it's kinda funny,' he said. 'I want to know everything but at the same time I want to hide what it is that I know. At least, I want to keep my secrets until I'm sure that I'll be seen as the owner of the patents involved.'

'You didn't even trust the people you experimented on?'

'They were all prostitutes. That's why I started talking about subjectivity. In those cases, I had every fifth level response from love to abject fear.'

'Fear of what?' the patent clearance officer asked.

'Evil,' Acme said, looking into her eyes, imagining what she saw in his.

'Does such a thing exist in science?'

Again, Acme was momentarily stymied by Normandie's questions.

'Um,' he said. 'I guess, I think, no . . . Matter is inert. It merely moves through time and space existing without intention. But life responds to this, um, the pressure of, the weight of the desire to survive. This desire, to survive, is paramount to all living things and the insouciant acts of matter and other living things against this desire can be, has to be, seen as evil.'

Normandie was suddenly overcome by the immensity of what Acme claimed and what she had just experienced.

'This invention, it's revolutionary,' she said after a long spate of gazing upon the brown man's face, feeling somehow that she was peering into a dark mirror.

'More than that,' Acme said. 'It's evolutionary.'

'What do you mean by that?'

Acme wasn't used to being questioned. It's not that he felt the arrogance of absolute certainty but rather rarely spoke to anyone, and never about science and his impression of its power.

'It's two things,' Acme Green said. 'They are interconnected but separate in their natures. The first is that we are not truly social beings but semi-social creatures that seek survival and domination, love and procreation. The second is that we are conditioned by our technology in deep ways that defy prediction. Never before in the history of humanity have we been able to empathize so deeply with another human being.'

'But that's just the beginning,' Normandie said. 'Now a patient can communicate with their doctor by allowing him to experience the symptomology.'

'Now,' Acme said as if denying her claim, 'we are on the verge of sharing souls; of crossing the barrier that every church, every love affair, every child born to woman and man has promised but ultimately failed to deliver.'

'Are you a scientist or a philosopher, Ace?' Normandie said on a smile.

'Is there any real difference?'

'Where are you staying?'

•

Normandie's husband, Bob Frisk, was not happy when Normandie showed up at 7:35 that evening with the squat Black man in tow.

'What do you mean you invited him to stay the night?' big and very white Bob shouted at Normandie standing on the trim lawn of the back yard.

'He's been sleeping in his car, honey,' the young woman told her husband of three years.

'Lotta people all over LA sleepin' outside. You never brought any of them home with you before.'

'Because . . .'

'What?' Bob clenched his big hand on her right biceps.

Normandie looked up at him. She knew that her answer wouldn't make sense and so was at a loss for words.

'Well?' Bob demanded.

'I can't explain it but, but I can show you.'

'Show me what?'

•

At a few minutes past eleven o'clock that night Bob, Normandie, and Acme were seated around a small sky-blue table in the dining nook off from the kitchen. They'd been sitting there in silence for more than a quarter hour.

'You want some tea, honey?' Normandie managed to say. Her voice seemed hoarse and Acme could see that her expression was strained.

'Uh,' Big Bob grunted. 'I guess.'

'OK,' she said as she rose and took the few steps toward the stove.

Hunkered over with one forearm on the hardwood table, Bob reminded Acme of a free-floating iceberg, mostly submerged and headed for collision.

'I never felt anything like that in my life,' Bob told Acme. 'I could hardly believe it even though I felt it in my shoulder. That's why I pinched her arm in the middle. I thought maybe you guys planned it somehow, that you made my shoulder hurt with something in that finger-cap.'

'It must be amazing to share pain with someone you have loved for so long.'

'I thought you showed her today in her office.'

'Yeah, but, we're strangers. You guys have known each other for years.'

'Oh yeah?'

'You're married, right?'

'So, what you gonna do with that thing?' Bob asked, his upper lip shivering the way some animals do when getting ready to defend their territory.

'I guess there's some medical uses and maybe, when we refine the fifth level, it might have some therapeutic psychological applications and maybe even have legal ramifications.'

Normandie returned then with a small cork-lined serving tray that carried three brightly colored ceramic mugs filled with steaming liquid. She placed a red cup in front of her husband, a blue one down at her seat, and then handed Acme the green tankard.

'Chamomile,' she told their guest.

Bob sipped, blew over the tea, and then sipped again.

Acme sipped and asked, 'What do you do, Bob?'

'I don't invent miracle machines if that's what you're sayin'.'

'No, I just wondered what your job is.'

'I drive a truck for Meadows Markets. Up and down the coast.'

'He took me with him one time all the way to Vancouver,' Normandie said, her eyes glued to her husband. 'The thing I loved the most was sitting up so high and looking out over the night.'

'Norm says that you been sleepin' in your car,' Bob said.

'Poor as a church mouse, my daddy used to say,' Acme replied.

There was hatred in Bob's big angular face. Acme felt the rage simmering but he wasn't afraid. When he was a kid in Detroit he'd been in many fights with bullies bigger than he.

Then Bob yawned.

This surprised the self-taught bio-physicist. He couldn't quite relate hatred with drowsiness.

'They offered Bob a managerial position at the central warehouse but he said that he wanted to be free, huh, honey?' Normandie's question had a note of desperation to it.

Bob drained the cup of tea, said, 'I guess,' and yawned again.

The man-berg put both hands on the table and pushed to rise. Acme expected the attack to come then. He didn't know why but that didn't matter. People fought for all kinds of reasons and sometimes for no reason at all.

Bob made it to his feet, said, 'you fuckin' shit,' and then fell sideways onto the too yellow tiled floor. His heavily muscled right shoulder landed with a thud. The big man flopped onto his back. His T-shirt rode up over a big pale belly and the right ankle was crossed over the left.

Normandie didn't move. She just stared at her behemoth mate with awe and terror in her eyes.

'I can't sleep sometimes,' she said.

Acme went to the big man and checked to see that he was still breathing.

'The doctor gave me these pills,' Normandie continued, 'these pills. He said to take one for sleep. Whenever I take one, I fall asleep real fast. The first time I was sitting on the couch and couldn't even get up to go to bed.'

'You gave Bob one?' Acme asked, still kneeling next to her husband.

'I put eight in his tea.'

'Why?'

Normandie stood and walked stiff-legged to a kitchen drawer.

'I felt him,' she said. 'For the first time ever I felt his heart, his rotten . . .' The clearance officer drew a large butcher's knife from a drawer and said, 'His rotten heart.'

She took one staggery step toward her prostrate husband.

Acme rose, blocking her way to Bob. The woman's eyes were not focused, her breath shallow.

'I have to kill him. He, he murdered them.'

'Who?'

'Bob,' she said, looking at Acme as if he were at a great distance. 'He's what you said. He's evil. He has to die.'

'No.'

'But he's full of hate. He, he was going to kill you. I know he was.'

Acme looked down on the sleeping mass and knew that Normandie was probably right.

'Come with me to the living room,' he said. 'Come with me and we'll figure out the right thing to do.'

'Right?'

•

They sat side by side on a pearl gray sofa in front of an 80-inch plasma TV. The TV was off and the butcher's knife was on the coffee table.

'I could see what he did,' Normandie said.

'Like dream images?' Acme asked her. The scientist in him took over and he began to think of Bob and Norma merely as a subjects of investigation.

'More real,' Normandie answered, wagging her head in denial. 'Young women. Young men . . . in a book. Page after page. They died horribly.'

'Maybe it was a book he'd read.'

'No, no. It was pictures. Photographs he developed in his darkroom, down in the cellar.'

'I've never seen an image through the e-projector.'

'It was pictures.'

'Maybe because you already know Bob you could see through his eyes,' Acme surmised. 'Maybe physical and emotional intimacy causes greater connection.'

'He has to die,' Normandie said with all the conviction of a one-woman jury.

'Let's go see the darkroom first.'

•

They were down there for more than an hour searching file cabinets and shelves, browsing through stacks of photographs and closets full of papers, chemical jars, and flat pans.

It was a very neat workplace. The blowsy truckdriver was immaculate as a spider in his own lair, that's what Acme thought.

'It's in a dark place,' Normandie said when they got to the fruitless end of the search. 'Up high.'

The two looked up at the hung ceiling lined with sound-proofing tile.

Because she was the taller, Normandie stood upon the three-rung, self-stabilizing aluminum ladder, moving it from place to place where she could rap her knuckles against the white bats above.

Halfway through the search a heavy thunk sounded.

'Don't do anything else,' Acme said as Normandie started pushing the panel up. He said this because he'd spent long hours listening to TV police procedurals while executing the detailed work of wiring and soldering his white box. Donning disposable latex gloves that Bob himself used for photo-development, Acme climbed up and managed to tease the scrapbook out from its hiding place.

•

The album contained detailed information, in pictures and in prose, of the slaughter of five young people – before and after their deaths. Acme was impressed by the specificity of the document. Here was a man who thought like he did but who used this knowledge to elicit suffering and terror.

Normandie threw up while Acme studied the document. He would have helped her at any other time but the album and its dark revelations resonated and even rhymed with Ace's obsessive pursuit of pain and its transmission. After nearly an hour of study he felt that he understood the difference between himself and the suburban serial killer. They were opposites and therefore had similar qualities. Over and over in his handwritten notes Bob would use the phrase, *people are meat*. Bob, Acme thought, objectified human beings where the short brown man from Detroit subjectified them.

This thought captivated Acme. It opened a pathway that he might use to consider the fifth level of his machine's output data. Bob's passionate concentration on his *study* might possibly have opened him up enough to transmit ideational material to his wife. Maybe Acme could devise a mental exercise to enable normal people to transmit thoughts.

'Goddammit!' The cry came from high up.

Normandie wailed in fear.

Acme looked up to the top of the banisterless staircase and saw Bob. The big man teetered a bit but his threat wasn't based on balance.

For a split-second Acme rued not letting Normandie kill her husband. But he abandoned that thought because the past could not be altered. He grabbed a large wooden mallet and, roaring as best he could, he ran up the stairs hoping that the hammer would even the odds between big and small, white and black.

'No!' Normandie shouted from somewhere behind Acme.

The Detroiter, also shouting, was ten steps up while Bob was four down when the solution to the impossible problem came to the homegrown scientist. Three steps away from the Brobdingnagian killer, Ace hurled his mallet and then dove low to hit Bob in the shins with his shoulder.

Though he didn't see it, Acme heard the crashing racket of Bob's tumble down the stairs. He also heard a frightened yelp from Normandie. By the time he'd made it to his feet, Acme could see that the big man was once again on his back and motionless. Beneath him lay the jangled body of his wife.

Acme saw that the woman named after a battlefield had come to the stairway to help him. That was the moment his heart was broken.

He approached the prostrate killer quickly, hoping, beyond hope, that his new friend lying underneath him had survived the fall.

But she had not.

The innocent was dead but her husband still had a pulse and his chest rose and fell more or less evenly.

•

'Emergency nine-one-one,' a woman's voice declared.

'He, he showed me the book and then tried to pull me down the stairs. He pulled too hard and then fell. His wife was behind him. They might still be alive down there but I'm afraid to go.'

With that brief description Acme went out to Normandie's

car and drove downtown where, on a sad whim, he boarded a bus to Phoenix, Arizona.

•

'So, what did you do with the white box and the loom?' Minna Two Chiefs asked after their thirteenth biweekly therapeutic meeting.

'I broke it into pieces and brought the parts to a recycling center,' Acme told the shelter's part-time psychotherapist.

'But why? If that man was crazy, it's not your fault.'

Minna didn't know if Acme was suffering from psychosis or not. The news about Robert Karl Frisk's death and the revelation that he'd tortured and then slaughtered five innocent youths had been a national news event. Acme could have read about it. The mannered and intelligent Green did not seem to be violent or psychotic.

'My father and his brother, my mother and all her siblings died before my nineteenth birthday,' Acme said. 'Normandie and Bob were just two more victims. It dawned upon me when I saw Normandie's crushed body that I was somehow unlucky, the bringer of bad news wherever I went and whatever I was doing. It felt as if the pain projector would somehow serve to destroy rather than heal. So, I shattered it when I got to Phoenix and then came to Tucson to live out my years in obscurity among those whose luck has been so bad I couldn't tear them down any further.'

BIOGRAPHICAL NOTES

THE EDITORS

MAXIM JAKUBOWSKI was born in England but educated in France. He enjoyed a long career in publishing, as editor to William Golding, Peter Ackroyd, Peter Ustinov, Patricia Highsmith, Michael Moorcock, J.G. Ballard and many others. Tasked by Richard Branson to start up Virgin Books, which he ran for several years, he left publishing to write full-time while setting up Murder One bookshop in London, the world's largest speciality bookstore. He has published books in the crime & mystery, science fiction & fantasy and erotica genres, as well as non-fiction titles about thriller writing, music, and books. He is also the editor of almost a hundred major anthologies. He is the author of 20 novels, including ten (in collaboration) as Vina Jackson, several of which broke into *The Sunday Times* Top 10 and sold to 30 countries, as well as half a dozen short story collections. He has won the Anthony Award for non-fiction, the Karel Award for SF and the Crime Writers' Association Red Herring Award for his contribution to the genre. He was for 10 years crime reviewer for *Time Out*, London, followed by 12 years at the *Guardian*. He also jointly ran the Crime Scene Festival of films and books at London's

National Film Theatre. He is currently the Chair of the Crime Writers' Association and writes a monthly review column for *Crime Time*, and contributes to leading British and US newspapers and magazines and appears regularly on radio and TV on matters cultural and criminal. His latest novel is *The Piper's Dance*.

He has been a past judge for the Arthur C. Clarke Award, the World Fantasy Award, the *LoveReading* Short Story prize and the Crime Writers' Association Daggers. He also translates from French and Italian. He lives in London just a couple of miles from where he was born.

www.maximjakubowski.co.uk

f https://www.facebook.com/maxim.jakubowski

·

VASEEM KHAN is the author of two crime series set in India, the *Baby Ganesh Agency* series set in modern Mumbai, and the *Malabar House* historical crime novels set in 1950s Bombay. His first book, *The Unexpected Inheritance of Inspector Chopra,* was a *Times* bestseller, now translated into 15 languages. The second in the series won the Shamus Award in the US. In 2018, he was awarded the Eastern Eye Arts, Culture and Theatre Award for Literature. Vaseem was born in England, but spent a decade working in India. *Midnight at Malabar House*, the first in his historical crime series, won the Crime Writers' Association Sapere Books Historical Dagger 2021 and was an international e-bestseller. Vaseem co-hosts the popular Red Hot Chilli Writers podcast featuring the world's best crime writers. He is on the board of the Crime Writers' Association.

www.vaseemkhan.com

f https://www.facebook.com/VaseemKhanOfficial/

🐦 https://twitter.com/VaseemKhanUK

THE AUTHORS

AMER ANWAR grew up in West London. After leaving college he had a variety of jobs, including warehouse assistant, comic book lettering artist, driver for emergency doctors and chalet rep in the French Alps. He eventually settled into a career as a creative artworker/graphic designer and spent a decade and a half producing artwork, mainly for the home entertainment industry. He has an MA in Creative Writing from Birkbeck, University of London. His critically acclaimed debut novel, *Brothers in Blood*, won the Crime Writers' Association Debut Dagger and was picked by *The Times* and *Guardian* as one of the books of the year. His second novel, *Stone Cold Trouble*, was longlisted for the Crime Writers' Association Gold Dagger. He is currently working on the next book in the Zaq & Jags series.

•

OYINKAN BRAITHWAITE is the author of *The Sunday Times* Bestseller *My Sister, the Serial Killer*, which was shortlisted for the Women's Prize 2019, longlisted for the Booker Prize and the Dublin Literary Award, won the 2019 *LA Times* Award for Best Crime Thriller, the *Morning News* Tournament of Books, the Amazon Publishing Reader's Award for Best Debut Novel, and the Anthony Award for Best First Novel. In addition it was shortlisted for the Goodreads Choice Awards 2019 in the Mystery & Thriller and Debut Novel categories, the British Book Awards 2020 in two categories, the Cameo Awards 2020 in the Book to Audio category and the Book Bloggers' Choice Awards 2020. *My Sister, the Serial Killer* has sold in 34 territories worldwide and has also been optioned for film. She lives with her husband in Nigeria.

HENRY CHANG is a New Yorker, a native son of Chinatown and the Lower Eastside. He is a graduate of City College of New York and his writing has appeared in 'Gangs in New York's Chinatown', *Murdaland Crime Fiction*, *Asian Pulp*, *The NuyorAsian Anthology*, and 'On A Bed of Rice'. His debut novel *Chinatown Beat* garnered high praise from the *New York Times Book Review*, the *Boston Globe*, and the *Washington Post* among others. His Chinatown Detective Jack Yu series of novels includes *Chinatown Beat*, *Year of the Dog*, *Red Jade*, *Death Money*, and *Lucky*, from Soho Press. The crime books are being considered for adaptation to movies and television series. Henry has been a lighting consultant, and a security director for major hotels, commercial properties, and retail businesses in New York City. His roots run through Chinatown forever.

•

S.A. COSBY is a writer from Southeastern Virginia. His short fiction has appeared in numerous anthologies and magazines. His short story 'The Grass Beneath My Feet' won the Anthony Award for best short story in 2019. He is the author of several novels including the award-winning *Blacktop Wasteland*. His most recent novel is *Razorblade Tears*. When he isn't writing, he is an avid gardener, hiker and connoisseur of both fine and cheap whiskies.

•

SULARI GENTILL is the award-winning author of 14 published novels, including the Rowland Sinclair Mysteries, and the Hero Trilogy, based on ancient myths and legends. Her debut novel was shortlisted for the Commonwealth Writers' Prize, her second was awarded the Davitt Award for Best Crime Fiction by a Woman. *Crossing the Lines* won the 2018 Ned Kelly Award for

Best Crime Novel. Sulari was an ambassador of the Emerging Writers' Festival, the inaugural Eminent Writer in Residence at the Australian Museum of Democracy, and one of four novelists who in 2019 undertook an Australian Arts Council tour of the US to promote Australian Crime Writing. Her latest novel, *The Woman in the Library*, will be released in May 2022. Sulari lives with her husband, sons and several animals, on a trufferie in the foothills of the Snowy Mountains, where she writes about murder and mayhem.

•

NELSON GEORGE is an author, filmmaker and cultural critic with a long history of chronicling African-American culture. Since 2004 he's published a series of music noir novels featuring the bodyguard D. Hunter: *The Accidental Hunter*, *The Plot Against Hip-hop*, *The Lost Treasures of R&B*, *To Funk & Die in LA*, and *The Darkest Hearts*. All are published by Akashic Books. He has also authored 15 non-fiction books on music, the black American experience and other topical subjects and was involved in Spike Lee's *She's Gotta Have It*. He has been nominated twice for the National Book Critics Circle Award.

•

RACHEL HOWZELL HALL is the critically acclaimed author and *Los Angeles Times* Book Prize finalist for *And Now She's Gone*, which was also nominated for the Lefty, Barry and Anthony Awards. A *New York Times* bestselling author of *The Good Sister* with James Patterson, and the author of *They All Fall Down*, *Land of Shadows, Skies of Ash, Trail of Echoes* and *City of Saviors* in the Detective Elouise Norton series, as well as the bestselling Audible Original, *How It Ends*. A former member of the board of directors for Mystery Writers of

America, she has been a featured writer on NPR's *Crime in the City* series and the National Endowment for the Arts weekly podcast; she has also served as a mentor in Pitch Wars and the Association of Writers Programs. Rachel lives in Los Angeles with her husband and daughter.
www.rachelhowzell.com

•

AUSMA ZEHANAT KHAN holds a PhD in international human rights law with a specialization in military intervention and war crimes in the Balkans. She is the author of the award-winning Esa Khattak/Rachel Getty mystery series, and the critically acclaimed Khorasan Archives fantasy series. *A Deadly Divide* and *The Bladebone* are her latest books, with her new *Blackwater Falls* crime series premiering in 2022. A British-born Canadian and former adjunct law professor, Khan now lives in Colorado with her husband.

•

SHEENA KAMAL holds an HBA in Political Science from the University of Toronto, and was awarded a TD Canada Trust scholarship for community leadership and activism around the issue of homelessness. Her bestselling debut *The Lost Ones* won her a Kobo Emerging Writer Prize, a Strand Critics Award, and Macavity Award for Best First Novel. The sequel *It All Falls Down* has been called 'a stunning, emotionally resonant thriller' in its *Kirkus*-starred review. *No Going Back* and her first YA novel *Fight Like a Girl* were released in 2020. Additionally, her writing has been featured in the *Guardian* (UK), *Bustle*, *The Irish Times*, *Writer's Digest*, and *Entertainment Weekly*.

•

SANJIDA KAY has had four psychological thrillers published by Corvus Books: *Bone by Bone, The Stolen Child, My Mother's Secret* and *One Year Later*. *Bone by Bone* went straight into the Amazon Kindle bestselling list. It was long-listed for the Crime Writers' Association Steel Dagger Award and nominated as one of the best crime and thriller books of 2016 by the *Guardian* and the *Sunday Express*. *The Stolen Child* has been optioned for film and published in Poland. Her thrillers are available as audiobooks. Sanjida also writes fiction and non-fiction under her own name of Sanjida O'Connell.

www.sanjida.co.uk

f www.facebook.com/SanjidaKayAuthor

🐦 https://twitter.com/SanjidaKay

📷 https://www.instagram.com/Sanjida.Kay/

•

THOMAS KING is an award-winning novelist, short story writer, children's writer, scriptwriter and photographer of Cherokee and Greek descent. His critically acclaimed bestselling fiction includes *Medicine River; Green Grass, Running Water; Truth and Bright Water; One Good Story, That One*; *A Short History of Indians in Canada; The Back of the Turtle; Indians on Vacation; Sufferance*; and the beloved mystery series featuring Cherokee ex-cop Thumps DreadfulWater. He is also the author of *The Inconvenient Indian*, a bestselling, multi-award-winning work of creative non-fiction that has been adapted into a critically acclaimed, award-winning documentary film. A Companion to the Order of Canada and the recipient of awards from numerous organizations including the National Aboriginal Achievement Foundation and the Western American Literary Association, Thomas King is a former Chair of American Indian Studies at the University of Minnesota, and is Professor Emeritus at the University of Guelph. For more information, please visit https://www.deaddogcafe.com/.

•

IMRAN MAHMOOD is a practising barrister with almost 30 years' experience fighting cases in courtrooms across the country. He hails from Liverpool but now lives in London with his wife and daughters. His debut novel *You Don't Know Me* was chosen by Simon Mayo as a BBC Radio 2 Book Club Choice for 2017 and longlisted for Theakston crime novel of the year and for the Crime Writers' Association Gold Dagger, and has been adapted for screen for the BBC in association with Netflix. His second novel *I Know What I Saw* was released in June 2021. He has been commissioned to write a screenplay for a third novel, *The Keeper* and to develop a legal drama for television. When not in court or writing novels or screenplays he can sometimes be found on the Red Hot Chilli Writers podcast as one of the regular contributors.

🐦 https://twitter.com/imranmahmood777

•

NADINE MATHESON is a crime writer who was born and lives in London. She is a Criminal Solicitor and also teaches Criminal Law. In 2016, she won the City University Crime Writing Competition and completed the Creative Writing (Crime/Thriller Novels) MA at City University of London with Distinction in 2018. Her novel, *The Jigsaw Man*, the first in the D.I. Anjelica Henley Series, was published in 2021. She's also a huge comic book fan and is waiting for the day that DC Comics gives her the green light to write for them.

•

SILVIA MORENO-GARCIA is the author of the fantasy and horror novels *Mexican Gothic, Gods of Jade and Shadow, Certain Dark Things*, and two noir thrillers *Untamed Shore*, and *Velvet Was the Night*, many of which have been bestsellers and nominated for a variety of awards. She has also edited several anthologies, including the World Fantasy Award-winning *She Walks in Shadows* (a.k.a. *Cthulhu's Daughters*). She lives in Canada.

•

WALTER MOSLEY is the author of more than 60 critically acclaimed books of fiction including his most recent *Blood Grove*, nonfiction, memoir and plays. His work has been translated into twenty-five languages. From the first novel he published, *Devil in a Blue Dress* with its protagonist Easy Rawlins, to his most recent short story collection, *The Awkward Black Man*, Mosley's work has explored the lives of Black men and women. Several of his books have been adapted for film and TV, including *Devil in a Blue Dress, Always Outnumbered, Always Outgunned* and the forthcoming Apple TV+ production of *The Last Days of Ptolemy Grey*. His short fiction and nonfiction essays have been published in the *New York Times, Los Angeles Times* and *The Nation*. He is also a writer and an executive producer on the John Singleton FX show, *Snowfall*. He is the winner of numerous awards, including an O. Henry Award, The Mystery Writers of America's Grand Master Award, a Grammy®, several NAACP Image awards, and PEN America's Lifetime Achievement Award. In 2020 he received the Robert Kirsch Award for lifetime achievement from the *Los Angeles Times* Festival of Books and was awarded the Distinguished Contribution to American Letters Award from the National Book Foundation. Born and raised in Los Angeles, Mosley now lives in Brooklyn and Los Angeles.

•

ABIR MUKHERJEE is the author of the Wyndham & Banerjee series of crime novels set in Raj-era India which have sold over 250,000 copies and been translated into 15 languages. His books have won a number of awards, including the Crime Writers' Association Dagger for best Historical Novel, the Prix du Polar Européen, the Wilbur Smith Award for Adventure Writing and the Amazon Publishing Readers Award for E-book of the Year. Abir grew up in Scotland and now lives in Surrey with his wife and two sons.
https://abirmukherjee.com/
🅕 https://www.facebook.com/authorabir/
🅧 https://twitter.com/radiomukhers

•

MIKE PHILLIPS worked as a journalist and broadcaster before becoming a lecturer in media studies at the University of Westminster. After a spell as Resident Writer at the South Bank Centre in London, he was appointed Cross Cultural Curator at the Tate Galleries in Britain, and then worked as Acting Director of Arts (Cultuurmakelaar) in Tilburg in the Netherlands. Later on, he lectured in Milan and worked as a freelance curator in London, Belgium, Venice, the Netherlands and Los Angeles, notably with the Belgian artist Koen Vanmechelen. He was awarded the Arts Foundation Fellowship in 1996 for crime fiction, and the OBE in 2006 for services to broadcasting. He served as a Trustee of the National Heritage Memorial Fund, but he is best known for his crime fiction, including four novels featuring black journalist Sam Dean: *Blood Rights* (1989), which was adapted for BBC television, *The Late Candidate* (1990), winner of the Crime Writers' Association Silver Dagger Award, *Point of Darkness* (1994) and *An Image to Die For* (1995). Later on there followed *The Dancing Face* (1998), a thriller centred on a priceless Benin mask, and *A Shadow of Myself* (2000), about a black documentary filmmaker working in Prague. *The Name You Once Gave Me* (2006) was written as part of a government sponsored literacy campaign. He also co-wrote *Windrush: The Irresistible Rise of Multi-Racial Britain* (1998) to accompany a BBC television series telling the story of the Caribbean migrant workers who settled in post-war Britain. *London Crossings: A Biography of Black Britain* (2001) is a series of interlinked essays and stories. Recently he wrote a series of libretti for the compositions of musician Julian Joseph, culminating in a version of *Tristan and Isolde*, performed at the Royal Opera House.

•

J.P. POMARE grew up on a horse-racing farm in small-town New Zealand with two brothers, a sister, two cats and two border collies. For the last five years he has produced and hosted a podcast, interviewing guests from Joyce Carol Oates to E. Lockhart. While working in marketing, he began to draft what would become *Call Me Evie*. His work has been widely published in journals including *Meanjin*, *Kill Your Darlings*, *TLB Review of Books* and *The NZ Listener*. He has also won, and been shortlisted for a number of prizes. J.P. has published three bestselling novels: *Call Me Evie*, *In the Clearing* and *Tell Me Lies*. His latest novel *The Last Guests* was released in August 2021.

•

JOHN VERCHER is a writer currently living in the Philadelphia area with his wife and two sons. He holds a Bachelor's in English from the University of Pittsburgh and an MFA in Creative Writing from the Mountainview Master of Fine Arts program and served as an adjunct faculty member at Chestnut Hill College in Philadelphia. John's debut novel, *Three-Fifths*, was named one of the best books of 2019 by the *Chicago Tribune*, a Best Debut

Novel by *CrimeReads*, and a Top 10 Crime Fiction Debut by *Booklist*, and has since been nominated in a clean sweep for most of the English-language crime awards and sold to 10 countries. His second novel, *After the Lights Go Out*, will be published by Soho Press and Pushkin Press July 2022. You can find John on Twitter and Instagram as @jverchwrites

•

DAVID HESKA WANBLI WEIDEN, an enrolled citizen of the Sicangu Lakota Nation, is the author of the novel *Winter Counts* (Ecco, 2020), nominated for the Edgar Award, Anthony Award, Barry Award, Thriller Award, Macavity Award, Shamus Award, and the Hammett Prize. The book was the winner of the Lefty Award for Best Debut Mystery Novel and the Spur Award for Best Contemporary Novel. The novel was a *New York Times* Editors' Choice, a main selection of the Book of the Month Club, and named a Best Book of 2020 by *NPR*, *Publishers Weekly*, *Library Journal*, *CrimeReads*, and other magazines. His work has appeared in the *New York Times*, *Shenandoah*, *Yellow Medicine Review*, and other journals. His short fiction is forthcoming in the anthologies *Midnight Hour*, *This Time for Sure* and *Denver Noir*. He's the recipient of a MacDowell Fellowship, a Ragdale Foundation residency, the PEN America Writing for Justice Fellowship, and was a Tin House Scholar. He lives in Denver, Colorado, with his family.

•

FELICIA YAP is the author of *Future Perfect* (2021), a murder mystery set in a near-future Britain where computers will be able to predict how we live and when we will die, and *Yesterday* (2017). Felicia grew up in Kuala Lumpur and resides in London.

She read biochemistry at Imperial College London, followed by a doctorate in history (and a half-blue in competitive ballroom dancing) at the University of Cambridge. She has worked as a cell biologist, a war historian, a university lecturer, a technology journalist, a theatre critic, a flea-market trader and a catwalk model. One of *The Observer*'s Rising Stars for Fiction, Felicia is a recipient of the Hawthornden Castle Fellowship in Scotland and the Ledig-Rowohlt Fellowship at Château de Lavigny in Switzerland. She has written widely for publications such as *The Economist* and *The Business Times* and her works have been translated in multiple languages.